Praise for Perdido!

Perdido

Jill Robinson

PUBLISHED BY POCKET BOOKS NEW YORK

*Grateful acknowledgment is made to the following to reprint
previously published material:*

Folkways Records: Lyrics from "The Songs and Stories of Aunt Molly
Jackson" (p. 152), Folkways Records, album #5457.

Harcourt Brace Jovanovich and Faber & Faber Ltd: Four lines from
"Little Gidding" (epigraph) in FOUR QUARTETS, Copyright, 1943, by
T. S. Eliot; renewed 1971 by Esme Valerie Eliot. Reprinted by permission
of Harcourt Brace Jovanovich, Inc., and Faber & Faber Ltd.

T. B. Harms Co.: One line from "Lovely to Look At" (p. 168) Music by
Jerome Kern, Words by Dorothy Fields and Jimmy McHugh. Copyright ©
1935 T. B. Harms Co. Copyright renewed. ALL RIGHTS RESERVED.
Used by permission.

Peer International Corporation: One line from "You Are My Sunshine"
(p. 11) by Jimmie Davis and Charles Mitchell. Copyright 1941 by Peer
International Corporation. Copyright renewed. Used by permission.

Robbins Music Corporation: Lyrics from "Hi-Lili, Hi-Lo" (p. 127) Words
by Helen Deutsch, Music by Bronislau Kaper. Copyright 1952 Metro-
Goldwyn-Mayer, Inc. Rights throughout the world controlled by Robbins
Music Corporation. Used by permission.

TRO: One line from "SO LONG, it's been good to know yuh," (p 123)
The original title, "Dusty Old Dust." Words and music by Woody Guthrie.
TRO—© 1940 (renewed 1968), 1950 and 1951 Folkways Music Publishers,
Inc., New York. Used by permission.

Warner Bros., Inc., and Chappell and Co. Ltd: Lyrics from "Just One
of Those Things" (p. 307) by Cole Porter. Copyright © 1935 Warner
Bros., Inc. Copyright renewed. ALL RIGHTS RESERVED. Used by permission.

Williamson Music Inc.: One line from "Tumbling Tumbleweed" (p. 87)
by Bob Nolan. Copyright © 1934 by Williamson Music, Inc. Copyright
renewed. International copyright secured. ALL RIGHTS RESERVED.
Used by permission.

To my mother and my father

This is the use of memory:
For liberation—not less of love but expanding
Of love beyond desire, and so liberation
From the future as well as the past.

—T. S. ELIOT

Part One

1950

HERE IS THE MOST AMAZING DAY OF MY LIFE.

I am Susanna Midnight and I have climbed right down from my room through the olive tree with my cloak wrapped around my red bathing suit which is my first real one-piece Lastex. My mother yanked up on the straps, my stepfather looked at the ceiling, and my grandmother said, "Such a thing for a fourteen-year-old." Mornings home at Perdido are like movie mornings in pictures about horse-raising families where Jeanne Crain gallops across a meadow to the loveliest sprightly music. The early fog still smokes around the cliff above the Pacific Coast Highway. The big trucks are hitting the road for the North, the morning birds coo, and there's a yawning sound under the grass.

There is time for an aquacade. I dash to the bike shed and whip my bike into position by the far side of the tennis court. I speed right across the lawn as fast as you can go. Cloak becomes wings.

It is fantastic. One hundred girls all going through the air on silver bikes with wings, flying to the music of our entire studio orchestra, flying right into the water.

Up through the water I come, spluttering and bubbling, and there he is, standing here, laughing down at me, hands on his hips. He is wearing white pants and a white shirt—and it is not Stanley who delivers for Cerise Dry Cleaners.

"That wasn't very bright," he says.

"Needs work," I say. He reaches out and grabs my hands in his and pulls me up out of the pool. I can feel heat through these hands come right through me.

3

"I'm Jackson Lane," he says, just like in his movies; he puts a lot into little things like that. His famous hair shines like splendid gold.

"Yes, you are too," I say. I am trying to untie my cloak which now weighs one hundred tons but my hands are shaking because of cold—because of him, probably.

"You must be Susanna." He helps me untie the knot, wrings out the cloak, flinging it across a lounge chair as if it is his own. Could have been, I got it out of Wardrobe a couple of years ago to wear to my twelfth birthday party.

"How are you going to get that bike out of the pool?" he asks me.

"Watch," I say, wheezing, which is what happens whenever I do anything swashbuckling. And I dive right back in again and, underwater, slide my bike up along to the shallow end and he helps me drag it up the steps and out.

"Nothing to it," I say.

"You can't breathe. Are you all right?" He pulls one of the terry covers off one of the other chairs and I pull my straps off my shoulders and pat·them dry like Lana Turner does and then wrap the cover around so it trails, very Nazimova, as I walk.

"Just a little asthma," I say. "There is a list of things —cats, dogs, chicken, string beans, chocolate, exertion, and angora socks."

"It must be hard," he says, "to be a teenager without angora socks."

He understands. Everything, probably.

"Yes. You can't do the dances without the fur flying up into your nose and you don't want to stop and say, 'Listen, I'm getting asthma from my socks.' "

He laughs. ("Imagine," I can hear him say to the trades when he is interviewed about us, "someone who can always make you laugh—she is young, but when I saw her first in her red bathing suit I thought she must be twenty-six.")

4

"Did you come to see my stepfather?"

My stepfather, Myron Howard, is head of Victor Levanin International—he runs my grandfather's studio, "Into the ground," as I once heard my grandmother say.

"Yes," Jackson says. "I wanted to talk to him about a friend of mine who's having some difficulty." I think he just thought this up. Just from tightness I hear in his voice.

"Well, Myron went with my mother to New York. He had to visit the New York office. She goes to concerts there. She's a pianist. Classical. Or she plays anyway. I hate it."

"The piano?"

"No, classical. But I adore music. I'm going to be a nightclub singer. Sit on the piano in sequins to the floor and tear their hearts out." I can see my cousin Val's right eyebrow skid up on that, and her grin scoot to the left.

"You probably could do that." He smiles at me such a smile.

"I'm sorry you missed Myron," I say, with absolutely no sincerity since I might have missed Jackson if Myron had been here.

"I must have had the wrong day. I wanted to catch Myron early, before I start shooting, you know."

"Well, you sure would have. But he's sometimes off and over to the studio by now anyway. He likes to make the rounds of the sets really early." And then "clean up his mail." Myron always makes it sound as though he and Fitzsimmons, his executive secretary, are hunched over shovels cleaning up stables when he talks about his mail. "Fitz and I really cleaned up so much junk today," he will tell my mother, as if that will make her love him, or my grandmother, as if that will make her proud of him. I wonder how Myron would feel about seeing Jackson Lane here. He is not, for one thing, one of our stars. And, except for Alan Benedict, who is my uncle (Alan is Val's father. I cannot wait to tell her about this. Watch how she will think I made it all up. This is precisely the kind of thing I do make up.)

The fog is going off to sea now. The help will be getting up. Bread will be toasting on the big restaurant stove we have and a vast pot of coffee will be brewing. Ethel, the cook, throws eggshells into it for "seasoning." I think that's her plan for slowly poisoning everyone. Dorothy, our maid, who is the only one who does not hate me, will be going through the upstairs galleries with her uniform thrown open over her bathrobe raising the shades which give our house a look that says "I refuse to see this." I would love to show him the house—the living room was just redecorated with a new chintz covered with cabbage roses. And the projection room, which is all wine-colored and paneled. Whenever the living room is redecorated my mother gets excited and sits in there playing her grand piano for days. She even files down her nails so they don't click. Much. She must—always—leave enough nail so when they're polished there's room for the white tip and the moon at the base of the nail.

And I would love to show Jackson my puppets and the stage Val and I use for shows. I remember (according to the movie magazines Dorothy keeps under her bed) he doesn't live anywhere that anyone knows about. Maybe he hates his house, which is why there are no "Jackson Lane at Home" stories.

We can't just stand here like this. . . .

"Would you like to come in for some breakfast?" I ask. Say yes. Say yes, I am hoping.

"I don't want to disturb anyone." But if he was here to see Myron he would have had to talk to one of the servants to know my stepfather wasn't here. What I think is, Jackson is a lot like me and likes to wander around and look at things and he sort of came up to look at the view, which is the best in town, and heard me splash into the pool. Of course, he could have come here just to see me because he heard I am going to be gorgeous. ("I must have missed that part," I can hear Val saying,

6

in her father's sarcastic voice, and I wouldn't think that was very funny if she didn't hug me quick or look like she loves me most of all when she can tease me—or because she can tease me.)

"Oh, Ethel would love to make breakfast for you. We'll have to go in the service entrance. My grandmother has to sleep late. She's not too well."

"I've heard that. I'm sorry. Are you quite sure I should come in?"

"Oh yes. I am absolutely sure—please." I give him my best appealing smile.

Grandmother just does not come downstairs the way she used to in the morning, which delights my mother, who can now have a tray sent up to her room too. When Grandmother was well, and especially when Grandfather was alive, there were real breakfasts around a table every morning. The only one who thought that was any kind of a good idea was Grandmother, who believed it was a fine time to discuss what everyone should think about that day and, during the war, to go over the latest overseas reports. No one except Grandmother talked. The others just rattled silver and china and crunched into toast. "You're all so quiet, you wouldn't hear a bomb drop," she once said, and winked at me.

I think she knows what's going on even when she's up in her wing. She might have been watching him come into the garden. Although you'd think that would have brought her downstairs and outside, heart or not.

Actually, she doesn't have to be watching to know things, which is the exact opposite of my mother who can be watching everything and miss the point . . . except if it's my table manners. I think my mother misses things because she is dreaming of being in the East or in Europe. She is beautiful enough to marry a European. Sometimes I think she dreams of my dead father.

Jackson Lane and I have crossed the lawn—I do love that: "Jackson Lane and I . . ."—and now we are walking under the wisteria arbor that leads to the back door.

We come in the kitchen door and Dorothy says, "Oh,

my God," and runs into her room to throw off her robe and fix her hair.

Ethel pretends she does not notice, but she does. She asks him what he would like and she never gives a damn what I would like and when he says, "Bacon and eggs over easy," she does not flinch even though bacon is not supposed to be had in this house because we are Jewish but I know she has some put away. Dorothy comes back and says, "Now you get out of that wet suit before you catch polio." I run upstairs and throw everything out of my closet until I decide on this blue Lanz peasant dress. Men love blue. And then I'm downstairs in a minute, shaking my hair so it fluffs and curls all blond around my shoulders and down my back.

I spill my orange juice down my front as I watch his throat as he drinks.

"Take it easy," he says, "don't drink so fast."

"I'm not." Here I am having breakfast with Jackson Lane. I cannot wait to get to school to tell Val even though at the same time I don't want to leave him.

"I wonder," I say. And stop.

"What do you wonder?" He puts down his coffee and looks at me, laughing. His laugh just fills his face, but it is not the laugh of someone thinking something is funny. It is more—more what? More as if he is triumphant. As if he has caught me at something. He has. Caught me loving him.

"Tell me," he says, leaning over the table, "what . . . ?"

"Well, okay, I was wondering, if it wouldn't be too much trouble, if you could take me to school?"

Dorothy looks at me with her I-think-you're-up-to-something look.

"Yes, I could do that. Get your stuff."

I dash up the stairs. And back down so fast, for fear he has been a mirage like the lakes you see in the middle of the highway driving to Palm Springs.

And before I am out the door, Dorothy pulls me aside and says, "You better not tell your grandmother about this because we'll all be in real trouble."

"Why?"

"Because . . ."—is she searching for a reason?—"because you're not allowed to drive with strangers. I don't care who they are."

"You sound like my mother."

"No wonder. I've heard it often enough and so have you. Now get." I flip my red plumed hat off the hook near the back porch and clap it on my head. And Dorothy takes it right off. "Now, you don't need to wear that." And she smooths my hair down right. My mother says she doesn't like me to be touched. Or her. And then she's hurt because she never is. At least, that's what my grandmother says: "You should sometimes kiss your mother good night."

"She doesn't like to be kissed," I remind her.

"She says things, you know her."

"Is everything okay?" he says as I run outside.

"Wonderful."

The contractor and his men are already here working on the foundations along the driveway which crumble after every rain. "We're in for a dry time," I say.

The eucalyptus leaves the color of his eyes are dusty; the pepper trees sound like tinsel on the Christmas trees you are not allowed to have in this house, and the bougainvillea which beckons over the front door like Basil Rathbone's hands in crimson gauntlets is falling down dry as Wheaties.

"Weather like this always makes me want to travel, hit the road, you know. . . . Morning," he says, walking by the workmen.

"Hey, Jackson Lane!" one of the guys says to him. People always look at my uncle Alan—but they wouldn't shout at him or anything. That's the difference. Alan says, "I'm the kind of actor who people ask for an autograph and then look surprised and say, 'Yeah—that's your name,' when you give it to them. 'But we love all your movies.' " He imitates a sort of Southern accent and it comes out very funny on top of his New York voice.

"How are you, nice to see you," Jackson says to the workmen, going faster, looking uncomfortable.

"Hey, kid, watch it. We just laid this stuff," they say to me as I step in the cement because I am so busy looking at Jackson and thinking how they are looking at me just getting to be with him.

"I am practicing," I say, "for Grauman's Chinese." And I bend over and put my handprints in too since my feet are already there.

And Jackson laughs.

We stand near the wall looking out over the view, the ocean to the right, Santa Monica and West Los Angeles stretching out to Culver City and the hills beyond. And when I stand right here I always think of how it must have looked to my grandparents when they came up the fireroad that Perdido Drive was and planned the house.

I like to sit on her bed with my grandmother, under one of her crocheted violet afghans, and look out at the sea and listen to her legends about Hollywood Long Ago and how Perdido came to be. . . .

"During the third decade of the twentieth century . . ." She likes to begin stories like that, as though she is taking a running jump at them from a great distance. It makes it all sound hundreds and hundreds of years ago, which when I was little I thought it was.

"It was custom for the new movie moguls like your dear grandfather to build summer cottages in the canyons and along the beach or these palisades."

"But why did you need summer houses? It's always summer here."

She thinks a moment. "Irony. And we had all come from a place where the rich went from the cities to the seashore during the hot summers and so it became the custom wherever one happened to be rich." I saw her stories move like Grandfather's silent movies which we sometimes run in the projection room. I saw everyone young and made-up and walking in the rapid way they did in those days, all angles and briskness.

Perdido was only sixteen rooms when they first built

it. The great colorist Hoyningen-Huené came to select the paint and wallpapers. And the cream color of the outside matched the shade of my grandfather's Bugatti.

My grandfather said that from each room he could see a different country, so he brought all of his set designers to Perdido and showed them how, at ten in the morning, the library seemed to overlook Colorado—or how Colorado should look in the next Western movie. And from the sitting room, Grandfather imagined he could see Naples; then, going down the one hundred and four wooden steps which used to lead to the highway, you could, if you looked between the cliffs and the hills, see a certain view of the ocean. And on a cold, foggy day it resembled the marshland in Russia where once my grandfather sat upon his horse and imagined Western America before they ever came here.

I used to braid the fringes of the afghan while Grandmother talked. Or strum on her balalaika and she would correct my fingering, as she went on ("And on and on . . ." Val would say). Val does not like the stories. Val is not patient about listening unless it is serious music. She goes to the opera with Grandmother when it comes to the Shrine Auditorium. I hate the opera and never want to see one.

"How do you know you hate it unless you have seen it?" Val says. This is exactly how Val is.

"I just know," I say. And that's how I am.

"That's really silly," she says.

I like to play cowboy songs on my guitar. Only Dorothy will listen.

You are my sunshine, my only sunshine, I think as I watch Jackson with one leg bent up, his foot on the wall. Even his bare ankle, coming out of his tennis shoe, is gold and tan.

On Sundays, Lancias, Daimlers, and Packards full of stars used to chug up the road here for the great luncheons and my mother and Aunt Lillian would look too much at the actors. That is why my grandparents sent them East to school.

"John Gilbert had the most magnificent Hispano-Suiza," Grandmother once said dreamily. If not for my grandmother's interest in cars, I would not be sure I belong to this family. All the others are small and dark and fold things before putting them in drawers. Even Myron, who is not much taller than my mother and has dark hair. His hairline forms a perfect M on the top of his forehead. "And where else would you find a hairline?" I can hear Val say and she would hug my forearm with her hand to show she loves me even if I am silly.

Jackson smiles up at the sun as though they are old friends.

"It's going to be a beautiful day," he says, and we start walking over to his car.

"Sometimes I used to imagine I saw Grandfather's studio down there. I'd stand here thinking I was looking out over our plantation. And I'd imagine the other children standing on their hills in front of their houses looking down at their studios and I used to think it would be funny to see us all going to war over Oscars and I'd imagine each of us leading our own army of extras into battle with our best stars riding up front."

"I always knew there had to be a more interesting way to win an Oscar— If you had a telescope, you probably could see the studio."

"Yes, Grandmother was going to get one for my grandfather, but he said he didn't need one to know exactly what everyone was up to. This car is beautiful. That's what I want when I'm sixteen. A convertible."

"You like it, huh?" Who would not like a '48 Lincoln Continental? He opens my door and closes it, locking my side. He cares.

"You're all right?"

"Sure." I lean my elbow out over the door of the car like a crackerjack teenager. And I watch him walk around to his side, with this kind of loping swing-gait, angling in on the corners. He doesn't waste a motion.

12

His belt hangs low around his loins. I adore the word loin.

"That's a great belt."

"They made it special for me in Wardrobe."

He starts the car, swings it back and swivels it around in one sweep, one hand dazzling over the wheel like he's polishing it, and we start down our driveway. I keep thinking I ought to be astonished to be in Jackson Lane's car, but it begins to feel like the most natural thing in the world. Now I sit sort of catty-corner on the far side next to the door with my left arm casually up over the back of this tan leather seat as if I've been here in this car all my life.

We pass Mr. Giordano the gardener coming up the road with his truck loaded down with flats of zinnias, which are not in season, but Grandfather always had zinnias and as long as Grandmother lives at Perdido the zinnias will bloom the whole year round down beyond the pool. In the afternoons, Angelo comes in his shorts to work with his father, flashing his tan young male movie star legs around. I would like Angelo to see this. Me here in this car.

"Hey. Do you ever play hooky?" he turns and asks me suddenly. But as though he has been thinking about it too.

"Not exactly. Well, sometimes I don't go to school. But it's hard once I'm there to get away."

"How would you like to play hooky today?"

"With you? Don't you have to shoot—could I go watch?"

"No, let's both play hooky."

"You're kidding." No wonder the trades say his pictures always go over budget. I am also thinking if he wasn't a movie star I would think I am being kidnapped.

I am trying hard to listen to everything he says. I want to remember every word the way he says it so I will believe it all happened when it is over. We have stopped by the side of the Coast Highway.

"Do you mind the top being down?"

"No, I love to ride in convertibles." I am actually not allowed to. Not allowed to ride in cars with strangers. Or play hooky. So why quibble about the top being down?

Who was the blonde with Jackson Lane? it will say in the trades. I wish I had lipstick and nylons so I wouldn't look like a kid. Robbing the cradle, someone is bound to say. "She is young—but has a woman's mind," he would tell them.

"I probably should call school. Do you think we could stop—and could I borrow a nickel for the phone? I didn't bring any money with me. They'll probably call home to find out where I am. I feel like I'm in one of your running-away-to-sea movies."

"What are you going to tell them? Won't they ask to speak to your mother?"

"No—they know my mother gets migraines and complexes from anything that has to do with me and school —but I can do a perfect imitation of Mary, my mother's secretary. So I'll just say, like this, 'Susanna's feeling poorly today.'" And he laughs at my sad, older lady's voice.

We are driving down the Coast Highway from Sunset, heading south along the short stretch of the public beach, too bad it isn't pitted with people today, I want the world to see me with him, to know I am something enough that Jackson Lane is spending the day with me. Part of it, anyway.

"Do you know what?" I say. And I'm going to say it even if it is kind of forward.

"No. What?" He looks at me with that amused-at-my-admiration expression. It is a lot like the famous one he gets when he has leaped down from the mizzenmast or a balcony and crunched up twenty bad guys in one great swashbuckle. It is usually accompanied by hands on hips.

"This is the best day I've ever had even if it stopped now."

He grins right back at me. And turns on the radio.

14

I would like to ask him what he is really doing with me, but I'm afraid if I ask he will wonder himself. It's best with surprises in life that you just take them as they are. I am never interested in visiting the Special-Effects Department to see how they really did that scene and I am not one of the ones who go up to Warner LeRoy at birthday parties to ask him how he does his magic tricks.

If you asked me what I suspect, it might be that this is a surprise arranged by Grandmother. Perhaps she wanted me to spend a day with an actor to see what they are really like so I will stop having crushes on them. Already that plan is backfiring.

"How would you like to go for a sail?"

"I'd like that very much. Can I ask you something?"

"Sure. I might not answer. I'm funny about questions." I know that—anyone who knows anything about Jackson Lane knows he hates questions, which I will try to remember. Watch how I will forget.

"Did you really run away to sea?"

"Where'd you get that?"

"I read it in a movie magazine."

"Well, I didn't exactly run away. I had the sea in my blood. A long time ago, my people were Vikings; they came from Iceland. So I love the sea. But I hated the Navy. I hated the engine rooms on ships. It was like being in a mine. Buddies drowning around me just like that when the pumps would bust."

"Wow. What a property that would make if you wrote it down."

I can see him writing in a garret. Me bringing him tea and toast. From listening to the wives of screenwriters I know you have to treat a writer the way you would a convalescent.

"Maybe I will some day. That's why I never give interviews. Let them make up what they want. I'm not giving anyone else my story."

"No, you mustn't do that. Do you have a family or are you an only child too?"

"Hey, let's not talk about that."

He looks at me sideways as he drives with that three-quarter profile, one eyebrow lifted, and the sun angles in behind, glinting through.

We drive past the great old Santa Monica beach houses where Jackson must have come for parties when he first came out here. I see everything now a little different and I'm wondering how it must have looked to him when he saw the ocean and all these palm trees high up on the Palisades. Did he walk along the park and look over the fence made of branches and imagine himself being in one of the fancy cars parked in front of the mansions on the beach?

"I was in the Navy when I was a kid before the war," he is saying. Men, and, I guess, even movie stars like to talk about the service, or sports. Or their work, I've noticed. My governess Tucky's sailor boyfriend hated going back to the ship, but he'd always talk about the war anyway, you'd think he'd like to skip the subject when he was on furlough. "But even in training it was taken for granted someone would get killed. We'd unload some big oil tanks down into boats from a ship with a big crane, some kid would get under it, and we'd go right on doing whatever maneuver we was doing, you see what I mean, the Navy wasn't heroic." He turns and smiles at me. "I'm not upsetting you, am I, are you all right?" I love when he makes mistakes with grammar.

"Yes, I'm fine. It's interesting." Jackson Lane could recite the multiplication tables and it would be interesting. In a way, I think he's talking to himself.

"They just toughen you up, and when they send you back, they don't tell you what to do with all that. I was always funny about being under orders after that. I don't like signing on for anything, don't like contracts. And the only boat I go on is my boat—maybe that's what we'll do today—" I hold my breath to keep from being too eager. He nods to himself and goes on. "I don't like being anywhere because someone tells me to." That's probably why he's always on suspension for being late. Or just not showing up.

"I know. That's school for you. Did you hate school too?"

"Never was one that could keep me." I see him small with a slingshot in his pocket. He was probably like Hoagy Bob or Randy Bix Carmichael or one of the other kids that used to tease me in the fourth grade. I was teacher's pet that year. Outgrew that fast.

"Me neither," I say. "I was almost expelled from this one last year for trying to fix the May Queen vote."

"How'd you do that?"

"Bribed the little kids with candy bars. The principal called me in and we had a talk."

"I'll bet you did." I love the way he looks back at me with one eyebrow up, still keeping his profile to me. That is some look.

"She wanted my cousin Val to win anyway. Her father's Alan Benedict, you know. . . ."

"He's a fine actor. Must be rough on him, the black-listing." He sounds really respectful about Alan. I wonder if he ever gets jealous of reviews actors like Alan get.

"It was just when it started and the school trustees didn't want a Communist's daughter to be May Queen, but Miss Duesen, she's the principal, wanted to take a stand, so she saw to it Val was elected. It was really fair. Even my stepfather Myron backed her up. One of the trustees had the lumber contract with our set department and Myron switched it."

"Myron must be okay."

"Oh, he's all right. My real father died just after I was born. Myron was working for Grandfather then and he went to New York to help my mother handle everything. So I was born in New York. My father was a doctor from the East. I take after his coloring. He was blond like you, I have some pictures of him. My grandparents really liked him. The last thing he said was my name: Susanna. They tell me. They never wanted my mother to marry an actor. Oh, I'm sorry. . . . Val says I talk too much, which is why sooner or later I say the wrong thing."

"No problem. I don't think of myself much as an actor. It's just the work I do. I'm not a serious actor like Benedict. I just fell into it, kind of by accident." He laughs as if he is remembering.

I remember: some accident. Suddenly I imagine Jackson all naked like my friend C.A. said he was that day, tan all over. C.A. is short for Carol Anne. She'll punch you if you call her that. She stands at the juice table in school and can skid a full glass of apple juice right down from one end to the other like Gary Cooper does with a whiskey glass. Her father is Jackson's agent, Alan's agent, and everyone's and she hears everything. They have forty phones at her house and an intercom even in the living room, which my mother says is in very poor taste. But my mother envies C.A.'s mother, who is Eastern Christian society and gets her picture in *Town and Country* in her riding habit. They own polo ponies and regular horses at the Riviera Stables. My mother would die to have her picture in *Vogue* or a little something about herself in "People Are Talking About." I watch her reading the magazine, clipping out dresses to order from Magnin's and biting her lip with longing.

Anyway C.A. figured out how to tune in the intercom into the living room, and her parents' bedroom. I won't go into what she reported about *that* except to say they do it (what exactly I am not certain, but Val and C.A. seem to think they know) *all* the time. Before dinner! All naked (C.A. says she can hear their skins rubbing), and that's how she heard one of the great storytelling ladies—whether it was Bubbles Hornblow, Irene Selznick, or Doris Vidor, I don't remember—telling the story about how Jackson was discovered and this is it:

He had come into San Bernardino from wherever it was (no one knows where he began and I'm not about to ask him today) on the early milk train and started off through the orange groves on his way to Hollywood. He was dressed, of course, all in white, and after walking

a long way, he decided to take a nap. Around noon he
was discovered by Pilar Perez, the Mexican film star,
whose husband, Whitley Ziebar, owns orange groves as
well as Ziebar Productions. She was out for a ride on
her horse when she came upon Jackson Lane, lying
naked under the trees with a half-eaten orange in one
hand. His white pants and sweater were spread about
under him like wings. She thought she had discovered
a dead angel. Then, and this is the terrific part, C.A.
said Pilar crossed herself and jumped on him.

And I remember—I remember thinking of Pilar
Perez Ziebar flying off her horse in slow motion and
lying on him. And I thought of his golden body. And I
think of his golden body now and keep my eyes on the
road as we drive along and I try also very hard not to
think about it in case he reads minds. Who knows what
a movie star can do?

He drives me out to where he keeps his boat, past
the oil fields. He salutes the oil pumps as we go by.
"Mornin'. Nice to see you," he says and looks over at
me to see how charmed I am. I've been down this way
with Myron and my mother when we went all the way
to the Hotel Del Coronado on one of our attempted
vacations where my mother worried about sunstroke,
her hair, or the crush I had on a nine-year-old Catholic.
And we went out here another time to Palos Verdes to
see a boarding school they thought I might like. Joan
Crawford keeps her kids there all year round. No one
could have kept me there. This was after I lost my sixth
governess in three weeks—left her wandering, looking
for me in Beverly Hills. I had slipped into a piano bar
and listened to some daytime drunks playing jazz until
I got bored and called home to be picked up.

We are standing now on this boardwalk looking down
at an entire yacht club. He points out his boat like a set-
tler saying, "There's our land, honey," as if we've come
over the pass after three months in a covered wagon.

"There she is," he says.

"Oh, Jackson, she's gorgeous." His boat isn't huge—

but it's by far the most beautiful one, which figures; it looks like a sleek little clipper ship.

"She's a very special sloop, Susanna, they don't make many like her. She's made by a company named Herreshoff. I went to Bristol, Rhode Island, and watched them build her—her deck is solid teak, the trim's mahogany—she's just the way I wanted her." He squints his eyes and nods to himself.

The wooden trim is all dark golden color and the rest is painted dark green with a maroon water line. We go down the little gangplank, and then walk along the dock and look at her from all angles. *Farewell* is carved on a little plank set up on her side. He climbs on the boat and helps me on.

"You have to be real careful, with those shoes. If I'd thought about it I would have told you to bring some sneakers."

"Well, I'll just go barefoot. This time." That is a hint. Which he ignores—or has not heard because he is checking this and that. He unlocks the door which leads down to a little room with two little bunks covered with a dark green and white striped canvas. "This is the cabin," he says.

That's right, I think. Cabin. Tucky's sailor friend gave me a book of words about sailing once—mostly to get me out of the way. "You never know when it will come in handy," he had said. That's for sure.

"Is this where you go when it says in the trades that you're 'unavailable for comment'?"

He's down on his haunches now, taking a sail from the locker. Haunches, almost as incredible a word as loins. Look at his legs. You could just die!

"What do you do, memorize those dumb papers? Hell, I don't even know what they say. If I had a lot of time I could go almost anywhere—and sometimes . . ." he says. He bundles the sail in his arms and carries it up to the deck. I follow him carefully. "Sometimes, I think I will."

"Where would you go—?"

"Everywhere." He flashes a smile at me, bright as the water. "I go to quiet coves on the other side of Catalina, listen, I'll show you how to take the cover off the mainsail here, and you can do that while I'm putting on the jib, okay?" He helps me get started. "That's fine," he says. "Sometimes I go down to Ensenada. No special places."

He must trust me a lot to let me help. I want to do it as deftly as he does everything. When he gets those sails pulled up, all flapping around him, and the boat dances under them like a horse prancing and pawing the ground when it's all saddled up and ready to go I wish a crazy wind would come along and whisk us down to Mexico. "HUNT ON FOR JACKSON LANE AND LEVANIN GRANDDAUGHTER—no trace of twosome missing since last week. . . ." They would interview Val and all my friends. "Twosome!" Val would say.

He touches places on the boat, rubs her wood and handles her like he loves her, looks at her like Grandmother when she puts new strings on her balalaika, like me with my puppets, like C.A. with her horse. Sailing ropes, musical strings, puppet strings and bridles tying on, pulling on, holding on, so you can hang on to the things you love. I would like to be tied to Jackson by a leash around his belt and follow him wherever he goes. I watch him moving around swiftly and do what he tells me as fast and quiet as I can. I love that he doesn't look to see if I do it right. "Hold this for me," "Lift that off," "Don't let go of that," "Throw me that," "Move over here now." His voice is low and steady and he even sees the wind. And shows me how. "See the cat's paws—the dark places on the water—that's wind walking over." And I can see the steely blue shadows on the gray-green ocean. It is like being in his own room, to be on his boat, and I don't want to talk. I just want to be part of his world as he is in it when he is alone because this is how you can see, I think, how he really is when he is by himself. I want to be the most quiet person he has had on his boat so he will ask me back again.

"There's no place so quiet, except maybe the desert at night, or when you're skiing, ever been skiing?"

"No." I don't want to say more than one word at a time, to let him guide the talking.

"Same kind of quiet. Quiet and moving fast at the same time. They got it in my contract that I'm not supposed to ski, can't get insurance on me if I do when I'm shooting."

"But you're a star—what if something happened to you?"

"What if something happened to anyone? It's not so much, being a star." I don't believe he really doesn't think it's not so much.

"I think it is. Everyone wants to be a star."

"Oh, they do—do they?" And I know he knows I mean me. He gives me his best grin, and that grin is like a present. You could get the feeling just from that of how it is to be a star and I'd trade being one for seeing him look at me like this once a week and so I grin back and then I have to look down and away from his eyes. You can't look in those eyes and breathe at the same time. And I look back up and he's still beaming wide at me with almost a laugh with his white teeth showing and I giggle and look away again and he laughs.

If you told me yesterday I'd be here sailing with Jackson Lane today I wouldn't have been able to live through the night for the fear that you were kidding and in the waiting I would have figured out something to worry about like being seasick, asthma, wearing the wrong thing (which I did. If I'd known I'd have put on my white slacks and sailor shirt and Tucky's friend's old sailor hat). If I'd known I would have imagined the day just gleaming like this, so much so that I would have been almost too dazzled by waiting to see it sparkle. A real person would be lost in a day like this; Jackson is as big and bright as the sun and the water and the sails. He goes with the day.

"If you're not afraid, go sit up there on the bowsprit; Herreshoff made it special for me so someone can do that; swing your legs over. It's like taking a ride on the wind."

Someone? Who else goes on this boat? I must not be like that. I do hope it is not one of the starlets I hate who drive around in powder blue Caddy convertibles with their monograms stuck on the door in chrome plaques.

I can't imagine why he has decided to share all his secret favorite things with me. It must be because he knows how I adore him. Does he pick a fan a year to surprise? But how would he have known? I wrote for his picture once, but I wrote for others, too, at the same time. I don't think he sees those letters. If you believe in shooting stars, then you can believe, I think, that this just happened. I tell myself.

I am the figurehead of this ship. I sit right on the tip above the carved wooden eagle with my legs over the edge and I spread my arms up and behind me like a bare-chested lady carved of wood riding this eagle and the boat parts the water below me, curling it up and back like long smiling lips and saltwater splashes up against my bare feet and onto my legs and now this— now this is flying. I am not just taking a ride on the wind, I am the wind. The boat dips and prances, the sails clap in the wind and the sea applauds and the sun casts down starry lace on the water like spangled handkerchiefs. The sun beats on my face. How to explain the fresh sunburn I will have? Outdoor classes, I will say. "We are studying the stars."

"In the daylight?" my grandmother will say.

"That's when they are so bright you really have to know to see them." And if Val is over she will nudge me and say, "Yes—it's such an advanced course, they're letting only Susanna take it. It's so advanced, in fact, no one ever heard of it before."

I turn to look at him, driving the boat around the ocean squinting his eyes at a road only he can see, his hair like tangled golden cords, his white shirt blowing out like a small sail behind him, unbuttoned now to get the sun, and his chest is gold. They made Oscar to look like him. (Why do they care that he cannot act? I wonder if he knows, or cares. They should give him an Oscar just for walking around so you can look at him.)

I look up at the sails towering and billowing above me, now *there* are wings.

"We're coming about now, Susanna," he calls to me. "Hang on." And I clutch onto the railing as the mainsail flips to the other side and we dip and turn in a wide sweep and head back to the harbor. I never want to go back. I see the Palisades like a low, russet wall ahead and somewhere Perdido is perched up there. I wonder if my grandmother feels someone out here is looking at her and if she sighs and hugs her arms and imagines it is Grandfather's ghost, skimming around out at sea. If it is, he's going to be mad as hell to see me here without my shoes and socks and my skirt bunched up above my knees. Above my thighs! And with an actor.

I imagine Grandfather flying by on a big silver dolly, sitting as he used to sometimes in the cameraman's seat, with the director gnashing his teeth (directors hate studio owners more than anyone, which isn't saying a lot, I guess, because directors, Grandfather said, "have feathered egos, always like tenors"). Grandfather is waving his arms at me. "What is the meaning of this?"

"Why does there have to be a meaning?" I say to him. "It's entertainment."

"Don't put my words back in my mouth."

The land comes closer now and the boat is so quiet it almost feels as if it is the land which is advancing on us. I wish it would snap out of sight like a Newcombe shot does when they turn off the film in the background, leaving just the close-up people against an empty electric blue world. I wish a monsoon would spring up and whirl us off to the South Pacific and we would live on an island and I would make a guitar out of a coconut shell with strips of palm leaves for strings and when I got to know him better I'd do the hula Tucky taught me and when we came back they would see how happy I am and

they'd let him pick me up at school and come over all
the time to Perdido and sit next to me on the big projection room couch and watch movies. I always want to be
able to stay at Perdido. When I'm married, Grandmother says I can live in her wing.

"But where will you be?"

And she smiled at me. "Oh, I'll be around. I just
won't need so much room."

"Yes, you will. I always want you to be in this same
place." I don't want her to ever have less room. I like
all her old things and the big gold-painted bed and her
boxes of old jewelry and her dressing room with its
closets full of old beaded formals which Val and I have
played dressup in since we were children. And all the
walls are hung with photos of their great old stars.

I come and sit beside Jackson now as we are coming
in and I imagine sitting beside him in our projection
room.

"Do you like to watch yourself in your own movies?"

"Not much," he says, angling the boat neatly around
a buoy. "Yes, no, yes, no," he goes, imitating the buoy
bobbing from side to side. His eyes are bluer now, with
facets like aquamarines. "They're not very good movies,
although I get mad as hell when anyone else says so.
They're getting too easy."

"Well, I like them. What movies do you like?"

"Not too many, watching them's kind of like work
now. Guess I liked them better when I was your age.
Here, now, you think you can hold her steady? I'm going
to take down the sails and bring her in with the engine.
Wind's a little unpredictable, it's coming in gusty. It
does that when it comes from the northeast. Gets all
confused coming through the mountains." I love to
watch him moving fast; I'm catching glimpses while I'm
holding on to the helm. He's pulling down the mainsail
and then he takes off the jib and flings it down into the
cockpit. I'm going to look at that book again and learn
exactly how to do everything. He will be surprised the
next time. He leaps down now and the boat is standing

25

still. It is completely silent, as though the sound has been turned off, and the mast looks so forlorn swaying there. Then he turns on the engine and we chug in and dock and I feel like I do when everyone's gone home from a party. Already I'm figuring how sad I am going to be when we're in the car going back.

"Now, Susanna, see if you can do this. Go forward now." I go. "Okay, Susanna, when I tell you, you jump off, and wrap that line around the mooring." I do as he says and then he swings up on the dock and ties up the stern. We wrap the big sail up again and he stuffs the little one into its locker, checks the cabin, and takes some suntan lotion out of his darling little hammock he has swinging in there. Puppets would be so cute in that hammock.

"Should have thought of this before—want some?" he says, handing the lotion to me after he's rubbed it over his face with both hands and put some on his arms and chest. I will remember the name, Sköl.

"This smells like the stuff they put in my asthma percolator," I say, putting it on anyway.

"What's an asthma percolator?" he asks.

"It's a machine I'm supposed to turn on at night so I can breathe. It has another name but I always forget it."

"Well, now maybe you'll think about it different," he says, and winks at me.

That is really something, the way he does that.

He doesn't like to leave this boat. After he has put everything away, including the cushions, he sits down again on the bare wooden seats. I think he is figuring out something else to do. "Hey, want to learn something about being a sailor?" He takes the little sail out of the locker. "I was going to tie a new line on here. Might as well do it now. Okay, there are about two hundred kinds of knots. I know about forty, but there are only three important ones. You already know a square knot."

"I do?" I say.

"Sure, that's a regular knot. Then there's the double

hitch," he says, "but I'm going to teach you the bowline.
Look, make a loop, then you take this end, see, now
watch what I'm doing, the snake comes out of the hole,
goes behind the tree"—he takes the end and pulls it
back through the loop—"and goes down in the hole
again. What's the matter?"

I laugh, but I'm squinting funny I guess. "I am scared
of snakes."

"Okay," he laughs, "let's say the long tall rabbit
comes out of the hole, got it now?" I'm doing it myself,
with his hand helping, trying very hard to think rabbit
not snake, but I'm mostly watching his hands. They're
big and squared off with the thumbs jutting out, not all
lined up smooth like gloves. Interrupting the golden
hairs on the backs there are tiny scars, almost like in-
dented veins, which are silver white in the sun.

"What are the scars from?" I ask.

"Oh—they're very old." He looks at his hands, and
flexes them. I probably shouldn't have asked.

He turns to me, his face close to mine, the tips of his
lashes are red and where his beard would be his face
seems dusted with gold. Under the Sköl I can smell his
skin and sweat. "You're supposed to be watching the
rope." He kind of half smiles. "You're not concentrating."

"Yes, I am."

"Okay, now try it again." I love his directions. His
voice gets lower and very slow and close, almost as
though he is speaking inside of my head. He could probably teach me to do anything.

I try the knot again.

"There, that's the way," he says, "just fine."

And he pulls on the knot to show how it holds. Then
he puts away the sail.

"Do you have double-jointed thumbs?" I ask him.

"I guess that's what you'd call them." He moves them
up and down.

"So do I. I can reach an octave and a half. On the
piano."

"You like music?" He's thinking of something. Us? In a musical together: "Jackson Lane sings, he dances and introduces a sensational new star. Ta-da!" That is ridiculous. They never let actors discover anything.

"Okay, now, before we go . . ." He looks around as though he is checking off a list. "We should hose her off—to clean off the salt. Can you hop up there on the dock, throw me the hose, and when I tell you, you turn it on—all right?"

"Sure." I climb up and unwind the hose. He holds up his arms and catches the end. I turn it on and watch while the water winds down and arcs out over him. He puts his thumb over the hole to fan it out and rainbows move across the water. I stand and watch him with my hands pressed close together as he moves around with the hose almost as if he is fencing, moving back, then thrusting it forward, then finding a new place to lunge at and the boat glistens with water and water runs down his arms.

He finishes and he looks up at the sun like an ordinary person would look at a watch. "Come on, let's go now." He strokes along the prow of the boat and touches her carved wooden name plate with his hand before we leave and then he stands for a moment looking down at her before we go up to the car again. I feel as I walk that I am not in touch with the ground. I am rocking; my rhythm has become the boat's.

I wait on edge for the words, "Ought to be getting you home now." But after we've driven a little way, he stops at a drive-in. I love days that go on and on like this. Just when you think it is over—like a great movie —there is more.

"How about a hamburger?" he says. And winks at the carhop who takes our order, trying hard to write her pencil shakes so when she sees who he is. She tottles in and tells everyone and soon faces are pressed against the glass as all the cooks and all the carhops and the drive-in manager take a look at Jackson Lane. And a kid from the next car comes and asks for his autograph.

I love how people look at you when you're with someone famous and how they look at famous people—they
cringe and smile and give you this knowing look like,
"You lucky . . . !" Although my stepfather Myron is
not exactly famous, when he takes me to premieres there
are people who know who he is and they come up for
autographs and he gets his picture taken—some of the
favorite V.L.I. stars come and slip in next to him—he
adores the ones who show up on the set on time.
(Everyone loves them. Ann Miller is a perfect example.
And Barbara Stanwyck. And Jimmy Stewart.) "It's
fine," Myron says, "to tell all these stories about eccen-
tric stars, just as long as you don't have to work with
them." That is exactly the kind of thing Myron says and
you just sit there and look at each other with eyes
glazed over when he says it. Or at least Val and I do.

Oh—I do want to be famous too, I think, as I watch
Jackson sign his autograph on a paper napkin ("Put it
under glass," I want to say to that kid), just to have
them look at me. They hate you when you're with
someone famous—they can see themselves doing your
place better—"What makes you so great?" they seem to
say. They also figure you can get stuff for them from
the famous one, that they can touch your arm and say,
like the drive-in cook, "Would you ask if I could have
an extra autograph for my friend Benny?" He catches
me on my way to the ladies' room while we wait for our
hamburgers. If you can't come through then you're stuck-
up. They're mad at you, not the famous one. So much
of a nothing you are—shows to go. Benny's friend gives
me the finger because Jackson won't sign any more autographs. The finger!

I take bites the size of peas and still get ketchup on
my sleeve.

"Can't take you anywhere," he says and kind of
reaches over and ticks my face with the back of his
hand.

Oh, God. My mother has told me:

"If you let a man touch you before you are married

your grandmother will know by the look in your eyes and the way you walk and she will have a heart attack and die. And it could be damaging to our public reputation." (This last part, I think, is my mother's idea that people would think she is not a good mother. It has nothing to do with wanting a child, which I doubt was her favorite idea; being a good mother is just a thing to be. I would not know how, but I think I would watch my Aunt Lillian if I wanted to learn. Or my grandmother.)

Public reputation! I see in my mind the headline in the Hollywood *Reporter:* LEVANIN GRANDDAUGHTER CHEAP. How disappointed Myron would be that I do not see it saying: HOWARD STEPDAUGHTER CHEAP. (Or would he be relieved? I think Myron would rather be competent than famous.)

And this is a man. Not a boy, even. But I also sort of know what my mother has in mind by "touch." And this is not *that*.

Jackson may be a little crazy. But I know that from before. That must be why this day isn't that strange. Unusual. I remember once reading that he rode this palomino horse down Camden Drive, yippi-ti-yaying, all the way, in his tuxedo, at six o'clock in the morning. The horse reared up and whinnied in front of a lady's house, then he galloped off again and no one even called the police because it was just Jackson Lane having a wild Hollywood party all by himself.

And Hedda Hopper said that two real New York socialites had killed themselves over him. I could see them, one after the other, catapulting out of windows in long Molyneux dinner dresses. I look at him, shining beside me here. He doesn't look like a ladykiller—just a little bit like a rascal who probably shakes his head and looks puzzled when people get carried away over him. I can't imagine him making promises he doesn't keep any more than I would.

I am lucky enough to have a day with him and you shouldn't ask questions, I remind myself when I think about it. And, God, I say, thank You. God, I will believe in You for years for this.

We are cruising through Venice now. Past the arcade. "My favorite governess brought me down here one day and gave me money to hang around the dimestore while she went upstairs to have a little nap with this sailor she was going out with. I bought a button there that says, 'Treat 'em rough.' "

I don't know why I have told him that. I will certainly not tell him I still wear it on my underpants. Sometimes.

He laughs. Switches the radio station to hillbilly music.

I bet Jackson can be a little rough. He's got rough cheeks, if you can call them that, since they're lean and angle inward. With the sun coming at a certain angle, they look like Keenan Wynn and some of his roughnecks might have ridden over them with their motorcycles. That was Tucky, that governess. She was from Australia and had a room full of koala bears and totem pole jewelry boxes from New Zealand. She had the best breasts, covered with freckles, but big and pink and they'd swoop around when she'd dance. Now that I've got them, I practice a lot in front of my mirror, lifting my arms up under my hair with a hibiscus bobby-pinned behind my ear. Tucky used to say sailors made her swoon. My mother fired her for taking a nap with Mickey, her sailor, in her room. That's what Tucky told me. My mother said I was getting too used to Tucky and she didn't want me getting the idea anyone else was my mother. I heard my mother tell Aunt Lillian, Val's mother, that Tucky was caught on the kitchen table with Errol Flynn at her next job and was fired. I had visions of them on our kitchen table with all the help walking around getting dinner anyway and Ethel muttering, "Trash!" She probably was just lying down in a swoon.

But I know what swooning is now. I feel I've got a

slide right inside me and my heart is swooping by at ninety miles an hour, upside down.

He stops at Ocean Park. "I don't think there's anything so seedy and rundown as an old amusement park during the day. Bad as an out-of-work actor with a three-day-old beard."

"Yes," I say, "oh yes." And I wonder why he hates out-of-work actors. You can tell by how he said that. I want to say, "Don't worry—you'll never be one," but I shouldn't even think such a thing would occur to him.

We go by the merry-go-round there. He's looking around for someone, he says. "An old pal of mine."

They tell him he must be looking for the Santa Monica pier.

"That's the one," he says. And off we go.

He stops and looks up these little rickety steps alongside the merry-go-round building. "This must be it. Scotty's an old traveling buddy. Just got a note from him a few months ago that he's been settled in an apartment above the merry-go-round. We hitched across country together a long time ago. Came into San Berdoo together on the morning freight. He walked one way, me the other. I sometimes wonder what would have happened if we'd walked the other way. He's a musician, when you said you liked music that reminded me. Scotty's a folksinger and I've been meaning to drop by. He's been blacklisted too, like all of them."

San Berdoo. That's where it was. To think C.A. might have been telling the truth for once in her life. I must stop thinking of him under the tree like that.

He knocks on the door and then smiles down at me. "You okay? Don't want to go on to school?" Even though it sounds like he is being serious, the way he looks shows he knows I'm having a wonderful time. I saw a clock in front of a drugstore on the road; it's only about two—I can still get back for my recital after school. I wonder why I even can think of that—why would that matter when I'm having such a wonderful time? Except it is the first recital Val and I are both playing in. I've always been in with two beginners before and I don't want her to think I chickened out; then she'd really think I made this up as an excuse. We were supposed to play a duet two weeks ago and I had an asthma attack.

Just before his friend answers the door I have a moment of panic. Can this really be Jackson Lane? Is it a double dressed up, and really a kidnapper? That's stupid, I tell myself, even if there was anyone else in the world who looks like this, there's that something else, that thing Myron calls "a motor." Someone has it or not and to be a star you have to have it and Jackson has enough to run seven hundred Cadillacs up this highway at seventy-hundred miles an hour. I love the number seven. I imagine a song called "Seven Stars." "If I had seven stars, they all would look like you. We would sail the seven seas in a ship with seven sails . . ."

Jackson's friend is a big man with broad, flat shoulders and a big face that has more of a landscape than features. He moves back gently when he sees me as though he is giving me a chance to get used to him so I won't be intimidated by his size.

Then after a moment of looking at each other, Scotty puts an arm around Jackson. "You sonofagun, I never thought I'd lay eyes on you again. Do you know you're impossible to get hold of—"

"I guess so," Jackson says, slapping Scotty back on the shoulder the way boys do when they like each other.

"Not," Scotty says, "that you ever were any easier to birddog. You're looking okay, for you." He teases Jackson, I see, kind of like Val teases me. He has a soft, easy voice, low and gentle for someone so big—but I bet it really gets strong when he sings, he wouldn't even have to stretch it to rock the rafters.

"This is my friend, Susanna Howard."

"Oh yeah?" He looks at me and then at Jackson and shakes his head and Jackson kind of glares at him as though he doesn't want any wisecracks.

"We're playing hooky today," Jackson says.

"Kid," Scotty says, still looking at Jackson for a moment or so, "you're learning from the expert. Sometimes I think Jack only goes someplace just to prove how fast he can leave. So, how d'ya like my place? I want to show you something." He takes us out on a balcony, more like a little catwalk. "Most people live on a merry-go-round. I'm a lucky man, I just look right down on it." We look down on the big painted tin top of the merry-go-round.

"How long have you been here?" Jackson asks.

"Oh, about six months. I wrote you, dammit, when I came out after the disaster at Peekskill. So you know. You just forget."

"It must be fun when the music's playing," Jackson says.

Changing the subject. He is good at that. I wonder how Scotty knew where to write Jackson. Probably studio. Probably Jackson didn't even read the letter.

"I'm usually down there when it is. But I like it."

We go back inside. Scotty has piles of sheet music and copies of worn-out songbooks and some old pamphlets around, and everything is battered a bit, except the beautiful guitar lying on a table.

"Can I look at your guitar?"

"Sure, you play?"

"Not really. I have a guitar and my grandmother has a balalaika. She's taught me some Russian folksongs. But I take piano lessons."

And I think about the recital again and get a catch in my breathing. I surely don't want to be the one to end this day.

"Whatever did happen at Peekskill?" Jackson says, lying back on Scotty's bed, which is right here in the living room, and stretching his legs out.

"I wrote you all about it," Scotty says, sorting through some things to show me.

"You know I don't pay attention to what I read. And don't say you can tell from the scripts I've been doing."

Just like me with Val, Jackson knows when he's going to get teased.

"How'd you know I was just thinking of that?" Scotty says, with a smile going sideways.

"I figured. So Peekskill. Did you get hit? I hear Robeson was roughed up."

"Paul Robeson?" I ask. "He's wonderful. What happened? Oh, I just love hearin' him."

"Well, you aren't going to be hearing him much for a while. He was okay, Jack, but they put a few in the hospital. This was over up at Peekskill, New York, Susanna. Paul was doing a big concert there, a lot of us were up there and the American Legion decided to stop the concert and some people didn't want them to do that and the police, of course, were nowhere to be found—they promised protection, too. Couple of kids got beat up real bad. . . ." Scotty stretches his big arms and shoulders. I have decided he is handsome in a very mixed-up kind of way. He does have a sexy look. Dirtier than Jackson in a way because you know he's taking off your clothes in his head and laughing about the fact you know that with his eyes. And Jackson's eyes know you want to take off his clothes. That's the difference. Of course, neither one of them is as completely dirty as Angelo.

"What did Paul do?" I ask, trying not to let Scotty or Jackson see by my expression I'm thinking of anything else (of *that*).

"Nothing he could do—oh, you mean, to get them so riled up?" (Riled up. I love that. I must remember to use it.)

"Yeah." I'm saying that slow and soft like he does.

"Not a damn thing except they decided he is a Communist. So, anyhow, Jack, that's what sent me out here. And I come here and it's just as bad. I hate those goddam Legionnaires—I hate their guts."

"Scotty." I want to change the subject now. And I have an idea (of course if they knew he is a Communist

35

they would never let me, so I won't tell them that part).
"Can you teach people to play guitar?"

Jackson's looking through a magazine now. "Scotty is
the best folk teacher anywhere, Susanna," he says.

"Cut it out, Jack," Scotty says, but with a blank expression so I can't tell whether he is annoyed or doesn't
like compliments. I have a feeling Scotty wanted him to
come down here to really talk to him about something
and Jackson has brought me along just so they can't
have that talk.

"And," Jackson goes on, "he's traveled on the road
with Woody Guthrie, knew Leadbelly and Fred Heller-
man and everyone else worth knowing, if that's what
you like—all those songs, with more story to them than
most two-hour movies."

"More story for sure than yours all put together,"
Scotty says and Jackson laughs and says he should have
felt that coming and Scotty says, "Jack always exag-
gerates—I only traveled once with Woody in his Chev-
ery, which is what Guthrie called his Chevrolet," he
says to me. Now he shows me copies of a magazine,
Sing Out.

"This is put out by Pete Seeger—would you like a
bunch, to look over?—there's probably some stuff you
can use in here."

"She can't take all that propaganda home, Scotty—
her family would hit the ceiling," Jackson says. "And
they'd start asking all kinds of questions." He had
moved off his back and is looking annoyed. I don't want
him to think he never should have started all this.

"I don't know what you call propaganda, Jack—don't
think you know either, but Pete told me once that every
folksong, maybe every song, is some kind of propaganda." Scotty still puts the pamphlets back on the pile,
or slaps them back down there, and I feel as though I
wish they would just ask me to go outside for a minute
so they could fight about whatever it is and get it over
with. But Scotty just picks up the guitar and starts strumming, Woody's "Hobo Lullaby" is the tune, and he says,

"Even lullabies are propaganda. No matter what you're singing, you're trying to get someone to do something, or feel something, even to think fallin' in love makes you feel good—now if that ain't dangerous propaganda, I don't know what is." And Scotty's strumming and tapping his foot for my benefit and he and Jackson are glaring daggers at each other. Maybe Jackson took away a girl from Scotty. Something. Stay out of it, Susanna, I tell myself. Scotty could well be a real Communist or sympathizer. He has that kind of wiseguy way like Uncle Alan and Norman Corwin and some of his other friends and I like it, that kind of way which probably means I'm sort of a pinkish person myself.

Scotty takes us down now to the merry-go-round. He's running the merry-go-round for the owners, doing all the mechanical stuff and touching up the paint on the horses and all of that. "These are the last of the horses with glass eyes," Scotty tells us.

Scotty turns on the merry-go-round and I pick a palomino horse with a harness of rubies and Jackson gets onto a white one with its head thrown back, he leaps from one to another as we ride and then, hanging way off a fierce-looking black stallion, he reaches out and grabs a metal ring as the merry-go-round whizzes by. He lifts me down from my horse when we stop and my skirt billows around me, and I would like to stay right here in midair with his hands on my waist looking down at him looking up at me and then he gives me the iron ring he has caught.

"They stopped making brass rings during the war," Scotty says, watching.

We go back upstairs and Scotty shows me the chords for "Good Night, Irene," Leadbelly's song, which is now a big hit, and I'm singing and playing as though we have all been friends for years. Then I ask Scotty if he knows "The Midnight Special," which is my secret theme song. ("Here comes-a-Miss Susie . . ." is how I sing it.)

"Sure, that's an old one. I don't know who made that

up, but Leadbelly did a nice job of it. . . . 'Here comes-a-Miss Rosie . . .' " and he sings, " '. . . umbrelly on her shoulder, piece of paper in her hand . . .' " and I do the chorus with him, " 'Let the Midnight Special shine her ever-lovin' light on me.' " Jackson just watches with his hands behind his head and says, imitating Scotty's drawl, "I ain't never been in no Pasternak musical before, by golly." Scotty gives him a look. "You're going to be kind of good. Nice style, nice tone to your voice. Never mind him."

"I have my own words to that. I guess you shouldn't do that . . . change them, should you?" I want Jackson to see I am serious, too. Not just a romantic child he can laugh off. Or at.

"Why not?" Scotty says. "These songs are all changed around from something. They're all there just to use as you like."

Then it had to come.

"Hey, Scotty," Jackson says. "Have you got the time? I've got to get Susanna back."

"Two thirty."

"Oh, dear." I clap my hands to my mouth. "Andrew will be picking me up at school and I won't be there."

"What time does he pick you up?"

"Three fifteen—Scotty, can I use your phone?"

"You sure could if I had one. There's a public one right down next to the hot dog stand, do you need change?"

"I'll get it," Jackson says, and gives me a handful.

Scotty looks at him. "I could have spared a nickel."

It's just as well, I think, to leave them alone for a minute or so and I go down and find the phone. "Mary, may I speak to Dorothy?" Mary is my sort of unofficial companion. They have finally given up trying to keep governesses for me.

"Where are you, Susanna? I've been frantic. The school said you had called in sick and they just phoned to see how you are."

"They have a nerve. Checking up. You didn't say anything, did you?"

"They're only following Mr. Howard's orders. But I didn't tell them. It's embarrassing not to know where you are. I'd really like to know what you do with yourself when you don't go to school. I really would. What do you want Dorothy for?"

"I just do." I will be charming. "Are you okay, how's Tom?" Tom is her husband who is either out of work or beating her up but she adores him anyway.

"That's very sweet of you to ask, he's all right. Just a minute, I'll ring for Dorothy. Now let's just not mention all this to your parents when they get home tonight. They'll have enough on their minds." I wonder what that means. I guess Myron had more trouble with the New York people over the blacklisting than he thought he would. Mary sighs. I have heard her say to Tom that I am impossible to handle.

"Now what are you up to, Glamour?" Dorothy says.

"Well, you remember this morning—there's a little problem with school. Could you tell Andrew not to pick me up, say I'm coming home with a friend, please?"

"Now, you know he's going to tell Mr. Howard, Susanna. I got no influence over Andrew."

"Yes, you do. Tell him— Never mind. I'll think of something."

Andrew's used to me not being where I'm supposed to, anyway, so it doesn't matter.

When I get out of the phone booth, Jackson and Scotty are standing outside on the pier and Jackson hands Scotty some money, which Scotty shoves into his pocket and I pretend I don't see as I walk toward them.

"So, let me know what happens," Jackson says, and Scotty shrugs.

"If I can track you down, I will." I guess, even for old friends, movie stars are hard to get hold of. Scotty tells me to come down anytime I want. "I'll teach you some of my favorite songs—you've got a real nice talent. I can see you pick up a tune real quick. Just don't try to get too fancy, d'ya g' wha' y' mean?" I like the way he swallows some of his words when he's enthusiastic—"D'ya g' wha' y' mean?"—I practice silently saying it like that—I want to develop a drawl or something so you'd just know I am a folksinger by the way I talk.

"Scotty's got a chance to work on this network TV show the Weavers are going to be doing," Jackson says, "so I gave him a bit of cash to go East. That's what he wanted to talk about. I hope it works out for him. I had to tell him there wasn't much I could do for him out here right now."

That makes me wonder why he was coming to see Myron this morning, or said he was. But I don't care about that. Thinking about reasons for everything reminds me of the math problems that go, "If Mary's mother baked six pies, how many miles would Ned have walked before Bill bought his bike for eight dollars?" You can faint from logicking everything out too much.

It's the same way I feel when people say why don't I go to school. I don't *know* why I don't like to go to school. I like to wander around in the hills nearby and think about things, look at things.

I love every red stoplight which keeps me with Jackson longer. I look at him as though I am taking snapshots of every expression. And I chatter too much—about the recital, about how I love his boat, about how interesting Scotty is, and about, about *anything* to make it last, not to say I don't want to leave him. He doesn't say anything—could not get a word in edgewise, actually, I guess. So I try to be quiet. He listens to the radio and when "Goodnight Irene" comes on I am just thinking of him. But I don't want him to think I am a sulky type so I say I love this song and sing a little in the rich singer's voice I do not have. He sings the chorus with me and we both laugh.

He stops at the foot of the driveway. "I'd better not drive you up. Is this okay?"

"Fine."

We sit and look at each other. I want him to hold me tight in his arms, in a real fade-out, close-shot kiss.

He leans over and just kisses me on the cheek and ruffles my hair.

I love how his hair has little waves near the neck. Not like most men, who have bristles. I reach out and touch his hair, to pat him and show him how I feel about the day and because I just want to touch him. It is so warm, the hair so soft . . .

He looks at me so astonished, so startled. For a second he is frozen with his lips just parted. I think he is going to grab me to him and kiss me like I want him to. I see the smoky look he gets in his eyes, that glint before he grabs his co-star.

Then he suddenly pushes my hand away. And he is angry. "Don't do that." He says it in a very low voice, but if ever anyone meant this, boy, does he mean it. "Don't ever do that, don't ever do that again."

Again? Does that mean I will see him? I will, Jackson, I want to say, I will wait for you forever.

"Will you wait for me to grow up?" I do not believe I have said it. How stupid. "I mean," and I stumble over the words, "I had a terrific time."

"You'd better go now," he says. I get out of the car and close the door gently and watch him drive away until the car is so small I could put it in my pocket. And he is gone as fast as that. With not even a "Take care of yourself, kid."

I walk backward up the driveway.

A few months ago Val and I put on a pageant for the family with my puppets—the founding of Perdido. I made up songs on my guitar (which Mr. Ruben, my music teacher, says is not a "serious instrument") and Val did the set. The house sits on top of Perdido Drive, which winds up from Sunset like a spiral staircase (if you ripped the street off the world by its roots it would look like a tornado). Val made a curved street out of wire covered with papier-mâché. She topped it with a fairly clever replica of the house. (Val is really good in art. And piano, and everything.) During the show, I swung one of the puppets too swiftly, too far back, and knocked down the set. No one really thought it was an accident, though, houses often fall down out here, and everyone always expects the earthquake. But Val said, "You have a way of turning everything into a disaster."

"And you," I said, and I was surprised because I am usually very careful with her, "have everything you want."

"I have everything *you* want," she said. "Difference."

Baby brother. Straight hair. Perfect pitch. No asthma. Own real father. That's the main thing.

Well. One thing I do have is an iron ring Jackson Lane caught for me, and I'm going to wear it on a string around my neck forever.

Of course if I were Val I would probably like to have a pool and tennis court and projection room and I would be envious if she had all that and I didn't—but Val is not like that and they are intellectuals, her side of the family, and these are not such interesting things to them, my mother says. But I think that's to make her feel easier about being the one who lives here, especially since I think Aunt Lillian is my grandmother's favorite, even though she did marry an actor. I also don't think Aunt Lillian would want anyone else running her house and Grandmother especially likes her better for that. My mother, however, was Grandfather's pet, "Because," Grandmother says, "she is such a beauty." I have a feeling he wanted my mother to marry Myron and probably didn't mind when my father died because Myron wouldn't mind living here where Grandfather could have my mother around to look at. I also think, and this is probably mean, that Myron was not miserable when Grandfather died because he would get more attention from my mother. He thought. But my mother still misses her father, more I think than she misses my dead father. She sure misses someone a lot because her basic expression except when she is looking in the mirror (and then it is just blissful, even when critical) is so mournful, and she adores herself in black, not only because it sets off her diamond clips so well, either.

I come into the house just in time to hear Grandmother shouting in the kitchen.

"Traife!" Grandmother says, holding up a large black frying pan. "Pork chops!" Her long hair is braided down her back. She loves to have kitchen tantrums. I think she would have adored to be an actress.

Mary comes clicking in on her high-heeled patent-leather slingbacks behind Grandmother and sort of reels back as she is confronted with the frying pan.

"Surely not pork chops, Mrs. Levanin. Surely not!" Mary always plays to her like Pancho to the Cisco Kid.

"Then bacon. I could smell it as I came down the stairs."

Ethel has rumbled down through the pantry and the laundry room and into her own room, slamming the door. Perhaps if Grandmother is in a firing mood she will throw in Andrew if I approach the subject delicately. But then she never really fires anyone—except governesses, and everyone took turns doing that, if they could catch them before they quit.

"Grandmother"—it really isn't fair—"Grandmother, it was my fault. I had a guest for breakfast. He asked for bacon. . . ." She always knows.

"There is always a choice," Grandmother says. "We could hire a good kosher cook who would not permit such a thing in the house, no matter the guest—who was this guest?" She's been threatening us with a kosher cook for years, but actually has very little interest in food any more since her heart attack diet started and since she had to give up coming here and making special dishes—which used to drive Ethel completely wild. But they were the best food we had. I think these kitchen fits take more out of her than cooking, but no one asks me.

I am trapped. I think fast. "Angelo. Angelo, yes, Mr. Giordano's son."

43

"He knows that this is a Jewish house. He knows not to ask for bacon." She is suspicious.

"Well, he forgot. I'm sorry."

Dorothy has been leaning against the sink, listening. She shows me her hands. Both fingers crossed.

Grandmother is trying not to show she is in pain and she is standing now very still with her hands on her hips just enough above where they would normally be to show she is hurting. Her great diamond and onyx rings glitter across her knuckles in a row like blackbirds with beady eyes.

"You be careful with that boy, now. He knows too much for a boy his age. You know how birds in the bush can lead to another."

"Yes, Grandmother."

"Now. Dorothy. Will you tell Ethel when she becomes available that my daughter called and the entire family will come for dinner tomorrow. The baby too." And her eyes shine. Grandmother adores Val's little brother, Theo. Everyone does—even Val, who, I think, was a little worried he would take Alan's attention from her. My mother says Alan was discovered in an acting class in N.Y.U. and that his family were "perfectly nice" people from Brooklyn. "Alan," she says, "just adores being controversial and that's why he says he's a Communist." Anyway, Val loves Theo and only gets the wry smile that shows she thinks something's foolish when Alan calls him "My Prince of Players."

"Men and sons!" Grandmother says and looks carefully at Val. Grandmother does not miss anything.

When Lillian and my mother went shopping one day, or Lillian went to watch my mother shop, Val and Uncle Alan brought the baby over—without his nurse. I watched, from my room, as they played with him by the pool until Grandmother got down there and you would have thought Val and Alan were the parents of this baby, even the way they grinned at each other when he'd do something cute.

"Angelo?" Grandmother says to me as I help her up the stairs—she holds her hand to her chest.

"Yes, Grandmother?"

"I don't think so. I don't know what, but I don't think Angelo so fast." She knows Jackson was here—Andrew probably tattled. But I'm not going to say—I'm going to pretend I don't know what she means.

THE FAMILY GATHERS FOR DINNER LIKE CAVALRY AND Indians assembling for a war, hitching around on their horses, checking weapons.

Myron drums his fingertips on the tablecloth. He is impatient with dinner when he is going to see dailies and rushes. He adores that part of his job and I'm not sure he is wild for this head-of-household part that came with it, which is why he plays it very seriously. He oversees the table like a gym teacher lining us up for calisthenics, and then having to do the exercises too. My mother taps her foot around under the table trying to find the buzzer set into the floor which signals the kitchen to start serving. My mother likes all the rituals, but I think she just wishes she had a better class of family to go with her—Grandmother is all right, except my mother winces when she uses Yiddish—but she could never get the rest of us into one of those family pictures in *Vogue* with everyone in black velvet and lace collar. I catch her posing sometimes in one of her dinner dresses with her fine white hands draped just so. She has the longest neck in the family and the finest features. They all have thick, silky dark hair (Lillian's and Grandmother's is curlier than my mother's and Val's) and very serious hazel eyes, and perfect mouths for lipstick. I, my mother says, should be pleased "You don't look like anyone else." But how can I tell what I look like then?

"You'll be just fine," she says. We often have this conversation when she is trying on new clothes in Grandmother's room and when my mother says, "You'll be just fine," she is looking at herself. Then my grandmother says, "There was, Vera, Victor's sister's family in New Jersey, who had fair hair and blue eyes." My coloring is like my real father's. My mother will not discuss my real father. Grandmother says, "It is a very painful subject." But sometimes she will tell me something about him. "He was very individual, a man who didn't talk much, a very appealing young man. Your mother loved him very much. And he loved her. I will tell you more about all this when you are older. Everyone fell in love with him, as everyone will fall in love with you."

"Oh, no one falls in love with me. All the boys like Val better."

"You must learn to think more highly of yourself. That is the secret: pride."

It's easy, I think to myself, when your father calls you Beauty, like Uncle Alan calls Val, and when your midriff swoops in neat and straight so if you wear a dress with a sash it stays there as smoothly as if the studio made it for you. Tarquin Olivier untied mine and put it in my mouth like a bridle when we were kids. He had braces before anyone; and Sean Flynn and I used to roll over and over down the grass slope in front of school while we were waiting for our cars to pick us up. But Tarquin would hold Val's place in line at lunch and bring her her plate. And Sean asked to be her partner in dancing class. Val has a figure like a little ballerina. I feel like Trigger next to her. She's one of those short people who when you're walking along gives the impression that short is taller. Val's short is like my mother's tall.

My mother thinks Aunt Lillian is too bohemian with her silver combs in her hair and even Val is too "fresh." I, of course, am never quite right. Tonight she tells me my hair looks "disheveled" and "what is that hideous thing around your neck?" It is the iron ring Jackson gave me, on a ribbon. "I found it," I say. "I think it's prehistoric or something."

"I think it's interesting, Vera," Aunt Lillian says, fondling the silverware she used when she was a child

47

here. Grandmother smooths her napkin in her lap and peers at my necklace. She is rosy from her visit with Theo, who is upstairs with his nurse, O'Connor.

"Bless that baby," Grandmother says. We are waiting for Alan.

"What is that thing? Paleolithic?" Val looks at me. You can't see her smile exactly, but I can just catch the dimples on either side of her mouth indent, tiny crescent shadows. She takes her dessert spoon, dips just the tip of it into her water goblet, and then flicks water across the table and it lands in my eye. Deadpan as Virginia O'Brien she sits there again, her hands folded in her lap, her gleaming black hair falling neatly from the center part right down her back. ("Now that hair must be a pleasure to comb," I heard one of my governesses whisper to Aunt Lillian at a birthday party once. My mother, Aunt Lillian, and Val all say, when asked, that their hair is really dark brown, but it gleams sometimes with almost blue lights—it looks black to me.)

I take my dessert spoon, dip it in my water glass, and flick the spoon in the wrong direction so it lands on Myron and while I am trying to rearrange myself fast before he notices where it came from I knock over the goblet.

"Susanna!" my mother says.

"Susanna, dammit!" Myron says. "If you're old enough to eat with adults, you're old enough to behave like a young lady." I sometimes think he watches movies with Walter Pidgeon so he can learn what fathers should say. He was nicer about it when I was little. Val and I are laughing so much I can hardly mop up the water with my napkin. "Typical," Val mutters, passing me her napkin across the table.

"I started it, Uncle Myron," she says.

"Then you're both wonderful paragons of social grace," Aunt Lillian says. "I think we'll send you two upstairs and bring Theo down."

I can hear the buzzer echoing in the kitchen as my

mother sounds the alarm, pounding her little foot against it furiously. Our butler, Frank, rushes in.

"Looks like we've got some two-year-olds here. I'll get a rag right away . . ." he says. Now, Frank I like. A lot. If he was not colored he would look like Errol Flynn and could be a big movie star. Myron says it's very sad that Frank is doing this, but on the other hand, he is a good butler. Frank despises Andrew. Frank uses the wagon for errands and ran into Andrew in the limo one day. I mean head on, right down there on Perdido Drive. Frank does not really hate me except he is the only one who scolds me about school and says, "You're real spoiled if you can't see what that education can mean to you. I know a lot of kids that would like to have your opportunities."

"But I'm going to be a singer after I'm married—or a musician."

"Yeah, and I'm going to be Ernest Hemingway. You can't do anything unless you get your schooling. It's just a waste."

"Frank, the girls will clean it up," Aunt Lillian says. "You're both excused," she says to us and Frank winks at her. He really likes Lillian and Alan, and Alan sometimes brings him a script to look at before he does a picture and they'll stand in the driveway together and argue about politics or talk about boxing.

"And take those wet napkins with you," Myron says to us. He cannot wait to get into the projection room, in the dark and the quiet, and watch the dailies.

Grandmother has been patting some of the water up with her napkin and hands it to me. "Accidents will be accidents. When I was a bride we had one plump chicken to celebrate the New Year and proud before the fall I slipped and the chicken flew across our room from the platter, knocking Zayda a zetz across the head, and landed on the floor. . . . We said the prayer for chicken picked up from the floor and cleaned it off. So!" She gives me a little potch and Val and I go into the pantry.

"I've got something to tell you anyway," I say to Val.

I put the napkins over the deep sink in the pantry where Frank polishes the silver. He always listens to the radio here, and throws the silver around when he gets mad at Winchell.

"Yes. I bet you do. What's going on tonight? Myron's got something bad to tell Daddy—that's why he's so cross, I'll bet."

"Oh—that? Yes." I really want to tell her about Jackson. "Well," I say, "I think it has to do with this telegram Myron got this afternoon that they don't think I saw. It was on Mary's desk, and it said that they're going to boycott your father's picture because he's— you know. But Myron won't go along with it."

"Who's going to boycott it? What do you mean?" She leans back against the tile-topped built-ins.

"I don't remember. I just glanced at it."

Now I feel as if it's somehow my fault, my fault for being related to Myron—and finding out things somehow becomes confused with making the trouble.

"Well," she says coolly, "it doesn't matter. Myron never hires Daddy anyway because he drinks too much."

"Really? Oh, Val. That's not true." It is true. Myron says Alan is a lush. When I was little I thought that meant someone who lay around listening to jazz and eating luscious food.

She turns and goes back into the dining room before I can even tell her about Jackson. I finish mopping up the table as Frank is serving the meat.

"Oh, a roast beast," Val says.

"No. Overdone lamb," my mother says.

"Maybe we could say the prayer for lamb," I say.

"It looks beyond hope to me," says Val.

"Valentine! It looks very nice," Aunt Lillian says kindly. It is traditional that our food is dreadful. Mabel, our other maid, who does the downstairs work, has started down the table with army green peas and Dorothy is passing mashed potatoes with lumps I can see from here. I am just waiting myself to see what shade of gray the gravy will be tonight.

We once had a cook who made a pie I still think about, but she was fired because Grandmother said to make a pie that good you had to use lard and lard is the most traife thing in the world.

Aunt Lillian fills Uncle Alan's plate. "He'll eat when he gets here, and if it's cold, it's cold. There's no point in someone having to make two trips." She smiles her broad, lovely smile at Mabel, who is not paying attention because Frank patted her ever so secretly as they crossed paths going around the table.

"And how was the recital yesterday?" Grandmother asks after we sit down. "Susanna had very little to say about it last evening—she was a very tired young lady. It must have been an exhausting day at school." Her eyebrows lift, otherwise her expression does not change. She knows I was not at school, I bet.

"Oh, very interesting," Val giggles. "Mr. Ruben was really surprised. Susanna played Chopin with a boogie bass."

"Well, I thought it would be different." I hadn't planned it that way, but I hit a clinker and just went with it.

"It was different," Val says.

I was late, of course, for the recital. And when I came into Mr. Ruben's studio, which smells of old wood and paint and wet paper and of Mr. Ruben, who also smells of all those things, and eraser breath, Val was already playing. She lifted her chin and winked at me without missing a note. I banged into a couple of chairs sitting down next to C.A., who only takes from Mr. Ruben because Val does. C.A. is tone deaf. C.A. and I had our first fight in the fourth grade when she said Val couldn't be my best friend because we were cousins and that was why she was Val's best friend. I waved to Aunt Lillian, who is the only mother practically who always shows up at recitals. She nodded and smiled as Val played. I think my mother does not come because she feels critical and gets impatient when I hit clinkers, although Grandmother used to come to hear her play. And Aunt Lillian does not play the piano, so clinkers do not upset her. I think that talent goes through the family on the diagonal. Val is a more serious person about her music. If I don't get into nightclubs I'd like to play with something like the Sons of the Pioneers and be in Westerns. I get car sick at real concerts. Here's a basic difference between Val and me. Practicing: She will practice for hours until she gets something just right. I play just long enough to get the feel of how it goes and then change it to something I like better.

While we eat Val is listening. Before anyone has heard a thing, she says, "Oh, I think Daddy's here—I'll get the door!" And she is up and running. She always acts as though she hasn't seen him in years even though she sees him every morning. It must be something to have your own alive father.

I start to go with her and Myron says, "Susanna, you sit right back down." It would certainly beat having a stepfather who is always yelling at you. Although that is not entirely fair. Myron just snaps at me when he is tired or when it would be inappropriate to snap at anyone else. He also figures it is fatherly. Shows he notices me.

They take their time coming in. Alan is probably fixing a drink. Yes. Because he has it in his hand when he comes in with his arm around Val. Alan has his sweater on inside out and his dark, handsome face looks a little more crumpled than usual. He looks like he always has a cigarette in the corner of his mouth, even when he doesn't, and as if he's just come from covering a big story—or from being in a scene about a guy who's just come from covering a big story. I think Alan would be a reporter if he didn't figure it would be harder work than playing reporters or tough guys who play poker and act like reporters even if they're gangsters or cops. He's probably no older than Jackson but I think people assume he is because he slouches, frowns, and winces a lot. He's the kind of actor who makes sure Makeup puts in extra lines, and has Wardrobe press wrinkles into his pants. But even when he's tired and just glaring around a room, you never forget for a second he's there and everyone wants to be sure he hears the smart or funny things they say. They search the deep lines around his mouth for the slightest flick of appreciation.

Then Alan kisses my grandmother on the top of her head. "Sorry I'm late, Luba, but then how would you know it was me if I had been on time?"

"Only with difficulty," Grandmother says.

"And Susanna, did you get in enough trouble today, or was it slow?" What does he know? "I suppose it's time to stir it all up with a stick." He swizzles his drink with his forefinger: I can't imagine Alan being a real Commie. Maybe it's his hair, being longer and not slicked back, neat. Jackson's hair isn't either. Slicked back. But he's blond and I haven't heard of any blond ones. All the ones who ever come over here are dark or gray-haired or writers, and they hold their cigarettes between their forefingers and thumbs and smoke them overhand.

Alan and Lillian know more of those people than we do. And they have foreigners over a lot. There was a man at their house wearing sandals without socks and his wife had hair right under her arms. Myron said he would not want her to come swimming in our pool.

"So where's the big shot?" Alan is asking about Theo.

"Out running the quarter mile," Val says.

"That's fast," Alan says. "Very good." He nods at her.

"Won't break any records today," she says, so pleased when she can amuse him and distract him from Theo.

"How did the meeting go today?" Lillian asks.

"Which meeting was that?" Myron wants to know.

"Nice of you to ask, Myron," Alan says. "We were expecting you. It went fine, Lily. We decided to overthrow the American government by putting Nixon and

53

Tenney in a 'Road' movie and sending Crosby and Hope to Washington."

"That's a funny idea!" I say.

"Be quiet, Susanna," my mother says. "Does anyone want seconds?" Firsts, I think, was quite enough.

"Thank you, Susanna," Alan says. "I thought so. The American Legion has decided to boycott my new picture."

"The American Legion!" I say. "They're dangerous—you know they stopped Paul Robeson's concert at Peekskill last year and beat up a lot of people and it was terrible."

"How do you hear such things, Susanna?" my mother says.

"I just read it somewhere— I don't mean to interrupt, sorry."

Val gives me a "likely story" look. She knows I've been dying to tell her something and I didn't have a chance at the recital with Lillian there and then C.A. butted in on us at lunch today at school. The last thing I want is for C.A. to tell her father and have it get back to Jackson that I can't keep a secret. And now here I am almost saying too much myself.

"Just to fill you in, Myron," Alan says, "there's talk about not releasing the picture at all."

"I am aware of the situation, Alan, don't patronize me." Myron is cutting up his meat into very neat little squares with short jabbing motions of his knife.

"Alan, what was the decision?" Lillian is trying to be very calm.

"Well, it looks fine—right now. They're going to write the Legion telling them if they do picket, the major studios or at least those represented—I wouldn't presume to speak for V.L.I., Myron—will put together a documentary about the Legion from newsreel clips, showing them in full flower, complete with cattle prods, and they'll play it at all the studio-owned theaters. At least that threat will keep them distracted until the picture gets into general release."

"I don't think it will do a damn bit of good," Lillian says. "The public will just look at the documentary and think they're having a high old time."

"I agree, Lillian," Myron is saying. "Well, we got the decision from New York today. They want us to continue the blacklist. I'm sorry. I tried. The confirming wire came to the house," Myron says, "if you'd like to see it, Alan. There have been meetings and calls all day. It looks as though everyone's going to have to go along with it."

"You're going to agree, of course."

"I'm afraid so, Alan. We've all gotten pressure from the stockholders."

"That's going to keep a lot of people out of work." Lillian looks at Alan.

"I couldn't encourage you to hold out," Alan says. "No, certainly not. Why would I even think of that?"

"Daddy," Val says, "how could they put you on the list?"

"It was just my friendly nature, Val. I'll tell you sometime." They always save the best for sometime.

"I think you should tell her, and you should tell her the truth," Lillian says.

"Listen, Alan. You can't say you weren't warned," Myron says. Myron is the perfect I-told-you-so type of person. I think he practices ways to say it in the mirror every morning. He never looks in a mirror like my mother does, to see how he looks, but to see, I think, how to be a certain way, how to seem taller, how to seem very sure of himself, how to walk with his overcoat swinging over his shoulder like my grandfather wore his. I don't think when Myron says "I told you so" or gets that expression where his narrow lips almost disappear like an angry little boy's that he ever really thinks anything he has told anyone would actually happen.

"No, Myron. I can't and I haven't, have I?" Alan bites at his words.

Frank and Mabel are clearing the table now and Dorothy will be helping Ethel in the kitchen, which she truly despises. Ethel will not permit her to have the radio on when she is cooking.

Alan is angry. He also wants to go make himself another drink. Grandmother says, "Alan, it makes me nervous to watch you stand at the edge of your seat." I think she says things like that on purpose to distract.

Usually the fights are about what Grandfather should have done with all his money. He should not have given so much to charity—or to *those* charities, whichever they are. Alan hates organized charities, although I think he likes organized unions and I don't understand the difference. Myron usually fights with him about that and Myron thinks Grandfather should have put more money back into studio stock, and Grandmother says it is a discussion for over the back fence for vultures. I think they like to talk about it to see if Grandmother will tell them how much they're going to have "some day" and that means when she dies. I hate that idea and I think she's right not to let anyone but her lawyer know anything. And Val agrees with me.

Then Myron and Alan argue a lot about movies and Alan tells Myron why all movies are lies. And Myron says they're in the entertainment business, not education. Alan just likes trenchcoat and hat movies where he lurks around in New York outside cocktail lounges because he is good in them. Actually, with all these meetings, and meetings about other meetings, I don't think they're making too many movies right now anyway.

"Susanna. Your fingerbowl."

My mother is wild on the subject of fingerbowls. "I remember," Grandmother says, "that Victor used to say, 'I think all she learned from school in the East was fingerbowls!' " You'd think they would have been pleased that she found a doctor to marry there. Even if he didn't last. Val would say, "That's a nice way to put it." Grandmother never has to bother with her fingerbowl. They've learned to give her just a dessert plate.

I always get the fingerbowl wrong and my mother

always watches. One long polished fingernail poised against the edge of her plate to tap. I can hear that nail against a china plate even ten miles away. First I take the dessert fork and dessert spoon off the side of the plate. And put them on the place mat. Then, I dip fingertips—do not make washing gestures or there will be trouble. My mother catches my eye and she gets her warning look on. Then dry hands. Then take finger-bowl off with doily and set it up to the left of place mat. My mother flickers her lashes like little dancing feet. I center the fingerbowl on its doily. The end. I look at Val who finished ages ago and is laughing at me. And my mother nods. It would have been the wrong night to louse it up.

You think with all of that that there should be a wonderful dessert. And here's . . . Jell-O.

When I have a wedding and I am the bride and they give me fingerbowls I am going to take them all and hurl them against a wall.

Grandmother has been sitting very quietly. She is drinking her tea now, sipping it through the sugar cube she holds between her teeth. She crunches the sugar now and speaks. "I don't see why Myron should not sign such an agreement, Alan. There has been betrayal on both sides—but the situation is very dangerous."

"But Grandmother—" Val starts to speak.

"Hush, my darling. Your grandfather once warned your father about being with certain groups of very cynical young people. You see, we worked hard to be accepted. Your father's early life was very easy in comparison. We do not remember the Russian peasants with the romantic simplicity some of his friends seem—"

"Luba," Alan interrupts, and he is really mad. "Since you're explaining my background to my daughter, why don't you tell her the truth? You, and my parents too, came here so we could speak out, or did you come here—have I been wrong?—to join the bourgeois upper classes, to take your own turn at oppression? It's really classic! Don't rock your own boat. Jesus Christ, Jell-O!"

"We always have Jell-O on Thursdays, Alan," my mother says, "and Nabiscos. I love these."

We each get one Nabisco sugar wafer. Imagine eating a small shoe box with the tissue paper.

"It's just, Alan, that Mother believes she owes a lot to this country," Myron says. "She pays her taxes," he says. If I said that I'd be sent from the table for being fresh.

"I can speak for myself, Myron."

"Jell-O's pretty tough tonight," Myron says, slapping at it with his fork. He looks at my mother accusingly. As though she has anything to do with it. My mother doesn't even like to eat. She says a lady should never weigh more than a hundred and ten pounds.

"I like mine more on the rare side," Val says to me.

"I wonder if it bounces," I say, pretending to start to throw it at her, and we get the giggles.

"I don't see anything amusing," Myron says.

"Ever," Val whispers to me across the table. Lillian gives her a warning look. Lillian catches more stuff than my mother but she also lets more go by.

"Alan," Grandmother says, "you wanted to be a star as much as any handsome boy . . . now you listen to me. You've said moving pictures are romantic lies."

"I wanted to be an actor. That's different." He really wants to be a director, Val says. For the stage in New York. I think that's more Val's idea because she would like to live there.

"But you found this alluring and that makes you ashamed. That is why it is so important for you fellows to travel with the underdogs."

"Luba, do I really have to listen to this?" Alan has his fingers doing a war dance on his glass now. Lillian has her hand over her eyes, elbow on the table. I can't tell who she is mad at, but she is taking very deep breaths.

"No, you do not really have to listen," Grandmother replies. "Victor used to say that some of you were arrogant in your unhappiness, because you were part of a world you found too attractive to reject. This made him very impatient."

Alan should never have said this thing about lies to Grandfather because Grandfather invented movies. Grandmother told me that when they were in Russia, he wished he could put his dreams into pictures on a big roll like the Torah so they could move past him like parades with voices and songs. He would keep the best ones in a pack on his horse to look at. It would take the trouble out of imagining and remembering. And she had said to him that if he repeated the wish often enough it would become so powerful it would have to come true. He imagined himself like a rabbi, pointing out the best parts of his dreams as they rolled by with a pure silver pointer like the big rabbis have.

Alan flings his napkin across the table. "Sign the damn boycott, Myron. Give me a pen and I'll sign it myself. To hell with it—I'll take my family to Europe and find work."

"To live in Paris?" Val exclaims. "That would be wonderful."

"Lucky!" I say. I can see her riding in a carriage and wearing kid gloves.

"Now that is all just talk," Lillian says. "I'm sure it will all settle down."

"And I'm sure it's just the beginning," Alan says.

I remember just before the start of the war when Val and I were really little and we were sitting in our vacation house in Palm Springs. They were all staring at the radio and the announcer said Pearl Harbor was bombed. I thought at first one of Grandmother's friends was drunk and I imagined her being found somewhere with her skirts over her head and her bloomers showing. Alan said then, in just this tone of voice, "I'm sure this is just the beginning."

"Something reminds me," I say now. "Uncle Alan, you were in the Army—you should tell them that. You weren't against us."

"No one is against anyone, Susanna," Myron says.

"Are you going to eat your Jell-O?" He is at his watch now, shaking his wrist ever so slightly, but enough so I see.

"That's a good girl, Susanna. You'll be my first character witness, okay?" Alan says.

"She's probably already figuring what she'll wear in court," Val says.

"Oh, black, of course," I say.

Now, after dinner everyone goes off in different directions. This house can seem empty even with twenty people in it. That's why I like visiting Val. You can always hear someone there. It's only a ten-room house but still nice. I think Perdido has twenty-two rooms. Sometimes I lie awake and try to count in my head—always comes out different. You'd think driving by and looking up at it that there must be a lot of wonderful parties up there. But these days it's mostly just us. I would certainly love to run a house like this for Jackson. Then you'd see some parties all right.

So Alan and Myron are off arguing some more. My mother and aunt are helping Grandmother get to bed, and Val and I are upstairs, helping Miss O'Connor get Theo ready for the trip home. I am holding him for a minute and I love the way he grins at everyone and the feeling of his hand, the way he grabs my finger. I love his soft little cheeks and the way he giggles when you bury your face under his chin and kiss at him. I hand him to Val and she holds him up over her with her two hands around his middle and he dances and laughs in the air. Then O'Connor wraps him in his woolly blanket and hands him to Lillian. He lies against her and puts his arms so easily around her neck as though they are made to fit each other.

Val and I go downstairs together and I say, "I have to tell you something."

"What?" She is scampering a bit, wanting to go with her family.

"Something incredible happened yesterday."

"I think there's been enough lately—what else?"

"I mean to me . . . I spent the whole day with Jackson Lane."

"Really?" I don't think she believes me.

"I really did."

"Where?"

"We went sailing and to visit a friend of his—at the merry-go-round."

"Susanna. You're not making it up?"

"Of course not. He gave me this. It's from the merry-go-round."

"Prehistoric! Post-Jackson— You'd better not say anything—to anyone. Susanna, what did he say?"

"Well, he said he'd see me again soon—and just before he left me off he kissed me very lightly, right on my forehead." I can't ever tell anything without exaggerating, even when it's good enough as it is. Now, why is that? That's why Val never believes me.

"Unbelievable." This is her favorite new word. We will all be using it soon. But I can't tell whether this time she means she doesn't believe it or whether she is just distracted.

"Well, I thought it was terrific," I say.

"I suppose it is," she says, "but why did he come? Did he come just to see you?"

"I don't know. It doesn't matter why. He was just here."

"Didn't you ask him what he was doing?" Val seems so angry with me. "Didn't you want to know?"

"I'm sorry. I just had a good time and I thought I'd tell you."

"Don't say you're sorry. You're never wrong, you're just always sorry."

"I don't know what you mean."

"Nothing. It's just you never think. How could you go off like that with a stranger?"

"He's not a stranger. He's a star. I knew who he was."

"Did you really?" She starts for the door. "Never mind," she says. She's probably just mad because I said "he's a star" and she might have gotten the idea I was implying Alan isn't. Val can be very touchy about Alan—maybe she thinks I meant that because Jackson's a star he's safe and that someone who's just an actor wouldn't be. You don't ever know with Val, what stirs her up. She's very complicated.

Myron and Alan have been talking in the projection room. I can hear the dailies have already started and it didn't go well because Alan has come out and looks annoyed. He picks Theo up from Lillian's arms and says, "Where's Val?"

"Waiting at the door," I say and I go quickly into the projection room.

Everything was fine with Val and me and then suddenly she's annoyed. Probably it's leaving this house—maybe it reminds her that she could be living here. Of course, she's worried about Alan and the blacklisting. Here I am having a great time playing hooky yesterday and her father is having his world torn apart. Or, his career anyway, but to an actor that *is* the world.

I never should have said anything about Jackson. It may not have to do with me at all. But nothing's going to really happen. It will be fine. I know it. They'll all go to Europe together and we'll stand at the boat and wave and throw flowers.

There's always a problem and then everything works out and the lights come on and everyone's smiling and wiping away tears.

It must be very late.

I hear something. It is not myself wheezing. It is the house. I hear it creaking around me like an old ship. But there is something else, like the sound of pirates sneaking on board. I check my room with my flashlight—all clear, as they used to say in the war. I turn it out and then I go out of my room and listen at the back steps. The help is sleeping. I walk past the big doors that lead to Grandmother's wing. Now I am moving in on the big oak floor to my parents' wing. The thick red plush carpet starts here. I open the door and get quickly out of the line of light that leads from Myron's door to the hall. My mother's door is open. Her room is dark.

I stand in the shadows of the main hall, just behind the banisters that begin here and angle along down with the stairs. I sat here once when President Roosevelt died and listened on the phone as Myron told my mother and I scratched my name on the bannister right here with a bobby pin.

"You come back upstairs," Myron is yelling to my mother, if you can yell quietly, and from the sound he is somewhere on the middle of the steps. I can hear his slippers. Even when the sirens announced an air raid, Myron would have his slippers and robe on. He may sleep in them.

I can see my mother down there, as I peer around. She is silhouetted against the windows leading to the wisteria porch. It looks to me like she has nothing on under her negligee.

"I'm suffocating!" she says, and she is crying. I have never seen her cry except when Grandfather died. And I have never seen her in her negligee without underwear.

"Stand away from the windows! Someone could see you!" Myron says.

"God forbid," she says, "he might be watching. Is that what you're afraid of, Myron? A threat? My God, now what could possibly threaten you about him?"

Him?

Her voice is slurred.

"How many Seconals did you take, Vera?"

"For me to know . . . you to worry."

He grabs her, I can see, by the arm. She strikes at him and he slaps her across the face. "Pull yourself together." I want to run to her and I want to run back to my bed and I cannot move either way. Andrew ran over a cat in the limo last week and I wanted to look and I didn't want to look. This is like that. I did look.

"You have a family to think of. . . ."

"Oh, a family, from the one who put his brother-in-law out of work."

"Look, Vera." His voice sounds like a clenched fist. "Alan got himself into this. I have a moral position—"

"Moral position, my ass. Your position is with your precious stockholders."

"Remember, my dear, they're your stockholders too, or is that only when it's convenient?"

"Nothing is convenient," she says, "except wasn't it convenient for you that we were in New York when Jackson was here, wasn't it?" I knew Grandmother knew. I didn't think she would tell them, though.

I cannot swallow my throat is so dry.

"I knew it," Myron says, hands to his forehead. "I knew you would use it for all it's worth." Is my mother in love with Jackson Lane too? Does Myron really think he'd be watching? Jackson isn't like that.

"Use it?" She opens her negligee in front of him. I look away and hold my nightgown tight around me. "Now there's an old idea for you. Oh, no one ever uses me. You never do, you know, never do. So I cannot be convenient either."

"Maybe it's because you think of it like that," he says and helps her up and then she slumps on the stairs and he sits down next to her. "I've only been loved once . . . only once," she mutters and begins to sob again. She really is being overdramatic. My father loved her, and Myron loves her. I think he's being very patient with her. I wonder how I'd feel if someone I loved cried about other people all the time.

"Come on, Vera," Myron says, "don't make it worse than it is. If he ever tries a stunt like this again I'll make up my own blacklist and Jackson Lane will be lucky to get on a set as a dress extra."

"Oh, such brave talk, Myron. If you can make your own little list, why can't you unmake one? Hire Alan. Take a risk. Just a little risk."

Myron puts his head in his hands. "I've always tried to do my best, Vera, but I'm not very brave. The only risky thing I did was marrying you. You're the one who liked to take risks—remember?"

"And I wish I never had. I wish I'd never seen him." She puts her head in her hands. Poor Myron. But I cannot imagine my mother really having an affair. She would never do that to Grandmother. I can see her making Myron upset, but not her mother. And would someone who cares about fingerbowls do something like that? My mother?

"We both do. Now it's very late." He helps her up and she shrugs away from him.

"It's too late, Myron. It always was."

"Oh, cut it out, Vera—it's enough tonight . . ."

Suddenly, as I am about to go, to run back to my room, Myron turns and looks up. I have already moved so I am a little in the light. "Jesus Christ—Susanna!"

"Susanna?" my mother asks. I want to say, yes, you remember me.

"I couldn't sleep," I say.

"How long have you been standing there?"

"Just got here," I say. "I'm going right back to sleep now."

That affair must have been the risk my mother wishes she had never taken. I will never tell her how I feel. How strange to be rivals with your mother, and it's all crazy anyway. It's not fair for her to like him—she's had two husbands. She's married and I'm really much too young for him, now. In two years, maybe. Even if she could be unfaithful, I can't imagine my mother with Jackson. She would never, for one thing, ride in a convertible—or be in a sailboat. And I can just see him taking her to see Scotty. "You live *here?*" she would say, arching her long neck, her hand curved up near the collar of one of her Adrian suits. But I wonder— did he mean to see her, and settle for me? If he knew her well enough for an affair he would know she never sees anyone before she's had her tray.

"It's time we all got some sleep," Myron says and he moves up the steps with my mother who is very shaky on her feet. He looks at her at each step as though he is dying of embarrassment because you can see through her negligee. I'm embarrassed too because he knows I can see and that I know he can see. The only one who doesn't seem embarrassed is my mother.

"We were just having a discussion, dear," she says as she gets to the top step and reaches out to pat me on the cheek and misses, patting the air instead. "Everything is just fine. Just fine."

"You remember, Susanna," Myron says, "anything you see or hear in this house is private."

I am hardly about to call the trades. I don't think I will say that. I could feel his slap just from the sound of it on her and that mood is not so far away right now, although Myron would never slap me. Not because he doesn't love me, but I don't think he would feel free enough with me—you don't slap a kid, somehow, who is not your own flesh and blood. Maybe you don't care, I guess, in the kind of way that would make you that crazy-mad with her.

"You wouldn't understand any of this, Susanna, don't try," my mother says, sweeping like a Looney Tunes broom into her bedroom.

"And try to remember, please," Myron says, "that this door is closed for a reason. Good night, now. Pleasant dreams."

And he closes the door to their wing.

"It isn't enough that you gave me only daughters, and daughters who had only daughters, but that you damned both of them to fall in love with actors."

This is one of the seven or eight deathbed statements Grandmother has attributed to Grandfather. He was talking to God.

My grandfather and grandmother always discussed things with God. I sometimes think I confuse the three of them, Grandmother, Grandfather, and God, which may be the way my grandmother wants it.

I never really heard it before. *Both* of them. So she

did love Jackson Lane too—I wonder if she ever really touched him, or just had a crush on him. She would be furious if she knew how I feel, if she knew I got to spend a whole day with him. And so my grandparents did know (and did not have heart attacks and die—over *that*). No wonder Grandmother was so angry today and would not tell me exactly—that's all she'd need—a second-generation Jackson Lane problem. Well, it's hardly *that*.

I go into my room and mark this date in my diary with stars. *Modern Screen:* I remember I was in Dorothy's room discussing how life would be when I am on the nightclub circuit and she was talking about how she wanted to be a singer once herself. "Yes," I said, "you'd be great in the Lena Horne parts." I told Myron to test her and he was furious. "Stop giving people ideas, Susanna. You mustn't make people unhappy with their lot in life."

I was going to say, "But look where you got from where you started. And just by getting married." But that is the kind of wiseguy thing he gets enraged about. Myron likes the last word, except when you say, "Oh, Myron, you're right." Which is why he usually does have the last word.

So Dorothy and I were thumbing through the movie magazines looking at pictures of all the parties both of us were not invited to and talking about what a drip Lon McCallister is when I saw this blind item in Sheilah Graham's or someone's column. Maybe it was Louella, who is big on blind items. "Not Born Yesterday: What Swashbuckling Star carries a torch for which movie pioneer's heiress?"

"See," I had said, laughing.

"See what?" Dorothy said.

"This. Me and Errol Flynn. Me and Burt Lancaster. Me and Jackson Lane. Wouldn't that be fabulous? To have someone carrying a torch for you?"

"Glamour, you know they just make up that trash.

And no one carries any torch for anyone he hasn't seen, no one I ever heard about."

"I know," I said, "but I can imagine, anyway." And how neat to think of myself as an heiress like Brenda Frazier or someone. She whipped the magazine away from me a little too fast, now that I think about it, and pitched it back under her bed. But he didn't even ask about my mother. And he's not even old enough for her. I don't know how old Jackson is, no one does, but he's certainly not her age. (Whatever that actually is—she's always taking a year off—Aunt Lillian says my mother is getting young enough to be *her* daughter.)

Now in my room, I get out my autographed picture of him—which is just one of those studio ones someone else signs. I'd had Mary order it in with a batch of others I had asked for. And I hold it and smile back at it the way he does—his sort of "aren't you glad to see me" smile. I wonder if my mother has a picture of him somewhere she looks at like this.

Well. One thing. Jackson certainly isn't an ordinary movie star with a real life.

God, I think we have to talk about this. If I were Catholic like C.A. is (on her mother's side) I could say something and They would all forgive me. All Three of Them: the Father, the Son, and the Holy Ghost.

But You. You never forgive anything. But I did see him before I knew she loved him. And it wasn't like that anyway. I didn't *really* touch him. Except a little on the back of his neck. I wonder if she touched him like that and if that is why he got mad. And I wonder if Val knows about my mother and Jackson and that's why she was so annoyed, and she would never say anything to me any more than I would say anything to her about Myron not hiring Alan because of his drinking. Is this the sort of thing one can talk to Rabbi Silverberg about?

"Rabbi," I will say, "Rabbi, I am in love with someone my mother also loves."

Yes. This will add a little something to my Hebrew lesson tomorrow. If I am that brave. Which I am not.

Do Jews swim? Rabbi Silverberg, in his black suit and yarmulka, and I are gliding through the pool where in Grandfather's little rowboat I am trying to distract him from the Hebrew I am supposed to be learning by telling him stories. He is the new rabbi in the temple my grandparents belonged to which is why he has to put up with jobs like this.

"Grandfather used to anchor this boat in the middle of the pool and read scripts. It was named *The Volga Princess* after the ship he built with his bare hands so all his family and friends could escape the Cossacks. It sailed them all the way to the Forty-second Street pier in New York where they went right into the theater business.

"That is one of Grandmother's favorite stories, something of an exaggeration," I add.

"Well," Rabbi Silverberg says, "a good story is a good story if you know inside where the truth ends and the show business begins."

"*Volga Princess.* Myron had it painted out—you know, the Commie thing."

"And he was worried about the name of a boat in the swimming pool? Well—perhaps. These are peculiar times."

"I am thinking of calling it *Farewell . . .*"

"That's nice, not an unusual name, but very nice." He is sitting here in the boat, getting the alphabet book out of his pocket. I have decided not to add that this is the name of Jackson's boat. Even before I heard about Jackson I wanted to run away to sea in a boat. This is what boys do in movies to grow up.

"Shall we get the show on the road?" he says. Like my friend Kitty Chapin's lawyer-father and all the civilians we know—the family doctors and our dentist—he likes to talk very show-bizzy. The worst is my grandmother's doctor. I think the main reason he works so hard to keep her alive is he keeps hoping she'll get him a part in a picture. And my dentist is always telling me things he thinks are wrong with Myron's pictures. He has the box office figures and keeps the trades and weekly *Variety* in the waiting room, which is funny for someone who has kids for patients—but then we're all movie kids and we like to read them—although I wouldn't mind an occasional movie magazine.

"Well," I lie, "I have been studying. I can write almost everything. I had a lot of trouble with the gimel until I decided it looks like an ankle strap suede shoe."

"Just as long as it is suede," he says. I wonder if rabbis know when you're lying, like God and psychoanalysts.

Paul Daroff, S. Leon Daroff's son and a friend of Val's and mine, even though he is a lot older, has gone to a psychoanalyst since his mother ran off to Mexico with a Communist ages ago, and he says they know exactly what you're thinking—before you do. Val says that's nonsense, that Paul only tells me things like that because it's so much fun to see me believe everything he says. Paul is so stuffy he'd never let Val see how he adores her, and he thinks teasing me is one way to amuse her.

God, I think, is probably the only one who really knows what you're always up to. I would never admit to Val—or Paul—that I believe in God. They are more sophisticated. Paul's father, of course, owns Daroff World Productions. Paul goes East to school and now has a New York psychoanalyst, but I don't think he'll ever recover from having Evelyn Ames as a stepmother. She once found one chocolate missing from her Old Vienna candy box and made Paul eat the entire five pounds standing right there in front of her. He was sick for two weeks. Plus he is allergic to chocolate and probably wasn't the one who ate the candy to begin with. And, then, of course, she made him pose, the next week, for one of those layouts showing "movie-star-as-darling-mother" with the two of them making fudge in the kitchen. He goes to an analyst because he has this dream of killing Evelyn—every night. I don't think that's very crazy at all.

I would like to discuss God with Rabbi Silverberg today but He is one of the subjects we don't usually get around to.

I try to concentrate on the alphabet. But the boat is leaking just a bit and the Rabbi suggests we row to shore. Now we are sitting on lounges by the pool, and the Rabbi has taken off his shoes and white socks to dry them in the sun. I try not to look at his plump little feet. I do not think you are supposed to see rabbis unclothed. Even the feet. I wonder if rabbis can quit on a person. I think they have to stick to you until you are saved or at least can read Hebrew. It is this kind of thing I am very interested in knowing about being Jewish. And it is this kind of thing which seems kind of out of bounds to ask.

I know a lot about being Catholic just from movies. But very little about being Jewish and, my god, I mean My God, everyone who makes movies practically is Jewish.

Maybe if you are Jewish the understanding should come with the blood. That is why there are no movies about being Jewish. If you are Jewish you already know. And if you are Christian you are not interested. What is the matter with me that I don't understand?

"I want to ask you something," I say. "Does God forgive you for wanting something you shouldn't because someone else does, but you didn't know it when it started—do you know what I mean?"

"Not exactly." He is leaning back now, and gazing over the garden, to the tennis court covered with Midascup vines and honeysuckle.

"Well, say you pray for something and you get it but you find out someone else would be upset—is He doing it to teach you something or does God occasionally mix things up? . . . I guess I'm sounding mixed up." I'm sorry now I started this.

"I'm not sure it is important—or possible to know. What is important is to be aware that we often do not get what we want because it is not what we need to grow. You can never go wrong praying for strength to handle what we do get."

This is probably why we have not discussed God. He doesn't know. Maybe he has not graduated to that level yet, and is just teaching.

"By the way, remind me to ask Miss Mary for my check, will you, Susanna? . . . I want to buy my wife a lovely pair of pearl earrings for our anniversary. We will have been married fifteen years tomorrow."

For their anniversary Myron gave my mother a white beaver coat, her white marabou robe, and a diamond necklace set in gold, not platinum, which means, she said, "I can wear it in the daytime, how thoughtful."

I think it is more romantic to have one present that has been very hard for the person to buy.

I am thinking as we sit here in the sun of the orange story Grandmother told me: In the olden days back in Russia, Grandfather tended horses for the Duke, and during the middle of the most bitterly cold winter, the Duke invited him to come to the Great Hall.

"Indeed," Grandmother said, "your grandfather imagined the Duke would ask him to sit in one of the great leather chairs which flanked the huge stone fireplace . . ." (in our living room at Perdido we have a great stone fireplace and it has these big leather chairs on either side. I think Grandfather used to sit there and imagine he was the Duke, if you want to know) ". . . he expected the Duke would offer to share some cherry wine and discuss his views on the political questions of the day. However, he only stood at the door and handed your grandfather an orange. But Grandfather brought it to the Sabbath feast. We gathered all our friends around the table, and by the light of the candle—for after the ceremonial lighting we would put out the other candles to save tallow—we shared the wedges like gifts of jewelry."

Another thing I like about Grandmother is when she tells such a story she does not say, ". . . so you should be grateful." One orange. One half an orange like Jackson ate in the orange grove. And one pair of pearl earrings. I am trying again to concentrate on making my letters correctly on the page. But I see myself in a little adobe house overlooking a sea as clear as a pool. Jackson Lane is under the water. He opens oysters on the bottom of the pool with his knife; he rises to the top with two lovely pearls . . .

"If oysters are not kosher," I ask the Rabbi, who is writing more words for me to copy, "how come pearls are?"

"Because," he says, as though this is a basic question, "the Talmud says we do not eat pearls."

It is like moving a rock to think of anything but Jackson Lane and where I have decided to go tonight.

I have seen it in the trades. And double-checked with his studio Publicity Department. (You should hear me when I talk like Florabel Muir.) Jackson is going to be at the party after the premiere of his picture tonight.

"And I," I say to my puppets, who are lounging around my stage like actors between takes, "am going to be there too." My prince puppet: no wonder I love his long yellow hair.

The bouncers will catch me as I rush to his table at Romanoff's. Jackson will turn to the men who are holding my arms and say, "Unhand her! That's the girl I love!" Hedda Hopper and Louella Parsons will race to the phones, trampling Sheilah Graham in the rush.

Here come-a-this Susie—How the world d'ya
*   know?*
Well, I know about her black hat and the sweater
*   that she wore*
Her geetar on her shoulder
Lot of star shine in her eye

PERDIDO

Well, she's goin' to see ol' Jackson, tell him, you
is my man. . . .
Let the Midnight Special shine her light on me. . . .

I am standing in front of my mirror in the dark in my
navy slacks and sweater with the buttons turned to the
back so they won't shine in the light. I have shoved my
hair into an old chauffeur's cap they thought Andrew
had lost. I pull on my black rubber galoshes. My eyes
are almost all I can see of me. Is it true that Jackson's
eyes glow in the dark? The bill of my cap shadows my
face, and my pale hands are hidden in my mother's
black kid gloves. I look dangerous as George Macready.

"Yeah . . . Let that Midnight Special shine her ever-
loving light on me. . . ." The trick is to make it out the
window and across the lawn without Watchman catching me.

I climb out into the olive tree and wait, holding my
breath. I see Watchman's flashlight swaying through the
garden like the searchlights used to sway through the
sky during air raids and I wait until he has gone around
to the front. Then I slide down the tree and dash across
the lawn to the cliff behind the rose gardens and over
the fence to the rickety wooden steps which lead down
to the Coast Highway. Jackson will say, "A kid after my
own heart."

Now I am walking along the highway to the service
station at the corner where I can call a cab. If there's
one thing Myron knows, it's when someone is using the
phone. My eyes, accustomed to the dark, now blink in
the bright lights.

"Hi," I say to the attendant, who looks at his watch,
wondering what some kid is doing wandering around at
night like this. "Got a phone I can use to call a Yellow
Cab?"

"Sure. In there. Any trouble?"

"Nope."

I listen to the waves across the highway as I wait and
wonder how my mother will feel when Jackson brings

74

me home. If he brings me home. We might just go to
Catalina. He is going to want to go away, from what
I hear about the picture. People get very embarrassed
around people who've just made a terrible movie. You
never know where to look. You can't say, "Well, *I*
loved it," because they usually know themselves when
it's bad and that makes you a liar or an idiot. I can't
imagine anyone not wanting to be with Jackson, but you
know Hollywood. Even if you're beautiful you're still
only as good as your last credit. And no one adores
Jackson as much as I do—there is no greater fan, no
other person who would die for him at this very moment, but even I think he should turn all these scripts
over to Rory Calhoun who deserves them and get a new
agent—Paul Kohner would be good—Jackson needs
some real grooming now. Movie stars, L. B. Mayer
says, are like race horses and you have to care for them
the same way. Myrna Loy was over one night telling us
that, lying on the couch in persimmon chiffon, and I
could just see her being curried until she gleamed by a
young groom while old L.B. bobbed around watching
like a penguin with spectacles.

And they've got to stop putting Rhonda Fleming in
anything Jackson makes. They should put *her* in the
Rory Calhoun movies and run them in Azusa.

The taxi comes and I get to Romanoff's just as everyone is beginning to arrive and I wait outside to see
Jackson.

I wait. The limousines come. The photographers close
in, the men sweep them aside so their ladies can walk
through. The stars blink at the flashbulbs, turn to their
escorts, then flash their public smiles at the cameras.

Then one of the photographers calls to another,
"There's Lane's car." They run. I stand frozen. Then
move to the edge of the crowd. I can see the white car
through them. Sam Zimbalist shoulders on by and a
columnist grabs him, his notepad out. "How's the picture, Sam?"

"How are you, Army? Nice to see you."

"Off the record?" Army asks, insistent.

Even though it's not his picture, Zimbalist is too nice a guy to say anything—even I would know not to ask Zimbalist if I wanted dirt. And at least he's honest—he just shakes his head and doesn't say anything.

Next Army gets hold of Charles Vidor. "Botchy," he says, "how'd you like that?"

"Come on, Army, I have only come here for a party. I didn't see any movie." And he's probably telling the truth. He makes his light blue eyes very wide. I love Botchy . . . he is the kind of man you want to waltz with. He was married to . . . my God—Jackson's coming. . . .

I see the top of his head, golden above the crowd. He moves swiftly through.

Now or never, I tell myself, and dive into the middle. He is wearing his white tux with an open-collared silk shirt so you can see his gorgeous throat. I am touching his arm.

"Hi," I say.

"Hello—hi," he grins at me. Movie star to fan. But this grin is just around the mouth. He looks at me, puzzled. It must be my hat. I pull it off and my hair comes down. My Jackson-Lane-blond-color hair and I never thought of it like that before. Anyone could see we match.

He turns to a tall dark girl who is standing beside him, looking impatient. "Just a minute, Betty." Then he pats me on the shoulder. "How are you? Up late—" He looks around. Does he think I am here with my parents? Does he really think they would bring me here?

"I had to see you again."

I follow him up to the restaurant door. He has the expression he gets when he's in an ambush: eyes darting, an extra little line on the left side of his mouth as though he's almost biting his lip. I think I've scared him. Or made him mad.

"This isn't a good time, okay? You ought to be—"

"Hey, Jack," the girl says. "I'm freezing. Come on."

I'd be freezing too if I had one foxtail around my shoulder.

"This is not a good idea," he says to me quietly.

He is being moved along now by studio people. The second-class executives like to pretend they're bodyguards in a gangster movie when they go somewhere with a star.

He stops for one second more and looks right in my eyes, but only for a second. "I'll be in touch, okay. Is that okay?"

"Tomorrow?"

"Probably not. I'll see. Now you'd better go on home." He shakes his head. He does not know what to do about me.

Betty looks over and down at me, and then back at me. "What does she want? Give her an autograph and let's go." I would think she is a studio contract player the Publicity Department wanted him to show off but they wouldn't do that to Jackson. He wouldn't let them except they put him in these lousy pictures and he lets them. I like anything he's in, of course—but he should be doing more dramatic things. Love scenes, of course, but not with people like *her*. Why am I fourteen! I am *always* the wrong age at the wrong time and it's always going to be like that. I know it.

"Just a minute," he says to her. She has terrible posture. "Forward head," my gym teacher, Miss Hamner, would say.

I'm starting to cry. I will not. I will not. "I can't go on home." I say, imitating his dumb way of saying it.

"Well, Susanna—I can't leave here now." He is trying to be patient.

"I guess it's over," I say.

"Oh, come on now," he says, and chucks me under my chin. Will not. Will not. Will not cry.

"Now you just go back to your house however it was you got here, okay? And don't do this kind of thing again." He doesn't sound angry, just sort of like that's what he should say. He actually sounds distracted, as though it doesn't even matter to him at all.

"I won't." I put my head down.

But it does matter, I think, because he looks back at me and I think he's going to come and get me when C.A.'s father, his agent, comes up and pushes him along with him through the big heavy doors and I am standing out here with the photographers walking off in bunches, lighting cigarettes and laughing.

"God," I say. "God, if this is Your idea it was pretty dumb. I don't mean it. I don't mean it." I take it back fast. The dumb ideas are usually mine. Val would never do anything like this.

I wish this was a bad dream.

I have no money left for the cab. Stupid. I imagined myself driving back in Jackson's car. Jackson's arm around me. And now all I've done is make him hate me.

"Out hitting the nightspots?" It is Uncle Alan, coming up the broad steps.

"I was . . . I was . . ." I look at him and cannot speak because I will start to cry.

"Never mind. I didn't see you and you didn't see me. How about joining me for a nightcap and we'll talk about it, and then I'll run you home."

"Not in there. I don't want to go in there. Listen, don't tell Val, especially."

"I said we didn't see each other. We'll walk over to the Derby. Okay with you?"

"Fine."

When I talked to Val earlier tonight she said he'd gone to another meeting. I'll bet he isn't even a Communist but just uses it as an excuse to go out and hang around, pretending he's a New York street kid.

I sit at the bar next to him. "I'll have a Jack Daniels," he says. "Make that a double, and a double ginger ale for my friend."

"Don't ask any questions, will you?"

78

"No questions. Sometimes it does help to talk about things." We sit silently.

Finally I say, "Do you know why I was there?"

"I thought we weren't going to have any questions."

"Well, I did something so stupid. I wanted to see Jackson Lane. He came over the other day, so I thought we were friends. I don't understand anything, I guess."

"Val told me about that. I should tell you—you know, we usually do talk about everything."

They are very close, just like real families in the movies.

"Well, tonight he just practically ignored me."

"Come on, you know how it is at a premiere, Susanna—for us, it's work. It's the same when Val visits me on a set and I can't concentrate on her. She always sulks until she remembers. It's the same thing."

"But that's different. She knows she'll see you later."

"She still gets mad," he says. I do not want to talk about Val.

"Uncle Alan, can you promise not to tell my mother and Myron something—I can't tell you how I know—it's sort of private." My mother would kill me if she found out I said anything about the fight. The thing about our family is, it is very proud that there has never been a divorce. And there has never been a scandal, which is a record for Hollywood. Until Alan, and his Communism—but fighting is worse. My mother has often said bickering is very middle class and she will not tolerate it. I guess her fight with Myron went beyond bickering and therefore does not count. Middle class— I wonder what class we are. Upper class is only Christian, and C.A. says just Episcopalian Christian. We were discussing this one day and Val said she thought it was ridiculous—"We're all show business and don't have any class at all, everyone knows that, except our mothers." We were just joking around that day—there isn't any class system here.

Alan and I are sitting kind of quietly like buddies and I'm trying to think, in that funny way you can, of two things at once—one, what you're remembering, and two, how you're going to say something that if it comes out wrong could make a lot of trouble. I wonder if Val could just sit at a bar with Alan and feel like a buddy like this. I wonder if I could have with my real father—Daniel Hartman—I wonder if he'd ever ever go to a bar. I think of him in his blazer and white trousers and my mother in her summer dress. He was perfect for her, stiff as Myron and "proper," a word which she loves (except, I guess, when smashed), and yet tall and blond like Jackson—no wonder she would have loved Jackson. I wonder if Dr. Hartman was alive if he would understand me having a crush on an actor. I wonder if Alan would understand if Val did something like this—would he raise the roof? I think Dr. Hartman would send me off to school in the East if I behaved like this with him. But if he hadn't died I'd probably be there anyway and I'd be good and quiet and Eastern and never get to learn how to drive or anything, just hang around operas and museums all day and go to Broadway at night. No dailies and rushes, nothing, and no movie stars to break your heart.

"What are you thinking about, Susanna?" Alan says.

"I'm thinking my mother was in love with Jackson Lane. Do you think he really came to see her? and would you tell me if they were in love?"

After all that I just blurt it out. Just like that—I think he's a little surprised because he lights a cigarette and he already has one going. He notices, shrugs, and smokes one, then the other, as he talks.

"Well, Susanna. I'm going to talk to you like an adult because that's a kind of adult situation. Remember what I tell you—some day you'll understand." He is drinking slowly—for Alan—and I can see him being very careful about what he's saying.

"There's a respect for certain kinds of gossip here. We all know something, but don't discuss it because we are afraid of other secrets which may be used against us."

"Like you're supposed to be at a meeting, but you're out, and I'm supposed to be home in bed?"

"Exactly. Hollywood, Susanna, is both a small town and a magical kingdom—both of these run on fear and a kind of simplistic morality." He's pleased with what he's saying, which I'm trying to understand because it sounds smart. He looks very intense and his eyebrows, like Val's, get very straight when they're talking seriously.

"They're also alike because they're run by the power of important families. Even though gossip is very exciting, it can also be damaging. I think your family was banking on people respecting that. Including Jackson. But he's a maverick, Susanna. And I'm not sure he really cares much about what they can do to him. I know this isn't a direct answer. But if something did go on with Jackson and your mother, that wouldn't scare him away. Want another ginger ale?"

"Sure."

"Another round," he says to the bartender. I feel very calm, very grown-up here with Alan.

"Jackson wouldn't even talk to me tonight."

"Well, maybe he thought it was the wrong time. You know you must have really surprised him. I'd try to see him more privately, if I were you. You'll figure out a way. You have to think about it carefully."

"I would go to his house, but the magazines say no one knows where he lives. Is that true?"

"You may have to wait until you're older to understand things, Susanna. You have a problem—and it isn't Jackson, it's reality. It's very hard to know what's real, living where we do. You have to learn, as you grow, how real people behave, not how they would do it in the movies. Difference." He says that just the way Val does.

"How will I know?"

"By watching people. Ordinary people who do not have power. Power makes people crazy. Stardom is a kind of power. I'm glad I don't have it." I don't believe that altogether. If he didn't want to be a star why did he let them change his name from Al Benjamin?

I think of Scotty. I bet he's real.

"I know Jackson isn't. Real. Not that way. But I still want to be with him. I hope he isn't furious."

"A lot of times people don't get what they want, Susanna. But I think that's just so we can see how well we can do without it. That's not my favorite way to look at things, but it might help. I doubt if he's furious with you. He's probably mad at himself because he didn't know how to handle the situation. He is not known for gallantry."

"He's not nice?"

"Nice has nothing to do with it. He probably wouldn't intrigue you, or anyone else, much if he was nice. You just have to see, as you grow, what someone's really like, and, if you do that, he can't ever disappoint you"—and he adds, muttering almost to himself as he scrounges in his pockets for some money, "I keep telling that to my remarkable wife, my Lady of the Lilies, when she says to me—" and he imitates her perfectly (the way Val does me . . . or her father when she's not busy protecting him), " 'Okay, Alan, you've been drinking, . . .' and I say to her, 'Oh, so that's what I've been doing. I had forgotten.' "

He doesn't come up with any cash and tells the bartender, "Put it on my tab . . . Time. Susanna. Take your time, everything comes along when it's supposed to. Just take it easy. Now—I'd better get you home."

I guess with everything else I've done. I can risk driving with Uncle Alan. My mother says he's a terrible driver.

"Can you get back in?" he asks as he drives me to the bottom of the hill. The house is dark, just a silhouette, like black construction paper against the sky high on the cliff above us.

"Sure. Same way I got out."

"Susanna . . ."

"What?"

He gives me a hug. "I wonder . . ." he says.

"Wonder what?"

"How much of all this you'll remember and use."

"Oh, I will. I really will. I hope things go better for you. I really love you, Uncle Alan." I pause. "Do you have to tell Val?" I know she would tease me.

"No. I told you. This was all between us. And it better be. Hell, if Lily heard I took you to a bar she'd know I was off the wagon, although," and he grins sideways, "I assume she guessed as much."

I get embarrassed when Alan talks about drinking, even though he's funny about it. I don't think they should bother him so much. He likes it and it's his life, after all. Except he does get slobby sometimes. Then he should just stop. He is an actor—I think he should try to look less drunk. I lean over and and kiss him quickly. Val hates the smell he gets from liquor. I don't mind it at all. Maybe if they ignored it, he'd stop showing off how drunk he can get.

Grandmother is standing in the front door and Watchman, who caught me at the olive tree on his late shift, hands me over to her. Her gray hair is flying loose from the braid she puts it in when she sleeps.

"Shena! What are you doing?"

"I decided to get an early start to school."

"No, that is not the truth," she says. "Now we will go up the back steps, so we will not wake your parents."

She leans on my shoulder and we go up one step at a time.

"You were running maybe to Val. But that is a long way to go, Shena. Remember when you were little and you used to run all the time to see what was there in the dark? How I called you Shena Middle-of-the-Night? I told you Baba Yaga would be out there, running along to catch you in her house on the chicken legs, or flying by in her mortar and pestle to get you . . . you remember the story of the little Vasilia who went out into the night forest to get light for her family? That seems so long ago. And still you are running. Still you run."

"It wasn't so long ago, Grandmother, really." I don't want to remind her she is getting older. I am just beginning, but she is near the ending. When I am with her I want to be like a child. And I am. Everyone is, with her, even my mother.

"So . . . and so . . ." she says, closing the windows. Now alone, maybe I can say something for Alan.

"I am worried, Grandmother, I don't see why it matters even if Uncle Alan is a Communist. He's not doing anything except going to meetings."

"Shayne, my darling, Uncle Alan doesn't understand. None of his friends remember the revolution in Russia, before it became the Soviet Union, but it is beginning here now. To some of us the signs are clear. The subversive ones are making movies the people do not go to see and this leads to something called a depression, where no one has any money, and then, if Hollywood, which speaks for the American spirit, begins in the movies to turn the people against the government, there will be a revolution."

In all the movies I've ever seen about the revolution, everyone gets beheaded. I think that was the French one, but I imagine they're all the same. Except ours. And we didn't do that. Unless that was one of the lessons I dreamed right through. I don't always know what I'm doing when I'm dreaming. "Susanna! You're dreaming —again," is how it goes—in class. But it's just suddenly they're talking to me and I haven't been there.

"But would the Soviet Union come over here?"

"No, my darling, that is why we are taking these steps now."

"But if he can't work, they'll have a lot of trouble."

"He should have thought of that."

She is being very stubborn. But it doesn't seem right. Uncle Alan is very smart; he wouldn't put his own family in danger, not Val—not little Theo. Boy, we should stop calling him "Little Theo," he's going to really hate that when he gets older. I think he's going to hate "Theo" enough as it is.

Grandmother starts to take off my sweater and I almost shrug away. Then I remember how my mother shrugged away from Myron and so I just let her take it off. Then she takes hold of my hands and sits me down on the bed beside her.

"This is a difficult time for everyone," she says, "but if there was not something, we would not learn. It is not for nothing that the best stories are full of troubles. But you remember, the brave girl always gets through. Now you'll go to sleep and in the morning you'll bring your guitar and I'll take out my balalaika and we'll make some music. That is why we have the songs, to make the waiting for the happy ending easier. You have to practice, look, the fingers are getting soft again, less mooning over someone and more practice."

I wonder who she thinks I am mooning over. Angelo? Jackson?

And does she know my mother is mooning over Jackson? If she is. Actually she had swatches sent over this afternoon for redoing her room so I guess she is not mooning. She adores redecorating and holding luncheon conferences with her decorator, George Hall, and the upholstery man and the drape man and the valance man, who carries the best swoopy valances in Hollywood. I think she feels as though she's running her own studio when she sits at the head of the table and gets all their reports and gives them orders. It's like when Grandfather would assemble all his producers here.

Grandmother gets up and looks at my puppets on their rack. She takes the prince puppet off and has him bow to me. "Don't go running after Mr. Charming, little one, until you are old enough to see who he is under the pretty uniform he wears."

Then she puts him back and he swings there, looking at me, and she leans over and hugs me and she feels so small under her velvet dressing gown her bones seem to float in the skin of her arms.

"Don't worry, Grandmother." I should probably tell her I was not running away. But what could I tell her I was doing? I'll wait until Jackson comes to get me again.

"What's to worry? Worry is a waste of the imagination. You remember that, Miss Middle-of-the-Night."

How different she is with me than Alan is. She can make me feel life is a storybook, older and odder than movies. She talks about "Mr. Charming" and yet it's exactly the same thing Alan said to me about knowing the person you love. Or almost the same. I wonder if they know they think almost exactly alike about some things—except this stupid Communism. Maybe Alan does that the same way he drinks, doing more of it when they notice. But I still don't see why any of this should mean he can't be in movies. He's not less of an actor because he drinks or is a Communist.

I dream I am playing tennis on a court covered with snow. A huge court with no fences. I cannot really see him in his white outfit way on the other side, but I know Jackson is there and I serve the ball to him and wait for it to be returned. It does not come back and in the snow and the silence I am frightened. I wait while more snow falls, and I try to yell to him, but I cannot scream. And I cannot run. And I know he is gone.

I wake up terrified. I lie in bed as cold as snow must be. Sunday there's a big match at the Riviera Polo Grounds and I'll bet Jackson will be there. C.A. has invited Val and me and—yuck—Kitty to come along and go riding after the game. If he isn't there I'll make another plan.

AND JACKSON WAS LISTED AS ONE OF THE CELEBRITY players but he didn't show up. I chewed up my entire program just waiting and wondering. Or almost. Val whipped it out of my hands. "Do you know what you're doing? You're crazy! Eating paper!"

Gilbert Roland and Cesar Romero are the last players on the polo grounds and the field is shadowed, except for a patch of sunlight on the southwest corner near the whitewashed stables. You can see dust coming up under the lawn as Roland gallops his horse down along the far side of the field. Bill, the regular stable boy, is telling Angelo, who works here on weekends, that they'd better sprinkle the field real well when the sun goes down. . . .

"As soon as we get you girls saddled up," Sim, the other stable boy, adds. "The wind has the horses all acting up. I'd hose down the roof of the stable real good while you're at it. It's funny weather." He squints up at the sky—Sim always has something bad to say about everything. If you're on a horse he'll tell you to hold up a minute: "Looks like he's gone a bit lame." Sim would love my mother, except she doesn't go around horses. "They go mad and suddenly kick you in the head. People were not meant to ride on animals. I never feel safe riding in anything but a limousine." She says that as if it is therefore a rule that no one else should be safe in anything else either. When I go riding she expects concussion, never broken ankle or arm—from falling off a horse the rule is you get a concussion. Just like you get polio from other people's swimming pools, trench mouth from tap water, and unspeakable diseases from toilet seats which are not prevented by any amount of paper covers. "Ladies wait." I don't think she ever goes anyway, her body would not dare to offend her like that.

"How's your father doing?" I ask Angelo. Mr. Giordano has been sick. Mary says it is quite serious.

"Lousy," Angelo says, "but thanks for asking." He walks over and leans against the fence, watching the movie stars performing for each other. I want to whisper to him, "I understand"—to speak to him with my eyes. But I stand there just like another cowpoke, chewing on hay, watching, eyes squinty.

Gilbert Roland leans over perpendicular to the saddle and hits a long shot the length of the field to Romero, who misses the ball, shrugs, and salutes Roland with a wave of his mallet.

"They move," Angelo says, "as though they're always being watched."

"It comes from being directed," I say. "You'll do it too."

He thinks I'm being snotty. But I mean it. I know Angelo is going to be a star some day. He isn't that much cuter than Sim or Bill, but he has that motor I was talking about.

The men are standing together now, drinking Cokes from the machine, with towels slung about their necks. I hear Jackson's name out of the corner of my ears. Gilbert Roland is saying, "He didn't show up on the set Friday, either. . . ."

I go by casually and say, "Oh, hi—I thought Jackson Lane was going to be here." At least I could have waited till the next sentence. "I loved the match, though," I add quickly. "You were wonderful."

"Thank you, my darling," Cesar says, "and how is your family, your dear grandmother?"

Gilbert Roland shakes his head and grins. "You don't need to see Jackson Lane when we are here, but he did tell me a couple—three weeks ago?—he would be here. I told him what a brilliant player I am, perhaps he is frightened away."

Romero says, "Oh, don't think about it, he doesn't even play—you know—they put your name on the list —doesn't mean anything . . ." He snaps his fingers to show how it does not mean anything. To him, maybe.

I think Cesar Romero is trying to change the subject.

But Roland leans back with his elbows on the fence, his very most elegant pose.

"You know, Jackson's a strange one. We used to play tennis when he first came here. I never knew where he lived. We have the same service and they say they don't even have a number for him—he always calls in. And not too often. And always pays with cash, no checks, no charge account. I never met anyone who's been to his house—and we were friends, I consider myself his friend. Strange kind of guy," he repeats, looking off in the distance.

"I don't know how brilliant you were today," Cesar tells Gilbert Roland, giving him a little hit on the shoulder the way men do. I love to hear stars talk about each other, and to see them look at each other—they become fans, but with a little edge of something—comparison?

Now Val comes over with a bridle draped over her shoulder. She sometimes does things just because they look good, but is clever enough to make you think she really was in the middle of saddling up and was just coming this way. If it was me she would tease me later about trying to look sporty and she'd be right.

Cesar Romero gives her a big hug. "How is your father? How lucky I am not interested in politics. They've been giving him a bad time. Give him my regards, will you?"

"That could be incriminating," Val says.

"So tell him privately, you're getting to be a beauty." He puts his hand under her chin and smiles down at her.

Kitty Chapin sidles up. "Hi, Mr. Romero, you may not remember me, but my father wrote one of your first contracts." Her father is a lawyer but she always pretends he is in the business and she talks exactly like he does, as if she's at least fifty and carrying a briefcase.

"Oh yes." Immediately his smile turns to her. "How has he been?"

Val whispers to me, "Notice how the smile moves by itself, not the attention, but just the smile—like a searchlight."

The actors leave in their Cadillac convertibles and the girls go into the tack room where C.A. is. Angelo is taking care of the actors' horses.

I go along after him. "Can I help?"

"Just fill these pails for me, okay?" He hands me two pails and I am off to fill them at the tap. I have to unscrew a hose, and the water splashes out and gets mud on my orange frontier pants.

He looks at my pants. "Sorry you asked, huh?"

"No, it's fine. They're just old work pants. Can you play polo?" I ask.

"Not yet. It's pretty much a rich man's sport."

"Oh, I think it only matters that you be good at it."

"That's a nice liberal attitude." He finishes rubbing down one of the horses and, with a solid pat on the rump, puts him in his stall.

"I'm not a liberal " I say. "I am not anything." That is probably the safest thing to be.

I follow Angelo to the corral, he looks up at the sky, stretches, and practices a few swings with a polo mallet. He puts it jauntily over his shoulder then, and walks past me. The night is coming down soon, dark and heavy, holding in the dry heat like a blanket.

"Wat'cha doing?" I say, very Western and horsey. And sniffy.

"Practicing listening " he says.

"Listening to what?" I ask.

"Crickets. Sounds You can hear the leaves rubbing together like an old man's bony fingers . . . even when he's unconscious his hands twitch—snipping and cutting at plants—tipping off new growth."

Mr. Giordano nearly killed me last year: I wanted to do a Hawaiian kind of aquacade and I cut off the heads of the zinnias, and made them into the most gorgeous leis anyone ever saw, threading them along on the string I use for my puppets—actually everyone was furious at me for that, but if you do something artistic you have to be prepared for criticism.

"Horses sure are restless tonight," Sim says, leading the other rental horses around for us. "I hope you girls get back soon. I don't want to hang around here forever."

"What time is Mac getting back?" Angelo asks him.

" 'Bout eleven, I guess," Sim says. Mac, his uncle, lives in a room over the stable and takes care of things at night.

"It's a real bad night. The horses smell something happening," Angelo says.

"They smell girls. That always spooks them. . . . Spooks me, for sure," Sim says. "Hope you all get going soon so's I can get back to my ball game." He goes back into the tack room with the others.

When we go inside to get the saddles for our horses, Sim and Bill are hunkered down against the wall with C.A. and, I could have told you, they are smoking. C.A. is sitting in the middle, her legs in real boys' blue jeans as long and strong as boys' legs. Mine are long and strong, but I have real thighs. I sometimes look at them and think one day someone is going to want to just bite them—they are so peachy.

Val is switching stations on the old radio the boys have perched up on one of the tack room shelves. She has a real Marlboro cigarette dangling at a perfect rakish angle from her lips. She looks twenty-one, which is the earliest you can be sophisticated. Twenty-six is when it's really great. When Val does things like smoke, she never looks cheap. C.A., my mother says, looks rather coarse. "It's so sad when a girl looks like the father." And she gazes at me. I don't really look like Daniel Hartman—but more like him than my mother. I don't actually think I look like anyone. Which my mother sometimes points out. Kitty just looks dumb when she smokes—she puffs like a little engine and her eyes go crossed when she looks at the smoke to see if she's blowing smoke rings the way Sim can.

I lean over to try a cigarette and knock over a paper cup full of beer. "Klutz," says C.A.

"Typical," says Val.

"Girls. Shit," says Sim.

(I hate that word.)

"Second the motion," says Bill with a laugh that's halfway between a crow and a whinny. I think it must be odd to be a boy and never know what your voice will sound like a minute from now.

I am furious at Val. Especially when she raises her eyebrows in a sort of well-don't-take-it-seriously expression. Angelo picks up a bridle and goes out again, whistling. I stamp past Val and get a Kleenex because I am sneezing.

Val says, "Lions again?"

She has always teased me since Paul Daroff's last birthday party when wicked stepmother Evelyn Ames had a circus show put on and one of the lions went crazy and started chasing us and I started sneezing. "A regular Circus Maximus," Alan said. "How cunning of Evelyn. She has always loathed children." No one knows that more than Paul.

"No. It's this dry weather." And I stride out. The Kleenex crumbles already into its own dust. I have forgotten my handkerchief and Kleenex, when you are sneezing a lot, is like rubbing a sieve on your nose. I shove a wad of it under my saddle anyway and we are off.

"Come-a-ti-yi-yippi-yippi-yi," I sing to myself as we ride out along the bridle path under the shady tunnel of giant pepper trees whose lacy branches meet above our heads. I pick off a bunch of small rose-colored peppercorns and put it in my hair, until I remember it makes me sneeze worse. I imagine the Spanish monks bringing in the trees from the beach on wooden carts, and trudging up the Santa Monica Canyon to plant them all along their new dirt roads. A lizard scampers across the path, dry and dusty as an old eucalyptus leaf. At the end of the path we cross Sunset Boulevard and ride up Mandeville Canyon, turning up and moving into the hills. "See them tumbling down . . . Tumbling tumbleweed . . ." Cowboy movie country, ruddy, empty, studded with brush, and sticky bushes of yellow broom, a few blossoms still hanging on like bits of scrambled egg. I guess I had planned that Jackson would go riding with us after the match; although after the other night I shouldn't plan—or expect—or hope—anything about him. I touch the ring which I put on my gold locket chain, under my shirt so Val won't tease me. I'll bet when the trade reviews of his picture were so lousy he just took off on his boat to get it off his chest. It would have been embarrassing to be on the set that day. I pretend we are a posse looking for Jackson Lane, and then I am singing, "I want my own cowboy all dressed in white linen, dressed in white linen as warm as the sun . . ." Which is not how it really goes, but I like to fool around with the words. It's Val who's able to make up new melodies, we could be Rodgers and Hammerstein except she can also do her own words. A coyote howls from another hill and the horses chuff and whinny. The bushes rustle in the hot wind, which comes and goes.

"What's that?" Kitty is scared.

"Werecoyotes," Val says. "It happens to Randolph Scott when his option comes up. Ever notice how furry his ears are?"

When we are up in the hills C.A. has this great idea to take off our clothes and ride naked. "No one's around, and it's so hot."

If anyone said no C.A. would say, "Chicken!" So we just take off our shirts and put them across the saddles. I can see Val in the moonlight and she looks as though this is the natural way to ride. I compare myself to Val and C.A., who have long lines, and I feel awkward. I think they can be naked and just have fun. I can't do it without thinking about sex and the warm wind feels like my hand on my breasts. I have absolutely adored these breasts since they began. I wonder if Jackson noticed. He could not have helped but notice, staring down at me in my bathing suit. Breasts are so comforting to sleep with. I almost have forgotten how it was before they came along to hold and cuddle at night.

I love the leather. When I get married I will ask him to wear chaps on our wedding night. I sneeze. Am I allergic to leather?—or wedding nights? I don't know exactly what happens on wedding nights. They have cut all that stuff out of our biology books at school. I think the teachers take those pages home and sneak them out at night to look at with their husbands or wives, underlining the best parts with their red and blue correcting pencils. I wonder if they give each other tests and the one who gets one hundred can do something really dirty to the other one such as touching everything naked with the lights on and the other one has to lie there and just let itself be touched and looked at. When I am "dreaming" in math, this is what I'm thinking about. You probably get to do this kind of thing on wedding nights. And then he lies on top of you. That's as much as we tell each other. I happen to think C.A. knows all of it from her listening-in, but then you can't always believe C.A. I think what you probably do is rub up against each other for this feeling I like. But I can't imagine how that works if you're lying under him.

I imagine I am in Greece, a person of mythology. This is the only part of school this year that I liked. The gods. It was easy because you just think of them like stars—sort of Hollywood with togas. The scrub oak here become olive trees and old columns and I am Athena about to be mated with Zeus, who has come to me disguised as an allergy. Does incest upset those gods? It has not come up in Miss Devey's literature class. Incest is, C.A. says, when you do it with your relatives. I can't imagine doing it with Myron. I can't even imagine him with my mother, which is probably what she was complaining about that night. I wonder if my mother ever really kissed Jackson—or if they just talked about it, and would that count as unfaithful?

Kitty sidles up beside me. "Do you think Alan Benedict is really a Communist?" she says.

"What would it matter anyway?" I say.

"Well . . . I've heard . . ." she looks around, "that they can read your mind, they're trained by Russians, you know, to know when you're lying. So everything you say goes right back through the channels, if you know what I mean."

"What channels?" Actually I don't care. I wish I hadn't asked. Now Kitty will tell me.

"Their TV channels, I think," she says.

"Oh, Kitty, they don't have any TV stations yet." Although we've all heard rumors it is a Communist plot— TV—to undermine movies and the American way of life. Myron won't have a TV in the house.

"Listen, I want to canter here . . ." I say. And I go off by myself.

And I am not sneezing. Maybe I am not allergic to horses. Maybe just the hay and all the people being around reminding me. This is the secret. I think allergists are paid off to say we are allergic to things our parents think are dirty. My mother thinks horses are dirty. I happen to think my grandfather would have let me have my own horse. And I think Grandmother would too, if she had the energy to argue with my mother. Grandmother is a lot more real underneath her elegant ways. When she used to cook she'd be up to her elbows in chicken. And she used garlic, which my mother hates. Grandmother would take a chicken and slide garlic between the skin and the meat and it was really great. And my mother would say, flinging her hands in front of her face, "Don't come near me—you've been eating garlic!" She sometimes makes me think I smell like a goat. She always smells like Shalimar. Has quarts of it.

I think my mother thinks it is higher class to be clean, which is why, when I really think about it, she would not have been unfaithful. That is not upper-class behavior, especially not with an actor and one who smells a little sweaty in the sun. I shouldn't even think about that—but I'll never forget how he smelled. My mother would say this is DISGUSTING. No. She would say REVOLTING. That's right.

Once I am really on the horse and away, I am fine. I love to feel his shoulders moving here under me. I love to feel how warm and big he is between my legs. It is like being in charge of an engine, my own car, or a whole studio. I kick my horse gently to get him to move like a rocking chair, like a big, strong hand. I saw a still photo once of Jackson holding a baby actor up in the air, balanced in the saddle of his hand. I am the baby in this saddle. I know why that baby crowed so, its little head thrown back, tiny teeth bared around the little wet mouth. The grownups do not want us to guess they remember too how much they felt when they were little. Will I forget I know? The Hindus, according to Miss Rentsch, our history teacher, say we forget our former lives when we begin the next ones. Will I forget when the time comes with boys, so I can pretend I don't know and so they can teach me?

I have not forgotten yet that I understand why they fired the nurses I liked the best. I know they did this rubbing then with their soft clean hands. This was way before Tucky—way before nurses became governesses and did not touch you (or weren't allowed to). I have seen O'Connor do it to Theo. But I wouldn't tell. They got into our pants before we could talk and when we learned enough to ask for more we were quickly told that it was dirty. I used to think up ways to drive my governesses bats for driving me crazy. Bats for crazy. Tit for tat. I hung all of my clothes upside down on the hangers. It looked like a possum dorm in my closet. They could not say I was not trying to put things away. Hanging is hanging, I said. Then I wrote *Keep Out* in the crotch of my pants before I put them into the hamper. They were always checking pants. Governesses think if you rub a lot there you'll get infections. I used to catch them coming into my room at night. I kept a flashlight under the covers and the minute I heard them rustling and breathing I'd whip it out and shine it in their eyes. One of them claimed I blinded her and she went around for weeks in sunglasses. But that was so someone would think she was a movie star. Sometimes I just crayoned the whole crotch ultramarine blue. They also hated you to suck your thumb. Probably gave them dirty ideas. God—I hope I don't die before I see a man naked. A man, a boy, an actor—anything.

I hear the sound of a horse before I see it is Angelo. He has come up on the butte above and is watching me. I catch my breath, as if holding my breath will make the horse be still and me less easy to see. I start to cover my breasts with my hand and then I figure he's been wanting to see them since they grew in or came out or whatever they do. So let him look. Is it cheap just to show? I pretend, of course, I do not see him looking. I hear the others and I see them standing in their saddles, and I can see them as he sees them and they seem even more naked. Suddenly, C.A., who is at the very crest of the hill, waves her arm and yells, "Hey, over there, a fire!" The others trot right up and they stand there, silhouetted against the night, raised in their stirrups.

"Susanna—where are you?" Val calls. I look back to see if he is watching, but he's gone. My face is hot and wet and I know I will not tell them Angelo saw us. I canter to the top of the hill beside them.

"Probably just a premiere," C.A. says, "or Aurora Borealis."

"I'm going back," Val says. "It's in our canyon."

"For God's sake, then, put your top on," Kitty says, already into her shirt.

"Maybe it's in the Glen?"

"No," Val says. "I must call home."

We dress and gallop back. I am hanging on for dear life. I know Angelo will be there before us. It will be interesting to see his expression.

"There's a fire," I say to Angelo, staring down at him

when we come riding in, and he holds the reins of my horse (which is mainly to watch me as I dismount).

"We know that," Bill says, "that's why we sent him to get you, Jesus . . ."

"Sent who? We just saw it from the bluff." Val looks at Angelo. And then she turns to me with her hands over her mouth.

What is really terrible is that I think it was wonderful when he was watching.

"Do you know what's happening?" Val demands. "Did you hear anything on the radio? Sim and Bill, you know something. I can see it."

They look at each other. "We've probably got to take you over there. It's pretty bad."

"My father? Don't tell me. Just take me home. Bill, you can drive." Someone has to stay. And for a few minutes everyone argues. No one dares to say it is exciting to go to a fire.

Angelo comes out from the stalls, gleaming in the dark. I turn away. This is not the time to think about whether he liked me the best. So why am I thinking it? My grandmother often speaks of people as "decent human beings." Such people do not think of such things in the middle of emergencies.

"But I want to go too," C.A. says, when the boys tell her her mother is on her way over.

"So, it is bad," Val says. "I just want Susanna." She is as calm as Aunt Lillian would be. I go stand beside her and try not to look pleased that she has chosen me.

"And someone has to stay at the stables." Sim looks at Bill and they both look at Angelo.

"Will you take care of the horses?" Val asks. "I'm sorry, but we've got to go."

"Sure—don't worry about it." He is already unsaddling one of the horses. He is looking at her the way he usually looks at me. He is as bad as I am, thinking of such a thing at this time. And I'm even worse, again, for noticing.

Val and I get into the stable's station wagon and she snaps on the radio.

". . . further notice. More bulletins on that fire after this commercial break."

"Jesus, I'll bet it's a monster," Sim says.

I turn and glare at him.

"Bastards," Val says, leaning forward close to the radio, switching to another station, ". . . blacklisted actor, whose infant son is reported dead. A housekeeper with the family is in critical condition, suffering from burns over most of the body, and has been taken to . . ."

Val pounds the dashboard with her hands. She turns to Bill. "You knew it, you heard it and didn't want to tell me."

"Val." I put my arms around her shoulders. "Don't, quiet."

She shrugs my arms away. "No, I want to hear."

I keep looking at the street signs going by to see if we are really here.

". . . the fire continues out of control at this time in the hills above the canyon, endangering acres of valuable cover. To repeat: The only fatality, to date, of this major disaster, is the infant son of the blacklisted actor Alan Benedict. The infant was alone in the house at Twenty-two Hundred Lookout Mountain with his governess when the fire erupted in the heavily wooded area immediately behind the house and spread to the rear of the home, gutting it within minutes. Mrs. Benedict, attending a party at the time, is at the scene of the fire now. Mr. Benedict's whereabouts are unknown, but attempts are being made to locate him."

"Look how they make it sound," Val says, her voice hoarse with fear. "Don't stop for any lights, Bill, just go —if we get stopped, they'll escort us."

"A police escort!" Sim shouts. He leans over the front seat. "Wow." He smells like socks.

"Shut up," I say.

"I know . . . I'm going, don't get upset now. You know what I mean," Bill says, gunning the dark blue Dodge.

". . . spectators are urged to stay away from the immediate area. The Canyon is closed until further notice by order of the Commissioner. You can view the fire from Mulholland Drive and . . ."

Val stares out the car window. I try to hold her hands and I want to hold on to my own hands, somehow, at the same time. We are just sitting here, staring, swallowing, hands balled into fists crushed into our laps, our shoulders and hips touching. If I had only been there I would have rushed into the burning house and rescued Theo.

Sim sits forward, elbows over the back of the front seat to tell us, "I have a friend whose brother is a fireman. He told me that when people die in a fire it isn't usually the burns, but the smoke inhalation. He said that usually people explode. They get all that smoke building up and explode all over just like a balloon. Pieces go everywhere."

"That's a stupid thing to say." I turn around and push him back into the seat.

"Jesus," Bill says, "you asshole!"

Val rubs her head. Then suddenly: "Stop the car. Stop . . ." Bill pulls over and Val opens the door and runs out through the bushes on the side of the road. I run out, yelling, "Bastard," over my shoulder at Sim. I can hear Val gagging.

"Go away," Val says, leaning over, holding on to a tree trunk.

"Boys are so dumb. Are you okay?" I ask.

"No."

"Oh, Val . . ." I try to put my hand on Val's shoulder. She pulls away and leans over again and throws up.

"Just go away," she says, kneeling now, with the dry heaves shaking her body.

"Okay . . ." I guess I wouldn't want Val standing there if I was being sick, so I stand by the car and wait.

Val comes back to the car. "Have you got some gum?"

I put my hand on her head. Her hair is damp. And she's pale.

"Bubble gum," Bill says.

"Look, I'm sorry," Sim says, hunkered down in his seat.

"Just shut up." Bill glares at him. We drive off again. I want not to be selfish. I am trying not to think about how I would feel if Perdido burned, if my room burned up and the dreams did not know how to get in. I used to believe that dreams were beamed into your windows by the stars. They would get all mixed up if they didn't have six weeks' advance notice of a change of address, like my mother's *Vogue* and *Harper's Bazaar*. I must try not to think of myself now.

I try to imagine the terrible things Val must feel. Theo exploding. I am trying to imagine where the bursting line forms, darkening like a flaw on a balloon on the small body. I am trying to imagine whether the body bursts first so that he could have watched these things like small terrible toys flying out. I see his little star-shaped hands reaching out to catch the toys before he knew that he was feeling pain. Or was he in pain and confused at the same time he was trying to reach these things? Or was his head blackened and addled with smoke and was his last feeling the feeling we have in a dream of falling and flying at the same time just before we wake up?

I put my arm around Val. Her shoulder blades are like little arrowheads. She tenses and I try to rub her back, to feel as motherly as Lillian would.

I will never ride on Sunset without thinking of this drive, without images of Theo laughing, Theo, fists full of crackers, Theo, little damp curls on the back of his neck—going along like a ghost on my shoulder. Baby ghost. Do not. Do not cry. If I cry it will be harder for Val. Why does she have all the trouble—why is one life lucky and one not? And why would a baby have to die—how do you live with that? And I am only his cousin. I wonder if Lillian's hair will turn white at this shock. I twist a strand of my own hair and bring it forward to see. How stupid. This is not happening to me.

Babies and fires; babies and wars. I think of the funny little perplexed look Theo gets on his face—got on his face—when he was being picked up and dressed to go somewhere.

Anything I say will be wrong or stupid. I don't want to be part of what she is upset about. I want to do something. My arm around her shoulder feels so useless and helpless. I try to concentrate on putting all my love into this arm to go into her. I think of how our art teacher, at school, Miss Lippincott, would tell us to hold hands in a circle and feel a whole world of love come around the circle and go through our hands like warm candlelight. She would have us close our eyes and think about it, and you could really feel it. I want Val to feel that now.

The policeman stops us at the mouth of the Canyon. "Only residents, may I see—"

"I live here," Val shouts across us.

"This is Mr. Benedict's daughter," Bill says.

"Oh yes . . . the movie star. I'm sorry, Miss Benedict. Go right on."

"Jeez—even the cops know who he is," Sim says.

"At least he didn't say 'blacklisted' movie star," Val says.

The hot night becomes stifling with smoke. The rest of us feel embarrassed. No one talks. Val leans forward and takes my arm off from around her and then she pats my hands. "I'm okay."

"I know. It's okay." I don't know how she can be so brave—would I pat her hands like that? Would I even notice anyone was there if this was happening to me? I would be screaming and crazy. But then, I think, she is patting my hands so I won't think she was annoyed when she moved my arm. I always forget she hates to be touched.

Bill turns up Lookout Mountain and then pulls over about three blocks away from the house. The street is partly closed off by wooden barriers; a fire engine comes rushing down away from the fire. The sky ahead still glows, but it is dark around us except for lights trained on the darkness by fire equipment. Val jumps from the car before it has completely stopped and runs up the hill.

What will it be like? How should I be? I remember Joan Fontaine watching Manderley, and Irene Dunne in *Anna and the King of Siam* listening to Tuptim screaming as she burned. I have never seen a movie where a baby burned. We burn Indians. Indians burn pioneers.

I should be calm and helpful now. I should not be looking around. I shouldn't be noticing anything, but I see everything. And it looks like a set for a war movie. The lights and trucks and hoses and wires, and the neighbors standing by like set tourists. I want someone to say, "Remember, it's just a movie."

"That's the daughter," someone says as we walk through; Val is clutching onto my arm. I put my hand over hers. I mustn't fuss about her too much—she hates that. How to be just right?

"I hate them," she says, "watching to see how we act." We. It isn't "we." They are watching Val. I hate myself for noticing that this reminds me of being with Jackson, watching someone being watched by other people.

We walk uneasily through the shadows and smoke. Moving lights twitch through the trees. The tall black sticks silhouetted against the sky are not burned tree trunks or telephone poles but parts of Val's house. Lights turn toward it as the fire engines move their positions, rumbling, pumping water. The dark windows like yelling mouths cough out black smoke against the darkened stucco. The Monterey balcony stands, but I can see, through the doors and long windows of the first story, right through to the hollow back as the lights flash by.

Lillian is standing by a group of neighbors, holding one of her begonias in its Mexican pot. She sees Val at the same moment and hands the plant to a woman and they rush to each other through the smoke.

They hold each other tight, rocking back and forth and crying and then Lillian holds Val at arm's length and brushes back her hair. She just shakes her head, pressing her lips together, her tears shine in the strange smoky light like satin ribbons streaming over each cheek.

"Oh, mother . . ." Val says.

"We'll be all right, dear. I thought you would go to the Morrisons'—I didn't want you to see it."

I wonder if she means the baby. I look about uneasily. Will terrible small things be found here and there?

"And . . . Susanna. Your parents are here somewhere. I'm glad you're with Val. That was nice of you."

I don't know what to say, so I just hug her tightly and say, "I'm sorry, I'm so sorry."

"I know, dear, I know."

"Did they find Daddy, where is he?" Val asks.

"I'm sure he's on his way. Don't you worry. . . ."

"Better stand back, ladies," a fireman says. "It's still live in there." What, I wonder, is still alive in there? What do they mean? Other firemen are moving in two's and three's through the debris with hoses and hatchets like shadows in the night. Will I dream about them?

"Now, I want you girls to go back to Perdido tonight with Myron and Vera. I have to stay here, at least until Alan comes, he'll need me."

I see my mother moving through the dark, her gown smudged, an evening bag swinging from a chain around her wrist.

"Susanna! What are you doing here? How did you get here?" What I am learning about my mother is that her first reaction to everything is always anger.

"Some boys from the stable drove us—"

"I told you you're never to drive with strangers. Some boys! What are you trying to do to me? There could have been an accident! That's all we'd need!" She takes me by the shoulders and shakes me.

104

I back away from her. I don't want it to be her that makes me cry. Not the fire and the death, but her.

Lillian grabs my mother's arm as she reaches for me again. "Stop it! Vera. Are you crazy?"

"Oh, Lily," my mother cries, "I can't stand it—everything's falling apart. . . ."

"Not your everything. Mine. Now snap out of it." Her neat chignon has come undone and her blouse has slipped out of her skirt, but she looks angry as a heroine of an epic and it is my mother who looks a wreck and I am ashamed of her. I hate for Val to be watching, as my mother sniffles and tries to find a handkerchief in the evening bag. She finally wipes her nose on her sleeve and gets out her cigarette case and then tries to scramble for her lighter.

"I'll get it," I say, and I fish in the bag, and find it and start to light it.

"No, you shouldn't fool with fire. Oh, hell," she says, "I'm sorry. That was an idiotic thing to say." I hand her the lighter, but Aunt Lillian takes it and lights my mother's cigarette. "You know it is harder, I think, when you're not involved personally. I know I would feel so helpless."

Aunt Lillian is the kindest person since Olivia de Havilland played Melanie.

"Come now, dears," and she puts her arms around Val and me and walks us back to the street, where beyond the fire engines and the fire chief's car I can see the limo.

And Myron, who has attached himself to the fire chief.

"This is Myron Howard, have you boys got a phone I can use?" he is saying, as though he is already on the phone. "I'm trying to locate my brother-in-law."

"Service is out all over the Canyon," the chief says, "but there's an alert out to escort him right up here, sir, soon as they pick him up."

"Lillian," Myron says, "oh, my God, Val, are you all right, you poor kid? What a shock." And he hugs her tightly. "Lily," he repeats, "why don't we wait here with you and send the limo home with the girls?"

We all jump as there is a terrible crashing noise, and sparks shoot up from the house. "That's the rest of the roof," a fireman says, and there is nothing standing now against the sky.

"Send up another unit up in back of Wonderland Drive," the fire chief says into his car radio, "and get me some relief men. It's going to be a long night."

"Myron," Lillian says, "I want to see these men get some coffee and sandwiches, may I send Andrew to Cantor's after he's dropped the girls off?"

"We want to stay with you, Mother," Val says, and I am glad she has spoken for me too.

"We'll all stay until Andrew comes back, then," Myron says. "Tell them to charge it—"

And Lillian interrupts: "To Mr. Benedict's account."

"Don't be ridiculous, Lillian."

"No, Myron. Alan would insist."

"All right. Whatever you want."

Lillian's face reminds me of faces in war movies where they've gone crazy from fighting and keep on going even though the battle is over.

"It was so sudden, darling," she says to Val, and puts her arm around her. "You see, it must have started back in the brush beyond the barbecue pit. I've been meaning to have it cut away, and then come right through the oleanders, down to that little patch of hibiscus. . . . Once that caught, sparks must have flown to the side wall, just under the baby's room, there was nothing poor O'Connor could have done. . . ."

Lillian is explaining it so calmly, like someone giving directions to a party.

"Is Miss O'Connor going to die?"

"I don't know, dear. The ambulance left before you came, just before. There was so much confusion at that point. I had just arrived myself. It's odd. I was thinking of calling home. We had just finished . . . why am I telling you all this? Come, I saved some of the plants from the patio—help me put them into the wagon. We'll keep them at Perdido until we decide what to do."

"Are you all going to stay with us?" I ask. I am terrible. I must be, because I am excited. The house will be so full.

"Well, I suppose we will," Aunt Lillian says, "I suppose we'll all be going right back home. Oh, God." And she pulls back on her hair with one hand, jabbing hairpins back into her chignon with the other. "Now, let's try to be busy."

Myron is walking along with us, watching her. Now he comes up beside her and I notice their shoulders are the same height.

"Lillian, you know, maybe one of us should go home to Mother now. . . . I can take care of things here. And you should get some rest."

"The shock, you mean, Myron? Oh, I am handling the shock my way."

"Lillian," he touches her arm, almost delicately, "you know how sorry I am."

"Oh, Myron, I know you didn't start the fire. Don't be overwrought, Myron, I'm not. It wouldn't be wise for me to rest. I might think. I don't want to think too much."

"If any of us had known," he says, stepping closer to her quickly as a group of firemen go by pulling hoses.

"How could you have known? Would you have waited, perhaps, for a decent interval, maybe until next week, to agree to go along with them? It's better this way. Look at the distraction we have."

"I guess bitterness is as good a defense as any," he says. "Use anything you need to, Lily, and I'll understand."

She turns and notices that the mailbox to the house has been knocked aside. Val notices at the same time and goes quickly, and I run along to help her set it upright. We hold it there, our hands touching, as a man who has been watching comes and moves rocks around the base of the post to hold it steady. Lillian thanks him, and brushes off the top of the mailbox, then closes the little door firmly. "Twenty-two Hundred Lookout Mountain Drive," she says. And her eyes fill with tears.

Some neighborhood kids come up to Val as we wait around for Andrew to come back. "Where are you going to live?" a girl asks.

"Oh, Daddy's been planning to move to England. I guess we'll just go sooner." She is saying that a little like an accusation.

"Yeah, it's probably best to go away."

"England . . . really, England? I'd love to live in Europe," someone says.

"That's not Europe, stupid," the first girl says, "it's an island, like Hawaii."

I feel lonely already. I want to close my eyes and when they open I want to see Val's house whole and dappled with sunlight, the begonias in their pots swinging from the balcony in their rope cradles.

I turn instead in time to see the balcony fold, almost silently, and fall off the front of the house with a crash.

When Andrew comes back, Lillian insists that Val go back to Perdido with us. "I need some time to be just with Alan," she says. "Go, for me, okay?" And she kisses Val.

None of us says anything as we see Alan's convertible careening up the canyon flanked by police cars with sirens screaming, just as we are driving down Laurel Canyon in the limousine.

Val turns in the jumpseat and looks back until she can't see the little red lights any more.

ALAN NEARLY WENT CRAZY THAT NIGHT. HE DISAP-
peared and went down to the hospital and Lillian went
to find him and he was in O'Connor's room and I heard
her telling my grandmother and my mother all about it.

"He was standing there screaming at her, and all you
could see were her eyes glittering out from the bandages
and he was shouting at her to tell him, 'Did he scream?
Did you hear him screaming?' Over and over again until
he had fallen on his knees by the bed crying and then,
just before O'Connor died, I saw her move her head
from side to side, to free him, and he didn't even see
that."

The service for Theo is being held in a small chapel on
the grounds of the cemetery where he will be buried.
Grandmother moves like an empress, all in black,
through groups of friends. She embraces Ethel Barrymore; they look at each other's faces, exchanging
strength. Barrymore's wily eyes flash with tears. "So how
are your famous Yankees?" Grandmother says, taking
her arm.

"We've had better seasons," Miss Barrymore replies.
She wheezes, but with elegance, as though she has in-
haled the dust of one hundred thousand velvet theater
curtains from the real stages where she used to act before she was a movie star.

Danny and Sylvia Kaye help Grandmother to her seat
in the front row. "He looks worse even than Uncle
Alan," I say.

"Comedians are always depressed. They have to
watch people very carefully," Grandmother says, "to see

little things they can exaggerate, and, in the watching, they pick up the sadness. Victor always said comics have no sense of humor. They are like dancers who off the stage make very bad partners. I could never dance with Mr. Astaire. He tripped me always."

Alan, Lillian, and Val walk in last and sit down next to Vera and Myron. Alan looks too carefully combed and Aunt Lillian's knuckles are white where she clutches the sleeves of his jacket. She is holding him up.

I cannot see Val's face. Her hair is hanging down like closed wings. She has been very quiet, watching Lillian and Alan closely. In a way, I think she feels left out of what they are feeling. She was in my room last night looking at my books and records and things and she said, "I feel so awful, missing things, everything that reminded me of when I was little. I didn't mind moving away before . . . I never thought of our house not being there. Now I don't really want to go. Do you understand?"

"Oh, Val. Of course I do. Your songbooks—everything." Only a couple of days ago I thought she had everything.

The Rabbi speaks briefly and reads something about God giving and taking away, and making it sound like this was something God just happens to do.

"But how," I whisper to Grandmother when there is a pause in the service, "can God just do this and expect people to believe in Him?"

After the Rabbi speaks two musicians come up quietly and play a Mexican song called "La Niña Perdida." One of the musicians explains that the song is about a father looking for his lost child. Two trumpets call to each other in the voices of the father and the child. Alan found them on Olvera Street the night after the fire.

Grandmother clenches her lips together tightly as they play. I hold on to her hands with both of mine.

"Maybe, my darling, some lives are like comets. The spirit is so bright that it . . ." She holds my hand and she sighs, and doesn't finish what she was going to say.

After a moment she whispers, "I don't know, Susanna." I've never heard her say she doesn't know.

I have noticed the Rabbi is wearing white socks with his black suit. I wonder how his wife let him go out with those. I turn in my seat to check if she is wearing her pearl earrings. So she is.

Every day women friends of Lillian's or Grandmother's come over, usually in pairs, with cardboard boxes of schnecken and coffee cake wrapped up with string. Val says she can imagine us doing that in thirty years.

And the big news is Jackson has not been seen or heard from for two entire weeks. It's all over the papers and not just the trades that he has left town. Disappeared. How can Jackson have disappeared like that? everyone wonders, and while they're wondering he's done it. We are not, for sure, discussing this headline story around the dinner table. Thank God, Val and Lillian and Alan have been staying with us and this is a terrible thing to say because they wouldn't have been here if it hadn't been for the fire, but it's been the only thing that's kept me from charging off to be the one to find him. I keep wondering if I was the last straw— showing up that night. It's been wonderful, the house full of footsteps and friends and the friends—once in a while—dropping something about "the Lane situation."

I heard William Wyler telling Buddy Adler, "They've had to shelve the picture. It must have been the reviews. I never had reviews like that on any picture, never saw reviews like that."

"Willy, you never made a picture like that." Buddy Adler touches his sterling silver hair. "I think Lane has been badly handled—but there may have been something political, or perhaps a friend was in trouble, you understand."

One could certainly imagine that, I think to myself. Practically everyone we know is in trouble. That must be it. I wonder if someone spotted him with Scotty. Someone standing around the merry-go-round that day. A spy for the Un-American Committee, which is a pretty tricky name for people who think they're patriotic. My God, when they call me to the stand, no matter what, I know nothing. I will take every amendment I can find, no matter how long I have to rot in jail. I will be the Hollywood Eleventh.

Jackson is smart. But he's not that kind of intellectual Communist type. He believes in having money. I remember what he said about being alone—and about out-of-work actors. But he wasn't out of work. Another evening I heard C.A.'s father say they had shelved his new picture too. Maybe he was scared it wouldn't be any better. But I don't care what they say. I know my Jackson Lane all right and he is no quitter—there's more to it than that.

Maybe he's on a secret investigation. A mission he couldn't tell anyone about, even me, because he didn't want to take the risk that I would be caught and have to testify against him.

So he had to brush me off in public the other night. Obviously. He would not want to incriminate a minor. That explains it. Alan said: look for the reality. Now I see. He only wanted to protect me. So it makes me furious when I hear someone I never even heard of say that he doubted if Jackson Lane ever voted. "All those political rumors are crap" (another disgusting word). "Jack Lane bitched about coming into the Guild. You know actors, it's some kind of grandstand play for attention. He'll wait around and then make a big comeback when the money's right. It's also a hell of a publicity stunt."

I point this person out to Val, who says, "Oh, that's Herbie Sacks, he produced Jackson's last picture. He's a schnook."

"That figures. What's he doing here?"

"Who knows? Half the people who are showing up wouldn't even hire Daddy and he says the rest come because you don't need an invitation to pay a condolence call. He says there's a whole group of people who just go to funerals and wakes to be seen places they'd never

112

get to normally and to talk to people they can't get in to see. A death, Daddy says, makes their week a social success. He's being so ghoulish. Which is probably a good sign." And she sighs.

"Do you think Jackson's going to come back?" I ask.

"I thought I changed the subject."

"I changed it back."

"Yeah. Well. Touch black, no backs." And she touches her hair.

Ethel has even allowed Lillian in the kitchen to cook with Grandmother. They took out all the big china mixing bowls and made more coffee cakes and Val and I were in there licking the bowls and the whole house smelled of raisins and cinnamon and warm almond paste and even Myron came into the kitchen and said, "Something smells great—it reminds me of when I was a kid." The main thing this house usually smells of is Shalimar, except Grandmother's wing, which smells of dried lavender, which she keeps in little china bowls and has sewn into silk sachets or into her padded satin hangers. He dipped his finger into one of the bowls and licked it and winked at me and then wiped his fingers on the kitchen towel Aunt Lillian had slung over her shoulder and she smiled at him, her face rosy from all the beating she was doing with a big wooden spoon. I have never thought of Myron as a kid. He would have been a monitor with a badge on—been chosen last for the baseball team and elected treasurer because trustworthy. C.A.'s father came over once to see Alan, "To offer his condolences on my career," Alan said bitterly. But C.A. told Val and me that her father said if Alan would make a public denial of his affiliation with certain groups, considering "the tragedy," he was sure he could have gotten Alan some work. Val said angrily, "Daddy would never trade off Theo's death like that. That is disgusting. I'm glad we're getting out of here."

"Well," C.A. said, hooking her thumbs in her blue jean belt loops, "well, hell's bells, Val, Daddy was only trying to help."

One night Alan got my mother to play the piano and they all sang songs they'd loved when they were young in the East, when Alan and Lillian had just met and when my mother and father were first going out, and Val and I sat on the steps listening to them and our bare brown arms touched and it was like having a sister. "I wonder if you can get tan over there," I said.

"They do have a sun over there, you know, and anyway there are more important things in life than suntans and swimming pools." Yes, I think, Jackson and getting my learner's permit next year so I can start driving. And falling in love and getting famous. In that order.

Now this morning they are leaving and I am up about six and go in to see Val who is sleeping in the room Aunt Lillian had when she was a child and I sit on the foot of the bed and watch her sleep, and I look at the suitcases of new clothes lying around the room and I don't want her to go and I want her to be going to a whole new life and all—at the same time I wouldn't want to be Val and leaving everything. I know she's still worried about Alan. He's been peculiar, singing with my mother one night, then the next night not coming home. Myron finally turned out all the lights and locked up and in the morning I saw Alan sleeping on one of the lounges next to the pool with an empty bottle. I watched from my favorite branch on the olive tree while Myron went out there before he went to the studio and at first he sat next to Alan as I am sitting watching Val now and then he woke Alan up and Alan held his head in his hands and then he looked for a cigarette. Myron gave him one of his and lit it for him because Alan's hands were shaking so and then Alan started to cry and Myron held him in his arms. I had the feeling then that under all the efforts everyone was making to make the best of it, somewhere, in separate rooms, at odd times of the day and night, all of them were crying and some of them crying all by themselves. I look at Val sleeping and wonder if she has cried alone here. No one should ever have to be alone. Not when you're crying. How would you ever stop without someone to hold you?

I leave Val's room quietly and decide to go crawl into bed next to Grandmother which I used to do when I was young, after Grandfather died. I walk into her room. The sun is already beginning to come in—she never pulls her shades—and there, lying on top of the bed next to her, with my grandmother's woolly blue shawl around her shoulders, is my mother, sleeping on her side like Val, with her hair lying spread out behind her as though she is running in her sleep. She has one arm over Grandmother's stomach and Grandmother is lying against her pillows. Grandmother sees me coming in and lifts her finger to her lips and smiles. I don't think I like seeing my mother here like this—I am jealous that she is Grandmother's child and I'm not. And I would never think of going in to sleep next to my mother and here she is—with her mother. Grandmother motions for me to come and lie next to her on the other side of her bed but I shake my head and go out, closing the door quietly behind me. Who takes care of who and comforts who and why, and when do you stop being the child and become the protector and when do you stop wanting your mother? And I wonder if Grandmother, with her tender bones, longs for her own mother, the forbidding lady in the old photograph she keeps by her bed. I wonder if, when she is old, I will come to my mother like that, but I cannot imagine my mother old and I wonder what my mother was so sad about that made her go in there, was she missing Jackson too, and wondering where he is? Or does she miss my father and is Myron sad that my mother does not come in and lie next to him when she is sad? That is unfair. I should be able to go to her and have her be all comforting and say, "Someone will come along who is right for you, and you're too young anyway." I wouldn't even mind if she said something like that.

I go back down the hall and Lillian is now in Val's room, sitting on her bed, bent over her and stroking her hair. It is like a silent dance, all of us moving through this house looking in at each other, lying down. If we could only sleep through the leaving. I wish they would just get it over with and go.

We are having our last breakfast together. "You'd better come back with an English accent," I say to Val, who is wearing this terrific navy blue suit for traveling.

"So you can imitate it?" she laughs. "Here's Susanna doing an English accent," and she does me singing "Goodnight Irene" with the accent over the Western one I've been using whenever I remember to.

VAL HAS BEEN GONE FOR TWO MONTHS NOW. IT IS still her phone number which leaps into my mind when I want to talk to someone.

Grandmother is going to die.

There are round-the-clock nurses who try to close the shades when they think Grandmother is asleep, but she always knows. "The shades are never to be closed."

My mother rushes in all day to Grandmother's room with little bouquets of flowers and bottles of cologne, as though presents will encourage life.

Grandmother watches my mother carefully. "My darling, I am concerned. You are getting overtired. Perhaps you and Myron should take a weekend in Arrowhead."

My mother straightens all the old silver brushes and mirrors on Grandmother's dresser and then lies down on her rose-colored velvet chaise.

"I'm fine, Mother. Just fine. And so are you. We are all just suffering from the shock."

"I've had shocks." Grandmother has been better about the whole thing than anyone. The sun dances through the chandelier and puts rainbows on the walls. I think of the rainbows I saw when Jackson was hosing off his boat.

"So, Susanna," she says, "what are your plans this afternoon?"

"She's going to make a condolence call to Angelo, Mother. We lost Mr. Giordano."

I did not want Grandmother to know he died of what she is having.

"No one told me," she says. "No one tells me anything. It won't kill me faster to know what is happening. It feels worse when I am left out."

"Mother, please. Don't talk about that!"

"I'm not afraid of it, Vera. You are. Death, Vera, is a very soft word."

"But there is no point in talking about it."

"My darling. Death is not distracted by your efforts to ignore him. He is, in fact, amused and we speak of it often. He sits here and watches as you all step over his feet. I've gotten to know him very well." A breeze comes in and makes the prisms on the chandelier move and the rainbows dance from one picture to another, like floodlights—the old stars are taking bows.

"Stop it," my mother says. "I won't hear you talk like this." And she rushes from the room. She will lock herself in the living room and play depressing music on the piano.

"Come, Susanna. Sit by me." I wonder if Grandmother ever was in love with a star like my mother was —one of these men on the walls with such formal faces—and I wonder if there was one my mother loved at the same time and if they never talked about it either.

Her hand feels like an old kid glove with a much smaller hand inside of it. Or a small, weak bird. I look away because my eyes have tears coming up.

Grandmother raises her hand and turns my face to hers and sings softly the song she always used to when I was little: "Oh, Susanna, don't you cry for me, for we're home in California where we will always be."

"Don't," I say.

"Not to cry," she says, the way she's said it all my life. "I'm still lying here, looking at you, in the house we love."

I don't want to leave her this afternoon. I look at her propped up on the pillows so she can see the ocean view she loves. Her profile seems even more sheer, like a shell, than this morning. You can almost see through her. Her eyes peer out from cups of skin. I can see why they are called eyeballs. I see them like two planets, slowly circling, as though they turn to the inside, looking at all the thoughts she has before she says goodbye to herself.

Her hand moves now to the peach silk coverlet. And I take it in mine. I have the feeling that if I listen I can hear all her thoughts, that she wouldn't have to even talk to me any more.

"I'll be back, Grandmother, soon." And I kiss her.

"I'll be here. Not to worry," she says and winks at me.

Andrew has driven the limousine from the studio to pick me up to pay the condolence call to Angelo.

I don't want them to see this car, so I tell Andrew to let me off at the corner, which he will not.

"I'm not supposed to do that, Susan." He never tries to get it right. I have stopped saying "Susanna."

So as he slows down to make the turn, I jump out.

"And don't wait in the front where everyone can see," I say.

I smooth my dress as I wait at the front door. I am wearing my bronze cotton that I wore to Theo's funeral. I think of it as my mourning dress with its black braid trim and its own matching bolero jacket. I look like a career girl in this dress. I bet they'll think I'm much older than I am. And if they are serving coffee I will have some as I have it all the time. He has wonderful peach-colored roses here, and some as dark as plums. The house is a small stucco bungalow with venetian blinds in the windows which give it a kind of modern look. I was expecting lace curtains.

Angelo's stepmother introduces me:

"This is Susanna, Victor Levanin's granddaughter." A man stands up and shakes hands with me. "Your grandfather was a wonderful man. Very famous, very nice man. I never had the pleasure to meet him, but . . ."

"Frank . . ." his wife says. She is knitting, looking over her glasses at me. Where is Angelo?

Another woman is sitting in the best chair, leaning back, filling it. The stepmother says, "This is Angelo's aunt, his father's sister, Signora Giordano, she is in the same business. The famous voice coach."

The aunt dismisses the introduction with a wave of her hand, and nods to me, taking a long puff on her cigarette which she is holding between the thumb and forefinger. I don't think this aunt likes me already.

"Would you have some lemonade and cookies?" the stepmother asks. "Mrs. Randall here made them." I sit on the edge of the couch and pick up a cookie, and Angelo comes in one door and walks right through the room into the kitchen. Signora Giordano puffs on her cigarette, jerking it in and out of her mouth, getting it very wet. She has on an expensive scarf, several strings of amber beads, and old gabardine slacks. She sits with her legs apart and has long front teeth.

"We all loved Mr. Giordano," I say, sounding just like my mother when she says something she doesn't mean, "I just loved him, I mean, and I love flowers."

"Do you?" Aunt Giordano says in a terrible deep voice. The others look at her. She snorts smoke through her nose, and regards the others on the couch. She seems to be used to being in charge. I wonder what Angelo is doing. I hear him moving around in the kitchen, slamming cupboards. Then I hear the squeak of a screen door, it snaps closed. I wish I had said I wouldn't come here. Somehow I imagined it would be just me and Angelo. Angelo and me?

"These cookies are delicious. I love cookies," I say.

"Also cookies?" Aunt Giordano says. "Such a loving person."

I am in quicksand. "Well, I don't love everything, I don't love some things, but . . ." Then I remember Aunt Giordano is in music. "I do love music. Dorothy says I have a nice voice, and that I should probably go to New York to study." That is wrong. I shouldn't say that when the aunt teaches here. "I mean, I wouldn't ever be right for movies. Dorothy thinks I'm more a nightclub type. . . ." I have turned to speak really to a neighbor lady who looks interested.

"Who is this great critic Dorothy?" Aunt Giordano pounds out her cigarette with a tobacco-colored thumbnail.

"Well, she is a friend." I do not want to say "maid."

"And what does she do, this authority?" I am getting the third degree. All eyes are on me like light bulbs.

"She works for my father. Actually, my stepfather."

"In which capacity? Is she in the music department?"

"Well, no. She works really for my mother." I feel hot. Even if I say the truth, I feel like I am lying.

"She works in your parents' household then?"

"Yes. I think so." I didn't mean that, but I feel like the words are stumbling inside me.

"You THINK so?" Aunt Giordano sits forward. This is the kill. I *think* Angelo's stepmother hands me the cookie plate again. I stuff one in my mouth—right next to my foot.

"Are you trying to say she is your *servant?*" Aunt Giordano's eyebrows shoot up. Can they go right into the hairline, I wonder, and disappear in a somersault over the back of her head? "Are you ashamed to admit that someone does your menial work? Is that so embarrassing an occupation to you that you cannot mention it? Are you so terribly afraid to see the reality?"

The stepmother says, "Oh, come on, Lina, please let's not have a political discussion. She is here to be polite."

"This is not political. It is time the child knew that there is a class system and she should not pretend it doesn't exist. I detest the lies these people tell children about democracy and race and equality. A servant is not a friend. A servant is obligated to flatter employers and you must not confuse this obligation with expert opinion. I would not build my ambitions, if I were you, on what this Dorothy tells you. Now if you sing for me and I tell you, that is reality." I am beginning to hate that word.

"That's not fair," I say, before I can stop myself. "How do you know she doesn't know? Dorothy probably wouldn't be a maid if . . ."

"If what? If she wasn't a Negro? That should tell you something."

She crosses her arms over her chest and sits back, leg thrown up across her other knee. I hear the needles clicking as the other woman keeps on knitting. I don't want to cry. I should understand things better before I talk. And I feel almost angry at Dorothy for pretending she doesn't hate me because she is a maid. I will never be able to even tell Dorothy I'm sorry. I know whatever I think about this is probably wrong.

Aunt Giordano is like Charles Laughton. I can see her pacing up and down, hands behind her back. I try to look ferocious.

"Why don't you go outside, dear, and see Angelo," the stepmother says, walking me through the kitchen to the back door. "Don't mind Signora," she whispers to me "She's just been blacklisted, you know about all that, and she's very bitter."

"Is she a Communist?" I should have known. The cigarette and the knitting. I am in a nest of revolutionaries.

"Oh no." The stepmother bites her lip and shakes her head. "No. She's just outspoken. That's just her way." She is trying to cover for them.

Angelo is reading a book on the little cement patio. There are pots of red and pink geraniums around the edge. *Amboy Dukes*. That figures. I heard Frank and Uncle Alan talking about that book. It is the dirtiest book in the world. And I would certainly love to read it and that's a secret.

"Was my Commie aunt yelling at you?"

"Well, not really." I have to be careful what I say, even to him.

"She's pretty smart, but she's mad now, especially at all you studio people."

"But I'm not a studio person. I'm just me." He is flipping through pages, not looking at me.

"Well, she lost her job. It's going to be rough. She's

old, you know, and kind of famous in her way. A lot of her students are really mad."

"I'll bet. I'm really sorry about your father."

"It's funny, being an orphan. I could go anywhere."

"You do have your stepmother." I am lifting one foot, then the other. I am tired, and this is a terrible thing to say, of being so careful with what you say because everyone I've been talking to lately, it seems, is in the middle of death. You don't want to use the word —like saying "I could have died" about this or that. You don't want to be your normal scruffy self. And I try not to talk so much because of interrupting the mourning.

"Well, I think I want to go to New York. I don't know. I'm sick of school, sick of the stables."

"You probably miss your father." I am testing. I am also looking for a way to leave without going through that room again. There is a gate at the far end of the garden, and a yard beyond that. I could circle around to the limo.

"I guess so."

I am trying to get a head start, so I kind of edge over to look at some nasturtiums, red ones, amber and striped like tigers. He only put in orange and yellow ones at Perdido. I put my hand out to touch one.

"Don't pick that." Angelo is standing right beside me, suddenly.

"I wasn't going to." I am not sure if I am lying. I am not sure about anything. Even Angelo doesn't seem dangerous in the same good sort of way. I do not adore him today.

"You know I was really mad at you for cutting the heads off the zinnias like that. That was really rotten. It made my father cry. Why did you do it?"

"Well . . ." I am trying to come up with a lie. "It was for Grandmother, to cheer her up." That was ages ago, why is he bringing it up now?

"It was for one of your costumes."

"I'm sorry. I know. I thought about it later." I try to bat my lashes in the irresistible Gail Russell way. But I have not mastered batting yet.

"Do you know what I wanted to do to you?" he says. He is standing close.

"No," I say, moving back. Not too fast. I must not be swayed by him. Maybe he wants to kidnap me and get the ransom to pay for the revolution. I wonder if the Communists have benefit lunches like Grandmother's charities.

"I wanted to bite the tips off your nice little tits, just like you snipped off the flowers." And he laughs as I put my hands quickly to my chest. Which is dumb, because he knows how it looks.

Communists and sex maniacs! I must get out of here.

"Angelo, would you get me some lemonade?" I say.

"You can. It's just inside." He picks up his book.

"I'm scared of her," I say. Boys love us to be scared. I hoped he would get the lemonade and leave the book here. I would swipe it. Well, not really. But I think about it, and that's probably just as bad.

"God, you're silly," he says, but goes in. I wait until the screen door snaps back into place. Now. I hope I make it. Here goes. And I am running across the lawn to the gate. Past marigolds . . . the gladiola bed. If it is locked I'm cooked. No—so far so good. Stealthily now and scrunched down through the neighbor's hedge, down their driveway. I am so glad to see the limo. I don't wait for Andrew to open the door. I don't look back to see if Aunt Giordano is looking out the window and shaking her hand, with cigarette, and saying, "She rides in a limousine. What can such a person know about life?"

"Come on, Glamour; they're all up the stairs." Dorothy's eyes are full of tears. She walks with me up the front steps and the carpet itself seems dark and brooding, our footsteps go like we are going to a ceremony.

Dorothy's body is warm and heavy and I lean against her.

"Is she still here? She said she would be."

"I think so, darlin'. She said she was waiting on you." Dorothy hugs my shoulder with one strong arm.

"I guess," I say, "this is just getting older. Everyone starts to die."

"Seems like, sometimes. But it reminds us to do our living while we're here. Got to keep that in mind."

"I wonder if they'll call Val and Aunt Lillian to come back . . . after."

"Mrs. Howard talked with them about it on the phone, just a while ago."

I stand outside the room and suddenly it is different. Now I don't know what to do. It feels different.

"What do I say?"

"Just say you'll miss her. She knows you love her, honey. Just be like you'd like someone to be with you."

My mother opens the door, her lace hanky dabbing at her eyes. She shakes her head. "She's gone, Susanna. I don't know what to do—everyone, everyone. They're *all* gone, Susanna."

I want to say "I'm here," but I'm not going to be silly. I know what she means. My father, her father, her mother, her sister—away. That's a lot for my mother.

Dust motes dance along a sunbeam that goes from the bed, where I cannot look, out through the window.

I reach for my mother, but she goes back into the room and is pulling the shades on the window down, and the room is dark and Grandmother is gone.

I am going to try, God, although why I am discussing this with You considering what's been going on, I'm not so sure—anyway, God, what I am going to try is not to annoy my mother at all. I will do fingerbowls. Everything. Socks turned down neat. Not twist my hair with my finger. Grandmother would really like that—so I'm going to try. At least until after the funeral.

And the women who come two by two with their boxes of schnecken and coffee cakes come back again.

WE HAVE A NEW GARDENER NOW, AND HE COMES ONLY three times a week. He leaves the sprinklers on and lounges on one of the pool chairs, reading the *Times* before Frank picks it up from the steps by the service porch where the paperman throws it from his truck every morning just after dawn. And I miss seeing Angelo, even though he is rotten. I miss, I miss everything. It seems. I was hoping Val would come back for Grandmother's funeral, but they've had enough of that, I guess. And mother told Myron that Lillian couldn't leave Alan and Val would not leave either of them now. Val wrote me a letter explaining:

You think when the worst has happened that you were clear for a while, but I'm afraid it just is like having an X for target area with a big red circle (Oops. Did not mean to write the word R.E.D., pls. explain to *THEM* if they censor this letter, as I know, my dearest cousin, only you can do), anyway, painted around our family. Daddy is not, you know what I mean, but do not let this go farther (i.e.: down your hall to their wing), *not,* as I was saying, too well . . . and Mommy, by being so concerned and understanding makes him want to kill her or run away or something. I wish—well —but England is terrific—unbelievable. WRITE, WRITE, WRITE; I guess it's really lonely there without Grandmother. . . .

I had written her about the coffee cake ladies and she writes back:

P.S. Is the pecan raspberry still the best—and do you think there'll be anyone left for us to visit in thirty years or will we have to eat it all ourselves and get fat in our mink coats and high heels? Vomitous thought!

In one way I am glad Val is away because she writes more in her letters than she says to me when we are together, perhaps that is because she thinks that I can see for myself what is happening. But I never see as clearly as she does—or as she thinks I do. But I think I know what she wishes about Lillian and Alan—I bet she wishes she would scream at him. When you're really being awful you want someone to shake you and yell— to show how they care so much you can upset them. That's why I never have really gotten to hate Myron for yelling at my mother. If she didn't matter to him he wouldn't have done it.

I am watching the new gardener from the wisteria arbor this morning, and he is turning over the zinnia bed, putting in ivy. He is Japanese. I wonder where he was during the war. I wonder if he knew babies who were burned alive in Hiroshima. I bet everyone in the world knows at least one burned baby. How I have decided to deal with You about this, God, is that You also have a kind of New York office and it does death, like our New York office does money, which is, by the way, Myron's new preoccupation. Grandmother did not like to think about it—which is another thing they used to fight about.

"We've been spending a fortune keeping up those flower beds," Myron complained last week. He misses tussling with Grandmother. He always could get a good argument from her and then they'd play cards to cool off. I think he misses her as much as my mother does, in his way. "I want to cut down maintenance wherever we can," he said. That's why this ivy is coming in.

My mother is not pleased. "There are always rats in ivy." But she does not argue.

I had asked her if we were getting poor. I remember Grandmother's warning about the depression. "Didn't Grandmother leave us money?"

My mother was sitting at her dressing table, surrounded by her jars and brushes and makeup tools. "She's left a small trust fund to Lillian and to me and for you and Val."

"How much?"

"It's not nice to talk about money, Susanna. If you're careful you'll have enough for the little extras you like, but not until you're twenty-one."

"Extras on top of regular things like dresses and cars?"

"No, dear, just extras. Stop twisting."

I took my finger out of my hair. I keep forgetting to stop doing it. At least where she can see.

"Then there wasn't a fortune?"

"No. Grandmother did what she thought was right with her money. Charities, a new wing for the temple, a row of theater seats at the Wilshire Ebell for the Handicapped . . . she was a wonderful woman—simply wonderful." My mother stared into her mirror, plucking out tiny eyebrow stubs one by one. "It was her money, after all." I think my mother was convincing herself.

"Well, if someone else leaves me money for the regulars, then I'd have enough. . . ." I wondered if Jackson was putting away money for me. When I am twenty-one, a messenger will bring it in two large round bundles marked with dollar signs. *A little reminder of a wonderful day,* and signed, *You know who.*

"I can't imagine who else would leave you money."

"My father's family might. I'd like to go see them sometime. Did you know them?"

"They have none to leave," she snapped. "I don't plan on dying for some time. So you'd best plan on marrying well."

"I don't want to marry well," I said. "I want to marry for love. You loved my father when you married him— didn't you?"

128

She put the tweezer down and glared at me in the mirror. "You know it makes me unhappy to discuss him," she said, "and you only want to marry for love because you're very young, Susanna." And my mother sighed and pulled back the sides of her face with her fingertips and smiled at herself, posing into the mirror with the skin smoothed back. "Very young." I don't think age has occurred to her much before. There is no one here now to remember her when she was a little girl.

The wisteria smells so sweet you want to eat the fragrance. I hold a branch down and feel the blossoms in my hand like a bunch of lightweight grapes. Tender things, you are, coming out of these tough old roots. I pinch my forefinger and thumb together and run them down the main stem dropping the flowers off into my palm. Then I blow them away, tiny chorus dancers flying off into the air. I walk across the lawn and down to the edge rose garden, with the flagstone wall border, and one gnarled little peach tree. I look back at the house to the olive tree and to the pool. None of this goes anywhere. It does not leave; it does not die. But then it does not live. Is the beginning of learning to live, learning to leave? Knowing, as Grandmother said, when to go? I cannot pretend this house is real. Or my puppets or guitar or movies. Only people are real. And the trouble with loving things which are not real is that you do know, even as you do love them, that they cannot matter as much. I sit under the peach tree which has flowers, but peaches you cannot eat, like the olives which fall like purple marbles from the olive tree and cannot be eaten either. Sometimes a bird eats one of those olives and you find him lying dead in the morning. Poison little green peaches, poison olives, rats in the ivy—and in palm trees for sure—and lizards crushed by tires in the driveway, and to look at it quick, you'd think everything was wonderful.

"Merry-go-round, sadly-go-down, lonely-go-by." I

sing the words to Scotty's carousel music in my head.
I'd like to try to get Frank to take me to see him. I
know he's not getting that TV show. I saw in the trades
that the TV network pulled out because the entire
Weavers were blacklisted. I bet he's not there either.
Probably used that money to go East and doesn't have
enough to get back. Jackson will help him out again.
Maybe that's where Jackson is, hitting the road with
Scotty. Just for the hell of it. Probably dyed his hair so
people wouldn't recognize him. I sure hope he gets that
dye out before he sees me again.

"Merry-go-round, lonely-go-down . . ." and, yes, "al-
ways-go-up." Yes, that is important to remember. And
"never-go-back." There's a lot out there and no one's
gone forever. Unless dead. And even then my idea is
when you dream of them they are alive for a little bit.

Even if Perdido burned up, I think, picking at one of
these little green peaches with a scrappy fingernail, even
if the Communists do take over and force everyone to
make black and white movies and ban all the sequins in
Hollywood, and I do not see how they're going to do
that if Scotty and Uncle Alan are any example. But say
the Russians did come over here, I would walk right
out that gate and find Jackson Lane. And we'd sail
around the south of France on a big clipper ship. And
he'd tell me that the only reason he really left was to
see whether I cared enough to try to find him. I wonder
if he's out there now. I think about when I sat out there
on his boat looking at Perdido. I wonder if he is looking over here now and am I thinking of him because he
is looking at this house, sticking like a tiny tooth out of
the cliff. Boy, Jackson's lucky. I mean you don't miss
things so much I don't think if you can go out running
around looking for them. Or if you know *when* they're
coming back—like if I *knew* Val was really coming
back, say for the holidays. Or Jackson. Someone . . .
someone, tell me when you're coming, won't you? Or
else—if I could just go. Get in a car. I'll *never* be sixteen, it feels like, but when I am, and when I get my

car (and I better get one), I'm going to call it *Farewell*. "Merry-go-round, east of the moon, follow the sun, I'll find you soon." I want to see the years go by like a montage, pages of the calendar falling off like silver leaves from the olive tree. If you could only lift the arm off time like I can lift the arm off the Capehart and put it ahead to hear the end of the song. But when I do that I sometimes scratch the record.

You know something, God, this sure seems sometimes like a so-long-it's-been-good-to-know-you kind of place to start a person out in. I walk over now to the big wall and lean out, looking out there just in case there's a boat and I'm singing, ". . . been good to know you, and I've got to be drifting along. . . ."

Part Two

1954

THE SONG OF LOVE IS A SAD SONG, . . . DON'T ASK ME how I know . . . hi-Lili, hi-Lili, hi-lo . . ."

I am singing and driving in my fast '53 Aztec Red Ford Victoria, a bomb, although not a convertible; but no one is getting convertibles after Barbara Weisman was beheaded when hers overturned on the road to Palm Springs. And I got my car for my seventeenth birthday instead of my sixteenth, and I suppose that was because I took the wagon out when I only had my learning permit and, what with one thing and another, cracked it up coming home from a sort of hootenanny up at Point Mugu. "What do you mean, sort of?" Myron had asked.

"Well, it was me mainly and a few sailors, and I was teaching them some chanties."

It all would have been worse and I might not have a car yet if Myron ever heard Oscar Brand's chanties. But, not one—not one sailor put even a hand on me.

Summer is here. After Alan died Val came back home, but she will be going again—to Juilliard in the fall. And we have had our first real fight. Actually, it's mainly C.A. I am totally furious at. And I could care less about her party. However, I will feel better about it tomorrow when it is over.

The Eastern boys have flown out again this summer to take us to movies from Europe where things are so depressed the films (and that is what the boys call them) are gray, subtitled, and small, rather like television, if you want to know. I am never so unconscious from boredom that I do not notice the arm creeping around the shoulder and the hand sliding under the bra strap.

135

I'll take sailors anytime. The Easterners are very peculiar. They move out here for the summer as if this is a resort. They never stay in their own cities in the summer, and the ones who come regularly arrive in collapse if their vacations start a week late.

"Isn't Fernandel a genius?" they say. Fernandel is Ivy League Milton Berle. *"Je déteste,"* I say back, and I flick up my bra strap and snap it right down on their fingertips.

They think we are fast and tropical and they treat us like Polynesians in *Mutiny on the Bounty,* but I get asthma from lying down in back seats and Val says they have to rush me to Cedars for Adrenalin shots so often I have a charge account in the emergency room. I do not know what becomes of the Eastern girls in the summer. Val says, "Martha's Vineyard." Well, you can send the boys to Ellen's Cabbage Patch for all I care. Except Paul Daroff who is almost Eastern now because of graduating from Harvard. He is Val's this summer.

I am going up Sunset. It is a gleaming summer day and it is a tease right here, just east of the Palisades. The late June fog is waiting behind me, waiting for everyone else to get to the beach. They will huddle against the wall at the Sand and Sea Club in the freezing mornings, wrapped in beach towels, waiting until it clears enough to bring the lifeguards and umbrellas out from the lockup room. You never see big, blond boys until the sun is out.

I am wondering if the fog reminds Val of England and Alan. It has been four months now. I am sort of on my way to see Scotty who is working in Topanga Canyon for the summer—and then he'll be doing college concerts and stuff in the fall again. But I saw a white '48 Lincoln Continental like Jackson used to have tearing up Sunset, and so I followed it; and now it makes a right on Rockingham and I go behind it past Betty Hutton's house where the red, white, and blue spangled curtains flash in the sun. I follow it by the place Rita Hayworth had and I wonder what happened to her kid Rebecca after Rita married the man my grandmother called Mr. Khan.

"You should marry someone like that," Grandmother said, when she first met him, long before they were ever married.

"But he is a prince, and there are no Jewish princes, Grandmother."

"All Jewish men are princes," she said.

"Myron?" I said.

"Do not nit pick with a sick woman," she said.

Actually, Paul is something of a prince now that he is thin. It is probably the bones, the way his hair looks red gold in the sun, the terry beach robe he wears over his shoulders, and the true fact that he does not put one toe into the ocean.

I know this is not Jackson's car because a couple of years ago the trades reported it had turned up on a used car lot in Tucson where it was sold to the owner of a rattlesnake, cactus, and curiosity museum and you wouldn't get me there not even to see Jackson stuffed.

"No. Really, Mary, it wasn't a boy."

Santa Barbara, that was another place I looked for Jackson. Once in a while I come across something, in the trades or *Confidential,* and I run down the rumor where I can. You can't believe anything in *Confidential,* of course, but it's something to do. They said Jackson Lane was at this party Farley Granger and Shelley Winters had at the San Ysidro Inn in Santa Barbara, so I had driven up there, just to see. This was only a week after Mike Connolly reported Jackson had signed with Harry Cohn to do a comeback. I had traced that easily enough by calling Columbia.

"Hail, Columbia," I said, which was just my little joke and they didn't get it. "I'm the President of the Santa Monica Jackson Lane Fan Club and we'd like to know when he starts shooting."

"Your guess is as good as mine, honey," the lady in the casting office said, cracking gum. "That column's the first anyone around here has heard of it. Listen, we've got a batch of old autographed pictures of him, lying around, gathering dust, if you want I'll ship them off to you."

"No, we've been making paper airplanes of the ones we got stuck with, thanks anyway," I said.

An axiom (the one thing I learned from geometry— just the word—no clue what it has to do with math): The only people you don't care about coming back always do. Such as Eddie Berlin. Yesterday I swung by Mary's desk to check out the mail. She slammed down a paperweight on one pile of letters: "No! Now that's your mother's mail and you know you're to keep your hands off."

"I just wanted to see if there are any goodies."

"Well, there's one letter—and a lot of bills. If you're lucky, they'll go right to the accountant. There have been quite enough goodies from Schirmer's and Music City marching in here this month. There are also some love notes from the Department of Motor Vehicles." And she hands me the letter.

"If you're not careful, cutie-pie, you're going to get your license suspended—I'll take care of these, but you ought to watch out. There's also a bill here from the Chevron station in Santa Barbara. What were you doing up there?"

Quick. Think of something.

"Oh, there was a horse show. That was it. The Montecito Jumping Association."

"The Montecito Jumping Association, really? Is he that cute?"

So I was standing by Mary's desk checking out the trades just in case, but it's been four years since he left town, and there's been nothing much to find out. An occasional shot they say is him, with a newspaper over his face bustling off a ship or plane, with some lady in Europe or South America. But I can't imagine Jackson just happening to have a newspaper with him. The best rumor was that he joined a Dominican monastery and there was this picture of a tall monk, from the back, with the hood up. They tracked down some lady who said she was his mother—or she tracked down some reporter—but that turned out to be a hoax. Wherever he is, the whole place is protecting him. I keep all the clippings in a locked box.

"How are you?" I remembered to ask Mary, as she handed me my letter.

"Coming along," she said.

"The eye looks better," I said. She had a lot of pancake covering up this shiner she got last week.

"Yes, wasn't that stupid of me, running right into a door." Last time she said she hit her head on the refrigerator.

"Sounds like something I would do."

"It's from a boy," she said, pointing at the letter I am bored with before I open it. She wanted very much to get off the subject of herself.

"Eddie Berlin. If you can call him a boy!" I said: "Stroble!"

"That's not nice, Susanna. That Stroble is a vicious criminal. You mustn't make jokes of everything."

Mary is always up on any stories involving men hatcheting or beating women. She is casing the coverage to see what they have to do to you before you make the front page and get Audrey Totter to play you on the screen. If he breaks her jaw, she might get Gloria Grahame. The Black Dahlia is her personal martyr.

"What did Eddie do to you?" she asked, putting on her glasses as though I was about to show her a movie of it. "He's such a nice person. Very polite when he calls. Of course, you never know, do you?"

"I couldn't possibly talk about it, Mary," I said.

And she catches her breath, "Oh, my dear."

It was actually the main back seat situation where I wound up at Cedars.

Eddie's father, of course, is the New York radio/movie critic, and Eddie comes out every summer to vacation with his parents and to talk about how weird we are and how surprising it is that we know so little about "film" and yet "you're all so sophisticated in certain ways." What he means by that, I think, is we have bigger breasts than Eastern girls and wear lower necks. I had hoped Eddie would drop me this summer. See, last year we were on a double date with Deedee Roston and a friend of Eddie's, and we'd left Wil Wright's after sundaes (no chocolate for me, of course), and were driving up toward Mulholland to neck. The first thing Eastern boys learn is where Mulholland is. And then, which girls have projection rooms, and then—the nerve —they complain about the "Hollywood mentality." Now most of us, if you can believe what anyone says, have been necking for a couple of years and there are rules. No one has written them down, but we all know what they are and if no one in the group goes farther than, say, letting him put his hand inside your bra for a little while and the boys get used to that, they won't give you any arguments. They'll know that's how everyone is. There are certain people, Deedee Roston, for instance, who go farther, but she also lives way out in Malibu, beyond the Colony. Actually, Trancas is where she lives, but if she wants to call it Malibu, I say let her.

She's not had a very pleasant time either, although Val says her father sold out which is why he's selling scripts under another name. But he looks terrible. You go out there to see him and he's always lying down drinking this terrible milky combination of ulcer medicine and Coke. And Deedee's mother drinks rum and Coke all day, and says when her husband can afford it she's going to get a divorce. And she's always asking him how many pages he's done and he tells her, and she says, "That's not enough, come on, Sammy, get back to work." And he practically crawls back to their old rattan couch, like the kind my mother threw out when lanais went out of style ages ago; and then his wife goes out and works on her tan, tapping her cigarette holder on the ashtray, which he can hear. I say no wonder Deedee is fast. The boys take distance into consideration.

Easterners do not love to drive just to be driving. When they want sex (they say), they go out with older women like Irish McCalla and other "starlets" who strip-tease and things. If you go steady and are "very much in love" you can go farther and even be naked with him, but Sharon Stea and Larry Waxonberg were caught in her father's beach cabana lying down with their clothes all off at night, by C.A.'s father (and a lot of people wondered what he was doing down there at night anyway). Sharon's mother announced their engagement the next day and hired the Crystal Room at the Beverly Hills Hotel for only a month later. They got a honeymoon and everything, even though there were a lot of jokes about how that trip wasn't necessary.

When I get married I want a real honeymoon. I want him to gasp with surprise and delight when I come out of the bathroom in my sheer white negligee and tell him he can open his eyes, and he will be the first person in the world to see me naked.

But I had decided I would neck with Eddie. He is cute and short with bright red hair, kind of a Cagney type, with strong little arms and legs. Eddie's friend from Yale, Sy Drinkwater, was driving in Sy's father's Olds 88 sedan, which is two-toned green. Easterners do not know anything about how a car should look. They also do not know how to drive, quite apart, as I said, from not loving it. We all were very quiet and Sy has the radio on to KFAC—the classic station which Easterners love—and each of us has said how gorgeous the view is and they started kissing up in the front seat. Eddie watched Sy and put his arm around me when Sy put his around Deedee, and we were all kissing at the same time and Deedee had her mouth open, you could hear the tongues, and then I heard Sy's hand sliding on her nylons, and then Sy moaning, "Oh, baby," and KFAC was playing a violin solo with sounds exactly like asthma and Eddie said to me, whispering, "What's the matter?"

"Can't breathe," I whispered back and then I saw

Deedee's head slide sideways and down probably onto the armrest and Sy was out of sight then too and so Eddie pushed me down and slid himself on top of me, only sort of to the side and put my hand on his fly and I thought my God he's got a cigar case or something in there, and then I realized what it was and tried to move my hand back but he grabbed the wrist and started blowing in my ear and thudding it against my hand while Sy and Deedee were making all these wet kissing sounds and then I heard Sy say to her, "Got a handkerchief?" and I turned my head and Eddie started blowing in the other ear until I was practically deaf and I pulled my hands out and pushed him off and one breast (my favorite one) came out of my strapless dress and I pulled up the dress before he could get at her and he started mouth-kissing again with this seedy wet look in his eyes which were half-closed like some gangster dope addict and I went into a fatal asthma attack. "What's the matter with you?" he whispered.

"I can't breathe through my nose."

"So, let's kiss noses," he laughed, with his Eastern kind of skipped caw of a laugh, which is just like his father's on the radio. And then I was honking and gasping for breath like a drowning goose as Deedee sat up with "Cherries in the Snow" over her face, in fact everyone had lipstick all over, and Sy said, "Jesus Christ, you picked a great time." And Eddie was all sweaty and Deedee said, "Susanna, you're such a child." And I said, "I'm sorry, I'm sorry." And I am feeling like a stuffed suitcase with three people standing on it. And Sy started the car and cut out, screeching, and I clutched onto the back of the front seat and tried to imagine breathing. And Deedee said, "Do you want to go home?"

"No," I said after finding the air to say it, "hospital, Adrenalin." And Eddie said, "I thought you were more mature." And so they took me to Cedars and I got a shot of Adrenalin and Myron came and picked me up. He shook hands with Eddie, which made me furious.

But then Eddie's father is important to Myron and he did not shake hands in a very friendly way and he looked Eddie right in the eye. I was feeling weak and whirly from the shot on the way home. Therefore, quiet.

"What happened, Susanna, did he do anything to you?" Myron said.

"No. There was a dog at the party. Two dogs, actually. Poodle and very large sheepdog."

"Okay. I told your mother there'd been car trouble. So let's not tell her about the hospital. He didn't bother you. You sure? I'd have a talk with his father if he did."

"No. I just hate boys. I mean dogs."

And when I got home my mother looked at Myron and said, "What did she do?"

"Nothing, Vera. Just a bit of car trouble. Those new Buicks are all chrome and nothing else."

"Oldsmobiles," I said.

"Well, you look just dreadful, Susanna. Didn't you have gloves?"

"They're in my purse," I lied. I had left them in the car—you never wear gloves, but to take them makes certain mothers I know very happy. What could happen to a person who wears gloves?

But nothing really happened, I told myself. Yes, but whatever it wasn't it must have been something because I didn't like it. Now I sound like my grandmother. I wanted so to have her there—to go in and sit upon her bed.

So later that night I was lying in bed, watching my collection of birds' nests which I have tied from my ceiling with ribbons so it looks like you're in a forest. They swing in the breeze and they keep my mother out most of the time because she is terrified of birds and convinced they have diseases. "Your room will be filled with trichinosis," she said.

"That's a pig disease," I told her.

"Never mind what I say, you know what I mean,"

she said. She is the main one who is getting like Grandmother in the way she talks, just the way Grandmother became a little like Grandfather after he died. I think people pick up the habits they notice to keep the person alive, especially the habits they used to complain about the most because those are the easiest to remember. My mother always corrected Grandmother, as Grandmother had corrected Grandfather and as my mother imitates Grandmother, so I will imitate her. Rather not, however. Have to watch that, as Val would say. So I was lying in my bed and my heart was still pounding from the Adrenalin, but it feels so good when you can breathe again you don't mind that you feel weak in the knees and a little dizzy. I put my hand between my thighs and turned on my side, which is my best hanging-on position when I feel as though I'm falling off the edge, and drifting off I felt so warm and cozy and imagined rocking and rocking put me back on Jackson's boat, and I could feel the canvas cover on his bunk and imagine the smell of saltwater and the house, creaking like a ship, was that boat and then he came bending down the steps, into the cabin, the sun like a halo around his entire body and he sat beside the bed quiet and airy as a ghost and talked to me so softly: "Lie on your back, Susanna." And I turned over. "Now what do you want me to do for you?" I shook my head and couldn't say.

"I love you, Susanna."

I nodded.

"Do you want me to take off my shirt?" he asked.

"Yes," I whispered.

"Okay, now you take off your nightgown. And just lie very still. Just breathe easy now. That's right. You are beautiful naked, Susanna. Now I'm going to take some Sköl you've got in your night table and I'm going to rub it on you. Is that all right?"

"Yes, please . . ."

"Just a little with my fingertips right along your ribs, and across your chest, here, like this. I'm just going to stroke it very lightly, and down the inside of your arms.

144

Now I'm putting some on your breasts. Now, that's all right, isn't it? You like that." He spoke very softly, like a director, in stage whispers. "Now just the tips, turning them like this, just relax. Now, don't move, Susanna. Don't move."

"Don't stop," I whispered.

"I won't stop, don't worry, I won't stop. That's a good girl. I'm going to make you feel something now. Can I do that, is it all right? I'm not ever going to stop. Is it right now? Do you like that? Tell me you like it."

"Oh yes."

And he was strumming down on me until I was humming so I thought the strings would break. It's like you start a little strum and then a group comes in and picks up the beat, picking up the tempo, then stopping, then coming in behind you even more solid and down and you put some percussion behind it until you don't know where you're going and he said, "Come on, now, there you go, easy now . . ." and he kneeled between my legs with only his white pants on and watched me, looking serious, never laughing, like I'm a boat he loves and was guiding into port. And I reached up my body for him and grabbed my hand between my thighs, and felt myself coming back again, kind of like unpacking after being on a trip, and felt just the same kind of leftover sadness because he wasn't there, and it was just me in my own bed doing that thing I am certain God hates and would get me for tomorrow. Something would happen for sure. I try very hard not to do that because I feel so sad afterward, just the way I do when I play a favorite song and it's over and you can just die I think from the confusion of happiness and sadness running into each other like that, and from knowing it's never going to be like that, or not soon enough, and necking is nothing like that and yet you do it because you hope maybe you're wrong. But necking is just panting and hoping and pretending because everyone else likes it.

When I got my first period, which was a year before Grandmother died, she kissed me and then she slapped my face, not too hard, but a slap is a slap and I cried and said, "Why did you do that?"

"Because, my darling, it is an old Russian custom, and this is so that the pain of being a woman will hurt you no more than that." It never hurt to have a period, but what hurts is the feeling that I'll never love anyone else again and never have anyone who is really there who feels so good to me or smiles at me like he smiled at me that day or smiles at me in these dreamy little things I make up.

Maybe the best of love is what you do make up, which is what everyone who writes love songs knows, or the best love songs wouldn't make you cry.

Susanna, I tell myself, that's ridiculous, you know something's coming, you know there's a lot of summer still to come and everyone falls in love in summertime. "You're going to see what you'll see," I hear Grandmother say, which she'd say before every movie when I'd ask what it was about.

And I got up and I went to my window and opened it and just leaned down with my hands on the sill and said, "Listen, someone. I just want to be loved. It's hot and summer's comin' and it's not fair to have these feelings and nothing to do with them. And lyin' down in back seats with some Easterner isn't what I mean. I want to be very much in love. I want . . . I want . . . Jackson. And I know it's no crazier than Leslie Caron and Mel Ferrer in *Lili*. He was older too. My mother already had her loving. It's my turn and I want it." When I talk to God and I'm angry I always go a little Southern country in my talk. Sometimes when I'm not angry but just want to discuss something, I talk very seriously and make my voice rather low and reasonable, sort of on the order of when I'm imitating Val.

Val. When she came home we went to the airport to pick her up and just to look at her standing there with Lillian at the top of the gangplank (gangway. What do they call it?), noble as Ronald Colman and Isabel Jewell on the guillotine, standing there—I did not think two people have ever had more to bear.

When Alan died we called and Myron and my mother wanted to go over there to help with arrangements, but Lillian would not hear of it.

Val wrote up until then and about a month after that, but never in writing about what happened to Alan. She wrote only a very short formal note during that time, in her perfect handwriting:

Dearest Susanna—thank you for writing. It helped so very much. And you know how good it was to hear your voice, even for a little. I guess I'll be seeing you soon . . . chin up gang. I do love you. Val.

"Save my place . . ." she had said to me once before she left for England. Needn't have said it. When she came back it was as though she had never left. We have all moved through high school and from summers around our own pools to the Sand and Sea Beach Club in Marion Davies's old Ocean House, and the formation somehow always held the center place open for Val and she swung right into it, teasing everyone—but never being teased back—not because of tragedy, but because of a certain swift delicacy. Like a little cat she charms and strikes out and then sits and observes with her large greenish eyes quiet and then she'll blink and challenge someone, with a glance, to say something she can catch and mouse around with, chewing up whatever you said and skidding it back, all used up . . . at first when she came back I sat too quietly and she'd be laughing, and leaning back with her hipbones and correct little breasts making her look especially trim in her dark cotton bathing suit—one of these Eastern ones she got when they were there finishing up her application to Juilliard. Actually, she was accepted a year ago. "Stop playing First Lady to Tragedy Queen," she snapped at me, and C.A. laughed and Kitty watched craftily, sizing up our friendship, and the boys who love Val rolled over from their tanning naps and Paul flicked grains of sand from her shins. "I'm not," I said.

"You stare at me all the time," Val said, later, on the phone, "as though you expect me to suddenly turn white and set my hair on fire and run screaming into the waves. Don't be so careful with me."

"Everyone's careful with you."

"But not the same way." She's right. Everyone else wants her to notice them. I want her to notice I love her the most.

"I don't know how to be a way I'm not, Val."

Now here is why I'm not invited to C.A.'s party. And I am not going to the damn beach:

In order to get accepted to Juilliard's composition courses, Val has had to submit several original serious music compositions, and she's gotten a special delay because of what happened to Alan, but she works every morning. She talks on the phone only from nine till nine fifteen—obviously not to talk, just to make plans—and will not take calls any other time. She hates to talk on the phone anyway. I don't want to be the first one to get on with her every day, but for one solid week Kitty or C.A. has called me at nine and then when I get finished with them I call Val and she's on the phone, and by the time I get through to her she's "About to go to work, Susanna."

Finally I got really angry, and I said, "You have to talk to me. You talk to everyone else and I think they call me just so I can't get to you. I feel like it's a plot."

"Communists under every bed. Shake your broomstick at them, Susanna. I haven't all day to run around. I'm going to Juilliard and taking it very seriously—grow up and get serious about something, will you. Hanging up now . . ."

"You can't hang up on me. You wouldn't hang up on C.A., you know." (And as I said it, I knew I shouldn't.) "Her father has offices in England and

Myron said if he'd wanted to help your father he could have."

"Don't talk fathers, Susanna." Her voice was icy.

"What do you mean by that?"

She paused, as if thinking what she meant. "Myron didn't exactly go out of his way—Susanna, skip it . . . it's no bloody plot. People are closer to some people sometimes. 'Best friends' is for kids. Susanna, don't you have friends that you can just be with?"

"Not really. No one more than you. You always used to say I never asked why, or never wanted to talk about things, but now I do and you won't talk to me." I was lying on my bedroom floor looking up at birds' nests and picking threads out of the cotton rag rug carpeting my mother selected because it was nonallergenic and chic. I would love a fluffy fur rug and it would kill me.

"I am talking to you. Things change. That was years ago. Maybe I feel reminded of those things and don't want to be. Have one thing on the mind, Susanna, getting the requirements done for Juilliard. They've been more than fair—and I want to have a nice time this summer. Okay, that's two."

"Could I come over and hear your songs then? I'd be quiet."

"They're pieces, not songs. I'm not ready yet, okay?"

"Okay, I guess. I'll see you."

"Yes. Soon. Take it easy."

So then I called C.A. to find out what she was up to.

"Oh, Val asked me to come over and hear her songs or something."

"They're not songs. They're pieces."

"Hell's bells. I don't know about music."

That. I think. Is the understatement. And I was furious. So I called Val right back and she answered the phone. "I thought you don't answer the phone after nine fifteen. That's one. And two, how come you asked C.A. to come over and hear your songs? I mean pieces."

Now we're getting to the part about the party and why

I am not invited and not speaking to anyone. Ever, probably.

"Don't know what you're talking about. I didn't ask C.A. to come over," Val said.

"Well, she is."

"Susanna. Cut it out. Stop checking up."

She hung up the phone.

I called C.A.'s house and Binky, her English butler, said (you know they are Republicans. My mother says only Republicans have white help. "Democrats like to give good jobs to colored people"): "I believe Miss Morrison has left for the day. . . ."

I was furious. I slapped my tan Stetson on my head and went right over to Val's. C.A.'s powder blue Merc was out in front. Enough is enough. I charged in through the little patio in front of the apartment Lillian and Val have and the door was open, and I went in and what did I find: both of them standing on their heads against the wall.

"Now, I've got you," I said. And I stood there with my hands on my hips and they were looking at each other upside down.

"Don't shoot, Susanna. We've got our feet up." And Val laughed at me.

"You get down and talk to me," I yelled.

"You can't just barge in somewhere and start asking questions," C.A. said, her face all fluffed out and red like a rabbit, and her frizzy hair which is turning dark and that just practically kills her mother, especially the orange parts C.A. peroxides up in the summer.

"You lied to me, C.A. Morrison. Val said she didn't ask you over. And Val, you said you were working."

"Susanna. When you calm down, call me," Val said, closing her eyes.

"Or don't call us, we'll call you is how it goes," C.A. said, and I lunged over and pulled her feet down from the wall and she leaped up about to go for me. And I jumped back because even though I'm taller, she's very tough.

"You've really hurt me. Really," I yelled, and ran and slammed the screen door in her face. Before she could see I was crying. And that is how come I am not invited to C.A.'s party.

"But that's ridiculous," Deedee Roston said when she called to ask who I was taking. "Even I'm invited and you know how everyone hates me."

"I know," I said. Without thinking.

"Well, you don't have to say so. Anyway, why don't you call Val and raise hell? Or, call C.A., that's what I'd do. You just say she'd better invite you or her father's clients will never work at V.L.I. again."

"I don't think I can get Myron to go along with that. And anyway, that's another reason probably. Myron banned Hedda Hopper from the lot and she's C.A.'s godmother." Hedda said something mean about the studio going broke because he hires too many friends. I had even complained to Myron, "How could you get integrity at a time like this?"

"If I'd known, Susanna, I would have waited a week." And he was grinning even though he was pretending not to. I could tell. "Don't be so upset. There will be other parties," he said.

"Never, never like this. It's going to be on Metro's river. Right on board the *Cotton Blossom* from *Show Boat*."

"Susanna," my mother said, "perhaps you ought to just call C.A., or write her a lovely note and say you are sorry for whatever it was." One thing my mother does understand is the importance of parties.

"I can't do that. It's too late."

"Well, perhaps I'll call her mother."

"Vera," Myron said, staring over his new reading glasses, "stay out of it."

"I'll just stay home and spend a quiet evening singing the saddest songs I know in the whole world."

"You can probably figure out something better, more constructive," Myron says.

"I DESPISE that word constructive."

"Well, do something destructive then," my mother snapped, "and take down those damned birds' nests. Dorothy says they're giving her asthma they're so dusty."

"That's not dust," I said. "It's disease. Trichinosis big as snowflakes floating through the air."

The thing is I try to tell myself that in the list of things in the world that can go wrong and happen to people a party is not up there even in the top eighty thousand. And how can I be the sort of person who wants to wander around the country with my geetar on my back, looking for Jackson or for *something,* and yet still feel this catch in my throat when I think of them all dancing. I mean that's the thing, too. It is going to be a splendid party. This is another thing God hates: people who give a damn about parties. I don't want to be one of those people.

And wouldn't you know, yesterday, just when I'm getting used to not going, Kitty Chapin called and said, "What are you wearing? Did you get something from Wardrobe?"

"That's really swell, Kitty. You don't need to rub it in."

"Rub what in?"

"I'm not invited."

"Not invited?" she said, with concern so sweet you could pour it on pancakes. "But everyone's invited. Even Deedee Roston."

"Yeah, that's exactly what Deedee said."

"Paul Daroff said Stevenson's sons are coming and Dorothy Warren. Arthur Loew, Jr.,'s bringing Joan Collins."

"Shut up, Kitty, I'll read about it in your column." She has a teen column in some fan magazine and no one knows how she did *that.*

"Well, don't get nasty, Susanna. I really didn't dream you weren't invited."

"Maybe I'll have your father sue C.A. I don't want to talk about it, okay?" And I slammed down the phone.

So I was on my way out and almost collided with

Dorothy on the stairs while she's on her way up with my mother's tray, on which her forget-me-not-sprigged breakfast set rattles daintily (forget-who-not?). I decided I would cruise by and see her before going up to Trancas to see Deedee and hang around Zuma Beach with her. I was hardly going to the Beach Club and listen to them talk about the party.

My mother was sitting up in her marabou bedjacket to which I am allergic, with her two white phones nestled in her ivory satin comforter like small pet dogs.

"Mmmmm, strawberry jam," she says as Dorothy puts the tray down in front of her. Then she lifts the round china cover off her toast plate and sits with her hands poised on either side of the wicker tray while Dorothy pours her coffee from the small china coffee pot.

"Is everything fine this morning, Dorothy?" My mother unfolds the small organdy napkin from the set Myron brought her from Leron in New York. It says *Good morning, Darling* in blue embroidery.

"Just fine, thank you, Mrs. Howard," Dorothy said. Which was not true; Dorothy's favorite nephew was in the hospital again, and Mabel and Frank had a terrible fight because Frank said he'd fix Mabel's old car and he got the engine taken apart for a valve job and couldn't get it back right, and Frank was furious at Andrew because he just stood there yesterday, watching, polishing up the limo with his chamois and saying I told you so. And Ethel's arthritis has been bad, so Dorothy'd been covering for her in the kitchen, plus doing her own work.

I think some of the best performances in Hollywood are given by servants. But the reason everyone stays here forever, my mother said, one morning, "is because I simply don't bother them and I don't know anything and so I don't interfere. It makes all our lives much easier." And she yawned and stretched her arms. Every time she shakes her marabou I get a feather in my throat. It is like having two families living here, politely ignoring each other's personal problems, like Lillian and Val's neighbors who just nod to each other even though you know they all hear everything that goes on.

"Susanna," my mother said, neatly cracking her soft-boiled egg with the side of her silver spoon, "why don't you send flowers to C.A.?"

"And why not run over to Ruser's and send her a little piece of jewelry while I'm at it? G'uy, Mother."

"Stop saying g'uy. I detest that word. I do not *know* where you pick up your slang. Now don't be sarcastic. The party's the day after tomorrow and there's still time and I think it would be a lovely and gracious gesture."

"And get me invited to the party. You want me to go. I wouldn't go if she did ask me anyway."

She licks a bit of jam which has fallen on the back of her hand like a ruby. "I am just making a suggestion. You may charge them to our account. Ask Mary to give you the number for the Brentwood Florists."

This, of course, is perfect. But I will not tell my mother I think so.

"Maybe I'll think about it."

"I wouldn't wait too long."

"All right!" I shove my hands in the pockets of my shorts. And start out.

"Susanna! You've got your shorts rolled up again." She pointed at my legs with her spoon.

"So I have."

"They're very short."

"That's right," I said, and rolled them down before I left her room, rolling them back up on my way down the stairs.

So I called the florist to send C.A. orange gladiolus with a note saying: *Happy Birthday. Have a wonderful party. Love, Susanna.*

"Orange? Gladiolas?" Mary said, when I ordered the flowers.

"Well, C.A. won't know they're supposed to be horrible."

"Her mother will." Mary tapped on her desk with her pencil.

So I called back and switched it to red garnet roses.

"There," I said, "and a lot of good that's going to do."

"You never know, honey-pie."

Well, of course, you do. I could imagine C.A. calling Val and saying, "Susanna's really rubbing it in now."

And she must have gotten them yesterday and I haven't heard anything at all and I haven't been on my phone all morning. Much. Deedee thought C.A. would be too embarrassed to call me now, anyway. "I mean, what's she going to say, that your invitation must have gotten lost? G'uy, Susanna." So that's where I got that. Sometimes I don't even know exactly where I pick things up. I sort of thought I'd gotten that from Scotty.

Even though Scotty says it is not true, I do believe that Jackson told him to keep an eye on me when he got back to L.A. and every time he does come through he gets in touch, and sends me copies of *Sing Out* from time to time and when he sends an address I send him a song and he'll write me about it—about whether the words work with the melody I'm adapting—I'm not like Val about making up my own yet. Not from scratch, which is why I stick to folk. Also I just like it— the songs can really say everything you want to about yourself. And they can tell real stories. And when Scotty's doing concerts at colleges he'll send me a postcard. And Mary will say, "Who is this Scotty Donovan?"

And I say, "Someone who is discovering me."

And she says, "Discovering what, I'd like to know."

"Me to know, you to find out. When I've got my name in lights, you'll see."

"How did you find me," I asked Scotty the first time he called a couple of years ago, "if Jackson didn't tell you and that means you know where he is?"

"It's not so hard to find someone, Susanna, when you really want to."

"Yeah, well, I've been trying to find Jackson, and so have a lot of other people."

"Well, some people don't get found till they're ready, either."

Scotty called me last week from San Francisco where he sometimes lives and told me that he was coming down here with Malvina Reynolds and some others for a big picnic hootenanny gathering for Aunt Molly Jackson and he said if I really wanted to see something I should come. So I'm going. Everyone's going to be swapping songs and everything.

"There hasn't been anything like this in years, Susie." He's the only one who calls me that. It's funny how you can have a friend like that who you never see, but somehow you know when you do it will be just like you saw him yesterday. And somehow keeping in touch with Scotty is a way of keeping in touch with Jackson even though I believe him—I think—when he says he really hasn't heard from him.

So now I am following this Continental down La Mesa, bumping along where the street has been thumped up by the roots of the magnolia trees, and onto San Vincente and up Ocean Avenue past the Palisades Park where the cliffs are falling away under the lacy tree trunk fences and I pull alongside at the light in front of the Santa Monica pier just to make sure it isn't because you can't always trust the trades. But it isn't.

So I head for the Hawes's house in Topanga where Scotty's going to meet me.

Driving. The true fact is I would go anywhere just to be driving. And this is somewhere I do want to go.

I wrote something about true fact something or other in a letter to Val and she wrote back there was no such thing. "That, my darling Hollywood-educated cousin, is a redundancy and, as my late great father once said, a Hollywood education is a contradiction in terms. Or was it my great, always late father." A true fact is inside and what you feel. A fact is what anyone else tells me.

I go down the ramp to the Coast Highway. I always

come here on Sunday mornings to get into the big Sunday-morning jam where the cars line up like the longest watercolor paintbox in the world. Everyone's there: Caddies, Chevies, big black Jags, Lorry Glass in his '36 limo with his St. Bernard sitting in back like a movie star; Connolly Oyler in his stripped-down, channeled, candy-apple Pontiac. We're all there, sitting, singing, and watching for each other, ready to blow our horns and ding our carriage bells and drive the Easterners crazy, pairing up in our cars ahead of them so they can't get around even if the traffic gets moving. You can talk from car window to car window up to Channel Road and have three invitations to brunch in the Malibu Colony by the time you get out to the Standard station at Sunset, where I can look right up and wink my eye at Perdido.

I turn right at Topanga and go past the trading post and wind around, a left here, another right, and then a left. I park on a big empty field under a lot of trees where a few other cars and a couple of very rockety pickup trucks are parked and I take off my loafers and put on the cowboy boots I keep in my trunk and walk to the big yard where people have already gathered together under the big old live oak trees.

Some are sitting around beyond the trees on a small hillside in the sun, some with guitars, some with banjos or harmonicas, some just lying there. And Scotty sees me and stands up and waves and I get this feeling, seeing him, that I had that day I met him, almost as if Jackson is with me. And the way he looks at me is just that same way he looked at Jackson. "Well, are you lookin' good," he says, and gives me this big bear hug and I feel like it could be Jackson hugging me—sort of—although it would be different, too. But I am almost in love with Scotty a little because he is Jackson's friend. And with me loving Jackson and him loving Jackson (in that way men do—like buddies, like it sometimes was with Val and me) it is natural we would love each other in the middle.

Scotty introduces me to the Haweses, who have this house, and to Lee Hayes, who is coming out of the house with a couple of folding chairs, and I recognize some of the Almanac Singers from back in the thirties and forties. It's like being at a kind of premiere.

Scotty has some ham and swiss cheese sandwiches on thick black bread which I tell him he must have cut with a saw, and a beer for himself and some Coke for me and while we're eating some people near us are singing Dust Bowl songs, and I sing very quietly and then they sing "Dust Pneumonia Blues" and I get the idea I could write a song about asthma with a couple of fiddles backing me up, wheezing away:

When a short-winded gal loves a dog and cat man,
She breathes when he leaves an' it's kiss as kiss
can . . .

"Back Seat Asthma" I would call it. My mother would be delighted to know I am allergic to kissing. Which is why I do not tell her. First on the agenda of all my days is not to delight my mother. Some days I do not think it is so amusing to be allergic to kissing. But I try not to think about it.

More of the people just sitting around are playing now, and they're swapping songs, giving each other advice. Some gather around the performers. Bess Hawes is showing her "M.T.A." song to a small group. And there's Malvina Reynolds with her guitar tied up with faded green satin ribbons. People stand with their hands in their pockets just looking at her. It isn't any different from fans hanging around movie stars. Except here everyone looks real. Except they have star expressions. Malvina, you can see it, she knows what she gives you when she gives you a new song. And she carries herself in this triumphant way—not arrogant, but she could lead me out of any kind of blues I was in.

So before I start to talk about Jackson, which I know I will, I will talk about music. I never want Scotty to think that I keep in touch with him just because of Jackson, just because he's the only one who can tell me that that was a real day, because he saw us together. If it wasn't for Scotty, I could get to a point where I'd be thinkin' I made it all up. ("Susanna," I hear my mother say, "do not drop your g's." "I'll pick them right up if you tell me where I left them," I say back.)

"So, Scotty," I say, "I read about this technique Maybelle Carter has in this last copy of *Sing Out* you gave me—where you use your thumb to pick out the tune on the lower strings. I'm having a hard time getting used to it. But I think it would make a difference if I wanted to play a lead guitar, don't you think?"

"You can do that if you want to," he says, taking a swig of his beer. I see a few gray hairs he didn't have and I wonder if he is older than Jackson. He has an older expression (although who knows what expression Jackson has by now?) but, with all the effect of crags, his skin is smooth, except for the lines which are like laugh reminders—sort of punctuation marks for laughing—and for after feelings.

"Main thing you got to remember, Susie, and Mississippi John Hurt told me this once, you just teach yourself to play the way you think the guitar should sound, you'll be all right."

"Who was Mississippi John?"

"He was one of the old boys. Used to do some of Jimmie Rodgers's songs. Worked for the WPA and then after the depression he just disappeared. I guess he's probably dead now. Dropped out of sight, anyway."

"You really knew everyone and remember everything like that —I wish I'd had all those adventures and known people in places like the South, people from the depression and all that . . . it really gives them something real to write and sing about."

He sees some people he knows and we sit down with that group.

"This is my friend—Susanna—makes up a song or two now and then." And he kind of rumples my hair.

I love the feeling of his big hands, no, it's not like that. Which is probably why I love it—I just feel so protected around Scotty. And I haven't even been around him at all.

We're sitting with some others who've gathered by to hear Scotty go into Leadbelly's "Cotton Fields" and a lot of people sing, and then he hands me the guitar and I am embarrassed but I play. "You're going to do just fine," someone says and I'm beaming, I'd love to see cotton growing, and rooms where one light bulb hangs down and you sing anyway. I need to get around to where the things that matter to Hedda Hopper and Evelyn Ames and all those people don't even occur to me. Things like trades and parties or columns. But they'd never let me. I can see my mother taking me to Miss Frenault in Saks Collegienne and saying, "We want something in a nice dressy sport hobo suit. Susanna will be hopping trains and hitchhiking around the country this fall."

And then people start putting their picnics back and I remember what I wanted to ask Scotty.

"Mississippi John? When he disappeared, did a lot of people know him? Has anyone special tried to find him?" (I have to get into this subject sideways.)

"I don't know, Susanna. That was a long time back. Boy, you don't let go of something once you put your mind to it, do you?"

"But, Scotty, wouldn't you know if he'd died? I mean, can someone really disappear if someone wants to find him?"

"You know they can."

"Someone famous?"

"Susie-anna—even Jackson's not so famous that people don't move on by with their own lives."

I know he'll change the subject soon.

"Does Jackson have a family—aside from me?"

"I don't recall." I know he has closed the subject. Never opened it actually. We're walking over now to where they're all grouping up to hear Aunt Molly. I wish

I could just be thinking about where I am and not imagining—but now I'm imagining that the people who heard me play just a few chords there are saying, "She's a new Malvina!" (and the real one is perfectly good anyway). Why are my dreams bigger than boots?

So here comes Aunt Molly Jackson. I watch her walk slowly across the grass—looking not really warm and friendly. She reminds me of that aunt of Angelo's. I wonder what happened to her? He's been at the Pasadena Playhouse and in productions already. I haven't seen him except on the Strip sometimes—I knew he'd wind up acting. How furious his father would get when I'd tell him that Angelo was going to be a star and he ought to be taking up singing and dancing lessons. I think I was twelve when I started doing that.

Aunt Molly's wearing a kind of plaid man's blouse and she's got a long old skirt on and a pair of old laced-up shoes and a canvas hat protecting her head from the sun. Her huge sharp eyes glare at anyone moving.

Now she's being introduced and the man is saying she's a woman with a just rage. She gets impatient with the introduction which is going on and on and just takes the mike away and after some coughing, and a pause for some water, she starts talking. "I wrote my first song about loving your neighbor when I was four." She's strumming along softly, her big old hands playing on the strings as easily as someone braiding a child's hair. "And when I was five I was standing in a picket line. Freezin'. It's always way too cold or way too hot when you're in line. Reminds you you ain't just there for the hell of it, making a promenade.

"I went to jail when I was ten and after the miners were blacklisted for joining the union back in 'thirty-one, the company doctor refused to come to any one of the miners' families unless they paid in advance." And she plays more here and as she talks she moves into the music harder and louder. "Thirty-seven babies died in my arms . . . their little stomachs busted open; they was mortified inside. Oh, what an awful way for a baby to die. . . ." Her father was blinded in a mine accident, and one of her brothers. She lost another brother, her husband, and her son to the mines. . . . She's singin' this "Poor Miners' Farewell," now with the mike adjusted down to her sitting height. "That's one tough, raw voice," Scotty whispers carefully to me.

I think, when she speaks of the babies, of Theo—Theo bursting from the smoke.

How bitter, how chilly to be one of those women who survive everything. Like Lillian and Lillian's friends, the widows who gather around her with their fast wit and season tickets to concerts, bringing their daughters and daughters-in-law to elegant little dinners with, as my mother says, "good china and reduced circumstances." Survivors. The women can't run away from home because home is us. A just rage. What are the outside limits—and how do you dare to qualify yourself? I wonder if my mother thinks she qualifies because she lost my father and loved Jackson. I have watched her when we go to some of Lillian's little dinners and she sits and bites her lip and looks at Myron with her eyes narrowed—the way she looks at a chair she is thinking about having reupholstered. And then she looks at Lillian who is very much the center of the survivors and at all Lillian's friends.

"I feel so uncomfortable there," she said to Myron one night as Andrew was driving us home.

"Why? I thought it was very pleasant," Myron said.

"All these women. I just don't trust women in bunches." And she moved her shoulders forward in a kind of shudder.

"You flatter me, Vera," Myron said, and smiled and put his hand on her knee. She just looked at his hand and he moved it away.

"That's not," she said, "what I mean. I'm just so bored with all their stiff-upper-lip bravery. I hate survivors. They're so smug."

I would like to remind my mother, and wonder why Myron does not, that if it weren't for Myron she would be a survivor. But then I wonder if after all she would. My mother does not seem the Aunt Molly Jackson, Lillian type. I do not think my mother is the "just rage" type who lives it and bears it. She is more the "How dare you" kind. I think she wakes up and says "How dare you" about something before she has even opened her eyes. I don't want to be either type. I don't know what other type there is to be except to be a man and say to hell with all of it and skip town. Like *some* people.

I still don't know how Alan died. The story in the papers said he died of heart failure. But the heart fails no matter how one dies, doesn't it?

I saw a letter Lillian wrote to my mother in which she said, "Peter Pan was really a story about a woman in love with an alcoholic. He stays in Never-Never Land and she must grow up."

So I suppose he died of the drinking. Val said in one letter that "they haven't even finished the opening titles of my life and I want a total rewrite."

The Skiptown Type: That's the type you are if you're a folksinger, I think as I'm sitting here listening after Aunt Molly finishes her special songs about the traveling they did to get away, and you can almost hear the trains clacking and whistling and see those long lonesome roads. It takes a lot, I guess, to get you going, but when a lot happens to me, I'm gonna git. I'm not gonna just sit still and be nice about it or let the cobwebs gather on my negligee.

Scotty and Bess Hawes and Lee Hayes are singing now and everyone's sitting closer together singing and those that have banjos and guitars are playing and we're all standing now, stomping our feet and clapping and I'm singing out, looking like I sing better than I do, cheering and crying, which I do as good as anyone, my clothes so dusty and scruffy you'd think I was too the salt of the earth and just like someone who doesn't give a tinker's damn about any old parties. When it's over and I see they're settling in for a more private afternoon with some business—and I hope they're not going to do anything political and get themselves in more trouble—I say goodbye to Scotty and hug him close again.

"I'll see you again."

"Yes—sure you will," he says. And Scotty I never worry about that way. He's a skiptown type but he keeps in touch.

I go home and come in the back door and Dorothy says, "Don't let your mother catch you looking like that. Now what you've been up to?"

"No good," I say, "and I love it. And I ate *ham!*"

"You take that up with your grandma late some night when you're up there singin' to her. Now, well, your cousin Valentine has been calling you all day. She said if it's before four to have her paged at the Beach Club—so you've just got time now. . . ." Dorothy is the only one now, since Alan and Grandmother are gone, to call Val by her real name—which she got, of course, for being born on Valentine's Day. You can imagine how she hated it in school. And I wasn't crazy about it either: looking at her perfect heart-shaped face, which was all the more noticeable when she wore braids, or now, when she sweeps her hair back and her widow's peak and perfectly shaped temples show—you'd think you'd have to have it done somewhere: to get a hairline like that. With my thick blond mop, I think, as I wait for Val to answer the page, you can't really tell about the hairline. I just swing it over, form a side part, and let it hang down as long as it wants to get, sort of as if Susan Hayward was blond and her hair was less curly—actually, I don't know whose hair it's like. It's just mine and it is my favorite—or almost favorite—thing about me. I can lie on it at night and it's practically like a pillow and a capelet of soft, thick silk all in one.

Now there's Val on the phone.

"Well," she says, "I was about to call you at Deedee's

and you know it must be important if I'd do that. I just wanted to tell you C.A.'s going to call and invite—"

"Oh, Val," I interrupt, "thank you. Terrific." Pause. "Do you think I should go?"

"That," she says, "is up to you. Suspect you will. Don't tell her I told you, can you handle that?"

"I'll try." I am practically flying with delight.

"Just wanted to say it's all been very silly. And I'm glad it's over."

"My God. Val! I've got to get to the studio to pick up a dress. It is all Southern Belle gowns, isn't it?—that's what Deedee said. She got something fantastic, she told me—from a friend in Wardrobe at Fox."

"Tell me. I hesitate to think what Deedee's idea of Southern Belle is—or yours. Just watch the sequins—"

"What are you wearing?"

"Something Helen Rose picked out at Metro—you know she and Mom have been friends forever. Good timing, one could say, with the flowers—a little time there to get invited, pick up a dress—and a date. Suspect fine hand of my Aunt Vera in all that, yes?"

I giggle nervously and she laughs and we both laugh together and I say, "Oh, Val, I've missed you. . . ."

And that embarrasses her and she says, "You'd better get your bomb on the road. See you tomorrow night."

"I'll talk to you . . ." I say. And then I remember that's how it all started and I decide I won't bother her tomorrow.

I ask Mary to call Wardrobe to pick some things out for me to try on while I'm on my way. "They know what I like."

"Yes, sweetie-pie, I'm afraid they do."

And I'm off again. Driving. To the studio. Up Sunset to Veteran. If I was going to Val's I'd go on all the way to Beverly Glen and then out over to Wilshire.

Practically the very day they moved into their little apartment in Beverly Hills, Lillian had the couches draped with Mexican shawls and pots of begonias and fuchsias hanging around the tiny balcony, and the walls were covered with pictures from Frank Perls and the other gallery owners who adored her, from before. And she has a job as a story editor at Metro, season tickets to the Hollywood Bowl and Greek Theatre concerts, which sometimes they take me to and which I always hate.

Val complained to me last week, before our war, "You ask when it's going to be over ten seconds after the overture, then you're at the snack bar, in the ladies' room, and you wheeze."

"I can't help wheezing. I get it from boredom."

"You get it from everything. People outgrow it."

"I'm not people," I said, rubbing my nose with shreds of Kleenex. "It's like listening to background music without the movie. Anyway, I liked Harry Belafonte." We had seen him the week before.

"Everyone likes Belafonte. Develop your taste."

Scotty tells me it's a wonderful opportunity to hear all these concerts. "That," I said, "is because you've never had to do it."

"Gotten to, y'mean. Friends and I used to hitch into New York and stand in the balcony at Carnegie Hall. You can't have too much background, you know. Don't be such a snob. You'd do well with some classical training—what you know shows up even when you're not using it—it gives you a kind of muscle." He chucked me under the chin. "Make a musician out of you yet, lazy ol' gal."

C.A. sleeps over at Val's a lot and they talk about sex. I am behind on the subject because when they come over to my house first for movie parties, I naturally do not leave my house to stay somewhere else. But I call them up as soon as they get to Val's and Val says, "Susanna, you aren't missing anything, and we promise not to say anything good about you behind your back."

"And, you know," C.A. will say, barging in on my call to Val, "we always tell you the bad stuff right to your face."

I detest hearing them laughing together. We may be

over the War of the Birthday Party, but I still want Val to be with me. Or alone—which is selfish. And it is the truth. But even though I know that I hate them there together I do not like sleeping in a room with other people, even if it's just Val and me. It is not like being married—I will adore that. I think. I do not like to hear breathing. I have enough trouble with myself, let alone trying, which I cannot help, to synchronize it with someone else's breathing. But sometimes I go over, knowing I will not sleep, just because I want C.A. to know I'm a permanent part of the picture. And I use Val's brush and poke around the apartment, being very much part of the family—going over boundaries C.A. cannot. Val can whip her brush out of my hand and say, "Don't use my brush! Dammit." Which she could not do with C.A. and C.A. knows that, but I just like to throw in a reminder here and there. And I do pick up stuff about sex then.

Sex: They know all about it. Until I steamed off the Scotch tape that kept the section on the Reproduction System closed up in my physiology text a year ago, I really didn't know how babies are put together. That is rather peculiar since I've been having these feelings for a long time. I'm still not entirely sure how the things I think about—and do—connect with intercoursing a person. I get everything—right up to that point and then, "Cut." I have an idea that is the least sexy part. When the time comes I'll wing it.

C.A. and Val were particularly revolting one night:

"You can do these things to them," C.A. told us, "they go crazy."

"They already are," Val said. "Faugh! It's disgusting."

"No, it isn't," C.A. said, "it tastes okay. It's like, you know, being with a Popsicle." I do not think C.A. can be a virgin. She swears she is, but I think it's right down to the wire.

"Lime or strawberry?" says Val.

"And you guys think Deedee is awful!" I've never heard her talk like this. And she is not a virgin. But we do not talk about how it was. Or is. I think it was just once in a moment of blind passion—or some other excuse you give when it happens.

"I don't see what fun I'd get out of it," Val said.

"Well," C.A. pointed out, "they can do things to you."

"I *know* that," Val said. "This guy, Colin, in England, put the finger. In there. Was supposed to drive me wild."

"What did it feel like?" I asked. Surprised Val would have done that. And in England.

"Like a finger in there," Val said.

"Then he wasn't doing it right," C.A. said.

How does C.A. know that? I wonder if she does what I do. Or if Val does. No. Val would not. She is too elegant.

"I could show you," she added.

"Oh, I think I'll skip that part for now," Val said.

"Okay, if you want to go through your life missing something."

"I'll pick it up along the way."

I think the closer I get to having sex, the more repulsive it sounds.

You would have to cut off my hands and feet with pinking shears to get me to say it, but I have a feeling my mother is right, it should be beautiful. That's all she has ever told me. Except not to do it, because until you are married it is not beautiful. Or I'm assuming that is what she means. I'm not certain my mother is the perfect authority on this, or any other, subject—with the possible exception of table manners and when it is appropriate for ladies to retire upstairs after a dinner party.

We had finished talking and I could tell by their breathing that Val and C.A. were asleep. Then clearly I heard Lillian sobbing. It was so quiet it might have been going on for some time.

I wondered if I should wake Val. Her breathing and the quiet crying made a kind of counterpoint, an odd lullaby. I reached out to touch Val's shoulder but stopped; she'd probably gone to her mother before in the night. I thought of Grandmother's pictures of Lillian and my mother when they were little girls and then young girls, like Val and me. I got up quietly and went into her room.

She was lying in her bed like a child, her long hair undone and falling forward around her face, up from her neck and the back of her neck looked so young. She was lying on her stomach. I sat beside her and patted her and leaned down to hug her, stroking her hair. In her arms she had an old picture of Alan, damp and bent and battered with tears.

"Oh, Aunt Lillian, don't. I love you."

"I just can't get over him," she said. "It is so terrible to be my age, Susanna, and have no one to love and no one to look forward to loving because you have already had your great love. And lost him. I get so tired. I just get so tired of being brave about it every day."

"I know it's hard, Aunt Lillian—but you never do know—maybe something will happen. . . ."

"Maybe, Susanna, maybe. I'm sorry—did I wake you up?" She smoothed the picture out and put it under her pillow and sat up, twisting her hair back from her face, looking so pale and mussed. I was surprised at how old she looked! It was not, I thought, that she didn't have makeup on, but that the sadness of her expression made her look old. I must try to be happy when I am older so I won't look old. Who tries to be sad?

"Let's go have a cup of tea. That's the least I can do for you."

"I wonder if my mother cries over Jackson like that."

"Why don't you ask her?"

"Aren't you surprised I know?"

"Not really."

"Did Alan tell you I knew?"

"Knew what, Susanna?" She had her back to me. She put her hands to her forehead, rubbing her temples.

"Oh, just that Mother had a crush on Jackson Lane. But I don't want to talk about it . . . I guess."

I saw that I was turning the conversation around to me when I had come in to comfort her.

Val once said, "Susanna, you must try to pretend to listen."

She is right. I do try to pretend to be interested in someone else.

"That's up to you," Lillian said.

She rubbed her hands together, then hugged her arms and rubbed her shoulders. I thought about this: there aren't any middle-aged unmarried women in movies who aren't crazy. I wonder how you learn to be a survivor. I know how to be young and in love from the movies, how to get married and have your wedding and live happily ever after, and then how to be a married matron and take care of everyone with a smile on your face like Irene Dunne in *I Remember Mama* (and I'd like to see my version of *that*), or how to be very old in a rocking chair and very wise because you have lived through everything and there isn't too much more that can happen to you before you die.

"Oh—dear, Susanna—sometimes I wonder if love isn't all just beside the point and I just wish I'd get to that point—I don't know." She sighed. "Now where were we? Where is anyone for that matter?"

Which reminded me, of course, of Jackson. And so I turned it all back to me.

"Did you know him?"

"Jackson?"

I nodded.

"Not really." I followed her into the kitchen. She made us tea.

"What was he like? Did he know how my mother felt about him?"

I watched to see if she was surprised that I knew about my mother having a thing for Jackson. She did not look surprised, but she was thinking very carefully as she answered.

"He was . . . he was difficult to know. I didn't see that

much of him. Susanna, I think you should discuss this with her—not me. When you feel you really want to."

"How do you know I don't? Want to."

"I know." She was smiling then, pleased, it seemed, with her new tea cups—and with me. "Knowing some things, Susanna, may be as good as being in love. It may be the compensation. God knows, season tickets aren't enough." And she shrugged and laughed.

Driving on regular school days I'd drive in to Dolores's after school, pick up a cheeseburger and shake; then back to Stan's for french fries, and circle around, checking out the crowd from Beverly High; down Wilshire to the beach for a cherry Coke at Jack's to watch the Samo greasers cruising in circles (like me), elbows hanging out the windows. Now it's bound to be different. Everyone at college. So far I've put up a good front. They gave up trying to get me to go East. My mother doesn't want me to go to S.C. because I am not allowed to drive in that neighborhood. And I can't get into U.C.L.A. Barely got out of high school; actually at the very moment, practically a year ago, that Val was applying to Juilliard, I was flunking math, Latin, chemistry, and fencing. "Doesn't leave much," Myron said. "Somehow, it's the fencing I don't really understand, with all those swashbuckling movies you love. We've produced three this year right here—I'd hate to think that was all in vain."

"It is not funny, Myron," my mother said. "She'll never get into college."

Well. I didn't flunk fencing because I wasn't good. They have this stupid grading on attendance and I was absent a lot. Thirty out of a possible forty classes.

I spin my wheel in the overhand style as I whip down Motor Avenue to the studio. I glare at MGM down across town, and turn down the main street. I think of Aunt Molly and I wonder if the people here think of us as bosses. Will I come down here one day and find nothing but the wind whistling through, and tumbleweed rolling through the streets and big boards nailed up over Grandfather's huge iron gates?

"Jezebel." That's me. I sing along with Frankie Laine going into a little harmony on the second chorus to impress the ducktailed boy in the channeled, skirted, dual-piped Chevy next to me. He has a network of acne scars on his cheeks—the burr that gives him S.A. I cut out, peeling rubber before the light changes, and rip through town, very brave and very sexy in my car. (And only in my car.) I go past the old closed-down movie theaters, past the ratty bars called the Cutting Room and Stage 530, and halt at the gates, where, up above, the letters spelling out Victor Levanin International dance like acrobats on the scaffolding.

George Tully, the gateman, stops me. "What's going on?" I say.

"Orders from the front office, Miss Howard, sorry. You're to park in the visitors' lot today. And I was told to tell you to report to Mr. Howard's office."

"But I always drive on the lot, George."

"I'm sorry, miss, I'm only following orders."

"There must be a terrible mistake," I say.

I zap her into reverse and fling us backward right down the road into the parking lot and drop her tight between a DeSoto and a Merc convertible in one swoop and George is holding his hands on his head. Then I start to vault myself over the fence which I cannot do and I see George laughing at me and I glare at him and walk around the fence and storm past the receptionist in the administration building and go on up to Myron's office.

"Your driving," he says, without breaking his stride as he marches across from his conference room to his private office, "is driving me out of my mind." And he slams the door. He must be having a bad day. He is usually very proud of my driving, and especially proud of the car he was able to get me. He tells people at dinner parties that he ordered it for me. I think that makes him feel like a real father.

I start to go in after him, but the secretary at the front desk, Linda, says he has someone in there. Like Grandfather, Myron has one private receptionist in a small waiting area, however there are now only two secretaries in the large central space between the conference room and his own office. Linda, who does mostly letters, sits at a small desk toward the front, and his executive secretary, Nancy Fitzsimmons, is in the back behind a huge desk. In Grandfather's day the office was all white and silver and there were Greek columns everywhere. The golden testimonial plaques and awards Grandfather won are still all over the walls along with pictures of the great stars, but all the offices are Early American and red, white, and blue and there are so many American flags it looks like a Young Republicans' Veterans' Day dance. I trot by the desks, saying hello, catching a look at mail here and there, checking out script titles and contracts.

"Hello, Susanna, dear," says Nancy, deftly covering everything on her desk that I could possibly read. But not quite in time. "Preview of *Sabrina!* I'm going."

"Susanna, please. That's just a censors' screening."

"So, I'll pull my hair back and go in oxfords. Listen, I just saw this incredible folksinger today. We ought to make a big folksinging musical about her . . . it's a great story. You'd open with a big 3-D shot of the Appalachians and shoot right down into a mine disaster, then . . ."

"I think, darling, 3-D's on the way out. The latest box office reports are lousy. Any other suggestions?"

"Yeah, me starring in anything with Marlon Brando."

"You and everyone else I know."

The intercom buzzes from Myron's office, and Nancy presses down the button. "Yes, Mr. Howard?"

"Would you call for a limousine for Mr. Schine? . . ."

"Schine?" I whisper to Nancy. "David Schine? You know Robert Ryan got so mad at him and Senator McCarthy he put a chair right through his TV set. David

Schine! Well, it could be Roy Cohn. Now he's what you expect to happen when you're fixed up on a blind date."

She laughs and places a finger over her lips as Myron comes out.

"Oh, Mr. Howard," Nancy says. "Dan Udell called from Stage Ten, the lighting people won't move until the union gives them the go ahead—they say there's only eight gaffers over there and the minimum is ten, we can bring a couple of men over from Stage Four, I think they finished retakes. . . ."

"Call Sullivan and send him down there. Most of those grips live better than contract players—geese that eat the golden egg."

Myron is also adopting some of Grandmother's malaprops. Perhaps it makes him more at home in this office.

"Yes, sir," Nancy says.

"Susanna, you may come in now," he says.

I would like to tell David Schine, who is standing looking out the window (tall and chilly, the eyes-in-the-back-of-the-head type, who has probably had a quick look at the papers on the desk), that he should take all the folksingers off the blacklist so they can work on TV and get their records on the radio stations again.

"I'll talk with you in a minute, Susanna," Myron says and introduces me to Schine. I must move fast. If at all.

"I went to hear some folksingers today, Dad; they were really great and I think it's a shame they can't get work on TV. . . ." I say this very quickly and with a lot of exuberance as though it just bounced out.

I look over at Schine, but after a quick looking me up and down (can he tell I'm a fellow traveler?), he ignores me, and says to Myron, "Can one of your girls put a call through for me? . . ."

"Sure, David, just use any one of the phones."

At least Myron is making him place his own phone call.

"Why didn't Tully let me on the lot? I'll have to walk to Wardrobe, and I'm late now. Nancy says they're waiting."

"That's your problem, Susanna. You should have thought of that when you drove through the lot last week. We had a report from the East Gate that you were doing eighty. We can't tolerate that."

"That's ridiculous," I say. "I was only doing sixty. It was on the straightaway, and no one was around."

Saved by Nancy who comes in and shuts the door behind her. "Excuse me, Mr. Howard, but it's that Russ Burstein again," and she lowers her voice, "that TV producer, you know, he wants to talk about leasing some offices and now it's two sound stages for an independent company he's—"

"I know, I know," Myron interrupts and goes behind his desk. "Which line is he on?"

"Three, sir—but let me pick it up." Nancy reaches for the phone and Myron pulls his hand back.

"Yes, of course. You're right, Nancy." And he grins at her. In his tight little shy way. Myron is more than a little embarrassed when his sense of humor slips out. Most of the time he has it perfectly under control.

"Mr. Howard will speak to Mr. Burstein now; will you put him on? Thank you. Yes, Mr. Burstein? Just a moment for Mr. Howard." Nancy covers the mouthpiece and stands looking at Myron who counts twenty seconds on his watch and then takes the phone.

"Yes, yes, we are very busy. It's all great—but busy. No, it's out of the question. Yes. That's my final answer. No, I'm not interested. Sorry." He hangs up the phone. "Electronic crackerjacks!" he says. "Damn TV!"

"Yes, of course, Mr. Howard," Nancy says, "but . . ."

"But what?"

"Well, Carol in the Goldwyn office says that she heard Mr. Goldwyn advising Jack Warner to pick up some Westinghouse stock and start thinking small. I just thought I'd mention that."

"Rumors. Everyone's acting like the Yankees have invaded Atlanta."

It would not be wise for me to remind Myron that they did do that. I also remember Grandmother's stories about the days before the talkies came in. "Victor," she told Grandfather, "hire some voice coaches."

"Now, Susanna," Myron turns to me. "The limit is fifteen miles an hour and you know it. This is a motion picture studio, not your own private Indianapolis, do you understand? And what are you doing in Wardrobe?"

"Going to C.A.'s party. Tra-la!" I smile my best smile.

"Well. See. I knew it would work out. Good girl! Now nothing too flamboyant . . . Susanna?"

"No sequins. Promise." I go out of his office. Schine is still standing at the desk next to the door. Probably heard everything.

"Now, will you please put me through to Piper Laurie, this is David Schine." And he tells her he can't take her to that party tomorrow night because something serious has come up in Washington. Something, I think, to do with the Army. Well, C.A. certainly did invite *everyone*. Obviously, her father is playing it safe; Hollywood politics; a little something from both sides of the fence and don't forget the ones sitting up on top. Paul Daroff and some of the Eastern boys say that all that's about over. That is because they read the *New York Times* every week. They bring pieces of it to the beach every Tuesday, hundreds and hundreds of pages of small print and Paul sits under an umbrella and reads every word, taking his long cigarette holder out of his mouth from time to time in order to bite a bit of nail.

On the way back home after picking up my dress, I cruise by Val's and really want to go in—but that's what she means she hates. Dropping in.

Invasion of privacy: I went by to see my mother at Ann Meredith's beauty parlor one day when Val and Lillian were on their way out here after stopping in New York so Val could take her exams at Juilliard. And only two weeks after Alan died she did that and *passed!* Val is dedicated, really. Which is why she will be actually famous. Very fast, too. I wanted to ask my mother why Lillian and Val couldn't have lived with us at Perdido. If you catch her with wet nails she can't get on the phone to avoid answering.

"I would have loved it, Susanna. But it would have been hard for Lillian. Life always seemed hopeful for us when we were little there—it would be hard to be reminded of how it should have been. And everyone wants her own place. We are all very private people, Susanna, and we dislike being crowded. Do you understand?"

"Yes, I guess." I looked at her—she even looks beautiful in a hairnet. Her face is a perfect oval and her eyes are hooded—like Val's, Lillian's, and Grandmother's. Ideal for eye makeup.

"Why are you looking at me like that?" she asked and anxiously looked at herself in the mirror.

"I was just wondering if you ever wanted to be a movie star."

"No, darling. I'm very grateful I've never had to work—and it wouldn't have been right to take a job from a girl who needed it." She smiled at her reflection and then at mine standing behind her. "Why don't you go over to Lanz's and see if there's something you'd like? If you wait we can go together. I want Andrew to run us over to Schirmer's and pick up the sheet music to a Sibelius piece I want to learn."

"I have my car, Mother."

"Well, you can leave it and we'll pick it up later."

"No, that's too much trouble. I don't want to wait."

She never goes anywhere with me. But now that I think about it—she was trying to that day. It was me who turned her down. We are like trapeze artists, just missing each other in midair. And each time we misconnect it finishes off the act. There's no such "I really meant . . ." thing. It takes forever to get us back to try again.

Driving again. With practically a ton of organdy, net, and taffeta in the back seat and the most gorgeous blue satin dancing shoes.

Here comes-a-Miss Susie,
Just look at them shoes. Shoes for dancin' by them
  blues,
Ruffles on her shoulders, Stars all over her hair.
Just too bad her Jackson ain't gonna be there.

I imagine a hundred songs and lose a hundred more just driving every week. And Jackson comes up somewhere in just about every single one.

I HAVE TWIRLED INTO GRANDMOTHER'S ROOM, WHICH
my parents use as a sitting room now, and I am wearing
a gown my grandmother would love to see me in—a
gown from one of Grandfather's epics. It has forty-eight
tiny buttons down the back, all the seams inside are
trimmed with lace, and it's all palest blue organdy ruffles.
And I have just told my mother that Marty, who I asked
to C.A.'s party, drives an MG. Marty's father is a doctor
and Marty is in medical school in the East. Marty is the
kind who always has his tux ready, which is why I asked
him.

"My God, Myron," my mother says, "that's one of
those little cars that overturn all the time." She is sitting
on Grandmother's chaise and looking at my dress with
her eyes narrowed, appraising.

"Every time you turn the corner, over they go," I say,
twirling again. I love the swish of the taffeta and net
petticoats. Ten layers! And a hoop.

"Susanna, be careful when you move. Isn't that a
little tight under the arms?"

"Now, both of you stop it," Myron says.

The intercom buzzes. Marty is here.

"Susanna, be careful," my mother calls as I dash out
into the hall.

"And have a good time," Myron calls. I wait at the
head of the stairs for the rest of that which comes just
as expected, "and don't be late."

"Wouldn't dream of it," I call back over my shoulder,
and flounce down the stairs, my hoopskirt billowing.
"Lovely to look at, delightful to know," I sing to myself.

I am Scarlett, Magnolia, and everyone gorgeous who ever floated down stairs in a perfect dress.

"I didn't know it was a costume party," Marty says. "Is everyone wearing that kind of thing?"

"A lot of the girls are. It's a *Show Boat* party."

"They did a terrible job on the movie. The stage play was pretty good, though." He's only in med school and he already feels competent to criticize movies.

"That dress is awful big, isn't it?" Marty says.

"No, actually. Tight under the arms," I say.

"I meant the skirt. How can you dance in that?"

"Beautifully." One more, just one more thing and I'm dashing back upstairs and putting on my blue jeans. It is hardly in a rush of confidence that I sweep out the door and stuff my skirts and ruffles into a heap around me in the car. The hoop pops up, covering my view of the road, and Marty glides a hand onto my knees. "Now that," he says, "is more interesting."

"Oh, let's just get to the party," I say, and try to reach around the hoop for his hand to put it up on the steering wheel where I want it to stay. Oh, to be going with someone romantic. Someone dashing. Someone else.

We drive in on Jefferson Boulevard to the back lot, and through the gate, past the guard. Then we go through a street in a small town with a bank and a pawn shop and a theater with an empty marquee and by the back of a Western town, past a Southern mansion and a warehouse where walls and roofs and windows are lined up like books in the school library and then over a Chinese bridge to a dock where in front of the *Mayflower*, we see the *Cotton Blossom* all festooned with tiny white lights and clouds of balloons. A car parker in a red jacket takes the MG and we walk out onto the dock where the water laps gently against the pilings like real river water. We are all coming up the gangplank and there to greet us is C.A. and her parents and her surprise, which is Angelo, who is wearing a tux with a T-shirt and the black tie draped around his neck like a scarf.

"Well," I say.

"Yeah," he says. "Last time I saw you you disappeared." He snaps his fingers. "Into thin air." I hate him.

C.A.'s mother flusters around, a wistful look at Paul who is every mother's idea of the perfect catch—even if Evelyn Ames is his stepmother. He may have his cigarette holder, but he still has the smile of a little boy who is trying to please, and the terribly bitten nails that show he is scared he won't. C.A.'s mother keeps one hand over her pavé ruby bracelets on the arm that is closest to Angelo.

C.A. has feathers on her dress to match the canary wings sticking out of her mouth as she looks at me.

Cat, I think to myself. "Happy Birthday. This is Marty."

"Howdy," she says.

"I like the way he stares you right in the breast," Val says looking at Angelo.

"Stroble," I say.

"Well, I wouldn't mind teaching him to tie his tie," says Kitty, "if you're talking about who I think you're talking about." She has come bouncing along between us rather like a balloon which has gotten loose from one of the clouds of white ones tied all about the railings among twinkling white lights. She has a little pad of paper with her and is taking notes. I am never so aware of how much we have grown as when Kitty is around, being suddenly shorter than everyone, even Val.

"Young for memoirs?" says Val, who is wearing Lillian's garnets with her dark red taffeta gown with puffed sleeves like enormous cabbage roses. She must have known everyone else would be wearing pastels. And she would also have known we would all have our hair curled and loose, which is why she has hers back in a perfect chignon. Grandmother had a photograph of Katharine Cornell in *Candida* and I'm sure Val had that in mind. She is a perfect miniature. Only more beautiful.

"Didn't you know?" Kitty says, "I have a teen gossip column in *Silver Screen*."

"Just another stepping stone to popularity," says Val.

"Well, as I always say, if you can't join 'em, lick 'em. I've counted five nose jobs so far. Ta-ta."

And she scurries off, scribbling along underfoot.

Paul and Marty have gone to get us champagne punch. A studio band is playing up on the second deck for dancing. And, with a lurch, the showboat starts moving, gliding out past a cyclorama of a night with moon and stars.

"How thoughtful of them to anticipate the fog," says Val, gazing at the turquoise blue moon going past us.

"Paul looks terrific," I say to Val. "Very interesting now that he has lost weight."

"I guess he got tired of people coming up and saying, 'Haven't you lost weight?' which, of course, no one ever says to anyone who doesn't need to."

Paul has a jawline I have never noticed before—next to eyes, I'm a sucker for jawlines. There was a song from *Finian's Rainbow* called, "When I'm Not Near the Girl I Love I Love the Girl I'm Near." I am just the opposite, or inside out of that, which is that whoever (whomever?) I'm near, I always see someone else I like a lot better. This guarantees only wistfulness. I'm sure I'd adore Marty, with his trim little body (he is not quite as tall as I am), if he was not my date. Well, maybe not adore, but he does have that knowing way of looking at you that med students get.

"Oh, my God," I say to Val, "did you see that!" Against the railing stands a riverboat gambler, in ruffles and brocade, blond as Jackson Lane, but fairer and delicate, a lower lip (right up there with jawlines and eyes are lower lips) with perfect squared-off edges, a little surly, a little sad about the eyes. And, oh, the cleft in the chin, a tiny dent to kiss.

"That must be someone's actor," I say.

"Little set decoration there. Not to fall in love with."

"Wouldn't think of that. Just looking, thank you."

"In the eye of pig," she says.

"Is he looking at me?" I whisper. One cannot keep staring.

"No. Currently gazing at its own reflection in the water. However, you have missed the chance. Great friend Roston is moving in."

And I see Deedee, in fringed lamé, done up like a gambler's moll, with plumes—the rat—approaching Gaylord Ravenal like a gold-plated torpedo.

And Paul and Marty are advancing on us with punch.

"Tasteful," says Paul, seeing Deedee.

"Punch?" says Marty.

"In eye," I mutter, taking the cup, imitating Val's way of dropping articles.

"Must have whipped it right off Jane Russell's back," says Val, sipping.

"I'm going to say hello to Deedee," I tell Marty.

"Give a little push for me," says Val.

I think Deedee has been saving this blond one up for this party.

"How nice of Duke Ellington to write a song for your house," Deedee says, introducing me to Bronston Sloane.

The band is playing "Perdido."

"Yes," I say. "He wrote it for Grandfather's first big New Year's party. A smash right from that night, Grandmother always said. What a coincidence they are playing it now." I am looking at Bronston to see if he is impressed.

"That's quite a good story," he says. Just the kind of thing Jackson would say.

"I can't," Deedee says, "imagine the Duke at your house. But I like the story, you're so funny, Susanna— Well, now, I'm going to tear Bronston away and feed him. You know actors are always starving."

"Oh, I'm doing all right," he says. "Who is your grandfather?"

"I'll tell you *all* about Susanna while we eat," she says and whisks him away.

I go back and find Marty waiting for me with two plates of food from the buffet line.

"Not eating?" I say to Marty, as I dip a fried chicken leg into pineapple-honey sauce.

"Not right now." He claps his hand over his mouth and runs out on deck.

"Tastes like it was left over from Chickie Slotkin's luau," says Kitty, balancing a plate and her notepad. "Aren't you going to hold his head?"

"He's a doctor; I think he can handle it himself."

"Young doctor," she says. "Parents must be pleased. I mean your mother and stepfather."

"They," I say, "are delirious. You can quote me."

Sparklers blaze on top of C.A.'s birthday cake which comes in on a trolley, a pink and white model of the *Cotton Blossom* the size of a pony.

"If this is eighteen," says Val, rustling by, "then ponder if you will twenty-one." This is her new Adlai Stevenson phrasing. And Paul lifts his head in a grin, his cigarette holder between his teeth.

Angelo stands off behind C.A. as she cuts the cake. Why did he come if he's going to stand there and look at everything with his Wolf gang sneer? This is our real life, I want to say to him, we can't help it.

The M.C. gathers everyone around for a little show. Howard Keel, Jane Powell, Ann Blyth, Carleton Carpenter, and Vic Damone sing songs from our favorite musicals, and I begin to think Angelo is right (notice how I know what he is thinking). This cannot be anyone's real life.

"The band is schizo," Val says, as it goes into its jazz mode after the show is over, something in between Freddy Martin and Stan Kenton, with a slight lean toward Martin. "I don't know how you dance to it. I can't distract myself. They're each playing in a different key," I say to show her I am learning to listen. "Only four of them. Three are playing the same key and it's wrong." I pick up the percussion, move to it and pretend it isn't music. "The drummer's okay."

In spite of hoopskirts everyone bops along doing the New Yorker, dancing side-side-back. I always imagine them moving, the New Yorkers, in their black outfits, down Fifth Avenue doing this dance, jerking and shifting through the crowds. C.A., with her eye out for Angelo who seems to have disappeared, stands next to me for a moment. "Val," she says, "is the only girl I know who can spend four years in England, have a major tragedy, and somehow come back knowing how to do the hitchhiker." And she does it without looking cheap, with her fine bones going into classy poses as she struts and her eyes off somewhere, looking like one of those sulky, silent girls in a foreign movie or one of those barbed-wire modern sculptures if you made a puppet out of it.

"Well," says Sherry Lemoult who used to be a child star and got notes from her agent to get out of doing arithmetic, "she's always been very musical. Do you still try to play that ukulele, Susanna?" she inquires before moving off, hoop twitching like a horsetail, to dance. "Guitar," I say to myself.

Gary Hollister looms up and asks C.A. to dance. They wheel off. He is an arm pumper. C.A. grimaces over her shoulder at me and, an instant later, beams up at him. My God. She's wearing her riding boots under her dress. And the spurs. Wish I had thought of that.

I think Marty has died. I dance with Wes Leahy, son of the newspaper publisher who is rarely seen west of Pasadena and then only at the L.A. Country Club where they do not permit Jews or show business people. It is in the charter, Alan once told us, "and of course it is a redundant exclusion." The band does a slow number, "I'll Walk Alone." I watch Deedee and her actor. It is not a good name, I must tell him, because I have already forgotten it. The name, but not this face. She has her head buried into his shoulder, eyes practically crossed from punch. He looks at me, our eyes catch, and I shake my head and just say, "Oh, God." I want to eat him all up. A cookie-face, he is. Sort of Jackson but silkier. Does he have a motor? Do I care? I don't want to cast him. I want to put him under covers in monogrammed silk pajamas.

Wesley is saying something. "Why are the best songs about loneliness?" Is he trying to be romantic or practicing interviewing?

"I didn't know they were," I say. He is holding me tighter, my heart is pounding. He is a sexy good boy. Sort of the Arthur Loew, Jr., type except not so despondent. Arthur's problem, we all have decided, is actresses. Any one of us would love to help him get over them. Why do I know actresses are bad for men and still want an actor for myself? It's not, I think, that they are so bad, but they just need all that adoring to keep the motor running and they don't do much adoring back in case you need some. Now, this is a terrible thing to say, but Lillian doesn't look nearly so exhausted now that Alan is gone. Easy to know—how to resist.

"Maybe," he says, "it's because we're lonely even when we're dancing, do you know what I mean?"

"I never feel that way," I lie. I know exactly what he means. "Actually, you shouldn't think when you dance, it throws your rhythm off. Or talk." Why am I mean to boys? Even before I think about it. And the nicer they are the more terrible I am.

"Can I have another one?" he says. The band is going into a fast number.

"I guess so." Now that's exactly it, why can't I just smile up at him and say, "Yes"? like Holly Butler or Lois Detweiler which, besides being beautiful, is why they are so popular. Am I nasty first so when they leave town without so much as a "See you around" I can say, well, I didn't like him anyway and he knew it? I do love everyone right now, however. Dancing, dancing. Cyd Charisse must adore her work.

"And the music goes round and round and . . ." and, and, here's Angelo, cutting in. As I said, when I'm not near . . . Now he is the perfect sexy bad boy, the Gloria

Grahame of boys. John Derek with dark eyes. My uncle Alan must have been like Angelo when he was young. I can see him in black leather, twirling something, like Brando in front of his cycle. Angelo used to twirl his yo-yo like that when he was a little kid. Born bad, as they say. He'd stand there beside his father in his little short pants, twirling that yo-yo and looking right through your playsuit. Dancing with Angelo is like driving a souped-up car. Everything disappears with the speed. He turns his back and twists me out and I go pivoting round and when we're face to face—those surly eyes— he throws me away again, working the floor while he prances in place, dead-pan, keeping the beat. He pulls me in and flips me up across his knee and my hoopskirt flies, my God, they'll see my stocking tops. My throat is hot and dry and he spins me out and back in tight and we do not stop, out and back, going with the drum solo. I catch a look at the drummer, watching us watching him chewing his gum. Drummers all get the beat from their jaws and move it on down from there. I bet they are great kissers. For people who can breathe through their noses. "Go, go, go," we're all shouting. I want to be right inside the sound. I pull out from Angelo, sweating, my fingers snapping, and he grabs me back against him. Music and moving. This is more like sex than necking. I look at him for an instant. He is laughing. Looking at me like someone looking at dirty pictures. "I'll bet," he says, "you look even better with your clothes off now than you did the last time I saw you."

"That wasn't the last time," I say between breaths.

"Yeah, the last time you tramped through the garden and disappeared. You're a hot little dancer." I feel his thighs. I feel—I feel a lot of things. And I cannot breathe. I feel my clutch. I tell myself it is just the exercise.

"I've got to find my date. . . ." I pull away.

"He's in the cabin upstairs, he's okay."

"Above, not upstairs," I say.

"Sorry. When my yacht blew up I forgot everything I ever knew."

"I've got to go now," and I wrench away. I hate dark eyes. You cannot see through them.

"So, go," he says, and holds his hands up and away from me. "I'm not stopping you." And he stamps and bends his knees and pivots around in a kind of sexy shuffle. Then turns and pulls me to him for an instant and wheels me out fast.

"I'm going." I glare at him and run across the dance floor and I hear him laughing even with the music playing, even as I climb—wheezing—up the steps to the top deck, my hand on my chest like Grandmother. He is not, I tell myself (repeat three times), my type. That's a definite not. He makes me feel like one of the girls who hang around Dolores's, girls with bleached hair cut to a sharp point in the middle of their backs, girls in tight gabardine skirts. He makes me feel like being fast. And I am not fast. Through the fog, from the top deck, I can see the MGM cities go by in ghostly silhouettes. Frontier towns, castles, bridges where a dozen wars from many centuries were fought, Indian tepees, Midwestern small towns with white-painted houses and elm trees, and thatched-roof villages. I can watch a weeping willow go by and almost touch the top. Below, the band is playing "Blue Moon."

"I saw you standing alone," he says. "Isn't that perfect timing?" It is Deedee's actor. "Remember, Susanna," I hear my grandmother say, "what you know of actors," and already I am not listening.

"Did you ask them to play it?" I say. Nasty, right off the bat.

"You're very young to be so cynical."

"I'm sorry. I forgot your name."

"Bronston Sloane."

"That's not the real one, is it?"

"No, the real one's Henry Simpson."

"Yes, it would have to be changed. Are you under contract?"

"Not yet. I'm more interested in the right part than a contract. You don't like my new name—it isn't convincing, is it? My agent thought it had the rhythm of a star name. Cary Grant, Alan Ladd, Jackson Lane . . ."

Oh, sure, that's why I had trouble with it.

"Yes," I say sharply, "but there's also John Wayne, Spencer Tracy, Clark Gable—there's no guarantee on a name."

"Can you think of a better name?"

Adorable. But that is obvious and he knows it. The lips. "Maybe," I say, "we could have a contest. Name this actor."

"It bothers me, not having a name. Names do define us, never mind what Shakespeare said." He smiles. Imagine such eyes across a pillow. I do not wheeze when I imagine sex. And when I imagine it I keep it in very soft focus. Or, best of all, above the waist.

"Where's Deedee?" I ask.

"Had a little too much to drink. Last time I saw her she was leaping over Gary Crosby's knee. You dance very well, by the way."

"Have you had a lot of training?" I ask. Look how I ignore the compliment.

"Acting? Four years; but I've lived a lot. I can't think of a job I haven't had. My family didn't approve of acting, so I've had to finance my own education. I'm a great reader."

"My family doesn't approve of acting, either."

"That's too bad. You'd be wonderful on the stage, you have so much vitality—it would be wasted in pictures."

I think I will make Myron give him a screen test. At the very least.

"I love to read too," I say.

"Gliding on this river here reminds me of a passage in *The Magic Mountain*. Do you know it?"

The Big Rock Candy Mountain? Night on Bald Mountain from *Fantasia?* Mt. Everest?

"Which passage is that?" There. Safe.

"A simulated winter forest all in silence . . . let us stray here at this hour—so soft the sand beneath our tread, so sublime, so mild the night! Far beneath us the sea respires slowly . . ."

Respires—is that a word? Does he mean to say reposes? But listening to him speak is like hearing someone else sing. His lovely hand lies on my arm.

". . . and murmurs a long whispering in its dream."

"Yes," I say—sigh—"that is one of my favorite scenes too." I drift in closer to him. *Photoplay* could do a layout on our life at home. No, *Life* will do it. Classier.

"Do you sing?" he asks. "You have a very unusual voice."

"All I really like to sing are love songs." Which is not true. I love to sing the traveling songs the best.

"I know," he says, "this is probably presumptuous, but if you aren't bored to death by premieres, and since we've been talking about Thomas Mann, would you like to go to the premiere of *Magnificent Obsession?* I have two tickets and I'd love to take you."

"Talking about *who?*"

"He wrote the original book. Of course, it won't be up to that, but I've heard it's not bad."

"I'm more a quiet evening reading type of person, usually, but that would be fine. . . ."

I give him my phone number, written in lipstick on a paper napkin which says *C.A. Happy Birthday* in metallic pink letters.

The band plays "Goodnight, Ladies" and the party is over. We wait for cars on the dock. Marty looks completely miserable.

"Real catch," Val whispers to me, raising one eyebrow.

I suggest to Marty that I ride home with Val and Paul. This will serve her right, having me along, no chance to be alone with Paul. Not that it's that sort of thing with them—but they like to ride together, sitting far apart, I am sure, talking like married people about everyone else at the party.

"Well, if you really wouldn't mind," Marty says.

I have decided I am not going to say I am going to the premiere of Tom Mann's (I wonder if he is Daniel Mann's brother?) *Magnificent Obsession*. Val will get it out of me that I adore Rock Hudson and Paul will laugh. I have also decided I will not discuss Bronston Sloane on the way home and then here I am saying, "You know Bronston Sloane isn't his real name. . . ."

"Never would have guessed," Paul says, knowing exactly who I am talking about; Paul, I see, is a terrible driver. He slows down and looks at you when he talks and he is driving his father's Cadillac sedan. You'd think Leon Daroff could afford to give his son something to drive around during the summer, such as an MG. Now see—here's exactly it—I'm with Paul Daroff and Val, of course, going home with really the best people at the party, and because of the car I am thinking I wish I was with Marty in the MG, bouncing along—roaring at every corner. But if I was with Marty I would look at this evil black Cadillac with Val and Paul sitting up front saying things (I would be sure) that I wanted to get in on.

"Can you think of a better name?" Now why am I doing this? I can hear it coming.

"Oh, many things come to mind," Val says. " 'Trouble,' yes, or, perhaps, 'Bit Player.' "

"Now there's one of your snappy names," Paul says. And it turns out they are not saying much in this car, with me along, anyway, which does not turn out to be about me. Or me talking. Which is the same. It does not matter. It was a great party. The test of a party is that you go into it as you and come out of it in love. And I am going to be in love. Hopelessly in love, which is the only way—to be positively faint with it.

So why is it when I am lying in my bed, in the dark, with my hand reaching down, dipping, rubbing, I see Angelo? Not Jackson. Not Bronson—not Bron*ston*.

At the beach the boys, just back from a trip to Tijuana, had talked about seeing a mother-daughter team of prostitutes. "In mother-daughter outfits?" I had asked.

"Oh, be quiet, Susanna," C.A. said. This was just before we went to war. The boys told us they sat in chairs, across the room from a huge old bed, and watched the woman and girl touching each other and touching themselves. Right in front of them! Dip and circle, and I see them, two tousled, black-haired "young lovelies with passionate eyes," which is how the boys put it, lying there on a red and green bedspread with sequinned black eagles just like the Mexican costumes we all had. Faster, wetter, I lick my fingertips and run my hand back and front and faster and I see myself. Faster, harder, diving, slick, slick, slick, and I see Angelo, Angelo, Angelo in all three chairs across a room, sitting there in a toreador suit, watching. A triple screen effect, castanets clicking in his hand. "Go, go, go," he says, leaning forward, jumping to my rhythm . . . images fade to one and he is watching, but will not touch, do it, babe, harder, harder and he comes closer, telling me to keep my eyes on him, ordering me to keep doing it but not to close my eyes. He's getting very close now and says, don't stop, don't stop and he leans over me, and I can feel the edge of his satin toreador cloak brush my breasts, and he looks me right in the eyes, his hands holding my thighs wide, don't stop, babe . . . and then I lose him, don't need him, as the feeling catches, strikes, and spreads like applause at a premiere, then fades with a clap here and there and my thighs clench against my hand and I am ashamed. I turn to go to sleep and it is the actor I imagine curved around me. Even in my fantasies, I keep my virginity. I don't know why. Grandmother is already dead. I imagine her up there playing gin with God.

"My God," she says, because she is allowed to use the familiar, "will you look at what Susanna is doing."

"Gin," says God.

I DID NOT REALLY THINK BRONSTON SLOANE WOULD remember about the premiere, although Val said, of course he would. Would one forget a screen test, would Evelyn Ames forget an interview with *Life?* Don't be a goose.

So we are going to the premiere. Bronston says he has left his car at the bottom of the driveway because it is such a beautiful evening for a little walk. I say to myself he has left his car there because it is such a terrible car and its hood is held together by string. One cannot drive up to the theater in this car, even with his profile and the blue brocade tuxedo jacket which is the same one he was wearing at C.A.'s, and that is fortunate because I thought it might have been rented. I wonder if one can rent actors like tuxedos. This is probably the sort one could. Rent. I feel unkind about him tonight. Am I looking at his wrong side? Fortunately he has the style to know one parks such a car in a lot and walks to the theater.

We get to the ticket taker at the door and Bronston looks for his tickets. He looks in all his pockets. He slaps the outside ones. He peers into the insides. He snaps his fingers. "Oh, my God, I forgot the tickets." He looks at his watch. "And there's no time to go back. . . . I'm so sorry," he says.

"Oh, that can happen to anyone," I say sweetly. "Don't worry, I'll call Myron. He knows the manager, he'll get us in."

"Are you sure that's no trouble?" He puts his lovely arm around my waist—I can imagine silken skin even under his jacket and my whaleboning.

193

"Oh, no . . . I'll be right back," and I start off for the manager's office. Myron will say I told you so. But I want to see the movie. I am a little annoyed that I have to do this while he gets to stand and watch the stars. Especially since he's the only one he really loves.

"I could have told you so," Myron says.

I told you so, I tell myself.

"Well, put Barnes on."

The seats are lousy. If I'd asked Myron in the beginning I could have been sitting up where the people are. But then Bronston folds his arm around mine. "You're a sweetheart," he says. And the lights go down and the music swells.

When the movie ends and I go outside everything seems dark. It is my eyes. . . . I was a Catholic for three days after I saw *The Robe* last year and now I am going blind.

"What did you think of the picture?" Bronston asks. I almost forgot how pretty he is. Takes me a minute to regroup. You could sit him on top of a Christmas tree and no one would blink. "Nifty angel you have there," they would say.

"It's very significant. Rock Hudson is astonishing," I say, "and powerful." You take glasses off an actress and she becomes beautiful and put them on an actor and he becomes a "powerful performer—or a brilliant eye surgeon." I do not point out that nowhere on the titles did it say "Thomas Mann." Unless he was writing this as Lloyd C. Douglas—it may be the name Mann uses for his movie books.

"Oh, Susanna—it's entertaining, but it's not half what the book is."

"Of course, one can never compare movies to books." I do not add that I cannot imagine reading a book if you could see the movie. No matter what the writer is calling himself.

"Listen, I'd like to go to Schwab's for a minute and talk to my agent," he says. Not a good sign. No one's agent goes to Schwab's. No agent with working clients, that is. But he is so affectionate as we are driving. An arm around the shoulder. I forget to be suspicious. On the way down Fountain Avenue he points out his apartment in a two-story Regency-Grecian-Ranch building.

Handy to know.

His agent is playing Klobiasch at a table. "Hi, Charlie," he says.

Bronston grimaces. I have not heard this name.

"Charlie?" I grin at him.

"It's Sammy's nickname for me," he says smooth as his calfskin loafers, which I now notice he has Vaselined tonight to look like patent leather. I do not miss anything until I want to. Or vice versa.

We sit around awkwardly while Sammy tells me how he was this great friend of my grandfather's. "Charlie wouldn't know this, but do you know her grandfather was a horse trader back in Poland in the old days?"

"Horse trainer. Russia," I say.

"Yes, yes," he says. "He used to tell some great stories about the old country. You still live in the house, Presidio, isn't it?"

"Yes." I am not bothering any more.

"Perdido," Bronston-Henry-Charlie says. He looks at me, his eyes going all soft with understanding. I love these kind of eyes, tough and suddenly warm. Liar's eyes. He is a bad man. But I am his woman. How nice he is embarrassed for me. How nice I can believe he loves me for a minute. Watch how I will talk myself into it. And out just as fast.

They slip away from the table for a minute and Charlie gets some cash from Sammy so he can take me somewhere nice. After all, he has probably left his wallet home with his tickets.

We are dancing at the Crescendo. His lips brush my hair. "You dance like an angel," he says, as I slip my foot out from under his toes for the third time. I am no good at this slow stuff. He whispers of the troubles the serious actor has in Hollywood.

He kisses me.

"What's the matter?" he says.

"Nothing." Why is it I only like the idea of it? Even someone this beautiful—the kiss still feels the same. Eyes open. Eyes closed. I cannot breathe.

We are driving home.

"Have you been working on your·songs?" he asks. He is interested in me as an artist. Val gets crazed when I say "artist."

"One is a musician, painter, writer—but not artist. Only Sunday people call themselves that."

I tell Bronston: "I am working all the time. I have written a wonderful song about . . ." It was about love. But he'll think I mean that.

"About what?" He is sitting away from me now on the bench in front of the house. He is slightly winded because we have walked up the hill.

"Nothing—really." I should begin to sing the song to him, the music would come up. I need to break off a rose to put in my hair. There are only oleanders. They do not break off easily. Only Oleanders. Possible title. About a girl in love with an actor.

He looks at his watch. "Well, it's late. I enjoy being with you. I'd love to meet the Howards."

"Perhaps you'll come to dinner." I will ask him to-morrow. I don't want to push. I like him because he does not jam into me so I cannot breathe, but kisses me lightly on the corner of the mouth.

Next day: Radie Harris in the Hollywood *Reporter* —a long list of celebrities and then: "ITEM: Handsome newcomer Bronson Sloan" (it isn't even his own name and already it's being spelled wrong) "with Levanin granddaughter Susanna Howard."

"Isn't that fantastic?" I say to Val, showing up on the beach with the *Reporter* in hand and my latest powder blue satin Lastex.

"If you like being used. I wonder what he did to which press agent to plant that."

"Radie never uses plants!"

"No, only long-stemmed roses—sorry. How was the movie?"

"Entertaining. Of course, it's nothing compared to the book."

"Yes, and a favorite of yours."

"That and *War and Peace*. Oh, well, I'll see it again if you want to go."

"Susanna, just keep your eyes open with that guy. Paul's heard some things about him."

"Val, I can protect myself. What could he hear? That he's a mostly out-of-work actor? That he's taking me out to get to Myron? Where do you think I've been all my life?"

"Hollywood," says Val.

Divine to be an ITEM. But what kind of an item is it if he does not call for two days? He must think I am embarrassed. Perhaps he is afraid my parents are mad and he is scared to call. I try to find his phone number. Unlisted. I try Celebrity Service.

"Never heard of him."

"By the way," since I have them on the phone anyway, "have you got a recent number for Jackson Lane?"

"Haven't had anything on him for years. Who did you say is calling?"

"Vera Hruba Ralston," I say.

"Oh yes," the girl says. "Didn't you used to go out with him?"

"Ve vere sumpsing of an item, sanks," I say in my V.H.R. voice and hang up fast.

I note that in my Jackson Lane file, with a question mark. Item, I think, is open to interpretation.

A week. Maybe I hurt him. I must grow up. I will go and give myself to him. More or less. He probably decided I am a prude. Or a baby. I pick up a black lace bra. I will do anything above the waist. I practice breathing while kissing my pillow for three nights. I put on my bra, black toreadors, navy blue sweater, and

Constance Bennett's old black velvet cloak. What I would not give for a black turtleneck.

I leave at midnight before Myron and my mother have come home.

Bronston's car is not parked in front of his apartment. Probably in a garage in the back, would not want to expose such a gem to the night air. He had pointed out his window. Easy enough to find the right door.

I knock in the "Oh, Susanna, don't you cry for me" rhythm. If you're going to go banging on doors in the middle of the night, knock cute.

Door flies open.

"Oh, my God!" We both scream at once.

It is a man. No clothes on. Anywhere.

"Where's Bronston?" I do not look below the waist.

"Bronston?" He is guarded.

I take off my hat and move into the light so I do not look so dark and dangerous. "Charlie. Henry. You know." I put my hand up to show how tall, and kind of do a quick study of his smile.

"All right, come in." I am still staring him in the eyes like I have never stared anyone in the eyes before because it is taking every effort not to look *there*. I caught only a dash of hair, shadowed flesh . . .

"Put something on, okay? I'm shy."

"Sorry. I'm not, I should have thought. Be right back. I'm Don, by the way."

"Glad to meet you. Is he out with another girl?" I shout.

He comes back in wearing a white terry cloth robe.

"Want a drink? I'm having three, myself. I've been wondering actually if he's out with another boy." He pours himself a drink. "Want one?"

"I'll take a Coke. I'm not old enough to drink. Much. And I'm driving." So Bronston is one of them. He hates girls. He must have been laughing at me all the time for being so dumb.

"Are you going to cry?"

"No," I say. Sniffling. "Just hayfever."

"You look like you're going to cry. I may myself, if you'd like to join me, Susanna."

Now that's a good sign. "He must have told you about me, then."

"I would have known you anywhere. You look just like your father, especially the eyes. Have you seen him at all—it's been years, hasn't it? Jackson Lane's kid—what a thing that must be to live with. Henry says you're very unspoiled."

Comes, as they say, the dawn; the other shoe drops. I do not want it to be—but there is not one second, not a beat before I know it is true.

Jackson Lane's kid. "You must be Susanna," Jackson had said. (Wise father that knows his own child.)

"Yes, I think so." I am answering Don and I am also in that pool again in my red bathing suit, looking up at Jackson. But now I must redo me. I am not the same Susanna I was five minutes ago. I put down the glass because my hands are shaking. What is it they say about wives being the last to know? Daughters, I would say, can also be. Why am I not in a dead faint at this very moment? I feel everything in my body revving up for emergency. A major alert is on. Heart right in there punching and troops marching up to get the head from lifting away like a balloon.

"Eyes the color of eucalyptus leaves, like mine."

"My father was blond, like you." Did he move a muscle in his jaw when I said that? I am running that day through my head like rerunning a movie you saw when you were too young. I have had it in storage because it comes back with every detail intact, and as I run it I go through the motions of being here. I don't want to go to be alone with this. Will I break like a very sheer crystal glass when you press it? I will not.

"Are you hungry?" Don asks.

("Both of my daughters fell in love with actors. . . .")

"Probably," I say.

("Do you have double-jointed thumbs? . . . So do I.")

"Me too, would you like to fix some scrambled eggs?"

(And Alan, trying to tell me without telling me: "Hollywood is both a small town and a magical kingdom.")

"I don't know how," I say.

(And Scotty looking at Jackson when Jackson said, "This is my friend, Susanna Howard.")

"Me, either. Henry does the cooking, when he's around. This is my place. He's sharing it until he finds work. Don't say anything about that joke I made about another boy, you know what I mean? I'd hate for it to get around."

"Yes. Amazing how things do that. Get around. I'll try to make eggs. Give me a hint: where are they?" I am in the kitchen now which isn't even in its own room, more like a little wing of the living room.

"Refrigerator. Here, I'll help. Are you all right?"

"Yes, I'm fine—" I feel sweat like a sleek sugar frosting on my face. "I guess it would be hard to be a major star if you don't like girls." Or to stay a star if you try to see your own daughter. Grandmother knew he was there that day. She probably heard the same fight I heard. And she had him threatened. That's one possibility.

"It's not exactly like that." He takes the eggs from me because my hands are shaking so you can hear the yolks slosh against the shells. Or at least I can. Don says, "Henry is very fond of you."

I think I've embarrassed him. We break eggs into a flat pan and then put butter in and stir it all around. He probably figures I'm upset because of Bronston. That already is a tempest in a thunderstorm—where to begin with any of it. He tastes the eggs.

"They look like scrambled eggs," I say.

"Taste pretty good. Well, we've learned something."

"I'll say." And I laugh—I sit down and he just looks at me.

"Sure you're okay?"

"Fine. Listen, one thing, how long have you known about my father?" I do have an alive father. Somewhere.

"Known what?" He hushes me a moment, finger, to his lips, as we hear a car go by and seem to stop. But it goes on.

"That he is my father—" Alive father—now I have one and Val does not. And in that same moment I know she has always known too. How could she not say?

"I guess everyone just knows. One of those great Hollywood stories you hear. I'm sure everyone tells you how much you look like him."

"No. Actually not." I am not even sure I have noticed. Refused to see it—more likely.

I am about to search out a mirror when we hear the car. The door slam. Key turns in lock.

"Well," Bronston says, "a welcoming party. Susanna, isn't it late for you to be running around?"

"Oh, it's never too late for practically anything." My heart does not leap to see him. I don't even know what I'm still doing here. Except I'm also mad. It's like everyone in the world has ganged up and said let's not tell Susanna the truth about anything. They are right. I am clearly too stupid to be told the truth or trusted with it. Too crazy perhaps—is insanity a result of mixed blood? Jew and Christian? Or could they have been afraid I would tell someone—let it slip accidentally late one night and ruin the family name? It appears the only one left to tell in all of Hollywood is me.

"That's not quite true; I've got a splitting headache." His face is flushed; hair all scattered as though he has a daffodil on his head.

"You look beautiful when you're angry," I say. Grant to Hepburn. How did I get to be Grant? Or, for that matter, Jackson's child? How do I get to be anyone when everyone I thought I was is something else? And who is everyone else? Now that they are all different.

"Can it. I'm sorry, I just don't like surprises." He picks up our glasses and puts them in the kitchen.

"Well, I'm not wild for some of them myself," I say.

"Want me to wait in the other room?" Don says, and goes—fast. Bronston takes a dishrag and wipes his kitchen counter.

"I guess it was a bad idea," I start to take the plates into the kitchen, "but I've had an interesting time."

"I'll take care of that," Bronston says, being kind of Henry now. "I'll be with you in a minute." It could be worse. He could have added, "Miss Howard." I'm starting to laugh again. I mean, I tell myself, think about this. It is a very unusual kind of evening, for me. For a lot of people, actually. Almost everyone would find it startling. Bronston goes into the other room. Their bedroom? I do not want to think about that (but it would be interesting to know. They must look wonderful together. Statues dancing). Why am I thinking that now?

I hear Bronston shouting, ". . . wreck my chances . . . all over town . . . and you've been drinking . . . she's not brought up to understand . . ."

No, I certainly was not brought up to understand anything—even that my mother could have done it with Jackson Lane. *That,* God. Stop thinking. I look at the hem of my cloak which is turning a kind of faint purple with age, as black velvet will. Blue ages fastest of all. My prince puppet's cape, for instance, was royal blue and after six months it became periwinkle and then purple. I wonder how many songs there are with blue in the title and does "Mood Indigo" count, or blues, like "Good Morning, Blues." I should just go. I take my compact out and am about to see myself when Bronston sweeps out of the bedroom brushing his jacket briskly with a small clothing brush. And I see he has combed his hair. He is beautiful, but he is no Jackson.

"I'm out of codeine. Going to Schwab's. You go home. I'll call you tomorrow. Wait until you're invited next time, won't you?" He slams the door and I hear his car take off.

I wonder if I must thank my host before I leave. For everything.

Don comes out of the bedroom. "He has a terrible

temper. He gets into blind rages. He'll never forgive himself when he thinks about it. He's something of a fraud, you know . . . see all these books?"

He starts picking out books from the bookshelves on the wall above the couch, opening them, then shoving them back.

"His precious library. Hear them all crack? He hasn't read one of them. I'm sure he's quoted you passages. He has just memorized one passage from each book . . . he isn't anything he says he is."

"Neither," I say, "are a lot of people." Why didn't Jackson tell me? Why didn't someone? Did someone, and I just never heard it? "Well," I say, half to myself —defending Jackson and Bronston, I suppose—"you do have to watch out for yourself as an actor, protect yourself, and all that memorizing . . . it's more than I could do. And it isn't easy to know which book to quote part of when. I couldn't do that. I don't even know the names of that many books. Just tell him he doesn't have to call. I won't say anything to anyone. He'll be back." I guess Don will watch out the window—hoping, missing, like I do for Jackson. And do I do it now that he is my father? Do I miss him the same way?

My face is hot with shame—over all my confusions.

"It must be a hell of a night for you. You could stay here until morning—I can make up the couch. Don't worry about Henry—he'd understand, if you're tired. Listen, we'll probably all laugh about it in the morning."

"I don't think I'd better—"

He looks at the clock over the stove. "My God! Look at the time. I keep forgetting you're a kid."

And *whose*—I want to say—that's the point—whose kid! "Tell Henry I'll see him in the movies. Maybe."

I'm down the steps to my car. I am crying. Sing, Susanna, singin' makes it better, I hear Scotty telling me. Top of my lungs:

A thief he'll just rob you
And take what you have

But an inconstant lover . . .
Will lead to the grave.

Scotty . . . Scotty knows. Knew that day. That's why he kept looking at Jackson like that, wondering probably if Jackson was going to tell me.

He'll hug you and kiss you
And call you his own . . .

He never did. He never really did. I didn't listen. I never do. And I think I mean Jackson, not Bronston. Who told me I never listen? Val told me. Jackson never called me his own. He never called me. Period. I get into my car. Perhaps this is the only place I belong.

Bronston could have told me the truth, not started me off with lies and kisses. But why should Bronston be different from anyone else I know and love? To know me is to lie. Because I'm so cute when I'm believing you. No one will ever see how darling I look in my black lace bra. I will die a virgin and a bastard. "The Illegitimate Virgin." Register that title. The Rabbi will say, "Believe it or not, no one ever loved her." (If the Rabbi can bury someone who is suddenly not a whole Jew.) Jackson will come to my grave with flowers every year like the woman who brings the flowers to Valentino. Will they wonder if he was my father or my lover. His white cowboy hat will shade his face. No, no one will wonder, stupid. Everyone knows.

A bastard. I wonder what the feminine is. *Bâtarde*. Sounds better in French.

I gun the motor down Crescent Heights and run right through the red light across Sunset. Then a U-turn in a driveway and up the hill to Sunset. "There was a young cowgirl all dressed in white linen, dressed in white linen, all cold as the snow."

I cannot remember the words.

"There was a young cowgirl . . ." Bronston: damn. Why didn't he say we were just friends to begin with?

How to kill a liar? I would tie him up and let him watch as I outline the plan on a blackboard. When he looks away, I will tie his head so he cannot move. I will sew the eyelids with black thread like mascara so that the liar cannot blink and look away. I will let him hear the sound of the sharpening of the knives.

But it is all my fault. Because I believe everyone. And what Liar do I have in mind?

Oh, God! I am this murderous concoction. My father with the wrong body. I could have fooled Bronston and pretended I was a boy and he would love me. "Listen," I want to say to this man in his Cadillac at the stoplight next to me, "if you'll take me to the Springs for a weekend and say 'I adore you,' I'll go all the way." I see myself in creamy white cashmeres being a well-kept girlfriend. He likes to see me trying on bathing suits with my high heels on.

He winks. I wink back. I said I am brave in my car.

Oleanders. If you eat the branches you die instantly. I see a Last Supper. Jackson in the center. I feed them all oleander Jell-O. After the fingerbowls.

I want to talk to Val. I feel like a puppet with all strings snipped. Someone has to tell me how to be. How do I feel? What do I do? Do they think my grandparents ended it? Do they think he walked out on my mother? Or didn't want me? Or that it's one of those neat bits of Hollywood gossip?

How I was made: in the back seat of a car? In his empty dressing room? Conceived in a trailer? (Does that destine me for stardom, like "Born in a Trunk"?)

Did he lie there asleep afterward, leaving you to find your clothes and go off to Grandfather's limo, smiling?

It would have been in March, I think, counting back from my November birthday. Perhaps an early spring passion.

Or did you walk down the wooden stairs to the beach and lie next to the jetty of rocks, chilly in the fog?

Was it a lot of times, or just this once?

I imagine me lying in his arms, like Gail Russell, or

Hedy Lamarr—or my mother. Do regular children imagine lying in their parent's arms, being the other one?

Was it an accident?

Just check yes or no?

And, by the way, were you both drunk and was I the side effect of a wild Hollywood party?

Val would think about these things. The things she says I never think about. I do. I just do not *like* to. I look at my face in the rear-view mirror. Did I love his face when I saw it looking at me because it was my face? I look like Jackson soft, and Jackson sad. I put a smile on to see if I smile like him. I do not see glittering assurance.

For an instant I feel excited. I should be, I tell myself, I know my father. My father is . . . somewhere out there.

My God, are You *still* my God? (Even if the Rabbi deserts?) Listen, don't get huffy because I'm illegitimate, You know. According to my father's people (my father!), Your son was like that—there wasn't exactly a wedding. Maybe Jackson is secretly Jewish. No. Let's not get carried away. There is nothing Jewish about Jackson Lane. Jews do not hit the road and run away. But the Prodigal Son was Jewish. Jackson could be the Prodigal Father. Listen, Susanna, I tell myself, heading down the Strip now, one thing—you can't be sure about anything ever again. Does it count that I didn't know, or is it like school where not getting the assignment is no excuse for not getting it right?

I pull into a public phone at the Union Oil station. It is late to call but this is something of an emergency. I remember sitting in the car with Jackson at the Standard station on Sunset, using the phone there. "Listen," I could have said, "I'm spending the day with Daddy." I looked back at him while I was calling, looking at him, his face turned toward the sun. Or were his eyes kind of watching me? Was he wondering what to do? Is he like me—I mean am I like him: we start something, get all wound up, and can't turn back? Did he worry about what he'd started? Should have—fourteen years before that!

Daddy. Did someone call Jackson on the day I was born and say, "Congratulations, you're a daddy"? A few cigars passed around on the set, perhaps. Or do they only do that with sons? Would he have fought more to see me if I had been his son? Would he have taken off with him, running around the country? Is there a son somewhere, another daughter, a whole tribe of us to carry on the face if not the name? I am Susanna Lane. But that's probably made up too. I see his hand reach out now to touch my shoulder and he looks around, and doesn't, and looks for an instant—now I see it—torn, and is that look behind his eyes a bit of sadness? Or is what I see now only me? Can I assume that his expressions can be interpreted the same way mine are?

I call Val. Lillian answers. "Hello, who is it?" She expects emergency, I can hear alarm in her voice. What can she ever expect but emergency?

"Nothing's wrong, Aunt Lillian. I just have to talk to Val." I hope she does not hear the cars going by.

"Susanna? My God, it's awfully late. What's happened?"

"Nothing, really. I just—can I please talk to Val?"

"But she isn't here, dear, she's at C.A.'s tonight." That, on the edge of everything, makes me mad. She says she never likes to stay overnight because she doesn't like to leave Lillian alone whenever I have asked her to stay over at Perdido. "Okay, well I'll call over there."

"Susanna, where are you?"

"Nowhere—really. I mean I'm fine. I'm sorry I woke you."

"That's all right. Are you sure there's nothing I can do?"

"No."

I call on C.A.'s own phone.

"What's going on?" she says.

"Nothing, I need to talk to Val."

"Val isn't here."

"Lillian said she was."

"Oh. That's right. Well, she isn't. But don't say anything. What's going on?"

"Nothing much. Do you know where she is?"

"Nope. Really don't. Val doesn't tell me everything, you know."

"Okay, okay."

Now I wonder myself where Val is. Not with Paul. They are, she says, just platonic friends. And Paul went with his father up to Sacramento for a sneak preview. You worry about a picture when they're sneaking it that far out of town. But I don't know even if that's true. Maybe nothing is true unless I see it with my own eyes. However, I saw Jackson with my own eyes and he wasn't who he seemed to be. Or did I just make it up my own way, while he was being a good father, teaching me about ropes and watching out to see I didn't get sunburned?

In my bed, I am trying to distract myself by working up a little number with Don and Bronston, trying to imagine them. I get as far as seeing them in a kind of tango, glaring at each other, grasping at the backs of each other's necks, their wonderful furred male thighs crossing and touching. I did notice Don's thighs, the long muscles sweeping down to his lean, perfect knees. I have probably not gone crazy from this if I can calmly lie here placing two beautiful men in different arrangements. Do men blow in each other's ears? Or is that something only girls are supposed to like?

"Susanna?"

It is my mother. Who else does she think is in my room at night as she tiptoes in?

I whip my hands above the covers and put clothes back on the men. I must clean up my imagination when she is in the room. She can see my dreams in the dark; I am always being watched. (For signs of her own tendencies? The tendency that resulted in me. One gov-

erness told my mother I had certain "tendencies" when
she caught me doing my Grable pin-up imitation in the
mirror naked. When I was ten. From the back I could
have fooled a sailor.)

"Are you asleep?" This is the major dumb question
of the world.

"Yes," I say.

"Well, good night, then."

Has she planned to come in one night and sit by the
bed and tell me what everyone else already knows?

Before she closes my door I call out to her, "What
was Jackson Lane really like?" Fan mag headlines flash
before me. She hangs against the wall, I sit up, leaning
forward in bed. "Tell me about Jackson Lane's private
life." I see her white gown lean to the side, her diamond
rings flash. "What is the truth about Jackson Lane; the
story no one knows; the behind-the-scenes scandal that
rocked Hollywood?"

"Who's been telling you such things?"

"Butcher, baker, candlestick maker. Everyone." I am
yelling.

She comes and stands next to the bed. "Don't wake
the whole house, Susanna. You know, children can be
terribly cruel."

"It's not children."

"People love to tease you. You are so gullible." I hear
her kind of waiting, wondering if it is a test, wondering
how much I really know.

I could say right out, "Am I Jackson Lane's daughter?" But I can't. Why don't I want to hear her say it—
or to hear myself say it?

"Do you want to talk reasonably, or are you just
going to scream at me?"

"I don't want to talk about it." Why am I saying
that? Do I want to hang on to him for myself?

"Would you like some nice warm cocoa?" She has
never asked me such a question.

"Yes." I pull down my nightgown and get out of bed.

"Do you know where they keep it?" she asks as we

hit the kitchen. She moves about it like a shell-shocked soldier in a mine field. "I'll get a little nightcap myself," she says.

I find the cocoa powder and put it by the stove. She comes back in rattling ice cubes like dice. We fool around the stove, turning knobs and darting back from it. If I knew how to work it, it would be amusing to get her to admit she doesn't know how.

"Don't ever," she says, "tell anyone." Is she talking only about the stove? Or her drink? Or about Jackson?

"Okay," I say, "it isn't so terrible not to work a stove. A lot of people can't. I'm sure Lana Turner can't. Or Hedy Lamarr, or a lot of movie stars, Evelyn Ames, a lot of them." My mother I'm sure enjoys being compared to a movie star. I could say I'm sure even Jackson Lane can't work a stove.

I want to say I like at least the way she knew the right thing to give someone late at night and that I know she meant to do it. But I am too busy thinking about how tomorrow I will tell Val that my mother doesn't even know how to work the stove. And then I will throw in a little something about Jackson.

I settle for some cold milk and we go up to her room.

"Hush," she says, "don't wake Myron."

"Doesn't Myron know either?—well at least I'm not the only one. . . ." I look at myself in the mirrored wall ·of closets she has. Does she flinch when I walk in sometimes, looking like him? How could I have missed it.

Now I sit in a chair, picking bits of gilt off the frame.

She sits on her chaise longue. "It was beautiful," she tells me, and turns away. Is this as much as she is going to say? I do not want to hear that. I cannot ever again think of Jackson and sex. How do you completely redesign who someone is in your life? We are talking about it without talking about it and I wonder if that is so I can never throw it back in her face and say, "But you told me yourself."

"I heard you come in very late," she said. But not scolding. She sips at her drink. "I always used to stay up waiting for my father to come home. Mother would go to bed early then—she felt it was important for him to preside over his business parties alone. She loved to be home."

I am not sure my mother understands what I have learned has anything to do with me.

"I miss my father so much," she continues. "I used to go in and sit with him late at night and he would tell me such wonderful stories. He was always so kind to me. So sweet and gentle."

I will not say I miss mine too. And I will not say that Lillian said Grandfather was a tyrant sometimes and had a temper like a fire-god.

"Did Grandfather say you couldn't marry him?" I do not mention Jackson's name.

"No. He didn't have to . . . Susanna." She snaps back into focus. "Don't pick at the chair. Look at all that gold on the floor!"

I cannot think of anything smart to say so I scoop it up and put it in an ashtray.

"I'm sorry," she says, "that you have been confused by someone. I wanted things to be so simple. I had a very simple childhood."

"I wonder why you think anyone's trying to confuse me . . . I mean, where would you get that idea? What is possibly confusing about making up a father who is dead? And how did Grandfather rig a birth certificate? What is confusing about having an alive father who skips town when he dares to see you—and what is confusing about a mother who wants you to have a simple childhood and never tells you the truth?"

"If you're going to be sarcastic then we'll talk about this thing another time. If you think you want to," she adds. I cannot tell if she is disappointed that we may have to, or disappointed that we are not talking about it now.

"This thing?" I say, raising my eyebrows.

"Oh, Susanna, don't be angry. I tried to do the best I could. Don't punish me by asking questions I'm not even

sure I know how to answer any more. It's too late."
Does she mean it's too late in the night, or too late for
her to remember?

"Okay. I just want to know—it's fair for me to know
something, only fair." I'm getting upset and she's getting wet around the eyes. I bet she wishes Grandmother
was here and she could go and be with her. (And so do
I.) "Did he try to see me before? Did you keep him
away? Did you really believe I would never find out?"

"Susanna, don't, don't push me, if I've only lied to
you before how will you believe anything I say now?
and I'm so tired—I didn't keep him away—when something happens long ago and you're young and in love
you don't think about what will happen much later,
and when you're hurt and frightened and guilty you do
things—you listen to people. Susanna, I'm not very
strong and I . . . God . . . why did you have to remind
me?"

She's crying now, but quietly. I know my mother's
capable of louder crying than this. I think of Lillian crying over Alan and now my mother's crying over Jackson. I put my arms around her as she buries her face in
her cream-soft hands.

"Careful, careful," she says, quickly moving those
hands to her head. "Don't mess my hair."

Does she intend to sleep only from the neck down, or
do her dreams only approach her when every hair is in
place?

VAL IS GOING EARLY TO NEW YORK. LILLIAN IS GOING with her to help her find a room in one of the places where students stay around the school; when Val is settled Lillian will come back to her job. How lonely she will be. We have gone shopping together for our fall clothes. Myron and my mother—it is now impossible to say "my parents"—are hoping I will catch the college thing. I cannot understand why anyone *wants* more school after an entire childhood of it. Val and I are standing in Saks trying on cashmeres; of course, it is the hottest day in August.

"I can see me walking into class with my rhinestone-studded silver-dollar loafers, none of this penny stuff, and they all stare and say, 'Oh, that must be the one from Hollywood. Bastard, you know.' 'Pity.' The others will say: 'Well, how did she get in?' 'Oh, pull. Lots of pull.' Do you think he really was scared of our family? Do you think that's why he never tried to see me again?"

"Oh, cut it out, Susanna," Val says. "Either do something about it or drop it. Do you think gray?" She pulls a pale gray cashmere over her head and looks at herself in it.

"Well, it's Eastern. I like it a lot in another color."

The only thing that makes me want to go to college now is that I will miss Val. The morning after I found out about Jackson she called me first thing: "Why were you checking up on me last night?"

"I wasn't," I said. "I needed to talk to you."

"At two thirty in the morning? It was a little awkward."

"Well, where were you?—never mind. I know. None of my business."

"All right. Now. What happened to you?"

I wait. I thought about how to tell her. How would she put such a thing? "About Jackson," I said.

"Oh, Susanna . . ." She is expecting my usual wail.

"No. I found out and I wanted to know why you never told me who he was. And how long you have known—"

"Susanna. Listen. We can't do this over the phone. Meet me at—not the Club—the Country Mart—okay? I'll leave now. I'm sorry. Now you'll be there? You're all right?"

It was almost worth it, feeling so hurt, to hear the concern—to have her rush to be with me. She did understand. Completely. When we met she told me she had said something to Alan when we were about thirteen, a year before I met him, about how I looked like a small Jackson Lane and Alan had told her "that's hardly surprising." Val said Lillian was furious and made her promise never to say anything. "And every time I looked at you, or heard you talk about him as though you were talking about a lover, not your father, I thought it was the craziest, saddest thing in the world. And I did plan to tell you myself, on your eighteenth birthday—I knew it would happen in some awful, dumb way. I told my mother that. And she said it was what Vera wanted."

"Do you think my mother would ever have told me?" I asked Val.

"Why don't you ask her that?" I told her about my mother's reaction. "She probably wouldn't remember what she meant to do about that either—Did they tell you anything else—about him, what happened—anything?"

"Nothing," Val said. "I think Daddy would have—but . . ." And she spread her hands out in a gesture of "There's no hope there . . . now." And then she said, "I'm not sure anyone but your mother and your father really knows and it doesn't really matter now. What matters, Susanna, is what you do about how you feel —I really know about things like this. You can't look back."

So now we're moving through Shoes, lifting, looking, rejecting. "Val. You said do something about Jackson or drop it— What do you mean, do something?"

"Okay. Once more with feeling. Susanna, listen this time. You take your past. Little jigsaw pieces put together day by day into a perfect picture. Not so perfect, but a picture. Gets kicked to bits. Won't go back same way. Plus pieces missing. Either throw it out because it is past; decide it's not needed. Or find pieces." She takes the shoes she wants to try on to a salesman.

"You mean I should find Jackson? Just take off? Like that?" And why not? I am thinking.

"I mean, figure out what you want and do it. You've always done that anyway."

Part Three

1954

ANDREW PUTS ME ON THE TRAIN TO DENVER. AND I
get off at San Bernardino, which is perfect, because
where Jackson got off when he came to Hollywood, I
am starting out my search for him. Then I take a cab
to Pasadena to switch my tickets around. I'm also going
to trade them in for coach tickets, which will give me
extra money just in case. You don't take this kind of
trip first class. Least I've never heard any songs about
anyone hitting the road in a private compartment. I wait
in Pasadena for the train to San Francisco where Scotty's playing at the hungry i. He would have met me if
I'd called or written, but you never know with adults
when they're going to check up with each other about
things they're not sure people my age ought to be doing.

And I wasn't so sure I'd be going. This isn't the kind
of thing you write or make phone calls about. When
I'm talking to Scotty, face to face, he'll be more likely
to help me out because he's going to see I mean it and
I'm going anyway.

Myron and my mother agreed with me that it was a
very intelligent idea for me to visit C.A. at the University of Colorado to see what that kind of college was
like and then to go on and stay with Val in New York
to look at some of the Eastern schools. Perhaps I could
find a college and get in for the second term in February.
They sent me off with traveler's checks and Mary ordered first-class train tickets, because, I said, "I might
as well see the country as I go."

Of course as I was packing, my mother decided to
think about it. "I'm not sure a young girl should just be

running around by herself. . . ." I had my record player going so my mother had to talk louder. I took a speaker out of an old phonograph, and Frank helped me put a real long wire onto it, hooked up to my record player so I can have music coming out on both ends of the room. This makes a lot of sound and drives Myron and my mother crazy. That and the song "The Huckle Buck," which my mother says is "filthy." Myron is calmer about that. He says, "Well, Vera, we used to dance to songs our parents hated. No one ever likes their kids' music." And my mother says, "I hate the word 'kid.' "

"Well, maybe you'd like to come with me," I said quietly, rolling my sweaters up and shoving them into corners of the suitcase.

She gave me this what-do-you-mean-by-that look and said, "I couldn't possibly go."

"Nothing can go wrong, Mrs. Howard," Mary said, seeing that I had all my tickets and her carefully typed itinerary in my bag.

And Dorothy stifled a hoot and said, but my mother didn't hear under the music, "Famous last words."

"The New York office is coming out and Myron will be very busy. He's worried. So I really don't want to leave." This is to convince all of us she actually considered going.

"What's Myron worried about?" I asked.

"Susanna—you're not taking those jeans?" my mother said.

"I'm going riding with C.A."

My mother, of course, did not tell me what Myron is worried about. Well, it would not be home without things I'm not supposed to know about going on.

Now I call C.A.—it is a fortune in change.

"C.A.—I'm not coming. I'm going right on East—I'll write and explain. But, listen, if my parents call . . . C.A., tell them I'm looking around campus or something. Or taking an exam. They'll like that."

"And they won't believe it. I'll think of something," she says. "Who is he? It sounds terrific."

"Well, it's someone very special." Let her think what she wants. I keep forgetting everyone knows. But not that I'm going off to find him.

"I'm sorry you're not going to make it. You'd love it here. Riding, great scenery, good driving, tennis, swell guys. And lots of movies. Everything you'd want in a college."

"Rain check, okay?"

"Suit yourself, pal."

I get on the train. I'm really doing it. I will call Val from Frisco, so she can cover for me.

I HAVEN'T REALLY TRAVELED SINCE I WENT EAST WITH Myron and my mother when I was ten. We had two bedrooms on the Super Chief and a drawing room in between. I had a governess on the way there—Mallory, who had big, warm breasts you could put your head right between when she hugged you. She was a relief from Emmalene the Enema Queen, which was what Paul Daroff called that one. She said: "Yes. This cures earaches, don't argue with me."

To protect myself against sneak attacks I used to put my overalls on under my pajamas and then I tied the lasso Roy Rogers gave me when I visited him on the set once from the door to my bedpost. You're never too sick to defend yourself.

Now, Mallory was terrific. She liked to hang around and play poker in the club car at night after my parents were asleep. And when she would swing out of her bed, which was the lower, I'd reach out and tweak at her hair and then pretend to be asleep and she'd say, "Well, you're not sleeping anyway, why don't you just come along for the fun," and I'd watch and drink ginger ale (I did not drink Shirley Temples. I wanted my own drink or forget it. Susanna Midnights: Coke, black coffee, chocolate syrup with whipped cream *on the top.* And one really great strawberry. That was my idea of the perfect drink—it included everything I was not allowed to have or was allergic to.)

When we got to New York my mother got a telegram saying that they'd found out Mallory was on parole for child molestation and so they sent her back. I think, now, that my mother wasn't so much jealous of the governesses I liked, Tucky and Mallory—which I used to think—but was afraid that I'd become a lesbian. This is how I have figured that out: Val and I once found some Havelock Ellis books in her old house and I remember reading that lesbians often got started because they were in love with their fathers and I guess my mother worried that if I found out I would be. Also a lot of them got started just from having general father troubles. And I would say, however you look at it, I have a father problem.

I saw a woman like that once. She arranges concerts in L.A. and my mother knows her from when she used to arrange these concert benefits. I think my mother hated doing that. I would if I was as good as she is on the piano. Someone should be arranging a benefit to hear her, is what I used to think. And she hated to hear that. I don't think Mother had a father problem. Although I haven't thought about that. Maybe she wanted Grandfather to herself. . . . So: this woman had on a black man's suit except with a skirt and she had on a white shirt and a tie and short hair. She had very intense eyes and she looked at me real close and invited us to come for tea. My mother said that would be nice in the way she does when she has no intention of doing something. And I felt the lesbian knew it because of the way she nodded as if to say, "Of course you won't come." And I felt embarrassed and wanted to say I would simply adore to come, because I was interested in the way she looked as if she understood me—even things about me I don't understand. Of course, like everyone else she probably was thinking this is *that* one. With the actor father. But my mother was breathing fast, getting ready to end the conversation and whip me on up Wilshire Boulevard.

Thinking about her now, I remembered Signora Giordano, Angelo's aunt, and the way she sat and the cigarette. I'll bet she was one too. Two important women in music and both like that. But you'd have to be if you didn't get married and how could you be important and be married? It doesn't work, having a marriage and a career. Unless you're a movie star, and that doesn't work too well. Except Evelyn Ames. But look how often she's been married.

I wonder if often counts as much as durability, or is marriage like clothes, as my mother says when her four-hundred-dollar suits arrive, and Myron says, "Vera!"

"One expensive suit is better than a lot of cheap ones."

I myself think I would like one good marriage like one good governess. Once you get used to one person touching you why change around? I say. Touching. I am not going to touch myself on this trip. Not even once. I have told God I will not do it if He helps me find Jackson.

I sit very far away from the woman in the seat next to me. I am thinking about people doing things at you, around you, on you. I love the idea of sex. But it's the touching . . . I want to float with someone, close as air and just as light, like ghosts we will be together. I want to see that look in his eyes that Marge and Gower Champion have, and dance, lying down dancing is how it should be. Some day I'll meet someone who gives me that feeling, all air and freedom and nothing yucky sticking into me. We'll float like phantoms, running to each other. That's why Bronston was a perfect person for me. But why do I dream about it differently? In my dream the man from the Chevron station opens me like the hood of my car and tests me with his dipstick, gently in and out, wiping and dipping and looking at me and he puts his hands on me and says let's take a look at that and I say sure and I'm just there like my car, and his face is right there at me with his blond mustache . . . and then everything gathers in me and warms and opens and I haven't thought of him in months. I get this feeling like sparklers spreading all over my body and it is like the engine starting and then charging off into the air and I rise and fall back in glittering pieces, shaking in little tics here and there until I come back together.

I am just remembering a dream, God. I am not. *Not* thinking about sex.

I think I am going to give the man from the Chevron station dark hair.

I can almost feel the rain through the window of the train. I wonder if people sitting next to you can pick up your thoughts. I'll bet people you're close to can pick them up all the way across the country. Like Val, knowing I was up to something. I'll bet Jackson somewhere feels all itchy, like I'm on his trail.

There were loads of servicemen on the train then. And my mother walked me fast on by them, Mallory following at a distance, hands in her jacket pockets, sauntering along. She was getting pretty rich from this trip with her poker games. Servicemen grinned at my mother and a couple of them winked at her. She liked it until she remembered she shouldn't and then she'd keep her eyes forward, not missing a trick, nevertheless, and not walking with any less of a sway in her sling-back high heels. I'd lie in my room in the hotel at night naked and imagine what hips and breasts were going to feel like when I got them. Then, with the New York lights which were so bright, I'd look in the full-length mirror and practice swaying and imagine servicemen looking at me. And I dreamed about them big and blond.

Yeah. Big and blond and looking like Jackson Lane.

I put my suitcases in a locker in San Francisco, which looks just like it did in *I Remember Mama* and *San Francisco* except it's in color and seems to be pretty much on its feet. I wonder, looking up at the hills where Tracy, Gable, and MacDonald were standing. I'm singing, "It's Susanna, don't you cry for me. I'm here to see ol' Frisco, with my geetar on my knee." The thing about being on a train is every time you get off you have a chance to be in a whole new movie with yourself. The train is the montage of the past and the place is the new start. That must be why Jackson keeps moving.

* * *

I check into the Fairmont Hotel where Myron stays when he goes up to Frisco for previews. I'm Susanna Jackson, I say, out from New York and I put down Val's address. It's too early to call Scotty and since I'm here I'll have a look around, so I pick up a tourist guide. I feel like one of the people you'd see looking down at you from their buses when they'd come gliding by the outside of the studio imagining what was going on inside, seeing glimpses of sequinned ladies glinting through the gates, plumes bobbing here and there above the crowds of extras and grips and assistants, imagining they were going to see Clark Gable or Lana Turner. Sometimes when we were very little, Grandfather would take Val and me around the lot in a carriage pulled by horses from one of the costume movies and you'd see Roman columns go by and men carrying SPQR banners, and trees on trolleys rumbling like giants past Indian tribes in gorgeous feathers, mingling with dancing girls in harem suits with ankle bracelets. And always visiting servicemen in full dress uniforms saluting warriors in Roman outfits and lancers and slaves in chains and prisoners in spanking clean jail stripes. Writers calling fast lines across the throngs to each other; directors marching along, barking orders to a covey of A.D.'s, and editors with secretaries tapping along on tippy high heels, taking notes. And producers and big stars gliding through the bright mobs in limousines (except Hepburn who always walked) like dark floats. And the tourists would peer in or go by houses with their movie star maps and look down at us in our limousines as though were were "attractions," and I guess they'd come back home and talk about this strange place Hollywood. But I get the feeling, looking out here from the cable car I'm riding, that a place is only strange when it isn't your own.

I've been to Telegraph Hill and imagined how the earthquake looked from here, and I've wandered around Chinatown, looking at dried ducks and trying on silk kimonos with dragons on, wrapping them around me

so I look very Chen Yu. I should really pick one up for
Paul, because the Daroff studio symbol is a dragon but
button-down people wear very few dragons, and I pick
up a dozen fortune cookies and open them all until I
find one I like: *Seek and it will be found,* and they must
have known something because right here I screech to
a halt: Jackson. On a poster in Chinese. I go into the
actual public theater by myself—if you're going to do
everything new, why not?

I pick up some popcorn and a Coke. *Wake of the Red
Witch* is on, not Jackson's movie but one of my fa-
vorites. I slide into a seat and there's Luther Adler being
evil and Gail Russell tormented. Look how he talks
about the "pearls." No one has ever gotten so much out
of the word pearls. I feel already more at home with
a movie I know and love. Now the previews of coming
attractions come on and here's *Clipper King.*

Jackson, I grin to myself, there's my Dad up there. It
is a message. I am on the right track. What did people do in a strange place before movies? *Clipper King:*
I loved Jackson in that. All in navy blue and gold braid,
and then here he is in his white pants with the black
boots and his shirt open all the way in the end when
they've won the battle and he dances this jig with his
men on the deck and then whirls around and grabs a
fid just in time to bean this guy who they'd thought was
dead but is sneaking up on him. And then, in the last
scene I remember, he comes home to Maureen O'Hara,
standing there with their little girl, and he lifts her high
over his head. How I wanted to be that little girl. I am
that little girl.

"Share the joke, sweetie?" A man sidles into the seat
next to me. My mother always said (whenever the subject came up), "No one ever goes to movies alone.
There are white slave traders in public theaters looking
for young girls."

And I would say, "Don't be silly."

I grab my purse and run, furious because I miss one of
the great close-shots of all time as I'm going. I look to

see if he is following. "They inject you with dope," my mother said—and I hate shots—"and then shanghai you away to where we will never find you." And here I am in Chinatown making it a cinch deal for him to drag me off to one of those opium dens I've seen in movies. And they would never get me back again. I imagine my mother taking a little nap. "Fiddle-dee-dee, I'll find Susanna tomorrow."

I've shaken the white slaver and I call Scotty. "Come right over," he says, which is just like Scotty. None of this "What are you up to?" business. He's got a girl-friend, Marcia, living with him in a copy of one of those houses in *I Remember Mama*. You can imagine Barbara Bel Geddes upstairs writing her diary. They only have half the house, but Scotty tells me right away to stay with them. "If you're runnin' away you can't afford the Fairmont." And Marcia says, "It's not in the tradition of any runaways I've ever known. You have to do these things right, you know." Marcia is a weaver, with really long red hair and bare feet in sandals. A definite bohe-mian. And she's kind of chubby—someone was prob-ably always saying, "She has such a beautiful face," which meant they would love her to lose weight. She's wearing a skirt she built herself—all purple and tawny with fringes and a black turtleneck.

Scotty doesn't ask me any questions at first and I'm not going to say anything until I'm sure he won't try to talk me out of what I'm doing. He shows me this in-credible shiny new Dobro guitar (you just say Dobro, of course, if you know what you're talking about). I've never seen one that wasn't kind of beat up. Looks like it's made out of Sheffield, like my grandmother's silver tea service.

"I'm not running away," I say, finally, as we're finish-ing supper, getting ready to go over to the hungry i. "Not really."

"We all do, Susie, one way or another. Some people just have adventures in their heads. Some guys run across the world and never find anything." And he leans back and looks at me. "So where are you going?" At least he waited to ask. And he's asking like he'd ask anyone, not just a kid.

"Well." I pause in this way I have, grinning at Scotty and Marcia, then beginning brightly like it says on lead sheets to cheerful songs: "Here's what . . ." And I stop —and I say it all at once very fast: "I found out Jackson's my father and I went to find him or our family— his and mine—and I figured you'd know as I'm not mad you never told me 'cause no one did—*but* I figure you're the only one now who can help and you got to. Okay?" Now I take a deep breath.

"Well, Susanna. Now, I don't know—and I'll tell you the truth—where Jackson is. I think we ought to talk about this tonight, I may be able to help you, if this is what you really want to do, and I guess it is— it's what I'd do—so don't worry. . . ."

I sure would like some of these wrought-iron earrings or hanging copper things like Marcia and a lot of the others are wearing at the hungry i and I have to get a black turtleneck now, and maybe a straight black skirt like some of the girls have. I adore it here—all smoky and dark and real hip. Scotty is wonderful—he dedicates "Lonesome Traveler" to me—"To my friend, Susie, who's setting out to see what she can see," which is a good sign he won't go back on his word and why would I think he would? I wouldn't be here if Scotty was that kind of guy. I also see myself up there—playing, on a high stool, with my foot up on the rung and everyone clapping. This kind of nighttime place is my kind of place. I like the dark in movies and nightclubs where you can imagine yourself up there.

We go across the street after Scotty's last set is over, and sit in an open-air cafe like one you'd see in a musical about Paris. San Francisco is just made to be in movies.

Marcia's the kind of girlfriend I'd like to be for someone—calm and gentle and always making nice things. Men love it when you make things for them. And I think it's only your girlfriends who want you to be real skinny, so you look real chic to go around with. If Jackson was my real, live-in father, I would learn to knit and make him thick white sweaters and afghans for his boat with its name knitted into one corner. I wonder where he did put that boat. When I called the yard where we went that day they said, of course, in a very guarded way, that they had no information on that subject. He would never have sold *Farewell,* but how can you say for sure "he never," or, for that matter, "he always," about Jackson.

"All right, Susie-anna," Scotty says, "the day Jack brought you to meet me, I told him he ought to tell you."

"Was that," I ask, "what you were arguing about?"

He puts six spoonfuls of sugar in his coffee and stirs it around. "That was part of it. I wanted him to take a stand about the blacklisting thing—but that's another thing. Anyway, he knew you'd find out when you were ready."

"That's what everyone says. Sort of. I just wish he'd told me—or seen me more—don't you think he wanted to?—was he scared of my parents? Did he say anything?"

"I think he got as close to doing what he could for you just being with you then, Susie. There are different kinds of bravery or honesty, whatever you want to call it, and, for Jack, that was a big deal."

A couple of kids who were at the "i" come asking Scotty for his autograph and I think Marcia looks more pleased even than he is. He signs some cards they give him, and continues, and I feel closer to Jackson already—it feels like when he was signing autographs. It must mean something. I know it.

"There are things some people just can't handle—and you get into habits or patterns of how you react to difficulty, or success, which for someone like Jack was pretty much the same thing. I think most people when they get to be stars of one kind or another think it's goin' to change them, change their whole past, take all the hard times away, and then there it is and no matter how many old friends they don't see much—"

"Scotty—" Marcia looks at him. She hears the bitterness I hear for the first time. I guess he must have been jealous of Jackson—I guess you couldn't but be jealous of a friend who gets to be a star when you're babysitting merry-go-rounds. But Jackson must have felt that. It must be awful to know how your friends can't help feeling; so no wonder you keep away—to keep from reminding them.

I am eating the most wonderful chocolate éclair. I have decided not to be allergic on this trip and to only eat everything I've never been allowed to, everything that is traife and everything my mother hates. I have had ham sandwiches and hot dogs already twice.

"Don't reach too much to figure Jackson out, Susie. And don't use him to figure yourself out. I think it's swell that you're trying to find him. Well, maybe not swell, but just natural. But don't lose sight of what you want to do—or what you thought about before— I don't think finding him will change you one way or the other."

"I keep saying I'm not running away."

"Susie," Scotty says, "now, listen to me. Do you have any idea what you spent today—what it costs to travel around? Taxis, restaurants. Have you thought how much it's going to cost every day?"

"Well. If I run out I'll find a job."

"Doing what?"

"I'll say I'm working my way through college. If worse comes to worst. And work in a diner. I can wait tables: take off from the left, serve on the right. I've watched that operation for years. Anyway, I'm not going to be on the road for days. I've got train tickets and I'm just changing my schedule around a little. It's nothing so drastic. I've thought about all the emergencies."

There's a long silence, and Scotty's thinking.

"Okay. Jackson has a sister in Illinois. Now, she's

married and she's a different kind than we are, so I don't know how she'll be about all this—and she's not likely to know where he is more'n I do—and . . ." he's thinking again, "there's . . ." Silence.

"There's what?" I say.

"I guess they have a kid. That's all."

"That's not all. You were going to say something else."

"No, I wasn't."

He was. But Scotty never tells you anything once he's made up his mind not to. And he's paying up our check. I start to put some money down. "Now you better cut out the grand Hollywood gestures if you're goin' to make this trip."

Probably this "grand Hollywood gesture" was the kind of thing Jackson did that Scotty hates.

"You know, if you'd been practicing, you wouldn't have to worry about waiting on tables, you could get yourself room and board, anyway, playing in little places. Long as you're near a college, you could even pick up some money. Not much. But it would be good experience."

"Am I good enough?"

"Unless you've got worse."

"I've not got worse."

"You can probably swap some songs, pick things up. Don't fool away this time."

"Well. I'll worry about that after I find Jackson." And it's not fooling away time, looking for a famous movie star everyone recognizes and no one can find. Aside from everything else, it's a terrific notion for a property which Myron would snap up. If it was anyone else doing the looking. I will try to explain it to him that way after I come back. There's not a question in my mind that I'm coming back. I'll stay with Jackson only part time, which he will probably like better anyway. But I will never really leave Perdido. That is for real sure.

So I sleep over with Scotty and Marcia, who gives

me one of her black turtleneck sweaters. "A friend who wants me to lose weight sent it three sizes too small."

"I'll wear it every day," I say.

"I'd have it cleaned every couple of months," she says.

I look divine in black with my thick blond hair pulled up in a pony tail coming right down my back, although what is really great is when I sweep it over one shoulder and let it all fan out.

The next day Scotty's singing at some post-registration rally at Stanford University and we set off to Palo Alto in his ancient blue-green Hudson, which sounds great because it needs a new muffler. The train East stops in Paly so I can pick it up later. We drive along the scenic route through mountains with pine trees and gates to mansions here and there and then the mountains slope down into soft golden hills studded with dark green gnarled old live oaks where real cows are lounging around like kids at the beach, and come to the university, all tawny stone and very serious-looking and full of students walking around with books. The boys all have blond crew cuts, white T-shirts, red and white baseball jackets, khaki pants, and carry their books under one arm, resting down into a hand. The girls wear Bermudas and carry their books in both arms leaning them on their stomachs as they walk.

As you walk along, everyone says, "Hi there," and every second I expect to see June Allyson and Peter Lawford dragging it up across the grass. And seeing the grass and the trees makes me miss my garden. I see the olive tree and the jacaranda, the three little birches Grandfather planted behind the projection room, and the eucalyptus and the peach tree—I see them like faces, going over old friends. There are even cheerleaders walking along with pompoms, saying "Hi there" so extra bright you want to put out your foot and trip them. The only cheerleaders I've ever heard about went to Hollywood High, were pinned to dental students at

S.C., and Val says, "They all crack their gum and have athlete's feet," which was, I think, to discourage me from being one. Not that I would. I detest football games and if you're a cheerleader you have to go to all of them. "The only thing about it you like," Val said, "are the outfits."

Scotty and I are having lunch at this hickory-smoked hamburger place in a shopping area near campus.

And I see something across the way.

"I'll be right back," I say.

"Where are you going?" He is eating the rest of my hickory hamburger. I have found something in the world to eat that I do not like besides Jell-O.

"Just something," I say.

I come back wearing my new red Bermudas with my skirt wrapped up under my arm.

"Now," Scotty says, "you better start staying out of stores."

"Don't you think they're darling?"

"They're bright."

We are standing, waiting for the train. Almost as if he wasn't sure until just now that he was going to do it, he hands me a piece of paper. "Don't say I never gave you anything. If you need me, you know where to get in touch."

Your Aunt: Thelma Williams (Mrs. Ken)
Davis Fields RFD 1, Motlin, Ill.

"It's about an hour's bus ride out of Chicago, I think. Don't be afraid to ask people for help."

He puts his arms around me. "Now hold on to your money. Don't forget to practice—that's going to mean more to you than any of the rest of this you need to see right now—you believe that, okay? And you be . . . you be all right." And he chucks my chin and I get on the train and wave at him and he's waving both hands over his head, like he's cheering me on, until we round a bend and I can't see him any more.

You never think, when you're imagining yourself on the road, of how much you'll have along with you. It's like Scotty said about Jackson not knowing he couldn't get rid of the past by being someone famous—you don't think it will stay with you when you're away—or by being a different you. And maybe being famous isn't being a different you—which is what he meant. Maybe there is no different you to be. Even in outfits I'm still me. I just pretend to be different.

It was my mother who taught me the techniques of train travel. And Myron taught me the song that does not leave my head for the first hour on this part of the trip:

> Passengers will please refrain
> From flushing toilets
> While the train
> Is standing in the station,
> Thank you, sir.

The drawing rooms and bedrooms then had little bathrooms, with pull-down sinks of steel over the toilets, which is where, Myron said, they got the name Pullman, "Because, you have to say, 'Pull, man,' to get those sinks down." Myron was good with children.

He should have had one. I wonder why they didn't. Perhaps she was wrecked having me.

My mother would sit on her bed with her train case on top of her hatbox and apply her makeup looking in the mirror, dipping her mascara brush in a glass of water left from her breakfast tray. Sometimes the train would jerk and her hand would slip and the mascara would make caterpillars under or above her eyes, which did not amuse her. Myron and I would laugh. I liked him better then. Maybe things looked better to him then.

In this roomette—I have traded in part of my ticket

to save money—things are not so simple. The toilet is under a carpeted lid, and you cannot get to it after the bed has been pulled down and made up by the porter. Not without an amazing amount of trouble. There is no question that the best thing about a train is the nighttime. There are small soft purple night lights above the bed and the sink and one round one in the ceiling which looks like the moon. It is a little like being in a miniature of the Griffith Park Observatory. I like being alone here because it is like being in my car and being able to play at the same time. Sometimes I get going so, with "Rock Island Line" or one of my other favorite moving-along songs, that I get a knocking from the next roomette and I remember to quiet down.

Scotty once told me the best people went out on the road on their own for a while. I think he does not want to remember now that I learned about all this from him—since I'm doing it.

Sometimes I get this feeling I'm really going to see Jackson. I always feel it, but sometimes it's so strong I get really excited and I want to dance along with my singing and twirl my guitar around like a jazz bassman, and I pound and strum and toke it like a wild person. And as I get closer to him, to really seeing him, I want almost to turn back. I won't. How good can it be? What is he going to say? Is it worse to be wondering than it was not to know at all? See, I have to know that someone who had me or started my life and then left me is probably not a perfect person. And yet? It doesn't matter. No one is perfect. Not to everyone. He will be scared that I'm going to ask him for things, make demands. I have to show him I won't. I won't try to hang on to him, or stay with him. I will not cling to him.

Look how convinced I am that just because I'm trying, just because I'm really doing it, I'm going to get to see him. And all I have is the name and address of his sister and Scotty says he hasn't heard from her or seen her for a "good eight years." She might not even still live there. Bet she does. People named Mrs. Ken

Williams in Illinois with Rural Free Delivery don't hit the road.

Other times I'll deliberately play something like "Streets of Laredo" or "I Know Where I'm Goin'" and I will know I'm going to start crying. "Hush, little baby, don't you cry, Daddy's going to buy you a diamond ring, and if that diamond ring is brass—Daddy's going to buy you a looking-glass . . ." And I'll smile right through the crying and say, "You are the craziest person. . . ."

". . . An' if you look and can't see me, Daddy's going to tell you where he'll be. . . ."

Daddy. Did I ever call Myron that? This morning I made up a whole story to drive myself completely wild. I decided Jackson showed up in Hollywood yesterday and called to talk to me and my parents told him where I was and he decided he would surprise me and hopped a flight with one of his old friends like Sy Bartlett, who used to fly with the Lafayette Escadrille, or Clarence Brown, who has his own airport on his estate out in the Valley, where he has a real river with weeping willows. And that was fantastic. When Val and I stayed out there one weekend at this huge house party—this was before everything—we had adjoining rooms and hers had a black marble bathroom and we found black nighties in the closet and put them on and lay down on this black bathmat and pretended I was Jean Harlow and she was Theda Bara and she peeled and fed me grapes from the fruit bowl in the bedroom. We laughed and hugged each other and danced around and we loved each other so much then. She woke me up real early, you could hear the first birds warming up, and we went outside and down to the river and Katharine Hepburn was up and just getting into this little rowboat; she took us both along with her and showed us how to row. No one else got up before eleven. It was like being in our own movie about a frontier woman and her kids.

So, Jackson has gotten one of these guys to fly him to Colorado to surprise me. And I'm not there. I'm here. The other version, which is terrific until we get to the next stop and he is not there, is that Scotty knows where Jackson is and called him and told him to get the hell on a plane and intercept this kid at the next stop before she does something crazy.

Even when I'm just doing what I do on trains, talking to people, singing, looking at the whole place going by, I have some of these stories going along in my mind, like background music—or, really, while I am traveling it is like having three movies running at once: the past, right now, and what I am imagining. And sometimes they all seem equally real and immediate—or equally unreal.

I lie awake at night, playing soft, with the shade up in my roomette, resting my head against the crunchy old pillows and watching the dark, sleeping land go by. We come into stations now and then, and men come out and hose down the train or just stand around smoking and talking to the conductor. The more I'm away, the more I'm used to traveling, the more accustomed I get to myself.

I don't wonder any more what made Jackson run like this. Or any of them. Folksongs are about moving and remembering what you're leaving and this is a country where if you're not moving, not on wheels, you're thinking about it or missing someone who is: moving. Maybe you only really love something when you look back at it after you've left. That's what they call homesickness, it feels like being in love, and if you're there you don't have it, you don't feel anything. I wonder if my mother only loves Jackson because she misses him.

I GET OFF THE TRAIN IN CHICAGO AND CALL FOR A reservation under the name S. Havisham Lane at the Pump Room, which is the only place I can think of to get something to eat, and I get past Irving Kupcinet's table fast so he does not see me and wonder what I am doing here. You always have lunch here with him, my mother said, if you're anyone at all coming through, and you have to wait over between the Super Chief and the Twentieth Century Limited. I remember wondering how Twentieth Century got to have its own train and we didn't. And I remember the smell of the hotel rooms and the huge white-tiled bathrooms and piles of thick white towels. We stayed in the vice presidential suite at the Ambassador East, all decorated in emerald green and white. And in every hotel we had baskets of fruit wrapped in yellow cellophane and one vase of American Beauty roses, which I do not much care for, and they certainly do not look like any roses I have ever seen growing.

I order the miniature hamburgers, which I adore, and they are so good I order them again. And drink quite a lot of Cokes. When I have babies I will bring them here for hamburgers. How cute they will look eating them. Small blond babies. Like my father was . . . did he ever *want* to see me as a baby? Or did he see me? I wonder if his sister, this Thelma Williams, has pictures. Mr. and Mrs. Ken Williams of Motlin, Illinois. Do I have a surprise for you. . . .

I shake hands with the headwaiter, a dollar folded into my hand like Myron always does, and leave the Pump Room. I wonder if anyone else leaves the Pump

Room to get on a bus to somewhere like Motlin, Illinois. I could be going to Athens, Harvard, Palestine, Geneva, or Genoa and it would sound wonderful, but they'd still all be Illinois. I wonder if the towns named after special places here in the Midwest have parts like those places, sort of excerpts, like the backlots. I mean if you were going to Paris in Culver City, I'd know you'd be walking under the Arch of Triumph. And in our Venice at home we have delicate little Italian bridges. It would be wonderful to roll into Athens, Illinois, and see the Parthenon above these drying cornfields with a sign saying WELCOME TO ATHENS, *pop.* something or other and *alt.* (practically no alt.).

MOTLIN, ILL., *pop. 6,735, Welcome to the home of Greenvale Corn Canning Co.*

At the bus station in Motlin, which is really no more than a corner of a small store, I get the directions to the Williams house. "Oh, sure, Thelma's probably home by now," the clerk says. It is exactly like a real small town where people know each other and you expect them to go into a song and dance any minute, with someone twirling off around the posts of all the front porches everything has. You could almost walk along from porch to porch and never get wet.

"If you're going over to their house, I'll have the boy give you a lift. It'd be quite a walk with that baggage. He's got a delivery over to the Moylans's—so it's no trouble."

I thank him and climb up in the small truck next to a blond kid about my age. I wonder if Jackson had jobs like this and looked out over cornfields longing to catch a look at an ocean and waiting for the right feeling that would tell him it was time to take off.

I ask to be dropped at a corner. I want to look a little. Size up where I am. Get a feeling about the sound of it. There's almost no sound. You could hear bugs walk through these cornfields. The day is warm and dry and very still. A little scritching of the leaves on the cornstalks like the sound—Angelo said—his father's hands made when he was ill and dying. I wonder if he has walked down this road. I wish I had my car and I could drive around awhile and listen to the radio and work up a little courage. She could hate me. Not believe me. Or get angry at him. Why do I have to tell her exactly the truth? She'll probably ask me to come in for a moment, look me over, give me some tea or milk and then, after she's sized me up, she'll go into her room and come out with a piece of paper with Jackson's phone number. Or address, more likely. Myron says nowhere in America does anyone use the long distance phone like certain people in Hollywood. Meaning my mother and me. My mother thinks nothing of having Mary call Bergdorf's or Tiffany's to find out about something she's seen in *Vogue* and wants to order. I sometimes wonder if she tries to find Jackson . . . but if she ever thought about it, she would pick up the phone, sigh, put it down and lie back against her pillows.

I have walked again to the end of the road where the cornfields begin. Far on the other edge you can see the canning company looming. There's probably a kid here who looks out at it like I used to look out over West L.A. to the studio and puts her hands on her hips and thinks about how some day it's going to belong to her and her husband and that they'll take their kid through there one day, like I will take mine and point out the places Grandfather used to show off. And the people working there will remember the old days and get all sentimental over the kid, the way George Tully, our gatekeeper, will get over my kid. Child, I mean.

I turn and look down this quiet road with the little houses spaced so far apart, each with only one or two trees, and I feel like Brandon de Wilde: "Jackson. Come back, Jackson."

Okay, Susanna, you just march right up to that door. You can't find out anything from not trying.

It's a darling little yellow and white house and the neat little garden in front looks all worn out with a few daisies, a couple of leftover roses, and what were probably some real vegetables. The geraniums are in pots, not growing wild like we have them on hillsides at home. Maybe they would like stories about California. Will I tell them where I am from? The door bell chimes, a sort of "How are you?" kind of song.

Maybe she's not home after all. I look at the steps. I could sit and wait there. Then I hear the footsteps, and a voice says, "Coming . . ." I wonder if he's ever stood here, smiling to himself about how excited she's going to be to see him.

"Yes?" she says, as she opens the door.

"Hi. I'm Susanna—uh—Haver. And . . ." And what? And I'm so crazy I almost gave my whole real name. And does it matter? She may know about me anyway.

"Well, hello, dear, Carleen's still up at school. But she's coming down for the weekend. You must be one of the new girls from the cheerleading squad. Well, my, don't just stand there with all that, don't you want to come in? I'm just in the middle of a new cake, but I can offer you some milk. . . ."

I was right about milk. She is like Jackson. Open and friendly and the same smile—my God, I have a family with characteristics.

She opens the screen door now and I see she has our thumbs. "I don't know Carleen, I'm afraid . . . I'm . . . um . . ."

"Yes?" She looks at me more closely now—her hair is grayed out; will mine? My mother's family stays dark late.

I put down my suitcase and train case and reach out my hand, not quite touching her but wanting to, wanting also not to look at her when I say it in case she doesn't believe me. "Mrs. Williams, I'm Jackson's daughter. I'm your niece. I'm sorry . . ." Now why am I saying I'm sorry? I look at her kind of sideways, with what I am sure is the stupidest grin.

"Good Lord." She just stands there too, with her hands also almost touching me. "You surely are, just look at you. He never said a word to me. But that's him."

"I guess so."

She's such a pretty woman. I think it's nice to be plump when you're older. She's not fat, just round, with all her features like Jackson's, but curved and round; but if you notice fast, when she is between smiles, there is a *giving in* to or acceptance (is that it?) of sadness in her face. Not just her eyes—in her *whole* face. Her hair waves around her face and it's wound in a soft, curly little puff at back.

"I was thinking to myself," she says, "that girl looks like one of us. Carleen will be so excited to have a cousin, we never thought either . . ." She pauses.

Either. Are there other children, aunts, uncles? I am going to have to listen carefully for things like that.

"I mean either of us had any relatives we didn't know about. He never did tell me he married."

As she speaks now, her voice is slightly more distant, because I think she is realizing she ought to be hurt. Then right away fast she is all bouncy and encouraging again. As though she snapped off those dark feelings like a light. Actually it is like watching an actress under the lights, before the camera one minute and biting her thumbnail in the director's chair the next.

"He hasn't seen me much either," I say. I don't want her to think he sees a lot of one part of his family. I don't think I can tell her he was not married. But what is worse—for her to know he did something immoral, or to imagine a wedding he didn't invite her to?

"He's very much a loner, I think." She looks at me, light snapped off again for an instant.

"I know that." I must. I bet the way she does this bothers him. This little switching of mood and this getting hurt fast . . . which is a little like my mother. Jackson and I (*our* part of the family. Listen to that! will you?) like you to be zippy and breezy. I wonder if she was the sort of little girl who would have all her dolls set up just so, having a lunch party, and he would

243

lark through accidentally and she would wail at him.
I'm the type that would give him a swift punch and that
would be that. But she would dawdle over dinner and
look at him a little hurt as though he meant to do it,
and how could he do something like that when she
adores him so much? Maybe that was the trouble. Maybe
I adored him too much that day. Has he caught me?
Loving him?

"I haven't heard from him in a little while," I say.
"And I misplaced his address with all this traveling."

There's that other look again. Either because I say
I had the address and she doesn't and that makes her
unhappy, which wasn't fair of me, or because, and I
can't tell for sure, she is a little suspicious—or possessive, and she's not going to tell me. I'm trying to imagine
if I was someone's sister—well, Val is a good comparison, if Val hadn't been around much and suddenly her
child showed up and wanted to know where she was.
No. I'd tell. I'd tell if I didn't know. I'd tell if I did. But
if Val was a movie star and this child arrived from
nowhere and I was older and Midwestern I might wait
a bit to get to know this child.

And as Scotty said, Jackson's strange. I wonder if
Jackson would be mad that I've come here. I wonder
if he'll say, "That does it!" when I find him. "I don't
like people who go around looking for people—my
own child, acting like some kind of legman for one of
those columnists."

My own child. Will Jackson ever say that to me? That,
I think, that would be almost enough. But when will
I start thinking of him as father? Not Jackson.

"Let's put your things in Carleen's room and then
we'll go out to the A&P, they've put in a lovely new
supermarket over in Dalehaven near the subdivision."

"Will she mind, do you think?"

"No, she's going to be real excited." I don't know if
I'd be real excited to come home and find a completely
new cousin using my room.

"That's a handsome suitcase," she says, as I put it on

the luggage rack Aunt Thelma brings out of the closet. The rack is maple with rose-embroidered straps.

"We'll hang a few things up so they won't get mussed," she says unpacking for me, as I guess she is used to doing for Carleen.

"My, my, a black sweater. Will Carleen be jealous of that!" I think Aunt Thelma disapproves. But so would my mother, which I will not say because I don't want her to think I'm the kind of girl who does things her mother does not approve of. Although, on the other hand, what can she think of a mother who allows a girl to have a black sweater? I am wanting her to approve of my mother almost as if Thelma is Jackson's mother, not his sister, and she does seem generations older than he is. Scotty said she was only a few years older but she seems much older than my mother. I thought at first it might be that she just doesn't have a tan, but my mother doesn't have a tan either. (How can you shop if you're lying on the beach?)

She is smart, Aunt Thelma, helping me unpack, instead of asking questions. I watch her casing labels. Glad I didn't try to hide where I was from. But she does it openly, like someone who is vastly interested in merchandise—not as if she is trying to find things out about me, and probably she isn't aware that that is what she is doing. And of course this is much better than asking questions because then I would get to ask some myself and I have a feeling she isn't much of a discusser. Which would drive Val crazy.

Of course, Jackson's not much of a discusser, either. He didn't discuss much while he was driving and sailing. Aunt Thelma bakes and, I learn, shops in the same way.

She wheels her cart now into the supermarket with that sort of look of adventure and happiness Jackson got on his face when we walked onto the dock and looked down at his boat.

"Wow!" I say, looking at the market. It's like a sound stage just filled with rows and rows of food. "I've never seen anything like this!"

"They must have supermarkets like this out there, Susanna."

"Oh yes." I don't want to explain that we have all our food delivered. "But my mother always likes to market alone." I can imagine getting into a kind of Aunt Giordano problem if I try to explain life at Perdido, or if I say my mother wouldn't set foot in a supermarket unless someone had a gun to her head.

Almost lovingly, Aunt Thelma looks over everything, examining packages, selecting, comparing, concentrating, as if she was listening to music. And she smiles and nods at other women, who drift by, smiling, gazing, with their wheeled baskets. So these are housewives. They all have wedding rings, some have babies. They all have their own little kitchens and own husbands coming home every night to a new surprise dinner. I cannot see Jackson being that kind of husband. No wonder he did not stay. I cannot even imagine how he came to be born here. Where did he learn to be magical?

Jackson in a supermarket. These carts would screech to a halt, pyramids of tin cans would tumble down. Ladies would yank out their curlers, he'd stand here shimmering and radiating. I want to be like that. I want them to look at Thelma and throw up their hands and say, "That girl doesn't belong here!" And at the same time, I am pleased when one of them says, "Well, she looks more like you than your own daughter!"

Aunt Thelma talks to a couple of women and introduces me. "This is Susanna, my niece from California," she says as if I have been expected. And in a way, I think she has decided to think of it like that. I am here. There is no need to worry about how or why.

My uncle, Ken, Aunt Thelma informs me, is a football fan and coaches the high school team. "That's along with being production manager at the company," Thelma says, and if Val was around I would have said, "Oh, makes documentaries about corn?" just to make her laugh.

One thing I do miss on a trip is seeing movies every

night. The last movie I saw was in San Francisco. I saw a drive-in theater on the way to the supermarket still playing *Niagara* and *The Beast from 20,000 Fathoms,* if you believe that.

"Aren't there any new releases playing in town?" I asked, planning to see whatever there was a couple of times.

"Oh—we just had one little theater and they tore that down when they put up the new savings bank, dear, we don't go to many movies now that we have the TV and can watch shows right at home—but you must see movies all the time out there, aren't you tired of them by now?"

"No. I just love them. I go all the time." Go right downstairs and put my feet up and watch them every night. I am not going to say that! I really *need* to see a movie the more I think about it.

I thought when I first walked in Aunt Thelma's home some of these things were very old and I wondered if Jackson ever sat on that rocker or if his mother had held him in it, but now coming back from the supermarket and really noticing, as you notice things you don't see in a movie the first time you see it, I can tell it's all really quite new. She has everything you can get that is maple, miniature, or monogrammed. It is as though Aunt Thelma has erased the real past and designed one which comes without memory, without flaws or evidence of any prior use. It is a house full of sentiment but no history. Like the artificial folksongs Scotty told me not to make up. I would like to know what that past was. Because it is my past too.

Even with my mother's constant redecoration, you can feel the stories at Perdido, and there are little enameled boxes, slightly battered brass candlesticks, the old Russian lamps—things which have always been there and always will be, as reminders. Maybe you don't need that so much when your people have always been where you are.

I can see now how Jackson must have been dazzled

by my mother and Perdido, and wondered how he
could bring her here and how she would be. I wonder
if he ever saw her get that look on her face when she
finds something distasteful. She looks as though she is
biting on a bullet to keep from yelling. She can get this
look when Frank serves to the left and takes off from the
right, which he does to make it clear he does not approve of serving dinner to Republicans (or people from
the New York office, which is often one and the same).
Dorothy told me that one night the foot buzzer started
going in the kitchen like my mother was playing the
1812 Overture and Dorothy and Mabel cruised into the
dining room. The wife of a Republican from the New
York office had made some remarks such as you had
to understand the Southern point of view—"The colored
themselves prefer segregation"—and Frank had spilled
a pitcher of cream down her back. And so there were
Dorothy and Mabel trying to do something about her
dress and my mother sat there biting away, the
energy it took you could always see in her throat and
the line of her jaw. That exercise is why her neck is still
smooth as a swan's. So I can imagine her here fingering
the silverplated flatware and gazing at the ceramic salt
and pepper shakers, which are two children and when
you put them together they kiss. And I wonder if Jackson would have put his head in his hands and thought
this was all a mistake to bring her here and that he knew
that in advance, which is why he didn't marry her. Or
she knew it, which is why she didn't marry him—she
guessed about his family and decided it would never
work. It doesn't matter what happened. They just didn't.
Get married. But I got here anyway.

Aunt Thelma cooks constantly. Even at the table that
night as she passes the vegetables she gives them a little
stir, and whips a bit at the potatoes, watching Uncle
Ken who is watching one sports program on the TV and
listening to another on a portable radio next to him on
the table. He was probably good-looking when they
met. Had more hair. He tastes the potatoes and nods at

her as she discusses them. "I put a little more cream in tonight, and some onion, maybe they could use a little more parsley, don't you think?" And he winks and nods. Probably played football then. I am not really listening to the radio but suddenly I hear, "And now this just in from Hollywood . . . Leon Daroff, famed motion picture mogul, dead at sixty-eight; Daroff was found by his wife, former star Evelyn Ames, near the staircase of their palatial Beverly Hills home . . ."

Uncle Ken switches the station. How terrible for Paul. But I notice Evelyn is referred to as a former star. I must remember to mention that part to Paul when I call him. I wonder if my mother will try to reach me to tell me to send a note. C.A. will cover for me. I'll try to remember to tell her. Paul will have his nails chewed down to the wrists by the funeral.

In the afternoon Aunt Thelma showed me pictures of Carleen's wedding dress in *American Bride* magazine. She has already picked it out. "I think it's important to get off to a good start. It's real slipper satin. Ken will be so proud walking her down the aisle, real proud. . . . She has a lovely cedar-lined Lane hope chest. With her own silver, some Lenox place settings, real hem-stitched sheets and cases, and a nice spread. Carleen started picking her heirlooms out for her hope chest when she was fourteen."

And I have five trees in the Cedars of Lebanon forest in Israel. I read about hope chests in *Seventeen* magazine. They are always full of heirlooms. I used to think heirlooms were only for Christians. But I could have half-heirlooms now. And I wonder if they're considered heirlooms when it's all new stuff.

After I have gone to bed I hear Aunt Thelma and Uncle Ken talking in the bathroom. Don't have to walk down any halls here to hear everything. They are in the bathroom together! I can hear him going—I put the pillows around my ears. When I was little, I remember I was standing outside Myron's bathroom one morning, to ask him to sign my absence excuse (this was before

I caught on to his handwriting and learned to sign them myself, and before the school caught on to that and sent them home by mail for Mary to sign, which worked for the school until I worked things out with her). So, I was standing outside Myron's bathroom and he flushed the toilet four times, which I asked him about.

"Why?" I had said.

"Because it's polite good manners, so people don't hear you." I wondered why no one had told me that before. But then I read something on water conservation in the *Book of Knowledge:* it takes seven gallons of water to flush a toilet; so I felt very confused about that. If there is a drought, I thought, it would be the end of manners.

I guess in Illinois they are more back to nature. Seeing each other, brushing teeth, and everything you can imagine. It makes sense to me to keep things to yourself that you couldn't put into movies. If it was anything great it would be in them. But then I would like, if I was married, for him to say he'd love me even if I do go to the bathroom and I wouldn't think anything of him doing it and we'd be really down to earth like horses living together. I wonder if you're ever allowed to just talk over those kind of things with a husband? Or do you pretend you don't even notice? Or, could you say, like with a song—this is what kind I want to make up, this is what kind of marriage I want?

Now they are talking about me: "Hush, she might hear you . . ."

"No, she's gone to sleep. She's an odd girl. Always looking at you but kind of distant, don't you think?"

"Well, I was thinking if Carleen went off somewhere and we didn't know. If I put myself in the same place, I'd want to hear." Uncle Ken is gargling now.

"I have an idea her people are in the movie business. See how she jumped when they said on the radio that producer died?"

And I didn't think Uncle Ken even heard it. He is

smarter than I thought. My people. What could be more movie business than Jackson Lane being your father?

"But," Aunt Thelma said, "we don't even know who the mother is. Haver—do you suppose he was married to that actress?"

"If Jack was married, Thelma, we'd have read about it."

Am I odd and distant? It's so hard to know how you are unless you hear it from someone. And then you have to be careful to size up who is saying it.

"Well, she's no movie star. Susanna says her mother goes to the supermarket. I can't imagine a movie star in a supermarket."

"You sure she's Jack's kid?" he says.

"She's his child all right. You can see that right off. Looks just like he did when he was her age." That's probably why she does let me be here—having me here must remind her of him. A little brother would be almost like your own child, and now I think of Val and Theo; I'll bet Val can't wait to have her own baby— and she's probably scared to death to lose it. Do you get so, after a lot of terrible things happen to people you care about, that you simply try not to care? Maybe some people do. (Maybe that's why my mother is so aloof—losing her parents and Jackson. Whatever happened, she must see him as lost.)

"I wonder," he says, "if she wants anything from us."

"No, you should see. She has very lovely things. He must have done well by her mother."

That makes me kind of sad, and she sounds so wistful, even through the wall. I'm sure though, if Jackson thought she needed anything he'd send it to her. Look how he paid Scotty back. He is generous. In his own way.

Now she is saying to Uncle Ken, "And I do wish you'd just talk to us during dinner."

"Now stop trying to get me to put on in front of her. You were all fussy during dinner—she's from out there—you don't have to impress her. They don't even eat their dinners indoors. All eat on patios or whatever they call it."

"I'm not trying to do anything. And I'm sure some of them do. She's got nice table manners."

Too bad Aunt Thelma does not have fingerbowls— some of them do! She should only know, as Grandmother would say.

My cousin Carleen and her fiancé, Duane, lead the cheerleading squad at their college upstate. Their team is playing a college near here this Saturday afternoon, and so they're both coming down. "Duane," Aunt Thelma says, "will stay with his family. Lovely people. His father is personnel manager at the company. High school sweethearts."

"Were you and Uncle Ken high school sweethearts?"

"No, dear. I grew up . . . somewhere else."

"Nearby?" I am already asking too many questions.

"Yes. Susanna, would you hand me the food coloring? Yes, that's it."

Aunt Thelma is making a cake for Carleen. Exactly the kind of mother you'd expect you should have if you ever saw any musicals. She mixes the green and yellow coloring to make chartreuse and drips it into the frosting. Then she packs it into one of her little cloth tubes. She starts a row of leaves around the top of the cake and stands back, the pastry tube held up in her hand and she squints at the cake.

"You could have been an artist," I say.

"Thank you, dear. I thought about that once. But you accept what you are. Whatever life brings. There is a reason." She dabs on more leaves. She flashes me her smile. There is something sad, or awful, in her past. Their past.

Carleen and Duane: I have never met anyone named Duane. Or anyone engaged (except Elizabeth Taylor.)

They're getting married next year, when they're sophomores, and they'll live in a married students dorm.

"Has Carleen ever met Jackson?"

"No, Susanna. She has *not*." Anything I learn I will learn, I guess, by accident. The one connection we have is the one thing she will not discuss.

Carleen comes bouncing in the door, all fresh outdoors energy. "Hi," she says, looking at me happily.

"Carleen, this is Susanna, your cousin from California."

"How neat!" She shakes my hand. "What a surprise." She doesn't ask anything. There's not even a questioning glance at her mother. She is everything you're supposed to be to read *Seventeen* magazine.

(That's if you don't read the poems, but Val says they just put those in to get subscriptions from the East. "This is the most totally Midwestern, California magazine."

"But Val," I'd say, "it's always about all those big Eastern college girls and everything."

"Yeah, like Midwestern."

"Well, it is in the East. Somewhere."

"Susanna. It's called Midwestern, does that feel like some kind of clue, some sort of indication? . . . I do not believe you." This goes with a long "lieve.")

Aunt Thelma has been cooking all day. She was reading a cookbook when I came in the kitchen this morning. "Chicken divan," she said, looking over her little eyeglasses at me.

"Divine," I said. I thought of chickens lying around on sofas eating parsley like extras in *Quo Vadis* nibbling grapes. She adores doing her cake decorating with an audience, I think, watching her, and watching Carleen as they perform for each other, I see it is not from out of nowhere Jackson became an actor. I could have been born right here and wound up wanting to be a singer, or something like that. It is genes. Not Hollywood.

"Carleen, honey, hand me my number four tube there, you're just in time. Do you think I should add some fluted waves right here?"

"That would be real nice. Hey, Mom, I did five forward leaps from a frogstand in place today."

"That's very good, dear. Now I'm putting on, watch this Susanna, a number six pinwheel feuillage—that's French—just around these rosettes. I believe that is the original French as well."

". . . and," adds Carleen, who is kicking and jumping around the kitchen, "Duane and I have worked out this real luscious swing kick on three, kick on four, then leap and down to splits bit. We're going to put it in right before half time tomorrow. It's very difficult timing, we have to be real super concentrating. One second and we'd mess everything up."

"Now, see this, Susanna, watch me here . . . it's timing, you have to move fast and with complete accuracy. . . ." I have to look before I realize it's Aunt Thelma talking about the cake, not Carleen about cheerleading. Aunt Thelma has covered her hair curlers with a lilac hairnet which is hanging close to the cake as she leans over. "If I lose the rhythm they get uneven, that's the trick to the triple scroll border pattern. Now, Carleen, just stop for a minute. I got to keep my arm real steady, see it's in the tiny movements of the fingers. Just like painting your nails."

"Now, see," Carleen is showing me, "I run forward five, then jump and he grabs my legs as I swing up onto his shoulders. Then two-three-four and I'm up standing right there . . . and we go into the big-arm pompom routine. With a kick, a kick, and a jump down . . . it's going to really be a show-stopper."

Saturday night in Motlin: Duane and Carleen have come for dinner. He is a paler blond than Jackson or me, and small, powerful in a neat, trim way. Duane and Carleen do one cheer for us before sitting down to dinner. I wonder if they will make love to cheers, doing it with lifts and flips and leaps and yells.

"Sick or dying"—Duane is telling me how it is to be a cheerleader—"you're never excused. It's not just a popularity contest, you know. We're an example." I think this is his recruiting talk. I could say, I'd love to, but I have this asthma see . . . Is there such a thing as too much energy? "I watch how the advisor treats us. You don't want any pansies letting kids get away with things."

"God forbid," I say.

"Noooo way, bob. It's a big weight for a kid to have on his shoulders. If we goof, our whole school suffers. Back in the twenties, you know, and the forties, you could get away with not having precision."

"Really?" That, I think, takes care of Rudy Vallee, June Allyson, and all the others. What did they know?

"Now you have to have real good flips and falls and big, ten-person stunts, you have to keep up with student feeling, with real pepsters. I mean you have to be ready. What if sixty-five thousand fans turn out for your pep rally?"

"Gulp," Carleen says, giggling, her hand quickly over her mouth.

"I have to be ready, with attention-getting devices," Duane says, looking at her.

As serious as she is about cheerleading, he is more. A lot. He will probably be running for President some day. Republican. I can hear it: "We're gonna vote, vote, vote, go-gettum, vote, heh-*heh!*"

"We're having a contest to raise money for our pepsters, we want a trampoline. We're having an Ugly Legs Contest, selling booster buttons, we got a Car Smash, with people paying a quarter for three hits . . ." Yes. Republican. Yes, rich. Duane will be very rich one day.

"How did you get to be a cheerleader, Carleen?" I want to say something to show I'm listening. I thought she'd say, "Oh, I don't know . . ." My mistake.

"Well, it's not as easy as it sounds . . . in high school it's one thing, but when I got to college, I was glad I was in the right sorority, you know what I mean. If you want to do it, Susanna, you've got to have more than talent. Constructive, positive, campus activities, good grooming, being style-conscious. You know."

I wonder if Jews can get into the right sorority. Or

girls who wear black turtlenecks. I'm not sure Duane approves of me. He cases me with his narrow blue eyes. Carleen said, "He is the cutest guy." I think he's something beyond cute. He's sort of a paled-out version of Angelo, and I wouldn't say this to Carleen but I'll bet he's one of those guys you read about in *True Romances* who takes girls from the "other side of the tracks" to roadhouses to do things his real girl won't.

Now Carleen has gone out with Duane, and Aunt Thelma and Uncle Ken have gone to choir rehearsal. Aunt Thelma said to Carleen, "Did you ask Susanna did she want to be fixed up?"

"Yes, she did, Aunt Thelma," I said.

"She says she'd rather just walk around," Carleen said. And we laughed.

"Also," I said because Aunt Thelma will appreciate this, "I must practice my guitar." Actually, I want to play it. When I call it practicing it's not nearly so much fun.

Duane stood next to Carleen looking me over before they left. Carleen's cheeks were rosy tonight as she listened to Duane and she tossed her chestnut brown hair. I look more like Aunt Thelma's daughter. Interesting how Carleen and I both take after our fathers. Do you take after the one who wanted to make love the most the night you were made? Did Jackson long for my mother because she was so different? Did he want me to look like her?—I doubt that. He did not seem displeased—with himself or me.

I think Aunt Thelma is a little concerned about leaving me here alone because I may look around a bit more than she'd like me to. And she's right. As soon as I feel they have been gone a respectable length of time, no echoes left in the house, I open the door to Aunt Thelma's room. They sleep in the same room and have twin canopied beds with ruffles in pale blue. Uncle Ken must look really wonderful in that bed. Like the wolf in Red Riding Hood's Grandmother's nightcap. By her bed, I see a small photograph, very old, of three children. Thelma—probably—Jackson, and a younger one, a littler Jackson. Jackson—I would have known that picture instantly—was standing there in a short-sleeved white shirt and long pressed white trousers, with his hands, of course, on his slim little hips. So he must have a brother. That's what she almost said—". . . either of them. . . ." I'll bet he died or something and she forgot that for a minute. Death again. There are other, even older, photographs of people in white summer costumes, sort of the style of my grandmother's time. A tall blond woman who must have been his mother. My other grandmother. Very severe-looking, though. What happened to them all? It was clearly not the pogrom or the Russian Revolution—they are probably, as Jackson said, Norwegian.

But this is not helping me find Jackson. I finally did mention it to Carleen when we were getting dressed tonight.

"Oh, you lucky! You've got a black turtleneck! Mom won't let me wear black. But once I'm married I'm going to anyway."

"Do you know my father—?"

"I know who he is. You can see that! I figured you were here looking for him."

"How'd you figure that? Did your mother tell you?"

"No—she hasn't said anything. But I know he stopped making movies, I read that, and I know if he was still with you, you wouldn't have come here—you never did before. Never even knew I had a cousin."

"Neither did I—Carleen, does your mother ever talk about Jackson to you—or about her life when she was little?"

"No . . . I know she had something real bad happen —but if she wanted me to know, she'd tell me. Soooo— Boy, when Duane sees that black turtleneck on you . . . Maybe you shouldn't wear it tonight."

"Okay. I won't." I look at her surprised—you wouldn't think Duane would have eyes for anyone else. "So you don't think they know where Jackson is—

honestly, Carleen, I just want to see him—Can you understand that? There's a lot I'm not saying, but it means so much if you could think about it—you know?"

"Sure," she says. "I can imagine how I'd miss my father. I'll think . . ."

If nothing comes up soon I'm just going on to New York anyway. I'm kind of missing Val. I'd call her to-night but she's probably out with this guy Chris she told me about this morning when I called about Leon Daroff. He's an older man, twenty-six she says, he was in the Korean War and is at Juilliard on scholarship. She says he's absolutely brilliant and funny and they make up songs together on their dates and I told Val I'd call that a busman's holiday. And she said, "Funny, that's what a lot of people would call it."

Silence.

"Got it?" she said. She must be happy—she's cutting me. When things are sad I can say anything really dumb and she doesn't pick up on it, right away; she'll store some things and get me later when she's in a better mood. Sometimes I'll throw out something deliberately when I can't tell any other way how she's feeling.

So now I'm sitting on the front porch about ten thirty, humming something or other and watching the moon turn from red-orange to white as it rises up over the cornfields, sort of segueing from the "shine on" in "Harvest Moon" to the "shine your light on me" in "Midnight Special," which I could do if I was working up a little act like Scotty suggested.

And I am thinking about that little boy in the picture and wondering about the people—my grandparents—in the other pictures and what happened to them. Dead is what happened, probably, but how and why, although there's no why to death, I think. I'm just sitting there when Carleen comes pell-mell up the path and bangs the garden gate and rips right past me into the house, and she's crying, so I go right after her.

She has thrown herself on one of her twin beds and is just sobbing: "It's all over. Everything." And she takes off her diamond ring and throws it across the room, which is no way to treat a diamond.

Doesn't life stand still and nice for anyone?

"What happened? Are you hurt?" She is lying face down on her bed, her straight brown hair tipped up and hanging off the edge.

"I'm going to die." It is probably something about Duane.

"Is it Duane?"

"Don't mention that name. I never want to hear that name again."

"What did he do?"

"He's just ruined my whole estimation of a human being." She sobs. In rhythm. Even her sobs sound like cheers.

I am sitting on the bed next to her, I put my hand on her back. "Don't touch me. I'm finished. I have principles, you know, as a woman. I have always been a morally whole person."

She is whispering. Still lying on her stomach, occasionally kicking her heels furiously into the air. "And he knew I will not be compromised. Not until we are married."

"Oh." Now I know we are related—this reminds me of my basic back seat asthma. "Did he try to go all the way?"

"Don't say the words. I told him, I am your bride-to-be, your fiancée, we have a moral responsibility to our entire spirit system, not only to our school, but if one teeny element goes against the principle of the thing—" And she lifts her fresh, tear-stained face. "And, he just said, oh, come on, honey, who's gonna know? . . . I'll know, that's who. And if I know, everyone will feel it."

"Gee, Carleen," I say, as much to distract her as to discuss it, "do you really think sex shows if you've had it? If you lined up a bunch of people, could you really see who's a virgin?" I used to imagine my parents' friends naked—I'd see them in my mother's room, for some reason, over on the wall where her fireplace was,

259

me sitting on the bed, telling them to turn around, do this and a little of that. I'd like to see the differences in how they looked. I never thought of doing it with my own friends. They would be hairless, without expressions. I figured that adults would have interesting characteristics on their bodies.

"Look, Carleen," I try to make her laugh, "you could have a kind of Ed Sullivan show with everyone naked. One of the specialty acts would be the virginity test: Ladies and Gents, can you tell? . . . will the contestants please walk across the stage and say a few words so the judges can pick out the virgins. I'm beginning to think it doesn't show so much, Carleen."

"How can you even imagine Ed Sullivan like that? It's not funny to think of someone like Ed Sullivan being with a bunch of nudes! And how can you think of that when I've just given up my life?"

"Oh, Carleen . . . I don't know what to say. I don't think it's really the end—it just feels like it. You know virginity is really rough for boys. Maybe you could compromise and do some other things." I'll bet he's out right now at some diner.

"What are you talking about?"

"Oh, I don't know. A little heavy petting, I guess."

"I let him touch me on top twice. I'm not from Hollywood, you know. I want to be a real bride. Someone he can be proud of."

Hollywood. The way she says it—like I say "starlet." I wonder if Carleen is jealous. Does everyone want to be someone else? Like I want to be Val—even with all her troubles. Does everyone have envy rising like salt in the throat from time to time? Did Lillian envy my mother when she fell in love with a big blond star who did not drink—there must have been a day when they talked like Val and I would talk and my mother told Lillian how lovely and wonderful he was—while Lillian was pregnant and heavy with Val and longing for romance? And my mother must have envied Lillian when she had Val and Alan was there with flowers and kisses.

And Grandmother must have envied them both for being young and having small babies to cuddle with. But does envy just float through most people like a sour note you forget about and try again, getting it right? Carleen quickly says, "I'm sorry, Susanna—I don't mean *everyone* in Hollywood. I'm just upset."

"That's okay, Carleen, I understand—it's hard loving someone and trusting and then getting surprised. But he'll probably apologize. I bet anything you'll be back together tomorrow."

"No. I will never speak to Duane Healy again as long as I live. Just leave me alone—"

"Sure." Maybe I should just go—here everything was so neat, so simple. . . . I go out on the porch again and listen to the breeze rustling the drying cornstalks. Then, after about a half hour, she comes out and sits beside me on the porch, in her pajamas. "If you're really trying to find him," she whispers, "I know my mother gets letters from all around the country, all with the same handwriting. No return address, but sometimes there's a postcard from a circus. When my mother gets one, she goes in her room to read it and closes the door. I don't read them, but I know the last ones came from Sarasota in Florida. If I was going to look for someone, that's where I would go. Oh—Florida . . ." she wails. "Duane and I were figuring on going to Florida on our honeymoon. We were thinking of starting a school for cheerleaders down there. Oh, hickies! Everything's ruined!" She's pacing now. "We were going to train them and then have national tours, we'd go to all different schools and recruit the best kids for teachers." She's got this excited tone back in her voice just thinking about it. And doing a little jump on the front porch. "Soon there wouldn't be anyone who wouldn't want to come down there and we'd take the best and go on the Ed Sullivan show. That was our big ambition. By the time I'm twenty-one I'm going to be on the Ed Sullivan show. Did you ever meet Ed Sullivan? I mean I really respect him, which is why I snapped at you before."

"No, it's not like that. You don't just know *everyone* famous because you happen to know some. A lot of movie stars don't know each other. I guess."

"Oh," she says, "I wonder if my uncle knows Linda Darnell—she's so sexy. I love the name Linda."

I don't want Jackson to be "her uncle" like that. What there is of him to think about is all mine. "My mother," I say, "looks a little like Linda Darnell."

"How neat!"

I'm thinking about how to get to Florida. I don't even know anyone who's ever gone to Florida. I just know it's way down there, the opposite of California. Florida. That's going to be hard. But I'll bet that's just where he'd be. Lying under an orange tree? What can you be discovered for in Florida?

"Do you remember the name of the circus, Carleen—was it Ringling Brothers?" Jackson is crazy enough, I think, to be with a circus. I am crazy enough to see him now to believe it. I see him in gold and white spangled tights, swinging onto a trapeze.

"I think it was Tinker—something like that." Then she's back to cheerleading. "Maybe," she says, "we'd get endorsed by Arthur Godfrey. Can't you just hear him saying, 'Aren't they cute?' And Ed Sullivan saying, 'Look at them. Aren't they wunnerful?' If I were you I'd just have stayed home and been a movie star. Have you ever had a screen test?"

"Oh, I wouldn't want to do that." I can just see my mother's reaction to that.

"Myron," she'd say, "Myron. You know how I feel about that." I think she really feels that since her mother wouldn't let her do it, she's not about to let me.

"Now, Susanna," Myron would say, "your mother and I can't stop you, of course, if that's what you want, but let's look at it realistically. Say I set up a test. We'd have to find a part that would be right, then you'd be up against a lot of highly trained, highly talented people. Naturally, I wouldn't have anything to say about it. It would be up to the individual producer, and then the director, and naturally you'd have two strikes against you; being in the industry to begin with, you'd have to be twice as good. It's just asking for disappointment, but if you want to take a shot, and it's a long shot, I'll see if I can set something up. Of course, your mother and I don't think it's suitable. Your musical talent is what you should be working on—you have a lot of potential, and you should look at the long-term goals, not the short-term gains. Do you understand?"

I can hear the speech just as though we'd actually had that conversation. Sometimes Myron, not God, not Grandmother, is what my conscience sounds like.

"I can see why he wanted to stop being a movie star for a while." Carleen pauses. "It's hard to be up there like that. Cheerleading is similar. Duane can do eighty yards of back handsprings. The rat . . . You ought to come up and see us soon, we're doing some new pom-pom routines. We'll have the best spirit spectacle this year you ever saw. . . . You're right, Susanna. I'll let him come over and apologize tomorrow." And she takes her ring out of her pajama pocket, puts it on, and watches it flashing in the moonlight. Oh—I'd love to have a real boyfriend with things we do together, fights, making up, plans.

Susanna, you don't really, I tell myself. I just want to see Jackson.

BEFORE I GET ON THE TRAIN GOING DOWN SOUTH, I CALL Val collect, which of course thrills her.

"But I wanted to find out if Paul is okay. I knew you'd talk to him."

"You could call him."

"Yeah. I will. But I'm not good at that."

"Like everything else. Practice makes perfect."

"Oh, Val."

"Okay. Considering. Paul is fine—he is currently fond of my theory that Evelyn jumped out from under the steps and frightened Leon to death because she's apparently getting practically everything. Paul is getting mostly four hundred old properties Leon had lying around in the files. *And,* in the great tradition you will especially appreciate, everyone's telling their children everything. Leon had neglected to point out to Paul that he had sold out Daroff Productions a few months ago to our great friend C.A.'s father—for television."

"My God," I say. "Not Daroff!"

"Tomorrow the world," Val says.

"But Paul just started working for his father," I say.

"Well, he thinks they'll give him something in television."

"Paul Daroff? Working for television?"

"Working, I think, is the key word there."

Val is always a little snotty about Paul. I think he has a lot of talent . . . but Daroff going TV? I remember my mother saying Myron was having some trouble with the New York office. I wonder. However, Daroff was a high-quality independent studio and it was all Leon

Daroff—without him it would have gone under anyway. V.L.I. is different. I will call my mother. When I get to New York. And I'll call Paul then. The more you like the person, the harder it is to make those calls and find yourself saying all the dumb, obvious things.

I think my grandfather and Leon Daroff's father and the rest of them invented the happy American family and put it into movies to drive everyone crazy. It's sort of as real as a musical number about falling in love. As real as Bronston Sloane. As real as my idea that people in slums wear bright-colored costumes and dance and sing up and down the streets about how friendly you feel when you're poor, as real as the blue-eyed Indians who look like suntanned movie stars and ride around on horses wearing a lot of crayon-colored feathers.

"Florida!" Val screams, just the way I knew she would. "No one goes to Florida." That's like "No one goes to the University of Colorado."

"Some people do. Or it wouldn't be there. Stop putting perimeters on everything. Uncle Ken drove me to Chicago. I'm catching a train to Atlanta or Jacksonville. I'll have to figure out the rest as I go along. It's really very simple. You just keep going South."

"Well, stop before you fall in the ocean. How's the money situation?"

"It's just fine. Now, don't act like a mother."

But how else can she act? Lillian is pure mother. Which means I will always be pure child if it is true that we learn how to be from our mothers. I will not. I will be like my father if I can find out how he is exactly. I'm already being like him. Going away. And every day I am not home I am becoming less like her. Why be mad at Val because she is so good at being what I wish my mother would be—wanting me to be all right, but not *afraid*. Wanting me to do things, but to think.

"If I get in trouble, Val, I'll call Mary and have her wire me more money. I'll say I got on the wrong train."

"And just got to Florida by accident?"

"Well, since no one goes there on purpose, I'll worry about explaining it when I have to. There's no point figuring out trouble before it happens or else you'd be ready for it and then it wouldn't be trouble after all."

"That's very logical."

"Have my parents called you?"

"No. Not yet. You're still supposed to be in Colorado for another week, you know."

"That's right. I forgot that part."

"Now, what are you going to do in Florida?"

"I'm going to the circus."

"Of course. Stupid of me to ask. Susanna . . . ?"

"What?"

"Nothing. Bring me some peanuts." She will be sitting there for a moment shaking her head and then she'll get up, pace around with her arms crossed over her chest and laugh, and then get down to work. She'll sit at the piano, her shoulders moving with the music, lowering her head and smiling privately under her curtain of hair, fingers flashing, and then she'll snap up straight and her head will be thrown back as she really moves through the piece, swinging with it, her whole body dancing it into the keyboard.

I've traveled enough now to look forward to new people to sit next to, new stories to hear. And I always have a new story to tell. I'm going to see my fiancé who is a trapeze artist with the circus and we're going to have a wedding with both of us riding in on an elephant. I'm not sure the man next to me at the coffee shop in the Chicago railroad station believes me. He is a Marxist on his way to Washington where his brother is a lawyer who will help him get clearance to teach again.

On the next train I'm sitting next to a teacher and I sit up very straight and explain I'm on my way back to college where I'm studying astronomy because I love stars. I had to come home for a short time because there was a problem in the family. Which is not a lie. There is. Me. Sometimes, I feel myself becoming these other people. It helps to be someone else because I don't get bored with my own company.

I got a rhythm to my traveling now. It's like playing, the more you practice the more you feel it. You get to a point where you can't imagine doing anything else. I got a train song in my head now, Chesapeake, Ohio, Baltimore, Lackawanna, Lackawanna, wanna, wanna get up and go. I watch the big trains coming, screeching in, pistons pumping, and I look up at the giant high-cheeked heads tearing down the track at me as I wait, and sometimes you can peer out and see another train coming, tearing up beside yours, cars coming parallel. Windows way up there at the top of their heads like tough-eyed Indian chiefs. We rip by little wooden stations, some of them abandoned, like kids standing there, old dogs or old cars and you see those too. And we go by the backs of towns and I see a light on in a window somewhere at night, always through a peach-colored shade, half-drawn, and I imagine someone sitting there, figuring out what to do about the trouble, waiting for someone who hasn't shown up. I don't see the light on so late as a sign of anything much good.

When Andrew would drive along Sunset I'd wonder how there could be so many rich people. Now I see it's a pretty small group of us. Most everyone you pass by on the train looks poor. And the people on the trains are neither rich nor poor, most of them going places they're not in too much of a hurry, too eager to get to. If you really want to go, I guess, you fly. So that brings me back to me: Your favourite subject, as Val says. Well, maybe I feel half and half about this. To tell the truth, I feel, on this trip, like I'm window shopping, just browsing through places and people, just to see if something catches my eye and says that's me.

The next train is older and rattles like a steel banjo, like twelve steel banjos. There are more older people on the train and the stations have fountains for white and colored, and the porters really lay on their accents. In the night we go through valleys and hills. I hear the train pulling and grinding and I imagine this is Southern mine country and I think of Aunt Molly.

How good you have to be on your feet on a train. Jigging and dancing your way along the aisles, the hissing of the doors opening and closing. I didn't stop swaying until it was almost time to leave my last place. If you work on a train, land must feel odd. It's like coming into silence after playing your guitar all afternoon. I like the rhythm of the train. I lie in my berth and rock. And I can hear the breathing and the snoring mixing in with the train song. One good thing about traveling this way is you're not so frantic thinking about what's going to happen when you get there because the traveling itself keeps you so busy.

Window shopping: Windows, looking out on possible places to be. People you talk to, like you do in a store, sort of like when Val and C.A. and I would go wandering around Westwood, except they'd always say, "Susanna, where are you now? . . . Susanna, come on . . . Susanna, jeez . . . Susanna, we were looking for you, are you still *here,* for God's sake?" No one's saying anything. No one's for sure saying Susanna, because I'm Suellen, or S. Havisham Lane like I was in Chicago when I called for the reservation.

I smile at myself in the train window, which is one of my favorite ways to look at myself, the lights and shadows of the dark going right through my face like thoughts. Like a movie called *Girl on the Train.* Of course, since I'm looking for Jackson, every time I see a tall man, blond hair, my throat catches. Flat, broad shoulders make my heart pound. Gestures, the way a man moves his hands, a guy with hands on his hips will bring me right back to the point and I race through a crowd at one train because I think I see him.

I have tried not to think about sex. Because if I do it will take over and then I won't think clearly. Boys who run away to sea don't think about it. Maybe that's the way to keep it out of your mind. Running keeps you distracted. You catch someone's eye, like this attractive man with silver hair, and I can imagine myself traveling with him; a young bride, all dressed in furs and diamonds and then we would make mad, passionate love in our drawing room and then he gets off at the next stop, thank God, so I don't have to talk to him and find out he is married, watches TV, and likes to hunt ducks. Maybe no one is as interesting as that expression everyone has one of for strangers—that sort of glamorous glint which seduces you for about thirty seconds until you can catch your breath and look him over, see the clocks on his socks and the hand-painted pheasant on his tie or notice how he snaps his fingers at the bartender in the club car and says, "Come here, boy."

Does Jackson travel around and have women looking at him like that until—older and wiser than I am—they figure him for a bounder, a run-out who left a towering career? But that's not what he is, there has to be something more to it . . . I try not to think of Jackson. So I look around the club car and try to figure out if we were stranded in a disaster who I would want to be with. I do not want to die a virgin. I wonder if conductors can marry you like captains can on shipboard.

How is it I am thinking of sex again so fast?

Perhaps it is the moving of the train, like being on a horse, you cannot avoid paying attention. I will try walking up and down. Maybe go stand in a vestibule and jump a lot. They hate you to stand in the vestibule with the wind in your face and especially when you play your guitar there, acting like you're some hobo on a fast freight.

I wonder if Jackson thinks about sex when he is traveling. Maybe Jackson doesn't like being jumped on, either. And runs.

Now in my berth alone and safe, therefore, I like it and can imagine the back and forth rocking coming from a man lying on top of me, holding me, rocking me, rocking into me. I lie there and clench my muscles and lift my hips against the rhythm of the train and I want to imagine who my faceless person will be. They are always faceless or hooded in black velvet. And it is easy to imagine how wonderful it would be to have someone lying on me when he is made of thin air.

Aunt Thelma said to me, between lunges at a cake: "You're a very curious young lady. And very stubborn. Does seeing someone really make the difference?" Or is it that I just wanted this time to explore . . . and that *that*, not where I'm going, is what counts? And I think it probably is also how you see it. Not what you see. Or who. Funny. I miss the powdery smell of her house, of frosting and old stockings.

She hugged me tight when I left. And Uncle Ken gave me twenty dollars and said to call them any time if I needed anything. I didn't want to take the money—but it meant something to him to be able to give it to me and Aunt Thelma held my hand tight over it and said to keep in touch, now. I want to find a present for them when I get to New York. What I really want is to find Jackson and bring him back to see them. But I didn't want to promise. How can you promise to deliver Jackson?

I'm rocking away down to Florida and I can feel, just feel the excitement gathering in my throat, but it's not a good excitement . . . it's a pounding . . . Lackawanna, Lackawanna, like I don't know if I wanna go. Circus! Jackson wouldn't be with a circus. Things couldn't have gotten that bad . . . but maybe it was what he always wanted to do. Always wanted to be . . . I think boys want to do that, like running away to sea, they want to run away and join the circus. From Jacksonville I catch the Flagler Eastliner. It's got old basketwork seats and smells of saltwater and therefore feels like home. Will a home that smells like a train some day feel more like home to me?

It is flat and plain all across Florida. It looks like a giant hedge clipper shot right across the state and sheared these bushes right down on a level. Once in a while you come to a quick orange grove, which is their favorite place to stick a lot of billboards. I have not been immediately aware of it but I am traveling down through the land of the World's Greatest: playground, waterways, alligators, oranges, genuine swamplands, cypress gardens, surfside auto raceways, Cadillac show-rooms, aquariums, nite life, water skiing, boating, low-cost resort-style housing, circus museum—there we go —and prune Danish. For which I would have to go to Wolfie's in Miami, which also has the world's greatest parade of luxury shops.

What I might miss out here, in the world's greatest category, I remember, I can find on the way to Palm Springs where Val and I used to go on the world's great-est burro ride and one Easter or Thanksgiving vacation we drank three of the world's greatest date milkshakes.

I look out the window of the car and up at the odd, towering, tropical clouds, like spiraling columns. World's greatest cloud formations.

Maybe Jackson's doing a high-wire act. Or he's a ringmaster. He'll be a star for sure. I get off at East Lake Beach feeling now exactly like Humphrey Bogart in *Key Largo*. There's a tiny little station house and a scrubby palm tree and one truck. I think there must be a mistake. It's been too easy so far. There's an old man flinging horseshoes around a water spigot that juts up in the middle of a patch of grass which is dead.

"Excuse me."

"What for?"

"Well, just hi, I'm trying to get over to the circus and I wonder if you have cabs here."

"Do we have whut?"

"Taxis. Someone to take people who get off this train that came in to where they are going."

"Someone ain't meeting you?"

"No. There is a circus here, isn't there?"

"Circus? They was a circus. You meant that ol' circus. They was it, but it's been gone now, two weeks. They pulled down about an hour or two south of here, probably down near Gulf Bay by now. Where y'all from?"

"Well, I came down from Jacksonville."

"You came all the ways down from Jacksonville to see thet circus? Whooeeee."

"You should only know," I say, reverting to my grandmother's dialect, which I think I do when I'm in trouble to feel less like I'm alone. "You should only know how far I've come to see this circus."

It's gummy and sticky, heavy in the air here and even the wooden railing I'm leaning against feels wet and there are dark water marks all over the planked floor, from an old hurricane probably.

"Is there a train to Gulf Bay? See, someone I know's with that circus and I just have to get there."

"The old Jacksonville-Georgia line used to run by there, but they haven't stopped down there for few years, since 'forty-eight, I think."

"Well, is there a bus?"

"If you kin wait till the afternoon, there's a bus comes by and stops down at the service station over across from the beach. You could sit there and wait." He looks at me now, stops throwing the horseshoes. I'm beginning to cry. I feel it in my jaw. But what kind of traveling is it if everything works out? So I lift up my suitcase and my train case and walk down the road and go out onto the beach so I can see the bus when it comes.

There's a kind of diner attached to the service station and I get what they're serving, which is fried shrimp, corn on the cob, a doughnut, and a Coke. And I get them to put it in a bag to take to the beach. I carry the paper bag in my teeth. A woman leaning on a backrest says, "Is that some kind of banjo? Kin you play that thing?" She says "thang." Actually.

"I sure kin. I play some really nice Southern folksongs."

"Where y'all from?" she asks.

"Well I came down from Jacksonville."

"Been livin' up there long?"

"No." Okay. Here goes—"I'm really from Hollywood." I just like to *say* Jacksonville. Obviously.

"I thought you said you was from Jacksonville, what you doing coming all the way from up there when you could have come right acrost from Hollywood?"

"Well, I had to go up north first . . . it's a long story."

"All the way from Hollywood. I hear they got a lot of building going on there. Going to be another Miami."

"I certainly hope not."

"What Hollywood you're talking about? You ain't a Southern gal?"

"No. I was talking about Hollywood in California. I've come here to see the circus. But it's moved. So I have to wait."

"Oh, well, see, we're talking about different Hollywoods. I'm talking about Hollywood Beach, just over acrost the state. . . . What you doing, a young lady like you, traveling all this way? Who you know in the circus? Some of them lions? That's just my little joke."

"No. I'm looking for someone who means a lot to me."

"Some fellow, I'll bet. Things you young gals won't do for some fellow."

I'm beginning to think this is crazy. If Jackson was with a circus they'd have publicized it. It would be all over the place. He can't exactly go around incognito. But he's an actor. He would know how to disguise himself. I might have walked right by him. If I do get to the circus, and if one of the clowns looks over my way and starts running then by God I'm going to run over and tackle him. Fat chance. Maybe Jackson won't know me. It has been, after all, four years. And I am a grown woman now. My lashes are longer.

This is a little beach with tiny soft waves coming up and shells everywhere you look.

"I've never seen so many shells. It's beautiful here," I say. She's resting now, but looking at me. It's not beautiful, exactly, but I like it. I take off my shoes and roll up my jeans and go down to the water, which isn't very far but you have to walk slow to keep from hurting your feet on the shells.

"At home," I yell back over my shoulder, "we mostly have mussel shells. And sort of thick shells." The water is clear and quiet, like a baby beach. The beach smell is soggy, not fresh. I don't care actually, it's a beach. I think I know what makes them so crazy in the middle of the country. They don't have any beach.

I sit on the sand and eat. And now and then someone else comes and asks me about the guitar. And I figure I'm not going to be stuck up or shy and so I play a few songs they're likely to know and get a couple of little kids singing and kicking in rhythm in the sand. It is, they tell me, unseasonably hot, and more families gather around with picnic coolers, the women in cotton dusters, sitting with their legs straight out, like my puppets used to sit, babies resting between their legs.

A young man looks at me from down the beach. He is wearing pink socks and black shoes.

I remember sitting on the Santa Monica beach one day the summer before this and I met this lady all dressed in black, walking right along the sand with her suitcase held together with cowboy belts. She was wearing mesh stockings, rolled down, and high heels.

"I have to catch the train," she informed me. "Have you got a quarter? I've got an apple." She undid her suitcase and handed me this apple.

"Yes . . ." I dug into the straw tea basket we were all carrying that summer and gave her a quarter. I ate the apple.

"It's a pleasure to work with Von Stroheim," she said as we sat in the sand, "but the business is changing. I'd get out if I were you."

"I've been thinking about that. But where?"

"Well, I'm going back to Broadway." She looked at a watch she was not wearing. "Garbo gave it to me." She pointed to her wrist. "Just listen to me, don't let it go to your head." She patted at the bit of hairnet she had covering her hair, which was red coming out gray, and she straightened the floppy black hat she had been fanning herself with. "There's the train," she said. "Now watch out for the sun. It destroys the skin." She picked up her suitcase and teetered down the beach on her high-heeled black dancing shoes.

And I wondered if Jackson was crazy somewhere.

I bury my corn cob under a sand castle I have been constructing. It is possible I think to make a rule that people who come to the beach with socks and shoes on are to be taken lightly. The man is reading a book by Jack Kerouac. Probably he is an intellectual.

Now, a couple of men are pitching cards into someone's old cap with white mesh cutouts on the sides, and they talk low and soft as the waves flap in whispers against the crunchy shoreline. One of the values, I'm seeing, of not belonging anywhere is that you can feel you belong anyplace you are. When the dusty old bus comes that afternoon and pulls up to the gas station across the highway, I feel sad and I say I'm going to come back sometime and sing them new songs and I know I won't ever be back. I wonder what kind of a girl I'd be if I had the courage to just stay.

I watch this long, flat beachland roll along on either side of the road as I bump along in this bus past green and yellow and pink painted motels, and scruffy little frame cabins, bleak against the big Florida sky. Shell stands for tourists, Stuckey's advertising saltwater taffy and pralines, and billboards for Sebring and Daytona. And I remember the record I left at home of Sebring sounds. Drove my mother crazy with that one. She came home one day and thought I'd really done it that time and got cars up in my room somehow. I was trying to figure out how you'd get music to sound like the roars of the racing cars.

I got Val, against her better judgment, as she said, to come over and improvise a solo with the steel string banjo and me with the guitar, using the car sounds like a big band behind us. I thought we ought to make a record of it. It was the kind of thing the Doodletown

Pipers would love, I said, and, after all, it's the sound of our time, which makes it kind of folk, just like some of the old songs which got their rhythm from trains, putting in whistles and steam engine sounds. I wouldn't have mentioned it to Scotty, of course, because he's such a traditionalist. He would have said you'd better get to be an expert at the basics before you get to start to improvise. If everyone felt that way no one would do anything new. I think the sound of any kind of car has a song in it somewhere.

I pick out a little motel called the Tumble Inn. I don't want Jackson to think I'm planning on moving in on him—if he's here, Susanna, he may not be—I want him to see how independent I am, like him. I don't want to stand there with my suitcases like a runaway kid in a movie. And if he isn't here—plan for that, Susanna—I'll need somewhere to go. I can always stay with him if he wants me to, later.

There's a nice couple running the place and they both bustle around showing me the little room, turning on the water (has no one stayed here recently or do they think I am one of those suspicious Northerners?), pounding on the bed, and lifting the shades. I thank them a lot, trying to sound Southern, and leave my suitcases on the foot of the bed. These suitcases look like I've been a lot of places.

With my guitar slung over my shoulder, I walk into the Tinker-Tanner circus grounds long about sunset, and they're just turning their lights on. They used to have a circus every year at the Shrine Auditorium, but I couldn't go because if I'm allergic to regular animals, it's for sure I'm allergic to elephants and tigers. So I'm kind of apprehensive and excited at the same time, even though something tells me this is a two-bit job as circuses go. The tent looks like giant webbed duck fingers pointing up at the sky with all these strings of little flags waving like charm bracelets. There's a calliope playing, and I think of the merry-go-round at home, and some out-of-tune brasses and percussion instruments playing like they never did it before and not one of them is listening to the others as they play. There are callers shouting with a kind of practiced jargon. "See the biggest rhinoceros in captivity, tusks big and round as my arm, yes, lady, big and round as my arm, that's right, in a cage made entirely of steel, ten thousand dollars for that cage alone . . . a genuine imported rhinoceros out of darkest Afreeca . . . only ten cents, same price to all."

All around the outside of the circus there are empty fields, like the farthest edges of our backlot. Grandfather used to take Val and me out there when we were small and I remember seeing all that dusty space and in the middle five or six different kinds of staircases standing there leading nowhere. And I wondered if each of them led up to a different part of heaven. I would probably, I think now, take the spiral staircase, so I'd have a good look around in all directions before I got there. The circus seems suspended now in twilight. Like those stairs. Isolated with its sounds and smells and the eerie glittering of the moving lit-up star on the Ferris wheel ride going round and round and the lights flickering now among the flags above the circus tent, and the lights racing around the various stands and the smaller sideshow tent which I am facing.

Children swirl by me through the dust and a mother stands near me with one child on her hip and another tugging at her, looking at cat-faced balloons bobbing on their strings in the air. The young vendor teases the child with the balloons and, as the mother walks away, follows behind, chanting, "Only half-a-buck, ma'am; half-a-buck, lady. Have a balloon for the little boy."

I walk past a cotton candy booth and I watch the candy whirling around like pink hair in a tin pan. My face is against the glass like the faces of small children, watching as the colored red sugar is hurled into the vat and is lifted as it becomes foam and is twirled onto cardboard cones. Damp sugar crusts along the counter like rosy sand, and in the change box and under the nails of the man selling cotton candy. I smile my best smile. "That looks like fun, what you're doing. Do you still like cotton candy?"

"Never touch the stuff."

With nothing but my guitar on my back I feel lighter about everything. I never feel its weight. It is part of me by now. About the weight that angels would feel from wings.

"Ladeez and gentlemen . . . Starting now in the Big Top . . . the Amazing Tinker-Tanner Three-Ring Spectacular, featuring international stars from all over the world . . . see death-defying feats, clowns, the waltzing ponies, Petunia the Elephant, famed on five continents, and those dazzling daredevils the Dynamic Damones. . . ."

I turn and go with the crowds rushing to the big top. I give the ticket to the usher in his blue cotton uniform trimmed with faded yellow braid. A man peddling dolls in pink feathered outfits walks by displaying his handsome, hairy chest under an open red and green striped shirt. He waves the dolls who dance on rubber bands suspended from wooden wands to the beat—or, actually, and even better, not quite to the beat—of the band, which is moving out, leading a parade around the outside of the three rings. Two dusty elephants with reddish blankets trudge out with girls on their backs, girls with muscular legs, peroxided hair, and gold sequinned briefs and pointy bras jutting out from an improbable position on their chests. The elephants are wearing also bad paper party hats. A clown comes jigging along with a purse swinging from his arm and a veiled hat, another clown runs by, waving to the grandstand, pulled along by a small dog on a leash who is wearing a hippopotamus mask with a huge open mouth and blinking red eyes. Ponies trot by, prancing, busy red feathers jouncing about in their manes. Then comes a group of cowboys in Wild West outfits on palominos. The cowboys gleam with greasepaint. I can see the harem girls in the wings handing their jackets to someone, standing around like extras and then throwing themselves into the parade, jumping out into handsprings and cartwheels and I think of Carleen. I keep waiting for the director to say, "Cut, let's take this one over." I can imagine Myron leaning across to the film editor who comes and sits beside him in the evening, taking notes on the dailies and rushes, saying, "Tell Finkelhoff I want to see him in my office in the morning." This is definitely a Monogram B-Unit number. Could Carleen be so tricky, could I be so dumb? Have I wandered into a black and white Dane Clark detective movie? I am Veronica Lake and I have been thrown a real curve.

But you don't go somewhere like this without a reason. Someone like me does not just wind up at this circus in Gulf Bay by accident. Or maybe that's exactly what someone like me does do. I remember Scotty saying, "Susie, some people get hooked on a person like people get hooked on dope or booze. And they do crazy things—go off on wild-goose chases. I'm not saying you're doing that . . . just something to think about." Wild-goose chase, and I am the goose. I watch the Dynamic Damones make a pyramid even Duane and Carleen and their whole pep team could be proud of, and Josef and His Beautiful Patti defy death on the trapeze and Marie and Pierre give a "French accent" to the high wire while jugglers throw sequinned rings around below them, and in another ring clowns in tutus play with spangled jump ropes, a ragged old bear rolls around in a wheelchair with a hospital gown on, and the band keeps playing, as though the players have never met each other, playing in the key of Loud. The animal act comes on. Clowns and roustabouts put up a big cage in the center ring and then: the ringmaster. I look at him. No. This is a shorter, wiry man. His three mangy lions and a tiger who looks like a mountain lion painted with stripes sit like people waiting for a bus after a long day.

I am getting asthma. My pills are in my suitcase back at the motel. It makes it worse to imagine the pills in

the right-hand corner of my train case. I feel my chest
tighten. People who have asthma do not run away. It is
a disease which inspires caution. For the first time, I
think of my bed, my blue and white room. My birds'
nests and the puppets sometimes swinging in them, their
heads and arms leaning over the edges like dazed bal-
loonists. It is just the air in the tent. I tell myself. And
the hair of the animals, and as the lions and alleged
tiger climb painfully on their perches while the ringmaster roars ferociously, cracking his whip to wake
them up, to distract them from their reveries, I can see
the hair, floating over, whirling around me, stirred up
by each beat of the drum, and I watch the clowns kicking up dust with their big, flapping shoes. None of them
moves like Jackson, even if Jackson was disguising how
he moves. Jackson was never that good an actor. The
little hippodog veers in my direction. The plumes on
the horses, waiting again in the wings near their riders
(who are playing cards at a small table back there that
I can see from here), are full of ages of dust. The grandstand is silty, the canvas is heavy with dust floating
down, and the hay is alive and wicked with it. My lungs
are like the insides of a vacuum cleaner. I used to watch
Frank dump our vacuum in the service yard. Even from
up in my window it would give me an attack. He would
look up at me and laugh and make a ferocious face,
holding the dust in his hand as if to throw it. And I
would laugh from behind the glass, and put a look of
terror on, crossing my fingers to ward off "Dustman."
That seems so long ago. I miss Frank—

I will call home and I will tell them I will fly back.
(From where? How?) And my mother will say, "But,
Susanna, you know you're allergic to the circus."

I come out into the air, and walk to the edge of the
circus grounds, very slowly, telling myself to go very
quietly, not to think beyond this particular breath. I sit,
gently, as though I am afraid to ruffle a mote of dust,
on a bench. I look at the star shape on the Ferris wheel,
the lights going round and round, and make my breath

go round and round, dipping down, moving up, down, around and up, and I think of ice, cold and clear as glass, and I listen, behind the sound of the band and the crowds and the animals—no, do not even think of animal—I listen, listen Susanna, listen, listen to the lapping of the little waves, cool and clear and salty, and think of the ocean across the highway, get with the pounding of the surf, the swish of it coming up and going back, breathe with it. I wait until it eases, until the packing breaks into a wheeze I can manage. And then I walk over to see the sideshow, walking slowly among the small groups of people, wandering aimlessly. A man is yelling at his son at the shooting gallery. "You ain't good at nothin'. Now, look here, I'll show you how it's done." I stand there hoping the man misses the tin ducks too. And he does, and cuffs the kid. "See, you make me so damn mad."

A girl in a blue nylon blouse walks by with her date who's holding a big stuffed teddy bear. She's eating a Good Humor. Her date . . . I might write a song called "What Do You Do on a Saturday Night When You're Running Away from Home?"

I get a Coke and a box of Cracker Jack and sit on a barrel next to the soda pop stand and look at the posters for the sideshow and watch the boy in the blue and white striped jacket with the megaphone. "See the Alligator Man, half man, half reptile, the astonishing Atomic Woman, ten thousand volts shoot right through her, the Tattooed Girl . . . and the Two-Faced Man, the shock of a lifetime, and the Boy with the World's Largest Tongue."

The posters are drawn by someone who hadn't learned to do hands and feet yet. The skin is painted in that funny orange they used to call *Flesh* on the label of the cans in Miss Lippincott's art class—the color Mary's makeup gets around her hairline by late afternoon. And all the pictures have round blue eyes and huge muscles. The Bearded Lady comes out in a harem suit to lure us in, she turns her back and then whips off

her veil and shows her long brown beard. She's taller
than the boy barker and has big shoulders and falsies
because her chest is flat around her bra and I wonder if
she's a man who loved to play dressup when he was a
little boy.

I finish my Coke and get the toy out of the Cracker
Jack, which is a small yellow plastic suitcase, and I
guess you could say that's appropriate.

Sideshow: It's like walking past a display of store
windows, each one has its little stall, with big painted
signs and a wooden platform to stand on under a spot-
light; there's a chair painted red on each platform, and,
because most of the crowd is inside the big top, there's
a kind of informal feeling, like a set before they start
shooting. The Fat Lady is eating a hot dog. I try to
avoid her little piggy eyes. No older than I am, she's
wearing a tight pink dress, and has a bow in her hair
like a pig dressed up. She sees a couple of other people
coming and she sighs and stands up, clutching her hot
dog in her hand, and says, "Ladies and gents," she
wheezes too, "I was a normal baby and when I was
fourteen I got sick and had to stay in bed and then . . ."

I am by the Snake Charmer fast, not so fast I do not
see her take thick black coiling things out of a wooden
box and start putting them around her body.

The Sword Swallower is just an ordinary guy, with a
paunch. "Now my wife's not much of a cook, folks, so I
just pick up a little dinner out, like this here tasty . . ."
And he picks up a sword and throws back his head.
"Like my friend over here, the Fire Eater, I've got unusual appetites. Like they say, one man's meat is another man's poison," and he thrusts that sword right
down his throat.

The Fire Eater, right next to him, says, "Yeah, Harry,
I like to do my own barbecue right on the spot." Have
they said these things a million times, or what? I don't
want to look at the Reptile Man or the Tattooed Lady
when I glimpse the snaky lines going up on her arms,
but she is speaking to me and I look at her eyes above

the tassel tattooed under them like long lashes. "It took one thousand and one hours total to get all this done. I had the best tattoo artists in the world do me. My belly here was done in Hong Kong, it's a genuine replica of a clipper ship and when I dance, like this, you can see the ship move, isn't that something? Honey, do you play that thing?"

"Yeah," I say. I want to say why did you do it, or do you really think it looks pretty or are you sorry now and are you stuck with that forever? "That's real gorgeous," I say in my Carleen voice, and I turn and stop. My heart pounds. I see the blond hair on his arm. The squared-off thumb jutting out from the wrist. The way he stands. One arm is bare. The other covered by a red cloak. I don't want to move my eyes up to see.

I LOOK AND FLINCH AWAY AND LOOK BACK. THE VOICE comes through the mask. I don't know whether I am relieved or not. It is not Jackson's voice. The mask is making it echo, but still the cadence is different. "Hiya, I'm the Two-Faced Man. This is my public face, and I wear it when I'm with people because when I don't they scream and run from me. And I'm really a pleasant fellow and I don't like for folks to run when they see me."

It is like a nightmare because the mask looks like a carefully made rubber replica of a face of a handsome man. But not a real man, a mannequin. It is not even a mask made to look like Jackson's face, but the hair is blond as his, or the fake hair. It is like a terrible joke.

"Now you-all just hold on to something, to each other, and shut your eyes because I'm going to turn around and when I come back, you'll see my other face, the face I see every time I look in a mirror. You can run away, but I never can. You holding on?"

"I'm counting to fifteen real slow. If you've got a weak heart, you've got time."

Jackson's brother. I feel angry—what do I feel angry about?—or is it fear? I am terrible because I feel angry at him for being Jackson's brother. For not being Jackson when I thought I was here to see Jackson—and I am afraid because I am not going to run.

"Now, if you have any small children, I'd move them out now. I am a Living Nightmare is what they used to call me back in school. Or the No-Face Boy." I can tell by the sound of his voice that the mask is off. The voice is flat and it has the sound of an Illinois kind of voice.

His brother is a monster. I feel sick and sorry I did this. But I don't go and as he turns around I lift my eyes and before I can flinch those eyes flicker out at me and catch me in their terrible stare, their terrible lidless stare. The lips which are not lips move. There is no upper lip at all and you see the teeth.

"There was a fire when I was a small kid. My parents died in that fire and I was burned. But life is what you make it, as they say."

Why do they all say, "as they say"? Who says? What kind of life? . . . And Jackson is an orphan. I complain because I cannot find my father. And he has no one. No wonder he cannot stay anywhere long enough to remember. No wonder he keeps running. And even running does not take away memory. What kind of a life do you have with such a memory running along with you? Interesting, he does not mention his brother. And there is no mistake. Look how he stands. Does he see that when he goes to movies? And does he go—or does he fear people will look right at him? There are small tufts of blond hair rising from a couple of places in his mottled scalp. I cannot stop staring.

"You just look real close, honey. And when you have kiddies just be sure you tell them not to play with fire."

It is a face of some terrible kind of heavy lacework, a layer of scars that stretches across the skull like wretched gauze, no nose, but holes, and the arrow of bone, the yellow, ivory, mottled and pale purple. The place where the lips would be is uneven and slants across the teeth, up from them so it seems contorted in a terrible permanent sneer. His head under the lights here is like a set designer's model of a drought-stricken terrain.

I stand. I want to tell him he is my uncle. But I can't breathe again. And I don't know what to say. Would he rather not know? Would he rather forget? What could I do with him? I walk out slowly. I try not to look frightened. But how does he want you to look at him? I get outside and I wish I had never come. And I remember the little scars on Jackson's hands. He must have tried to save his brother.

I try to smile at him. I feel I have slapped it on my face, the smile, like a piece of gummed paper. He has no ears, wads of scar tissue on one side. My God, my God. I think of Theo and O'Connor—O'Connor bandaged and dying with Alan screaming at her. Did Jackson scream and run from him? It is better to be dead. I look back down the row of stalls. Some of them don't have to be freaks. Why do they do this? Why does he put himself on exhibit like this? This, my other family, is suddenly a bizarre mirror image. I am suffocating from their craziness. They have gotten together to plan this nightmare to get back at all of us because they don't fit. I imagine them all saying, "Well, we really scared hell out of that one." The night is hot and still, and the breeze has died down. People are coming out of the big top. God, if You're up there, why do You invent such lives, why do You maim and make people crazy and allow them to just go through it, knowing, feeling it? How they must hate us to put themselves on exhibit, so we SEE it.

I know why Jackson runs and hides. If he stands still too long he sees that face. I want to find him and tell him I understand. I bet he wishes his brother was dead. And he probably read about Val's fire and it reminded him. It must have been like a nightmare to hear about it. And it probably reminded him he wished his brother was dead once. He must have felt guilty wishing that. I can imagine how outraged Aunt Thelma would be at him for feeling like that. I've got to tell Jackson I understand.

I lean against a tall chicken-wire fence. I feel I could be back in school. I cannot breathe. I am gasping and people are looking. The more I think about it, the worse it gets. "God, get me out of here and back home." I pray very hard when I cannot breathe. It is the time I most believe in God. And when I pray to Him when I am in trouble I always promise I'll remember to thank Him when things get good again—but sometimes I forget. Is is possible that when you get to the point where you always do thank Him He makes everything perfect? Sure, like the nuns who get raped and shaved and burned in wars. Or like Theo who couldn't talk or O'Connor who was always discussing things with the Virgin on the beads. God, I'm sorry for everything I thought back there. I cannot say this, but I think it, because until I get back to the motel and get my pill and until the Tedral begins to work, I will not be able to talk out loud. I feel so little and dumb and so lonely. It wasn't supposed to be like this. I wonder if Jackson's brother thinks that. I wonder if he dreams every night of his old face and sees it burning away. I wonder if he ever made love. I wonder if anyone ever kissed him. And could he feel kissing? Could he forget, in a moment of sex, how he is? But how odd that he writes his family. But Jackson doesn't. I wonder if Carleen knew. I somehow don't think Aunt Thelma would have told her.

The Tedral is taking forever to work. I fill the sink with hot water and cover my head with a towel, making a tent, bending over to let the steam surround me. I see the faces float and bob until I will them away. And I put Jackson's face there and I cannot make it have an expression. I see him as a sequence of the old stills I have in my scrapbook, at home, under my bed.

I have to call Val. When I can breathe. I will go to the managers' cabin. I think I saw a pay phone there. I wish I could get out of here now. When I take the towel away, my face and head feel chilled, but I can breathe easier. I sit on my bed and play, tuning her, playing nothing really yet . . . "I went to the circus, and what did I see? Tell you a story, you tell one to me. . . ."

I wonder what he feels about the Fire Eater standing right there. I wonder if he flinches every time that little flame goes up. I wonder if he looks at himself through the eyeholes when his mask is on and imagines himself playing Jackson Lane in the movies. I wonder if Jackson sends him money. I wonder if he sends it right back. I wonder if he knows where Jackson is . . . bet he doesn't. Bet there's no return address on the envelope.

The managers are watching TV, laughing at Ernie Kovacs. "Sure, honey, you just use the phone anytime. Y'all get somethin' to eat?"

"Yes. Thank you. Could I call someone?"

"Sure, don't mind us, then. There's some fresh pie on the stove, if you'd like. Here, you get the phone, I'll get the pie for you. You been eating that carnie food . . ." The lady bustles about.

"Thank you very much. That's very nice."

I listen to the accents change as I get the operator in Jacksonville with her flat Florida country drawl and then the elegant magnolia sound of the soft-voiced Atlanta operator and now here's New York for you: "I can't hear you, operator, speak up, will ya." And she's cracking gum in ears right down the whole Eastern line.

Hildy, the teacher Val is living with, answers the phone and calls Val.

"Where are you and what's the matter?"

"Why is something the matter?" I am twisting the cord of the phone around my fingers. Hearing her voice makes me want to cry.

"It always is when you ask how I am first. Besides, you're breathing like a horse."

"I went to the circus. I'm allergic to lions."

"Well, I'm certainly glad you're catching a little entertainment on your grand tour."

"I saw Jackson's brother." And I wasn't going to tell her. I have no control.

"I thought he didn't have one. Susanna, when are you getting here? Vera calls every night. She's beginning to think something's up. My mother called last night and said Vera's really hurt."

"Hurt—but not worried. I should have known."

"Of course she's worried, but I'm a very good liar." I wonder if she's lying to me. If they know exactly where I am.

"You didn't say anything to Lillian? You did. I'll bet you did."

"Look, Susanna, you're almost eighteen. You made up your own mind to do this. Are you doing it because you want to find Jackson, or because you want to see how much everyone will worry? You're not a little girl, and, even if they knew where you are, they're not going to come and drag you back home."

"Okay, okay. I didn't call for a lecture."

"I know. Listen, don't spend any more money on the phone. I'll see you when I see you, okay?"

She doesn't sound angry. But distracted again. A wall is between us.

"I guess I have been whining. I'm sorry. But you were the one who said they were worried."

"Well, I'm just tired of being the middleman. What I'm trying to say is if you're doing it, do it, and to hell with the effect. . . . What's his brother like? Does he know where Jackson is?"

"I didn't ask."

"Well, that's wonderful! What's the point of going there if you didn't ask?" I can just picture her, with the phone held in the crook of her neck, her chin tilted down and her arms busy working on a piece. She wants to end this conversation and not just to save me money.

"It's a long story." I wouldn't be mean enough to tell her over the phone. She will think of Theo and O'Connor—I mean, what could I say to her? That my uncle is something like what might have happened to Theo if he had lived? That's what she would think even if I didn't say it like that, which of course no one would—but you wouldn't be able to keep from thinking about it.

"Oh, listen, before you go. Chris and I were down in the Village the other night at this place called the Improv. We did a song we wrote, kind of a parody, nothing serious, we just do these as a kind of game"— which means it's probably a song I would adore; she also knows it's good or she wouldn't be singing it somewhere. Val is very careful about being just right. Even when she's funny.. She's never silly. "The stuff we're doing is kind of like the guy in Cambridge I told you about, Tom Lehrer, but I think we're more New York—funny song about Hollywood—you'll like it. . . . Anyway, what I was going to tell you is that we saw your former great love Angelo."

"Angelo . . . my God. What did he say?" I am instantly jealous. Not of her songs or evident success—but she saw Angelo.

"Well, he looks fantastic, he's left the Playhouse and is studying at the Actors' Studio, with Strasberg. And even I have to say he is very, very good. He's really matured. Very interesting. Very." I can see her narrowing her eyes.

"Did he ask about me? . . . What did you tell him?"

"We hardly had time to talk, but he did, I think, ask what you're up to, and I said you were traveling."

"Traveling! Didn't you tell him I was coming there? . . . Val!"

"I'm sure I did. I'm having coffee with him tomorrow, so I'll mention it."

"You and Chris?" I ask.

"No. Just me and Angelo. Susanna . . ." I know. She's bating her breath against the tone of jealousy she hears in my voice. Easy to hear. I catch it myself. It is like asthma. I feel it come over me the same way. And I despise it the same way.

We hang up. The operator gets on. "Honey, you done? That'll be fouah dollahs and sixty cents mowah!"

I stand there for ages putting in coins. I feel so strange, after talking to Val, as though today was a dream. Her life seems so connected to our past, sort of appropriate. Mine has nothing to do, these last ten days, with my real past—has it really been ten days? It feels like a month. It's more about a past I've just imagined, or wanted to discover, and I'm not sure what it's told me about myself except I get along on my own pretty well, all things considered. And that's something to learn.

I go back to my room and play my guitar quietly. "Nine hundred miles . . ." How many miles has it really been? How many more to go? . . . And I haven't even begun to sort it all out. And all it's done is make me want to see Jackson more. It's been like skirting around the edge of his life.

I'm doing too much thinking. I love Jackson. I love him because he's my father and I loved him before I knew he was and isn't there such a simple thing as you just love someone because he's the kind of person you love and that's that? Like I love Scotty—not the same way—not for any reason but that he's my kind of person and I would like him anyway. Even if there never had been Jackson to begin with.

Scotty. Scotty knew all about the brother. I bet not from Jackson. I bet Jackson never talks about him at all. I bet he knew from Aunt Thelma. I think of her decorating everything within sight with ribbons and shells and domes and triple waves and templates of sugar coating, covering, masking, hiding, embellishing. Could it ever be pretty enough or busy enough? I go back to what Uncle Alan said to O'Connor when she was lying there dying: "Did he scream? Did you hear him screaming?" How old was Aunt Thelma? Did she see? Did she hear? No wonder he loved my mother with her skin like milk. And yet I see why he would be scared to be attached to anyone again. I wouldn't go back there. And look how guilty I feel. So maybe since he won't go back to see his brother he won't permit himself the pleasure of going back to see me. Maybe he would feel he doesn't deserve to do one if he can't face the other. But then I remember what Scotty said about circumstances not really changing us. A skiptown type is always going to move around. Like me.

Since I really only have enough money for the train to New York I ask the managers in the morning if any of their roomers are going up to Jacksonville because I can catch the Orange Blossom Special right from there to New York.

They set me up with this salesman who has a rack of sport shirts swinging across the back of his car.

"What is that you got, a geetar or a banjo? Can you play it?"

I wonder why that is the first question people ask. "Play what?" I have wanted to say, but I won't, because I am always asking for favors all the way across the country and up and down. What do they think I am doing carrying this guitar around all over to hell and gone if I cannot play it?

"It's a guitar," I tell him, and, "Yes, I play it. Every night before I go to bed and every morning when I wake up and whenever I can in between, and I sing for my supper, and for my bread and butter and so forth." I sit far over near the right-hand door, all hunched together. I would like to put my legs up, Indian style, which is how I like to ride, but he has plastic seat covers and people who have plastic seat covers don't want you putting your feet on them either.

"Well, I didn't mean to get you all huffy. I was jus' askin'. Where y'all from?"

"Hollywood, California."

"You in pictures?" This is the other question, next to "Do you know any movie stars?" (Or "Can you play that?")

"No. I'm just a kind of traveling folksinger." Sometimes I think I would like to tell the truth and see if anyone would believe me.

"I don't know much about that," he says. "I see a lot of movies, though. And I get to talk with a lot of people in my line of work. I could tell them out there what people really like. People I talk to like to see movies about someone wronged and then getting their revenge. They used to make more of those movies and that's when people stopped going to so many movies, when they stopped telling stories like that. You can't beat a picture about a woman scorned. Everyone knows someone like that and they can look at that movie and really say, 'Why, that's true.' You want to see someone really get out and get after someone else because no one really does that, but they all want to. And that way you get some adventure in it, some big scenes of places no one has been to. You put some of your big stars in it and that's what a movie ought to be."

I can't think of any movie like that, except he's talking about my own real life right now. It even has a big star in it. Except the star hasn't shown up on the set. This morning I woke up hating Jackson. And thinking, more than I did last night, that my uncle hangs on to his sanity by his teeth by doing his bizarre act. Everyone plays a little game to pretend a kind of satisfaction. I would rather see someone screaming and yelling. I would like to plan a reunion of Thelma, Jackson, and his brother and make them see each other and tell each other what they really think. Except none of them would show up. I wonder where the Boy with the World's Largest Tongue was. I may be going up to New York with more questions than I had to begin with. There's only one person who can answer them—God knows where he is—and God, I say to Him, You are neither showing nor telling . . . although You have given a few pointers. I'm sure my grandmother is furious. Slammed her cards down on the table—is it His table and are His possessions capitalized too?—and rattled her rings at Him. "What," she is saying, "is Susanna doing in Florida with a traveling salesman in a Nash? We never rode in such a car. If this was Your idea, I'm leaving."

"So," says God, "so call when you get there to let me know you're all right."

Watch, I think, how He will have all His lines busy and then complain she did not call.

I must call my parents. I mean Myron and my mother. Parents, somehow they *are* my parents. I would never call Jackson Lane a *parent*. He is my father. That is different.

WHEN I FIRST VISITED NEW YORK, WHEN I WAS LITTLE, we stayed in the Sherry-Netherland Hotel and my room had field flowers all over everything. I could look out at this big park in the middle of town and see Broadway just on the other side, where the Eastern stars were all dancing and singing in their musicals. And down below the taxis went like little tin toy cars in every color you could want. We saw *Annie Get Your Gun,* which was great except, frankly, they should have put Ethel Merman on a diet and done something with her hair. And *Oklahoma!* and *Carousel.* And *Call Me Mister,* which was terrific. I adored Betty Garrett, and how could they say she was a Communist? That was a very patriotic musical. Funny how I am sitting here remembering. When I was on those trains when I was small, I did a lot of remembering and at the same time fixing pictures of what I was seeing to remember later. I have been going back to my old past, to get pictures of things and people and places that were part of it. Will they some day be so mixed up together that I will remember when Carleen and I were girls together and playing in the Midwest town on the backlot and will the fire I think I remember be the one where my uncle was burned? Will it all come together like a song, where what you hear you come to believe you really do know and will I tell my children about things from the past as if I had been there—will it get mixed and moved and rearranged to become legend like Grandmother's stories?

I arrive at Penn Station. And Val is waiting for me. I see her up ahead, standing, arms crossed, ankles crossed, angled against the wall, examining people going by. I don't know why I do things like this but I know she sees me and I pretend not to see her, to be looking around and then be startled to see her.

This is the first time I have been met on the whole trip. Which makes tears rush to my eyes. I blink them back. She will hate that. But she looks at me softly and reaches for my suitcase.

"No, I've got that. You can have the train, case, if you want."

"Oh, thanks. You picked up a little sun down there."

"Well, what's a cruise for?"

She looks terribly pale, in fact. They all do. Packs of gray people, floods of them. Mostly men in raincoats rushing by, like turtles walking on hind legs.

"Val—are you all right?"

She looks at me steadily. I love her face. The straight dark eyebrows, the amused tiny lines on either side of her mouth. Her square lower lip. This is the most reassuring face. Almost too reassuring an expression right now, as though she is reassuring herself.

"I'm fine. Exhausted. I've got a paper on harmony due tomorrow, so I'm working hard. I have the most incredible teacher, someone who knows so much more than you do that he makes you want to work. It's such a different feeling here, Susanna. It's more like England. I'd missed that. I mean, people really care about the quality of thinking. Everyone has read so much. You are going to love it. Not at first—but you will. I really want you to."

"Val. I haven't even thought about that. I'm really just here to see you. Don't make plans for me. Okay? So much has happened. I can't just drop the whole thing. One thing I've got to do is call home and get some more money. I may tell them I have to take a look at some places in the Midwest before I make up my mind."

"Well, you won't have too far to go. I have some news for you."

"Val. Why didn't you tell me?"

"I am telling you. Look, we can't just stand here."

"Is there somewhere we can grab a cheeseburger? I'm really hungry."

"There's a coffee shop, but it's terrible. We could go up to the West End near school—but I'll see people and I'll never get that paper done. We'll go in here."

We sit down and order. Val orders two lemon Cokes for herself. Nothing else.

"Now. Don't say I never did anything for you. I was in Saks the other day and something happened . . ."

"What were you doing in Saks? They have one here?"

"Of course. It's the biggest one. I needed a new black turtleneck. I'm into my all-black period. I don't believe I'm about to tell you something you're dying to hear and you're asking me about Saks. Yes. I believe it. God." She stops and laughs, putting her hand on my shoulder.

"I got a black turtleneck too. In San Francisco." I'm very pleased I have done something on my own that is just right. You can't make too many mistakes with a black turtleneck. I'm not going to spring the red Bermuda shorts on Val right away. They look so great with black knee socks and my red fringed loafers and a few red beads looped around the neck.

"We have so much to talk about. I have to tell you about Angelo too. He is terrific," she says.

"But what about Chris?" I ask. I hope everything is wonderful with him. For me. Maybe I am smart enough to handle Angelo after all this. But then who *handles* someone like Angelo?

"I don't know . . . I'm going with him. I guess. He's very talented too." Val continues, "But I want to hear everything, about your relatives; do you feel different?"

"I don't know how I feel. I'm kind of numb. . . ." I'm thinking about Angelo and Val. How can that even make a dent when so much has happened? I do not feel different. I am here with Val and just as jealous—and eager to please and excited to see her, all at the same time.

"So, what happened at Saks?" I ask.

"Well, I was in a fitting room trying on a very tasty

black wool, and from the next fitting room I heard two salesladies talking in the middle of the clanking of the hangers.

" 'Do you remember my customer Mrs. Rodgers?' one of them said.

" 'How do you expect *me* to remember *your* customers—?'

" 'Out of town, ten top, twelve bottom? Loaded?' " Val is doing these New York accents perfectly.

" 'Oh, that one.'

" 'See, I told you you knew her.' You know how they talk."

"Yes, yes," I say.

"Well, this one said she read that Jackson Lane was living with this Catherine Rodgers in her ski lodge somewhere in New Hampshire. 'Remember him?' she said. And I thought—do we ever . . . so."

"My God. Val. You're brilliant! How wonderful!"

Skiing. Why didn't I remember? He loves to ski.

"So I leaned my head around the door, and said I happened to overhear them and that Catherine Rodgers was a great friend of my mother's and did this woman happen to have the name of the town, because my mother would love to write her. And she said it wasn't really the store's policy—"

"Oh no—" I put my hands over my mouth.

"You don't think I'd leave it at that do you? I said my father and Jackson had known each other in Hollywood and I even told them who my father was and she said, 'Such a tragedy,' and I got to listen to a story about her brother-in-law who was blacklisted for teaching Russian history rather too thoroughly in New Jersey and then I bought the damn dress and—"

"Val—I can't stand it!"

"Well, you'd better pick up a ski outfit, because here it is. And don't say I never did anything for you." She hands me a piece of paper with *Mrs. Catherine Rodgers*.

"Oh. Val. I love you!" And in reaching forward to hug her, I knock over one of her Cokes. "What can I do to thank you?" I'm babbling as I'm mopping up Coke with a handful of paper napkins.

"Not throwing Coke all over me would be a beginning—well. The seasoned traveler returns," she says. "We could pick up your trail just by following the wads of wet paper napkins."

So I will spend the rest of the winter skiing with my father. And then I'll go to a college in New Hampshire and come next fall we'll walk through autumn leaves together and he'll come to my graduation in four years, walking in, in a white suit, while they play "Pomp and Circumstance" and everyone will say, "We never knew," or, "We always knew. How wonderful you found each other after all these years." And I'll be a cheerleader, although not full-time like Carleen, and he'll throw out the ball for the first game. I can see him. He'll bring me a chrysanthemum. And we'll have a huge family dinner at the Lodge. East meets West meets Midwest. Thelma will do a cake in the shape of a ski mountain with feuillage or whatever she wants and it will all be wonderful.

I hope it is not an unlisted number. That wouldn't stop me.

Val rents a room in Hildy Aaron's apartment. Hildy Aaron (at first I thought it was one word) is a history of music professor at Juilliard and Val says everyone adores her. Because the rent isn't much, Val helps Hildy with some chores. "But every time I decide to really fix the place up, Hildy decides there's somewhere marvelous that I must go. I think she's terrified I will wreck her filing system, which, as you'll see, is pretty informal," Val says. "Get ready. You're going to hate it."

Hildy Aaron lives on Claremont Avenue. Her building is across from Juilliard and "That," Val says, "is the best of it."

"Well, I won't mind—I've been around."

"Actually, I love the Village a lot better," Val says, as we rattle north ("uptown," Val says) in a taxi.

"Charming old houses, you can just imagine Henry James walking around."

"Henry James?" A musician? Brother of Harry? Who?

"Susanna—*Washington Square, Portrait of a Lady, What Maisie Knew*—you would love his books."

"*What Maisie Knew?* The old Ann Sothern picture."

"Sorry. I forgot for a minute."

"What?" I am looking at the way everything is getting more massive, big buildings like prisons in dark brick— no trees, no windows to look in. And it breaks your heart to see how they try to trim up these places with snazzy canopies and cement trimmings—pieces of sculpture here and there, like fat old men wearing boutonnieres, and sticking out their chests to show how proud they are.

"Love his books. Probably. Well, you would if you'd ever just read. You have so much you could learn—it's like going into another world. It's like music."

"I'd rather learn by watching real people, here. Now. There's plenty of time to read when I'm older."

"But if you read you can bring so much more to what you see." I'm having enough of a time just seeing with my own eyes. I don't want anyone else's ideas coming in. But this is not what Val wants to hear. I must try not to seem dumb or stubborn about Eastern ideas, things, and places.

Hildy has long grayish red hair piled up sort of askew and glasses on a black cord because you can see right away she'd lose them if they weren't attached. I've never seen so many books. Even the kitchen is piled with books. Cabinets where dishes would go have the doors open and they're filled with stacks of papers. The sink is full of dishes from Mexico and old cups without handles and battered little pots and bulletins and announcements of intellectual-looking events are tacked onto the walls. And there are pictures of Adlai Stevenson all around.

"That's my man," she says. And she looks at my

guitar. "Are you good?" That is a relief after everyone else in the country asking if I "can play that thing."

"I'm good," I say. "For me."

"You'll learn," she says, "not to qualify."

Val is going out with Chris for a while. "Be right back," she says. That's what's good about college. You can just come and go like that. But I've always done that anyway. Hildy helps me make up the big old faded russet velvet couch in the living room for a bed. I can just imagine my mother letting someone sleep in the living room. Even if it was the only room she had—she'd sleep standing up herself. Hildy says, "Now, Val gets what she wants from the store. But I've always got Coke on hand. It takes a while to absorb things when you're in a new place, but from what Val tells me, you're used to that. I've got plenty to read, just help yourself."

At least Val has not told her I don't read. Much. "If you wouldn't mind, I should call my mother. I'll call collect."

"Just go ahead. The phone's here, somewhere. Yes." She scuffles around in a huge basket under some newspapers, and pulls out the telephone. "And here's today's *Times,* did you see it?"

"Of course—thanks—can't get my day started without it." They are wild about their newspaper here. I know that from Eastern boys. And the New York office used to carry it out with them.

I call my mother, who sounds completely distracted. Does she miss me so much? "Of course, I do," she says, "but we've been so busy—I don't want to get into it—" (Probably too many dinner parties. Not enough jewelry to go around.)

"Sometimes I forget you're gone. Except it is quiet. I must admit that. Now—have you settled on a college? I talked to C.A., to tell you about Paul's father, but Val told Lillian you had called—I do hope you've written him. . . ."

"Well—I'm going to. Now the thing is, I need more

money because I have to go up to New Hampshire. There's a school there that I'll probably go to."

"Susanna, you had plenty of money—what school in New Hampshire?"

"Rodgers-Conway, it's a junior college. A lot of music. Very strict." That was probably not bright. My mother may know. If Saks knows, can Mother be far behind? "Also, I need to get things for winter. I may take up skiing."

"Skiing—that's very dangerous. I don't know anyone who skis. Don't be ridiculous."

Oh. Yes you do know someone who skis, I almost say. Know very well, in fact.

"Well. I can't worry about that now. I'll send a check, and . . ." she adds, "charge everything else you need at Saks. All right? They have a lovely store in New York."

"Yes. They seem to have everything I need. Thanks a lot, Mom, really."

"And get yourself settled in college—please—we want to have everything organized. . . ."

"What do you mean? I'm not disorganizing everything. I'm trying . . . I haven't even called."

"I know, Susanna. It will be all right."

What will be all right? Skiing?

"I'll be careful. I won't ski too fast. Promise."

"Oh, I'm not worried about that—you get a nice outfit. That will be your Christmas present."

"We have never had Christmas," I tell Val when she gets back, "and she is not worried about skiing. Something is peculiar."

"She probably has just decided to let you grow up. They do that. And I think it's harder on us than the fussing. You'll get used to it. Don't worry about it— it's good for her. My mother says Vera's whole problem was Grandmother never let her grow up. So enjoy it."

"I will. Now where can I get skiing lessons here?"

"Bonwit's fifth floor—they have a refrigerated run. It's terrific!"

"Val—really?"

"No; not—you can't get lessons in the city. Why don't you wait until you talk to him?"

And so I dial Information and get Catherine Rodgers's number. With teeth in my throat I call. Someone young answers.

"Oh—are you the daughter?" I ask.

"Oh—no, I work at the Lodge. I'm just staying here while Mrs. Rodgers is away. Who's calling?"

"Miss Valentine, from Saks in New York. Something just came in that I thought she might be interested in—"

"Well, Mrs. Rodgers is away for at least another two months. I'm sorry."

"How nice. Well, if Mr. Lane is there I could send it on approval, I suppose."

"No—I mean, you could—but he won't be back either, they're in Spain."

"I see. Thank you very much." It is lucky for them I am not someone casing the place. Two months!

I hear the tone of his voice and the small cotton sound of his sleeves as he bends his arms and the high, slight jingle of coins in his pockets as he reaches over to lock the door before we started driving that day. I can pick it up at any point and rerun it, slow it down or run it on ahead.

Sometimes Val goes out alone with Chris—or meets up with Angelo, I think, which is when she tells me she didn't "do anything special." Chris is smart and funny, but mean around more than the edges, although these songs they make up are pretty good. And a little dirty in an intellectual way. Dirty, but not sexy, which I guess is how they are out here. I've had a couple of dates but they just go places and sit, drink, and listen. They tap their wrists like they're really so bored on the edges of these little tables, sort of in rhythm to the jazz they like. It's that cool, blue stuff, Condon, Brubeck, you know, that everyone in the world in the East adores. Then they get at you in the taxi on the way home. *That's* why Easterners like back seats. It's all they know. Some of them cannot even drive a car, which is disgusting. And most of them do not want to dance or walk around. They always know what time it is even when a little drunk. And you cannot get them near a real movie. So I go myself. Sit on the aisle and put my coat and stuff on the other seat, eat popcorn, slug down Cokes. I guess I'm just waiting until something happens or I feel like I know what I want to do. Sometimes Hildy and I go up the street and eat pizza pie, which you would not think she would love, but she is the one who got me liking it. Sometimes when Val is hating Chris she comes along. Tonight it's just Hildy and me. And I've been thinking about it, so I finally tell her about Jackson. About how nothing else matters.

"Well, it can't if you won't let it. If you try you can make a commitment to something else."

"Like what?" I knew it. Music. Here it comes. I take one of the crusts of the pizza she has left on her plate.

"Something you believe in. I couldn't tell you what. I was in love once." I cannot imagine Hildy in love. Too smart. "It was a different thing, but it felt like what you're describing. I wanted to pull myself apart to keep from missing him when he left me. I'm not easy for a man to live with. They like order—even if they're disorganized, you must be orderly. I remember I wanted to be a fish. I thought to myself, fish don't fall in love, how wonderful for fish. They have all the luck, not to know about romantic love. God, and I believed in God then, would not waste a gift like that on man. Look what we have done with all His other gifts. So He made the fishes free. I was very bitter then. You do change your feelings about all these things. Or they change."

I just want to see Jackson. Now that I have stopped moving. Now that I'm getting used to the city. Visiting classes here and there. Listening to the Quartet rehearsing Bartók until I want to bust out into my new imitation of Fats Domino at the top of my lungs, which Val's friends think is funny.

"Up to a point," Val says. "You don't need to do a

whole song. If we can call it that . . ." (Her latest way to talk is using the royal "we.")

I do not do this Domino imitation, obviously, anywhere on Claremont Avenue. Only when we go down to the Village. I did it once at this club, which was my first public appearance you could say, and "probably the last of many," Val said, which was funny, and she squeezed my arm and grinned at me, but I didn't laugh too long and asked her too many times on the way back uptown if it was any good at all.

What if he figures out it was me calling, looking for him, and never comes back? What if something happens to him before I can talk to him? What if I get there and it is a moment too late? Like Norma Shearer waking up and Leslie Howard has died on the sword. Or am I Leslie Howard and he is Norma Shearer? I have thought of me dying and Jackson being there. What if I lie there across his grave, sobbing, and they all say, "His only child, and he never knew her . . ."? Or would they say, "One of those Hollywood publicity stunts, you know. She's a folksinger looking for a break, what these kids won't do. But she looks like him."

"Yeah? A lot of people look like a lot of people."

Her parents, Mr. and Mrs. Myron Howard said, "No comment," and remain in seclusion. Seclusion, that's one place I never want to be, hidden out in a big old house covered with vines and unavailable for comment. I am always going to be available for comment when I'm famous. And I'd better get famous, because when I am they'll interview me and I'll tell, and then they'll smoke him out for me. Maybe I should call a press conference. "Girl triggers worldwide hunt for famous actor. Claims he is father."

My mother will say, "This is in very poor taste."

Hildy is in her bed in her tiny bedroom, rustling papers, listening to classical on the radio. (Val hates when I call it that. "Not a noun, Susanna. Never has been.") No wonder they all look so pale here. All that reading. But what else would they do, stand around and look at trees in cages? Watch the numbers go by in their elevators? When I was a child I thought New York was just Central Park surrounded by hotels, F. A. O. Schwarz, and Broadway. And there was Harlem, because my mother mentioned it when we went by it on the train, with buildings marked SHAFTWAY, which I asked Mallory about. "Oh, that's an empty space—like a stairway with no stairs." So many stories high, I thought. And I imagined how it would be if you were a child and got up in the middle of the night for a glass of water, or to hear what your parents are saying, and the stairs were gone—and you just fell.

God—I want to discuss something. I am not going to ask You if I can be famous by tomorrow at seven thirty, I'm not going to discuss a convertible, or even actually seeing Jackson and having him take me to live with him tomorrow. You've already put all that on the spindle, and I know you'll get to it when your secretary gets back—no, sorry God, I know You have a bigger staff than that. I know You're a Chief Executive. Do secretary angels wear spike heels and glasses and wear their angel hair in chignons? Are my requests like unsolicited scripts that Myron's executive secretary just sends down to the readers? Do I have to have an agent? Are priests, rabbis, and ministers sort of the Ashley Steiner, MCA, and William Morris? Is Rabbi Silverberg shiftier than Swifty Lazar in dealing with You? Sorry, God, I was doing a little riff, nothing disrespectful intended. But, listen, what I want to say, all I want to ask is just a sign, just to know, really know, that I will see Jackson again. He loved me so—I knew it—or was it that I loved him so much I made it reflect right back?

It was probably touching him on the back of the neck before I said goodbye to him that day—touching his hair—that did it. He probably has a phobia about that. Like me with snakes. But he could have just said so. Touch me anywhere, kid, but not on the back of the neck. Feel the sun. Smell the saltwater. Hear the sails. Miss the day. *Do* I! .

Sometimes I get so crazy I feel I am being drawn around a corner because he is there. Or I should rush home because he is going to be there, or call home because he has called and is waiting for me. Ever since I started driving, when I'd drive up the driveway I'd expect to see the white Lincoln parked there even when I knew he wasn't driving it any more.

I have sometimes thought—without the thought being there, if you know what I mean—that if he was dead I would know it was over. I would stop imagining. Except. I know me! If someone said he was dead and I went to a funeral even, and saw the gleaming white covered coffin with a basket of white roses, I would figure it was just a trick.

I'm mad as hell. Sitting in Val's room on the end of her bed. She is trying to work. I know I'm interrupting but sometimes you get started on something like that and you just can't stop.

"Where do you think I should try to call him in Spain? Should I ask when he's coming back?" I start to strum my guitar.

"Thoughtful," she snaps.

Well, I've had it with New York. I want something to happen. It's one of those days when you're just restless. "Couldn't we go out for a while and do something?"

"I've got to study, Susanna. You go out. And even if you did call him in Spain, did get hold of him, would he tell you the truth?"

"Yes he would! Damn! I'm always going alone. You've been studying enough."

"There's no enough here. Do you know, do you have any idea how hard it is? Do you know two students kill themselves every year? Just from the pressure. Do you know what this kind of work does to you?"

"Well. Don't do it. Quit. No one's making you stay here."

"I am. But you wouldn't understand that. I am not going to give up. I am not going to be like my father. You talk about your father, you talk about rejection or disappointment, you don't even know what that is, you have no *idea*—do you?"

I've never seen her like this. This angry.

"Here." She shoves a piece of lined paper with lyrics on it into my hand. "Want to hear how it goes? I know it by heart." And she takes my guitar and plays as though it is her own.

" 'Cold one English morning, shoulder to the door . . .' " She stops. "I call it, 'Good Morning, Daddy.' "

" 'Colder down there, Daddy, what you doin' on the floor? He doesn't answer. Hey, I said. So, yes, I said—and, good morning, Daddy.' "

She stops. "This is the chorus here: 'And let's hear it for the red, white, and blue. Oh, say, can you see, what they did to you?' "

It's about Alan and I think I don't want to hear it.

She strums, retunes the guitar. "I haven't worked it out here, but it's something like this." She doesn't look at me.

Have you ever seen a cheek
Shirred up like curtain on a rod?
Ripped right up above the top of the teeth?
I can see right up, Daddy, underneath your face.
Daddy, Daddy, you're really quite a case.

She stops for a minute, breathing hard. "That part's not right yet, but I go into chorus again here: 'A case of whiskey, rye whiskey and rye . . .' "

"Val—it's terrific." I don't know what else to say—it's so ugly. Is a song so ugly a good song? Well, I don't know why not—look at the Dust Bowl songs—look at the songs about murderers they used to make up.

"It goes on here," and she shifts the guitar, playing with one foot up on her desk chair.

PERDIDO

Went in to see my mother, Mom, I said.
And I held my mother's hand.
Mom, I think Daddy's killed himself.
All together now, Mother, Daddy's dead.

Alan killed himself. Did I always think so and didn't want to see? I guess it shows on my face. Everything always does. Poker face I'm not.

"You just got it?" Val says to me, strumming. "No one told you that, either?"

"No, Val. No one told me that either." I'm not sure it's possible, but I may be angrier with them for not telling me that Alan killed himself—I was old enough to trust.

"Have you played that for Chris or anyone yet?"

"So far I'm just keeping it for me. . . . Then I go into another chorus, and here's as far as I got."

She turned in her sleep.
How'd he do it this time? she said.
And she looked at the clock by the bed.
Six in the morning and half of it's gone by.
Oh, that's no time at all for this.
That's what she said.
And she reached across; thought she'd been
*   dreaming.*
When she saw that bed was empty
That's when she began screaming. . . .

I don't know what to say.

"Now," she says, "I've got another idea for the chorus, which is to use this old nonsense song Daddy used to sing when he was a kid. They'd sit around on stoops in the summer and make up songs, I guess. See what you think."

And the horsie flew around
With four feet on the ground.
Why do they build the shore so near the ocean?

308

Go get an axe
There's a fly on baby's mustache.
A boy's best friend is her mother.
Three cheers for . . . da, da, um da.

She sort of does a little Ella Fitzgerald thing at the end. I can see Alan in a tough kid outfit, sweating, leaning against an iron bannister with a cap over one eye, singing such a song.

"Val, was that how it happened? You saw him like that?"

"You think, Susanna, you've seen a lot. I can't do the part about how he got sick from the pills." She's casing my reaction, watching to see when I wince. "Or explain exactly how it was that he got his head wedged in between the metal leg of the sink and the bathtub and how the leg shirred up his face."

I put my hand to my own cheek. She notices. I put it down fast.

"Tissue—that's not just skin—pulled right away all up from his jawbone, and all the blood under him. And . . . *So,* what do you think of the song?"

"Well, it sort of is blues, sort of folk—really different—almost a little rock 'n' roll beat, I'm sorry to say, but there is." Val usually detests rock 'n' roll.

"No. That's all right. Supposed to be there."

"Why didn't you tell me?—he killed himself. My God."

"Does it make any difference to you?"

"Well, when you care about someone, you want to know. . . . How awful—that you found him—oh, Val." I want to reach out for her. "Did Aunt Lillian really talk like that?"

"She was trying to be so calm I thought she'd flipped." But that is exactly how Val is being. Think of how calm you have to make yourself to write that song. And angry. How could he do that to her?

"I walked around there not wanting to tell her. I wanted to have it taken away. That wasn't Daddy. I wanted to pretend it didn't happen so we could go on pretending he was off on another drunk. Men do disappear, I would have explained, just look at Jackson Lane."

She has had all of this to live with, all of it kept to herself.

"I tried to keep her from going in there. . . ." Her eyes are glazed now, and like I do with Jackson, she has turned in to herself, running the scene in her head. "I thought silly things like maybe she won't be able to find her slippers. And she did silly things like pick up each slipper and put it on with her hands rather than shove her feet in them, or go barefoot, and then when she had them on, she stood up and tied her robe and pulled the collar around her throat. . . ."

"That's like *my* mother does," I say.

"That was it—she was acting much more like Vera." And Val looks down at her lovely slender hands with their long deeply set nails. "So," she says, "she then stood by her dresser with her elbow up resting on the top—it was a highboy like she used to have at home—and she went back to her nightstand and picked up her phone book. She placed a call to our doctor—Dr. Perriberg—although I hardly thought we would need him. 'Would you be good enough to come round soon as possible? Yes. It is rather an emergency.' I remember she got terribly British there. And then she sat for a moment with the phone book. I mean, I couldn't believe her until I noticed how her face was just covered, covered by sweat and she looked at me in such incredible terror and went in there and started screaming. Her scream began with a whooping sound and whirled around like it was being spun through a funnel, circling back into her throat and coming out, airier and fuller each time. It was as though every time she never screamed, like the fire, and the hospital—just had built up there. She never did it before, never wanted to upset Daddy. She just stood there screaming and I went and called Dr. Perriberg back and he had not left yet, and told me he would call the police and get them to send an ambulance and would come himself to see things were quiet because 'We shan't want any photographers.' I remember I thought Daddy doesn't have a really good side left. I can't stand people who won't grow up. And that's why I get so mad at you for living in a dream world—for thinking Jackson could care about anyone—for not planning anything for yourself except where you're going to look for him next, and for being also so jealous of anyone I see. I'm sorry. That just all came out. If I didn't care I wouldn't say it—"

"Well, it sure does cover everything! It's okay—what happened after you talked to the doctor? Tell me."

"Okay, I went in and while the water was boiling for coffee I washed the dishes and then I fried two eggs and toasted some scones which were slightly stale and buttered them and put raspberry jam on them, and I sat down and ate and waited for the doctor to come. I remembered Grandmother saying, after the fire, that it was important to eat to keep up your strength. And my mother was just standing there shaking and screaming. And when she did come in—I didn't want to go back out there—I gave her a cup of tea. She held it with both hands, which I noticed were covered with blood, and there was blood on her face. But she quieted down then and drank her tea. And she didn't get up. So I let the doctor in. I try never to think about it."

I can't swallow. My tears in my eyes won't even move down.

"I didn't want to come back here," she says, "and I didn't want to stay there. I think I'm going to throw up." She says it straight and steady and cool with her deadpan voice. Her green eyes go blank. You have to listen to catch what she says—most of the time, if you think about it, you get what people are saying from expression, tone of voice. With Val you can't rely on that.

She runs out of her room into the bathroom. I know better than to go with her. And she runs water so I will not hear her being sick. We have both been very carefully brought up.

It was not enough for Val just to take the music course. She is going for a degree in everything, as far as I can tell. I am flicking through one of these massive philosophy books she is studying—underlining, underlining, all the time—it is the abstract art of thinking—the perfect Eastern thing to fool around with all winter. They get crazy from the cold and from being inside too long and they think up things like this and musical theory and math. I watch it get colder and bleaker out and listen to Hildy's old radiators doing their cool jazz numbers and I think about Palm Springs and would give a year of my life for a traffic jam. Just to be stuck at Sunset and Sepulveda by the poinsettia fields would be heaven. No wonder Jackson went to sunny Spain. He is not back yet. Twenty-five times I have called.

Then one day I call and a Japanese houseboy answers the phone. "Is Mr. Lane there? This is Ramona Delgado from the Montezuma Script Service." I have on my Rita Moreno voice.

"Yes?" In his own voice, "This is Jackson Lane."

"Hi. This is really Susanna. I forget you can do voices too."

A beat. Then, "Well. My favorite sailor. How are you?"

I was going to say "older and wiser" but I am disarmed. "Fine. I found out . . . do you know what I mean?"

"Yes, Susanna. I think I probably do. You're okay though?" His voice is warm, close, a little grainy like a bad sound track. Probably snow sitting on telephone wires.

"I'd like to see you." I cannot breathe.

"Yes, well, I'd like that too. It's been a long time."

"It's been the whole time, actually." I can hear him really breathing. Daddy, I want to say, come and take me to be with you.

"I'm going out of town for a while . . . but after . . ."

"I thought you just got back." I must not whine. Scratch the Margaret O'Brien voice, Midnight.

"No, no . . . I have some dubbing to do. They drive you crazy over there. The labwork is rotten. I expected to spend the season skiing, and now I have to go back and work . . . do you ski?"

"Naturally." There has to be somewhere in New York City where they teach you. With a lesson every day, I'll ski.

"Good, then when I come back we'll have you up. Okay? Call me in about ten days. What are you doing here? Visiting?"

"College. Sort of." *Wel* I don't want *her* to be there.

"I thought you hated school. How'd they rope you into that?" He remembers! He remembers things about me. So he has been thinking about me.

"Well, they haven't yet—roped me in. But they're working on it. I have an idea though—"

"Well, good for you. Listen, don't be shy about calling, you know."

"Oh no."

Val and I are sitting in the West End Cafe that night. "Well, I talked to him."

"What did he say? Was he surprised? Oh, just a sec. I'm dying to hear, but I'd better call Chris. Right back!"

She is not in her best mood because Chris is late and she has a big exam to study for tomorrow. Her songs are so good I don't know why she doesn't leave school and be a songwriter for money. I said that once and she said, "What, hang around in the Brill Building turning out tin pan alley rock 'n' roll for a bunch of thirteen-year-olds?"

"No. That's not what I mean." That's probably what I'll wind up doing if I don't figure out something—but my main idea is to work at Mrs. Rodgers's ski lodge. They must need an entertainer. What is a lodge without someone playing a guitar or piano and everyone standing around singing along with you? My mother's reaction? Trained nurses round the clock would be only the beginning.

But Val could do real folk concerts—or little clubs where they want original material for revues. That's what Chris wants her to do. Because if she doesn't do it with him, he'll never have the energy to do it on his own.

"Okay. Tell me now," she says, coming back.

"He didn't say much. He has to go away again. But he was wonderful. He's dying to see me. We're going off skiing together when he gets back and really talk about everything. We're going to have dinner at some little place. He wanted to know everything about me."

"Susanna? Really?"

"Really. I felt like it's always been the same. You know, it wasn't strange or anything."

"Did you ask him anything, like about why he disappeared that day . . . why he never called or anything?"

"No. Of course not. I didn't have to. It's really fine between us."

Val is always suspicious. She hears between the lines. After I finish talking to her I am furious. I cry just out of frustration. It's like talking to a blank wall with her. She asks questions with shadows. Something like philosophy. You can't really hang on to what she's saying. She tries to pick at things until they bleed. I like to leave things as they are. This is why I hate that analyst who was taking Lillian out this summer. He was always trying to figure out what you're thinking. And meanings. I hate meanings. And when they ask what I think, what I tell them I think isn't what they think I should be thinking. They, for instance, would not find that confusing at all.

I do not know why but then I am at the public phone in the West End Cafe with a handful of change and calling Jackson, back with my heart pounding as it always does when I call his number—or even a number just to ask about him. I can tell by the ring that he is home. You know those things. Finally he answers. I love how he says "Hello." So soft and low.

"Hi, it's Susanna again. Did I bother you?"

Sound of cornered breathing.

"Not at all . . . I was just reading one of the new scripts my agent sent me."

"Anything good?"

"Well, they want me to star in a new Western. But it's reminiscent of *High Noon*. I've suggested some script changes so we'll see what they come up with." Myron says actors aren't that bad until they pretend they can write.

"Great." Silence. I continue. "So how's the weather there?" Stupid.

"Fine. Good powder." Silence.

Okay; I'm going to say it: "Listen. I want to see you. I've been chasing all over the entire country looking for you. Can't I come up there even if it's just for lunch?"

"Well, okay. If you get on the next train we can probably have some time tomorrow and the next day—before I have to go. Maybe I'll take you up to one of my favorite runs."

"Oh, that would be super." I will worry about that when the time comes. Perhaps I have a trick knee. "Ski on the wrong day and all these rabbits pop out," I will tell him, so he does not think I take it too seriously. Jackson is not, clearly, wild about people who have problems.

"Just come right up to Catherine's house. Everyone knows where it is. And we have a couple of guest rooms, so you can stay here. Or I could get you a room at the Lodge—it's a little livelier."

I don't think he understands. "No. I want to stay with you." Mistake. Why do I get this feeling I should be playing hard to get with my own father?

"Well—that's okay, too."

"So I'll see you when I get there," I say. Then very quietly, "Thought I was joking didn't you?"

"About what?" He sounds distracted. He does understand. That's why he would like me to stay at the Lodge. So we will not have too much time to talk.

"Nothing." I want to get off the phone and get going before he changes his mind. I wonder if I will tell him about the trip, about everyone I saw. I decided I will not. But I make a lot of decisions about what I will not say. Maybe I will call him back once more and tell him I will stay at the Lodge after all and he won't feel so smothered. No. I'll see how it goes when I get there. What he would hate the most is another phone call.

The waitress comes by now. "Looks like we might get more snow," she says.

"Isn't that something," I say. Easterners like to pretend their winters are a daily phenomenon. Except for the Arctic exploration movies (which were more accurately about New York), Hollywood versions of winter in the East are crazy. I believed the idea that snow would come, once a winter, in soft, small white balls, like the cotton they use at Ann Meredith's to remove my mother's old nail polish, and lie there nicely until spring. But it comes and goes and leaves a dreadful mess; it's cold as hell and no one ever told anyone west of Figueroa Boulevard about ice.

Val orders her fourth Coke of the evening. She's going down to the Village later to meet Angelo when he's finished rehearsals. I think it is quite over with Chris.

"Well, so you'll be going tomorrow," she says.

"Yes. Isn't that exciting?"

"I hope so. Why don't you think about staying a bit—"

"Oh—I am. You know that—" I think about what she is saying. "I've been driving you crazy, I guess."

"How could you say such a thing—listen; hint: no expectations, okay?"

"None. It's just a little trip to New Hampshire. Somewhere I happen to have missed."

"On your grand tour!" she says. Slight smile.

I AM ON THE TRAIN AT 6 A.M. IN MY SCARLET SKI SUIT,
red boots, mittens—"My," Val said, "too bad they didn't
show it with a little white fur and you could go right
down his chimney. A little late, but he's never been
exactly prompt himself." She's nuts, of course. I look
absolutely sensational. The whole train looks at me and
smiles. And guys hang all over my seat all the way up.
There is, however, not one other good thing to say about
that trip except I am *finally* here.

The house is more like a modern chalet than what I
expected, which was sort of a large German-looking
mansion with dark beams. This is wood and glass,
angles up on a hill, tawny against the white snow and
almost black pine trees. There's a perfect dark green
Mercedes roadster in the garage.

"Susanna—I'm so sorry . . ." She opens the door. She
is a regular person. Not gorgeous. Not made-up. Her
hair isn't even done, just pulled back softly—straight
and light brown. Not as tall as I am, but very slender.

"He's gone? He didn't even wait? The train out of
Boston froze and then we had to wait for another one to
come because . . . it wasn't my fault. I tried. I've been
all over this country trying to see him and he didn't
even wait for me." I should have known. It was too
simple. "Damn this East! If I was home I would have
just gotten in my car and been here."

"I know, dear . . . please, come in, I'll make you
some hot chocolate." I look at her to see what he sees.
She has a round, flat face with a square jawline, sort of
a flower face. She is suntanned and has tiny wrinkles
under her eyes, but she's probably about forty, so that's

to be expected. She looks like a friendly gym teacher—
if there is such a thing. Hot chocolate is what my mother tried to make me the night I told her I know. I'll bet
Mrs. Rodgers at least knows how to make it. My
mother would be so jealous of all of this, I bet. And of
another woman's thoughtfulness to me. Does Mrs.
Rodgers make this for him? Does he love the kind of
lady who can do that—who cooks and cares? Like his
sister who he never sees.

The furniture is modern, white fur rugs, white tex-
tured fabric on the couches and Indian blankets. I can
imagine him sitting there, one leg crossed up on his
knee. Imagine him standing by the fireplace warming his
hands.

"But he said we'd have time. I got the first train I
could."

"He waited as long as possible. There's a blizzard
coming and our little airport could be snowed in for a
week. So he had one of the boys at the Lodge drive him
out to the airport. He wanted me to be here at least—
to explain."

Is she annoyed that she didn't get to drive him—
missed that extra time with him? Am I supposed to be
grateful?

"I hate it here . . . this would never happen at home.
When did he leave . . . ?" Did I pass him on the way
up the mountain in the cab? (Which was just someone's
ordinary Chevy—God! I hate being a *passenger*—here
I am doing the most adult things in my entire life and
always being driven.) Did he see me and scrunch down?
I would have felt he was going by.

"He left just a moment ago—a few minutes . . ." She
looks at me. I'm shaking, with cold and sadness. She
thinks for an instant. "Come on, I'm not promising anything, but maybe there's a chance." She takes a fox fur
parka from a hook by the door and puts on boots and
gloves and grabs a bag. She looks like the kind of person who buys clothes at Kerr's, the sporting goods store,
not Saks. But she does buy clothes at Saks. She wants

318

people to think she is simpler, more down-to-earth than she is.

"If I could just see him for a minute."

"We'll do our best," she says. "Just leave your bag here." We get into the car, which crunches along down the driveway. "I can't go any faster," she says, "these chains drive me crazy—but without them the Green Hornet would slip and slide right down the mountain." You have to like an Easterner who names her car, I tell myself. So I smile at her. A first. It is like the road to Arrowhead at home, except I've only been there in the summer. But on one side you're only inches away from huge jutting walls of gray rock, which here are bearded with icicles, and on the other—there is no other side, just an edge, a shelf, and far below, a town and miles of snow-covered hills.

"My father used to try cases in the courtyard in that town down there," she says. "I've lived here all my life."

"That's some backdrop," I say, trying to sound normal. Like Lillian, she's one of those reasonable people who can bring out the best in you. If you let them. Maybe that's it. She makes Jackson feel like a regular person. That must be what movie stars long for and never find—while everyone else wants only to be treated like a movie star. I wonder why Lillian couldn't do that for Alan—because he wasn't a star, all the way up there? Because she did want him to be—you can't come from our family and not have some of that. Now, I love Lillian but she is a secret pusher—a little like Thelma. That's why Carleen and Val will be somebodies. My mother is no stage mother—she knows if I get famous it will not be the same as if she had become a concert pianist. Who else can I think about, what else can I pull at and poke over as we crawl down this mountain?

"You never get anything clear here, except just what you don't want to listen to," Mrs. Rodgers says, switching stations around.

"That's exactly what I do," I say, "always looking for my favorite song."

319

"And when you find it you come in right at the end!" she says, turning hard around a real hairpin curve.

"Yes. Last chords," I say, gripping the armrest, trying not to do the foot-on-brake imitation which drives me crazy when someone's driving with me. She hears a time signal and leans over to adjust the Green Hornet's clock. He must love the way she drives. I do. Although it's scary when it's not me doing it.

"Jack says you're a talented musician."

"He does! Well, I'm trying." He did remember.

"It must have been very hard on you—not seeing him."

"Well. You get used to things. And when I decided to—well, here I am."

"If it's any help—and it isn't—he really did want to wait." I think she wants to believe that as much as I do.

Finally we're down the mountain and we are coming to the town. "Damn," she says, "first light's red—that means with these chains we'll miss the second one too." The light turns green and we have to wait for a group of people with skis who are walking across. Then, just as we're picking up again, a car with a New Jersey plate spins and swerves in a complete circle in front of us, coming from one side of the road and around to the other and back again like a bump-em car at Ocean Park. It sets itself right and moves ahead of us, slowly. "Tourists!" she says. Sounds like me. Well, if I do miss him, I just have to start planning for another chance. The failure of each try starts the hope for the next. It is like how you look at Sunday—it's either the end of one week or the beginning of the next. All in your attitude. What I'm doing is pretending I won't mind missing him so there will be a better chance for him to still be there. It is a kind of inside-out wishing trick. It does not work.

"Maybe the plane won't be able to take off," I say.

"Maybe," she says, "but they try to keep the runway clear, and they'll try to get everything out before the storm."

"You don't want me to build up hope. I'm not. Everything's gone wrong so far. I mean, except you. You're really great to try."

I see a sign with an arrow saying AIRPORT. Six miles. That would be nothing in real weather.

"Think positive, Susanna, but you should know it's harder to see someone for a minute than not at all. I know you don't understand that, but it is. . . ."

"Did he tell you about me before I called?"

"Yes. He said he had a daughter and had only seen her once. But he didn't say anything else about you. I asked him why he never tried to see you again, and he said he felt it was better not to disturb your life, not to get in the way." I hear a plane overhead and she sees me looking up, my head against the side window.

"That's crazy, didn't he know I'd try to find him?"

"I don't think he understands that kind of feeling, Susanna." She looks at the car clock again. "That might have been his plane—but I doubt it." And she smiles at me, downshifts, and we slip a bit even with the chains on a patch of ice that didn't glint at all until we were right on it. This never happens with cars at home. Something gleaming in the road is a mirage at home. Roads and cars are not out to get you.

The sky is lowering, dark gray—almost black at edges where it meets the snow and outside you can feel the silence. I remember dreaming of a tennis court in the snow, and not being able to reach him. Is this like a movie stored in my head, coming back as memory of a dream, when it was actually just a movie running ahead of schedule? Schedules. Time. "How much longer?"

Flat stretches or almost flat, except suddenly there's a clump of snow to avoid, and in every dip, I now understand, a terrible patch of ice.

"Almost there."

"Why does he want to make that movie anyway? He hated making movies. That's why he left Hollywood."

"He can't help it, Susanna." She shifts down to go around a curve and we go into another small skid. I

321

watch how she steers into it. Jackson would not live with a bad driver, of course. She's good.

"He jus. wanted to go, I think." I am holding on to the dashboard. I don't blame him leaving the snow. Except he like to ski. He must like the snow.

"It's not you, Susanna. He always wants to go somewhere. I waited for him a lot. I understand how you feel, that's why I'm doing my best. Well, I don't know *exactly* how you feel, but I understand something of it."

We go by the third sign saying AIRPORT and turn down a road which is even more narrow if possible than these bridle paths we've been going on. Why can't they even build roads right here? Your snow is real cute, and I like how it glistens just when you think you'll never see anything sparkle again, but would it kill you to put in a freeway?

Finally, and I am practically out of the car before it stops, we pull into the airport, which is more like a parking lot with a hangar and a little pre-fab building like the writers' building at V.L.I. Jackson—taking off from such a place—? Talk about having trouble getting insurance for skiing!

"There's the plane. Thank God. You get out. I'll wait. . . ."

I already have the door open. I turn to her, poised . . .

"Now go on. But, Susanna . . ."

"What?" I have my foot out of the car.

"Please, don't expect him to stay." She reaches across and clasps my arm, briefly, firmly.

"I know." But I do expect him to come back with us; me in the back seat, jumping around, imitating Carleen (but nicely) to make him laugh, him turning with one arm over the seat, Mrs. Rodgers driving, smiling—not jealous. . . . I run across the black-top that's surrounded by neat ridges of snow which have been plowed away. Even close up, the plane looks like a toy you could roll up and down. The propellers are turning. The mechanics are standing by the gangway stairs.

And I see him. He's walking out of the building and

toward the stairs and the wind is ruffling his hair and he's wearing a tan sheepskin jacket, like a cowboy, with a white furry collar turned up.

"Jackson . . . wait." He can't miss me, trotting along, afraid to slip even with this sand on the runway, this ice thing here scares me. But he can't miss this red outfit. I probably look like a giant cardinal in a Marilyn Monroe wig bobbing across the field.

He can't hear me, but one of the mechanics points and he turns and stops and walks toward me. He is not running. But he opens his arms and waves them in a big, swashbuckling way. It is so awkward walking toward each other, both wondering, I guess, if the other one is mad.

"Well, you made it!" He stands for a second looking at me, and for an instant, like his sister, annoyance, or fear, crosses his face, and then that smile. I want to throw my arms around him, but I wait. We stand here with the wind blowing, the propellers roaring, smiling at each other. He has not changed. He doesn't even seem smaller as he should because I am even bigger than I was. He still towers above me—above everything. Look at this face! This is a person's father? I can get the idea —but seeing him!

He puts his hands on either side of my shoulders. But we do not draw into each other. "I thought you stood me up," he says, and then he touches my cheek with the back of his hand almost as you would a guy friend. I want to say you can hold me and I won't keep you. Just hold me against you. He doesn't know how to play this part. It's called Father, I could tell him. How come I know and you don't and I'm not even an actor?

"The train got stuck. We had to get out and wait for another one. I didn't know you were going so soon."

"I didn't either. It's one of those things."

"Just one of those things." I didn't want this to happen but tears are coming. "Flight to the moon on gossamer wings and all that." I wipe at my eyes furiously with my mittens.

"Susanna. Now you know about shooting schedules." He looks up at the sky. "If I don't get out now . . ."

"I know all about it. Mrs. Rodgers told me." I notice her there standing next to her car. How nice she is. She must want so much to come over here. To look at him. I must ask her if she ever gets tired of looking at him. . . . Does she wake up at night and smile across the pillow to see him sleeping there?

"Well, then, you understand."

A mechanic comes over. "Mr. Lane, the pilot says we've got to take off. I'm sorry." He looks at me sniffling, my hair whipping around my face and turns away, embarrassed. I am making a scene.

"I don't understand," I say. "I don't understand a lot of things. I don't even understand you. Especially you I don't understand."

"You're a young woman now," he says. As if that should make everything clear to me. He has an awkward, but, of course, charming half-smile on his face, and one foot is kind of kicking, shuffling. Does he have any expression that is not guaranteed to charm?

"You noticed!" I mustn't do this. This is probably exactly what he feared and expected, and that's what I'm doing. "My God, whoever had a father who wears a white cashmere muffler with his cowboy jacket?" I flick at the muffler, laughing, to change the mood.

"Listen, I'll be back in a month." He puts his arm around my shoulder, but in a herding gesture, and I see he is walking me to the car. "And I'll give you a call and you can come up and spend a couple of weeks with us, we'll go skiing . . . I'll show you some of the greatest runs you ever saw. . . . What kind of skis do you have?"

Now there's something I've really been waiting to discuss. Are there kinds . . . what?

"The best," I say. "Like sailboats, you have to have the best. Runs in the family, having the best."

His breath is coming in puffs of smoke. His eyes are, here, like ice. He turns me over to Mrs. Rodgers like a runaway.

She looks at him anxiously. "She wanted to see you so much."

"I understand that." There is one of those we'll-talk-about-that-later looks. "Now, Susanna, you keep in touch."

"I've been trying to do that for years." I'm sulking now and trying to smile anyway and he knows.

"Hey, very few guys have daughters with bright red ski suits, either. Now, I'll see you again, all right?" He puts his forefinger under my chin in the chins-up way. And I feel all wonderful again. He has actually said it. Said "father" and "daughter," and in the same sentence —except it was "guys" and daughters. I know that. It's not that I don't listen. I just listen selectively. But then he does something I hate—for an instant I think of Bronston—he kind of stoops from the knees down and looks at himself in a window of the Mercedes and pats back his hair with both hands. He is a star. I keep forgetting that means he is also an actor. And then he looks from his reflection to me and smiles with a short little nod. So. I will have that at least. He is pleased I look like him.

He puts a hand on each of our shoulders. "Drive safe," he says, and looks at the sky. "It's going to be a bad one."

"Can you see cat's paws?" I say.

"You don't forget a thing, do you?"

"Nothing." I catch myself before I add, about you.

"Well, I'll be in touch." And he flashes his smile, his teeth as white as the snow, and snaps his collar jauntily.

"Kiss goodbye?" Mrs. Rodgers says. And he puts his fingers to his lips and touches her mouth, and she closes her eyes and takes a deep and, I think, terribly disappointed breath. He notices I am watching and he touches his hand to my cheek and it is cold. (Of course, what else could even *his* hand be in this lunatic place?)

He turns now, and walks toward the plane, breaking into an easy run, going faster as he gets closer to the plane, like a horse goes faster when it knows it's going home. For Jackson what feels like home is going away, anywhere. I see it. I know it. And I think I understand it. Although I hate it. He bounds up the steps three at a time with his long legs and stands for a moment in the door of the plane, waving down on us across the field, waving now and grinning freely. Breathing easy, now, I think to myself. And they close the door, and move the stairs away, and the mechanic waves to the pilot with both his arms, and the plane taxis down the runway. I think I see that face, and the arm, still waving through the window. And I can almost hear the sigh of relief as he settles into his seat, unflicking his muffler from where I flicked it over his shoulder. That sigh comes across to both of us like the wind whistling over the snow.

"Are you all right?" Mrs. Rodgers says. Her eyelashes are frosted. Tears frappé. Wil Wright's could sell it for $1.95.

"Well. I saw him. I never thought I would, so that's something."

"With some people, Susanna, something is everything. Now let's get into the car and turn on that heat." She gives me a little rough, warming kind of hug, and clutching her arms around her shoulders, rubbing them hard, through the fluffy soft fur, she runs around to the driver's seat.

Something is everything. And for some people, too, everything is not enough. He didn't say we'd talk about things. He didn't say he loves me. He didn't say he's been wanting to be with me so much he didn't know what to do. He didn't say any of the things I knew he wouldn't say but always somehow thought he might say by accident, just because anyone would. Anyone else.

He didn't. But he might next time. He said he'd call. He asked me about the skis. Maybe I should take some lessons. He'll expect me to be good. Maybe I'll hang around. I can probably get a job in a place here where the kids go. Scotty suggested that kind of thing might be possible. I can stay with Mrs. Rodgers. I'll be like part of the family. Not like, Susanna. I am. And I'll be someone who belongs here. People will say, when I come to pick up things for us, "Hi, Miss Lane, what do you hear from your dad?"

"Oh, he's fine. Coming home next week . . ."

"Well," Mrs. Rodgers says, "now it's my turn to pack."

"Aren't you going to wait for him here?"

"Wait for Jackson?" She gives me a sidelong, are-you-crazy look. "No, I'm closing up the house and getting down to my Palm Beach place for some sun next week."

"What about the blizzard?"

"I'll worry about that when it happens. I'm not, thank God, much of a worrier, Susanna. I'd never have lasted so long with your father if I was."

My father. At least I have that. I have seen him. And people say to me, "Your father." I feel as though he had hugged me. Almost.

I am wondering about that blizzard. It sure looks like something's coming. And I sure think Jackson willed it to look that way. And I think Mrs. Rodgers—Catherine —is telling me not to hold my breath until he comes back.

Maybe I should stay around anyway. I could do something in exchange for room and board. Play "thet thing," wait tables. I'll tell my parents I've found this wonderful little college in the mountains. And I'm a ski major.

Val will have an idea. I promised to call her if I saw him. We had a bet I wouldn't. But I saw him. And why isn't that enough? Why am I now thinking it is worse, like Mrs. Rodgers said? It isn't. It's a beginning all over again. I will say that twenty-five times every hour until I believe it.

I call Val in New York. Hildy answers the phone. "Susanna. I'm so glad you called. Are you on your way home?"

"What is it, Hildy?" I can hear something urgent in her voice. "Something's wrong with Val. Where is she?"

"It's nothing serious. But she's in the hospital. Mount Sinai. A little operation. I'm not supposed to know, dear."

"I'm on my way." I don't know how I'm on my way. But I am.

"Susanna. Don't tell Val I told you. She is so private about everything."

"I know. I'm coming."

Mrs. Rodgers takes me down to the next big town where I can catch a train going right on to Boston.

"You could wait with me and fly, Susanna. I've chartered a plane for tomorrow if the weather holds out." She smiles wryly.

"No—but I'm really grateful, Mrs. Rodgers."

"Catherine," she says. "Listen to me, Susanna—don't expect—oh, you understand—"

"Miracles or phone calls—or ski weekends?" I say.

"Something," she says, and hugs me, "like that."

Of all his people I've met, she is the most like family and the least related and the one I feel the best about, even maybe including Scotty, and I have to say definitely that includes my mother, who is sort of one of his people. Was.

Such a bleak event their winter is. When you come by places where the snow isn't. If you took the sun and the orange trees and the horses out of Palm Springs you would have winter here. The trees remind me of my birds' nests and the houses look like the nests have simply been organized into neater piles of wood. It is an elderly, brooding place, this East. Such effort it would be to leave those houses on these bleak days. Their spaces here are forlorn, not invigorating. You have the feeling there is nothing better over the next hill. No wonder they love foreign movies here. Big houses look collapsed as shacks. And they don't paint anything in colors. It is all white. No wonder Technicolor came late to Hollywood. They would not have gotten the idea

328

from fall. It does not last long enough and the need for color movies would never come up here—you just look at the way they dress and you know. They must read a lot of books.

It is too late to see Val when I get into town, so I call Angelo at the Actors' Studio from the train station. "What's the matter with Val?" I snap.

"She'll tell you," he says. "Where've you been?"

"Just away."

"Did you see him?"

"You could call it that."

"What are you so goddam mad about?" he says.

"I don't know. But if it's what I think, I'll kill you."

"Hey, wait—Susanna!" he says.

"Never mind." I slam down the phone. And right there in Grand Central Station I just stand there and scream, "Actors! Damn them! Damn them!" at the top of my lungs, waking up this nice old woman who was sleeping in a phone booth and scratching her crotch with a pink terry cloth bedroom slipper at the same time. She catches my eye. "I'm so poor," she says, opening the door of the booth and putting out her cold bony hand and I give her a dollar. Do the crazies always catch my eye because they see a kindred spirit? Is it playing with myself that does it? Or being illegitimate?

I am a lovechild. I have not thought of that. Lovechild; why does the word remind me of wanderlust? Because lovechild is the dressy sport version of bastard, and wanderlust is the same for what you'd call just running away, which is how you can wind up with a lovechild, or you can get one right at home. . . . I could make a round out of this: "Now, you people to my right sing, 'Lovechild'; and the folks on the left sing, 'I'm just running . . .'" What this country needs, I say, looking down the row of phone booths, is a musical number right here in the Grand Central Station phone booths. Up on your feet, ah-one, ah-two. . . . If Gene Kelly can get a whole French supermarket dancing then watch Susanna Lovechild, girl choreographer.

I GO TO SEE VAL THE NEXT AFTERNOON: "VAL?"

"I know, you were just driving by." She looks so pale and weak. There is a long tube extending from a bottle on a metal rack to her wrist.

"Let me guess. Hildy told you, but I'm not supposed to know she said anything. Just promise me, if I die, don't tell my mother."

She won't really look at me. I sit on the edge of the bed and touch her forehead. She turns the other way.

"Officially they're calling it a D. and C. It's actually your basic botched abortion."

"Oh, Val." How can you be living with someone every day and not know something like that? It's me. Not listening. Not paying attention. That's what she's been worrying about. That's why she threw up when she was singing her song about Alan. Or partly why.

"Don't say it like that," she says.

"Well. Just think, you could have had another me."

"Caught it right in the nick of time. Aren't you glad you dropped in?" She has become so bitter.

"Were you in love with him?"

"A question only you would think of." She must be wrong about that. Somewhere someone else would ask that question. "No, we just got drunk one night and I forgot to put in my diaphragm."

Val has a diaphragm! It's one thing if you do it in the moment of passion we all talk about. But premeditated! I guess she reads my expressions too well.

"Not to spoil your illusions, but that's usually how it happens, Susanna. As you can see, I can't recommend sex highly enough. And don't you think it's thoughtful

330

of them to put me on this floor. I get to hear the babies going by. Just think how terrific that is for the hysterectomy patients. Stop staring at me."

She does not cry, but her eyes are red. Beautiful people when they are hurt look so much more hurt than the rest of us, so astounded. I am wondering if they get hurt because people hate them for being so beautiful, or do they put themselves in places where they can be hurt so we will think they are just like us?

"That rat," I say.

"No . . . as he said to me, 'Look, kid, that's life.' "

"That certainly sounds like him all right," I say. I think I will punch Angelo. I will find the strength and break his jaw for Alan.

"Bravado . . . Oh, for the little mother?" Val flashes her best fake smile at the nurse who comes in with flowers. She reads the card. "From Chris. Without whom this never would have been possible."

"Chris!" I say and hand it back to her. "I thought it was Angelo."

"Of course you'd think that. No. Chris . . ." She flicks the card. "He drinks too much. Can you possibly figure out whatever attracts me to men who drink too much? I haven't slept with Angelo."

Yet. I think. She loves him. I see that.

The phone rings. "Ginny, darling. No, no. I really feel sensational. Chris just sent flowers—Did you finish that paper? You know you could use some notes I have. . . ."

I remember suddenly how I hate this—when I am with Val and she talks to someone else as though I am not there. You think you are her best friend until you hear her talking to someone else. Yet I feel so ungrateful thinking like that. She has such terrible things happen to her and yet she is always asking about you, helping, giving advice.

Terrible things. Somehow, I cannot help thinking, Val is the only person I know who would have an abortion and somehow wind up with a roomful of flowers.

"Ginny, as a favorite friend . . ." she says into the

phone. It is not so much what she says, but this certain tone of voice she gets when she talks to people she loves which infuriates me—it gets lowered, fragrant like peaches, and private, or charmingly motherly. "No. Insecure, I'd say. We haven't cornered the market on that. Emotionally they're not much different. Stop thinking of him as one of them, just think of him. Reverse the situation. How would you feel? That's right. Going now. Tired. Love, love. Thanks for calling.

"Well," she says, "if you get it over with, you can get on with your work."

"You mean Jackson? I'll never get it over with. He's not 'it'!"

"No. God, Susanna, I mean all the curiosity about sex. Love is just curiosity. A terrible interference. When I'm really stuck or the challenge gets too big—feels too big —that's when I give in, that's when I get vulnerable. You've always done that. You used to be absent for ages and get guilty and then later you convinced yourself it was all about Jackson, or you'd get a crush, like that ridiculous thing with that actor. Love is an alibi for creative fatigue. You're lucky Jackson keeps you running after him, you don't have to deal with yourself."

"Let's not bring all that up again, Val."

"Listen—did you ever call Paul?"

"Why'd you think of him?"

"Oh, I guess, thinking of all the fathers dead or missing—the only people with perfectly orderly lives and two real parents are *in* the movies, not making movies, Susanna, or going to movies. And I was just wondering about Paul . . ."

"Paul and me?" To distract me from Angelo?

"Not really. Just thinking." She lies against the pillows and closes her eyes for a minute.

"Does it hurt?"

"No, just uncomfortable. It's not terrific to know you've just killed your baby. Have you ever thought how brave your mother was to have you in those days? I wish I'd had the courage." Her hands fall limp on either side. She looks so flat—like a spill of milk slid under the covers.

"Oh, Val. I'm sorry . . ." I try to hold her and she just looks away and stiffens herself. "I think you have courage to do this—I was thinking of Carleen, how she wouldn't take that risk at all."

"What risk?"

"Sex. I guess."

"Well," she says, "we thought it was a lot of things—but not exactly a risk. I guess that's mainly what it is. Even if you don't get pregnant—there's always the risk you'll fall in love and wind up obsessed and crazy and unable to think straight."

"But it's wonderful too—it's not just like that—it couldn't be or people wouldn't do it all the time."

"Wouldn't they? People do a lot of self-destructive things."

Obsessed. Crazy. Unable to think straight. Sounds like a description of how I am about Jackson. Maybe what I need is to fall in love with someone. Else, I mean.

Angelo is coming to see Val as I am leaving. He comes breezing through the front doors of the hospital. Nurses turn heads. Reception clerk nods—buttons her uniform up one more button and blushes.

"Look," he says, "I'm going to give her this." He pulls a little antique ring from his pocket, very thin gold with a slightly worn engraved pattern and a turquoise. "It's not that Navaho stuff. This is from Persia, the guy told me. Do you think Val will like it?"

"Oh, it's beautiful . . . she'll love it." I feel very, very sorry for myself, which is hateful. Why can't I be a nice person and be pleased when something good happens to someone else? Why do I immediately see it mostly as something which is not happening to me? I do have a lousy character.

"I thought the least she ought to get out of this deal is a ring. Why don't you wait for me? I won't stay long and we'll go for a walk or something."

He comes back down after about twenty minutes.

"She really likes it," he says, looking very pleased with himself. But he always does. And we walk along by the Park, looking at the huge apartment houses with their uniformed doormen across Fifth Avenue. "Some rich cat's wife was slumming one night, down at the Gate, and picked me up. She lives in one of these places, you know. We went up for dinner there. Her old man was out of town and she had a maid serve us. I was wondering what that maid thought. She wouldn't have let me in the front door if I'd just come up there. Even the peas were mashed. All this heavy glass and silver and hardly enough food for a bird. Weird."

"What did she want?"

"To ball me."

I wonder if that is a special way of doing it. Sort of face to face, rolling?

"Did you like her. Wasn't she old?"

"She was all right. She was lonely."

"That is weird."

"I don't like to miss anything."

I remember a story Angelo's father once told about him when he was little. His mother was preparing a party and she put a bowl of fruit out, and when she looked later there was one bite taken out of every piece of fruit.

I'm beginning to freeze. The stones we're walking along are slick in places with frost and the Park is bleak and bare and colored a faded peach from the late daylight. If I don't inhale and just sort of puff occasionally as I walk, warming the air before it gets to my chest, I can keep it from clutching on me. But when the cold air gets in I can feel my bronchial tubes become as narrow and dried out as the branches on the trees. A breath too deep and I feel they will crack.

"I was watching you girls that night of the fire. You know, when you took your shirts off?"

"What made you think of that?"

"I guess thinking of the two of you here in New York.

Val there. You running all over the country, still a virgin."

"How do you know that for sure?"

"I'm just guessing. What do you do, play with yourself a lot?"

"Angelo!" Was Grandmother right after all? Does sex really show? Any kind. And does that count? Maybe I'm not a virgin in the strictest sense. I keep my eyes on the pavement.

"Well," he says, "you've got to do something. I remember that night after you guys left to go to the fire. I took the hose to water down the roof of the stable, just in case."

I can imagine him standing there, the hose arched high above him like a silver rainbow, the water sliding like a sheet over the roof. I walk along faster. My cheeks getting hot. I wipe my nose with my mitten.

"I wanted to run that hose up someone until she'd be bobbing above me like a balloon, screaming with sex. I wanted to do it to you hot little girls with your cold smiles. I was thinking, when I was watching you all, that I'd like to leap from my horse with my pants off and get behind you and lift up your hips and do it to you with that horse bucking along under us. I held that hose and thought about that, about having two of you at once, astride both the horses, and I went off there just thinking about those neat little curved backsides. I was still holding that hose, and when I came I shuddered and the hose twitched and the water came down all over me."

"You're crazy." I shake my head and want him to think I don't know what he's talking about, which I don't really, except the things he says, the way he says them, make me feel like buckling down under him right here even in the cold.

"Everyone thinks like that, except no one talks about it. I just think you should know that."

"Gee. Thanks." Even for him to talk to me like this, after he's just given Val a ring, is disloyal.

And it's more disloyal of me to want him.

"Are you cold? We can catch the bus downtown."

"That's probably a good idea." We run to the next bus stop, and my breath flies behind me as though running from me in terror. The bus is warm. He pays the driver and we sit down.

"What's the matter?" He grins at me and takes my hands in his and rubs them together. It feels so good I don't want to pull them away which I know I should because the next minute he's got them pressed down into his lap and he just laughs at me. I look up at the ads. I wonder if they have a Miss Bus like they have a Miss Subways and I imagine Vera-Ellen and wonder when someone of my own is going to be in love with me. I wonder what happened to nice little games like Pediddle, where if you were driving with a boy and you saw a car with one light and he said "Pediddle" before you did he got to kiss you. Except Eddie thought if he said it twice that meant he got to put his hand up under your garters. And nice little games like Pediddle wound up in the back seat. It's different how I feel with Angelo. He's direct and dirty and you know he knows how—I mean really how. Every woman on this bus knows that. One look at him and every woman crosses her legs. You can hear the sound of nylons.

I want to do all of it with him, even things I say to myself I don't really believe people actually do. I mean, if he ordered me right now on this Fifth Avenue bus to get on my knees, and with my hands on his thighs put my head between his legs—or if he said, take everything off from the waist down. Which would be cold. And drape my stockings over these bus handles so they dangled down and people would have to brush them aside and he said I don't care if that seat is cold against your ass, and he might say a worse thing than that and if he then took his lean dark hands and put them so firmly on my thighs there would be marks for a week and put his head between my legs so I would feel his dark silky hair on my thighs and see it against my blond hair there and feel—stop it. This is the trouble with being around him. He wets his lips, too. Just to drive me crazy. He doesn't seem to be doing it on purpose. It's just how he is. Made for sex. Which sounds like some Barbara Payton–Scott Brady B movie that even I would know was trash. And I'd love it. I love trash as trash. And sex as sex. Not Easterners in suits suddenly pretending they're animals after a whole evening of throwing intellect and culture and foreign film directors in your face. That's why it's never worked. It's like driving a four-door Chrysler with skirts and a dual carburetor—it's even weirder than when it was a plain Chrysler.

Oh, God. Look how he does it to these women. Keeps his eyes moving so cool from about breast level to crotch and up again—but not like a creep.

He is only trouble for me. And he is right for Val. And she for him. Actors need women who can help them become stars. Who can make their lives more orderly. He sees how Val is with her friends. Like Jackson choosing Mrs. Rodgers. They want you calm and direct and motherly. I am maybe direct but even that only part of the time when I forget to design a lie. But what will Angelo be to Val, or what will he give to her? And how will that go if I'm hanging around watching them (him) when I'm not calling to see if Jackson's back?

"You know, I think Val's going to be famous. Did she play you her 'Good Morning, Daddy' song? I think it's really great." I say this very fast and slip my hands out from under his.

"Are you changing the subject?" He laughs right next to my ear. I can smell his skin, feel his ear just brush my cheek.

"Damn right," I say, looking at two young New York ladies in their suits and mink coats. Such people would have two parents, and orderly lives. And Carleen has that. Do I want an orderly life? They are looking at us. Do they imagine we are in love and are they in love or just married? And is that enough? Are such ladies ever obsessed and would one miss the feeling if one never had it?

"Won't you be jealous?" Angelo asks. He is looking at one of the ladies' legs. She looks at the bus ads, her eyes glazed, and squirms in her seat.

"Of Val? Would you? If she's a star before you are?"

"It's a different thing. She's a girl. We're not in competition. Music and acting are different."

"I don't want to be a star, anyway. I'm not in that league," I say. Maybe he also means be jealous of her with him . . .

"Well, she's always been more serious about her music."

I wish he hadn't agreed with me so fast.

"Someone once said," I say, watching the ladies who are getting off the bus—one turns and gives Angelo this quick, smoky look—"if you're the kind of kid everyone was always in love with you probably have the makings of a star."

"That's a Hollywood idea. I don't think everyone was in love with Bogart . . ." he says.

We're passing the great part of Fifth Avenue now and they're taking down their Christmas decorations. At home the triangular green paper trees will be packed up on trucks and carried away down Hollywood Boulevard and the streetlights in Beverly Hills will be stripped of their little lanterns, and the forests of pink, blue, and white Christmas trees will be empty lots again. The beach is wonderful now for walking alone, thinking of sad songs. I miss Perdido suddenly, with a rush—I miss it more than Jackson. I miss my room and movies every night and the busyness when there is a dinner party. I even miss dinner being served by Frank and Dorothy gently—not briskly along by waitresses you don't know. I miss the crocheted place mats Grandmother made. And oh, my God, do I miss my car!

We've taken the bus now all the way down to the Village and we're walking into the Italian section.

"I'll show you Sullivan Street where my family started out," Angelo says, "and we'll walk down Bleecker and get something to eat."

"Hey, look at the face on that guy," Angelo says. "Is that a great face or what?" I see a tall colored man standing by a wall with a length of that brown stuff we use under carpets wrapped around him. He is drinking from a paper bag. He reminds me of the old veterans at home who hang around Sawtelle near the Veterans' Hospital with its view of thousands of white wooden crosses in the dead soldiers' cemetery. Not a promising view for the guys up there in the hospital.

Angelo walks over to him—is he going to ask the man if he's ever thought of going into the theater?—he hands him a dollar. The man looks at it, and bows to Angelo. "I thank you, my friend. We all thank you."

"Why did you do that? He'll only drink."

"He's going to do it anyway."

"But that's helping him die."

"Isn't that his choice?"

We are sitting now in a cafe in the Italian section and drinking espresso coffee, which Val loves. It tastes like transmission fluid. I put a lot of cream and sugar in mine and Angelo says, "You've turned it into a Crumplar's milkshake."

And I miss Tom Crumplar's where we were not supposed to go because of Wolf gangs—and guys Angelo was pretending to be like then. Everything today reminds me of home.

"Virgins always drink espresso this way," I say.

"I haven't met one except you in years. I've got to make a rehearsal soon, but why don't you come by later and we'll go hear some music, or hang around with some people. There's a place down on MacDougal where they'd let you sit in on the guitar."

"Sort of amateur night?"

"No. Not amateur night, just like real informal. Pete Seeger used to drop in there. It's up to you." The espresso comes with little bits of lemon peel. He tears his in even smaller bits and chews them up one by one.

"Okay . . . maybe I'll go."

"What are you going to do now anyway? Hang around, watching Val—calling up north every day—waiting?"

"I don't know."

"What's going to happen? You'll spend a couple of days with him. Maybe. Meantime you're just hanging around. You know you remind me of these kids who hang around the studio having a vicarious career. So you'll play father and daughter for a few hours—big deal—he doesn't want to make a whole scene of that. He's as much as told you. And you're—"

"Stop it. Stop it. I'll do what I goddam want to, okay? He's my father and I know—Well, I know what I know. Just drop it!"

There is a long silence. He's doing it again, those fierce dark eyes fixing my eyes, I feel his legs reaching out and circling my knees. The table is too small. Our chairs too close. His knees press around mine tightly. I remember every curve, every dark shadow in those legs. I remember him working the garden in his shorts. And I look at the Christmas lights hanging still around the cafe twined with tinsel and think of how Tucky and her sailor drove me around one year to look at all the lights up and down the streets in Beverly Hills. And how Val and I used to touch the ornaments, little glass houses and snowmen on C.A.'s tree. And how from her bedroom window in the house on Lookout Mountain we could see the Christmas tree in the next door neighbor's house.

"What are you thinking about?" Angelo says.

"Being Jewish at Christmas."

"That's right, man, change the subject."

"You always accuse me of that when there hasn't been any subject." Except sex. I do not say. I stare right back at him and move my legs out fast and around to the side of my chair.

"Do you give each other un-Christmas presents or what? I never thought about that," he says.

"Well, you're marrying someone Jewish. So maybe you should think about it."

"Are you kidding? I'm not marrying anyone. I'm too young to think about getting married. Jesus, man. Val would be crazy to marry me. Is that what's bothering you? Just because I love her doesn't mean the world has to stop. Like just because you love someone doesn't mean your life has to stop and wait. And you're only half Jewish, so you can have half a Christmas if you want."

"That's not very funny. I'm probably not anything." Scratch that, I tell God. I didn't mean it.

"Well, you think Jewish." He takes the lemon peel from my saucer and starts tearing it up into little confetti pieces.

"What's that supposed to mean?"

"Just the way you get all involved in things. And all defensive about being Jewish."

"Look who the hell is talking!" I practically yell at him.

"Well," he says, doing this hip kind of jazz nodding of his head, "if I'd been Jewish, I'd be scared as hell—like when the right wing talks about Communists, they usually mean Jews. And when they talk about Hollywood they mean Jews, too. Yeah, I'd be scared—and what did you think I did this afternoon? Run in and say, 'Will you marry me?' hand her the ring, and run out?"

"Look who's defensive! I think it's wonderful, whatever you did. Something good should happen to Val." A waiter walks by with a frozen orange, hollowed and filled with sherbet. I cannot take my eyes off it. I want to see California orange trees with big ripe oranges under the shiny dark green leaves. (And not Jackson. Try not, Susanna, to think of your father naked. I don't. I just don't see that any more. Much.)

"What gives you the idea that I would be so good for her?"

"I don't know. I think you love each other. You're interested in the same things. You look good together."

"Now, there's a reason. Man—the main thing is Val always gets what *you* want, is how you see it. That way you don't feel guilty for being jealous of someone who hasn't had it any easier than you have."

"I'm not. I love Val."

"That doesn't mean you can't be jealous at the same time. And you're probably jealous of me. And she's probably sitting there in that hospital room wondering what we're up to. That's one thing I'm trying to work on at the studio—to figure out what other people are feeling. I never thought about that, man. That's Hollywood, that's why they couldn't pay me enough to go out there."

(They wouldn't have to pay me anything. I want to go home. And I have just enough money left.)

"You can only be good if you do it from the inside out. Look, you want to be a singer . . . ?" He makes the gesture with his hands of someone telling everyone to please rise.

"No. I don't know what I want to be. I'm a lousy singer. I know that. Well, that's not what I mean, it's not that I don't know what I can be, it's just I don't think I can be it, Angelo, and that's worse." I watch a couple walk out who can't be much older than we are. She's pregnant and holding one child by the hand and he's carrying another and they are all stuffed into eighty layers of clothes.

"That's because you see it from the outside. You see yourself being a singer or whatever. You don't look at where the music comes from. You're too busy acting like it. That's why I think you ought to come with me tonight and see—they just play, they just listen to each other. But like you said, you'll do what you want to do. You know something?—everyone does."

He finishes his espresso and stands up, he shifts into his slouch, and shoves hands down into pockets. He leans into the glass door as we go out, opening it with his shoulder, and turns and stands for a moment, looking at himself. He pushes his hair back and then forward with both hands. Men always use both hands for hair. He kind of bares his teeth at his reflection and realigns his shoulders. I am almost as tall as he is, I see in the glass. I fluff my hair before I wrap my muffler around it. I look at myself in windows too. I must go easier on these actors.

"Well, you may be all screwed up, Susanna, but you still have great tits."

"When you're famous I want that in writing." I sort of jab him in the arm the way guys do to each other.

"Sure thing. I'll see you later."

"Probably," I say. Probably not, I know. He shows me to the subway and explains where to change and gives me a token and I run before I get kissed. I don't want to start with him. I wouldn't stop. CALIFORNIAN LOSES VIRGINITY ON IRT STEPS. Or whichever one this is.

I pick up some flowers for Hildy in the Times Square station. Tunnels and warrens—these Easterners live like moles and rabbits. Once you actually get on the subway though, it's a pretty good ride. They should have such a thing all the way to New Hampshire.

Hildy is not home. I put the flowers in the kitchen and start to clean up for her. I make up my bed, which means folding the stuff and putting it on the end of the couch. I know as I move around that I'm really packing, getting ready to leave. Angelo is just being himself. He doesn't long for me. I want someone to long for me, not to just flirt, but to grab me. But, then, why when he touches me, do I run? Because he does not belong to me. He belongs to Val. And it is a little too tricky.

Val would leave Hildy a real present, not just subway flowers—these roses with their dusty, slope-shouldered leaves. These roses a shade paler than they ought to be. These roses who live like underground fugitives in the World War, whisked from trucks to tunnels. Val has always been expert at presents. She gets what she knows you want, not just what she likes. Like when she bought me this silvery beaded collar for my seventeenth birthday. "This is just the kind of garish thing you adore. I would not go in and buy it of course, so that is why it is in this plain brown wrapper, which is how they sent it to me." I still have that card somewhere at home.

Grandmother always said, "You never go (or leave) anywhere empty-handed." And, Val, of course, is the one who remembers that. On the night she brought me back to Hildy's she brought a prettily bound copy of some poems by Shelley or Keats or one of those people.

"Val," I call her at the hospital, not sure as usual whether I am going to tell her the truth. "How are you doing? Angelo showed me the ring before he went up to see you."

"Oh, right—he said he ran into you."

He clearly did not tell her he told me to wait. What was that nonsense about her wondering what we were up to?—it is exactly smart to leave before I say or do something that would hurt any of us.

"He's rehearsing tonight," she says. "You ought to go down there and watch him. He's so good. I mean he's really good."

"I might. I'm going to go now." And now I can't tell her I'm leaving. She might talk me out of it.

"See you tomorrow. When I get everything sorted out, I'll help you figure out what to do—about Jackson and everything. Entire life, you know—I'm sorry. This came at a lousy time. It was really brilliant of me."

"Don't worry. I'm fine. I think I know what I want to do about some of it."

"Well, that's good. Have a nice evening . . . if you see him, say hello. We'll probably get together tomorrow night anyway, although, God, I'm going to have a lot of catching up to do."

"You'll be all right." I'm anxious to go. I don't want her to say anything which will change my mind.

"Bye-bye, Ginger." She hasn't called me that in years. I'd forgotten about that. She started calling me that when we did this dance number—it must have been in the sixth grade. And I got all wound up in my dress, and wrecked her impression of Fred Astaire. She just stood there with her hands on her hips and this big black bow tie making her look like a sleek young cat and said, right in front of everyone, "Ginger, you've never been better." And we both doubled up with laughter and never did get it straight.

I call up the Idlewild Airport and make a reservation for the next flight to L.A. If I had been so sure, however, that I did not want to be talked out of leaving, that I did not expect her to ferret it out of me, wouldn't I have made that reservation before?

The guitar sits on the empty airplane seat beside me like a silent child with exceptional posture. I wonder about this secret departure. It beats explanations I don't have. And avoids possibly alluring arguments to stay. It avoids Angelo's fierce bright eyes.

Did Jackson feel this way when he crept away from Hollywood? Have I inherited from him the art of running away? But I'm going home, not running away.

The plane is like a shark gliding through an upside-down sea. It is easy to imagine I am in the coach car of a train and the bumps and bounces as we hit storms are just a rocky bit of rail. We come in above a storm which skids across the Pacific, leaving trails of light like mercury on the water. I can see the Palisades, and if I could open the window here I would tumble out and over the tiled rooftops the color of the brick buildings I have just left. I would turn and twist and float down; and land in the green and golden country where I really live.

I STAND HERE IN MY SKI SUIT, WHICH IS THE PERFECT outfit for airplane travel, and I look at my house and my trees and hear the Western sounds I love. Our birds —the cars running fast below, big highway trucks. Home sounds. Wind in palm trees.

The hydrangeas have turned pale again. Angelo's father used to put nails in the ground to keep them cobalt blue. Bougainvillea, who has clipped you back so far? I remember when she seemed to be so high above me and now I can reach up and touch her little paper lantern flowers. The shrimp plants are blooming with their tawny flowers that look like miniature paper fish kites I saw in Chinatown, and the tiny begonia border— how you get to love plants, like Aunt Thelma watering her geraniums, asking them if they were going to be around for another month. Just seeing the trees is the main thing. Coming in the cab up Sepulveda and through the most boring parts of town, I thought of the trees. And touch the trunk of the jacaranda asking if it plans to flower this year—you never know with it— sometimes it becomes a ferny umbrella covered with lavender blue blossoms which fall fast and make a carpet on the driveway, which Angelo's father used to love and never rake until the last blossoms had turned brown. And sometimes jacaranda is just like now, a— well, a ferny umbrella. And to hear the waves—and smell the sea—I skip to the edge, to my wall, and look over at my view and the only thing better would be to have Jackson with me. Don't think of that. I love to be home. I do. I had to go away, Perdido, to know how much I missed you!

My parents must be out, the limo is not here. I ring the front door bell. Dorothy opens it. "Oh, my God," she says. "Susanna, honey! look at you. What are you wearing? what are you doing here? Now, just come in, I'll get those bags."

"I thought I'd just drop by." I laugh and we hug each other and I look beyond her and through the double doors to the living room and I see the furniture is covered with sheets. There are tags swaying from Grandmother's Russian sconces above the table in the entry hall. Two of the paintings are gone and I can see the marks on the wall like shadows.

"What's happening here, what's going on? Where's Mary?"

"It's Sunday, honey." But I have looked into the den where she always sat and the files are gone—and most of the things from her desk. The philodendron my mother always hated is even gone.

"Where's my mother?" I'm going to scream.

"I'll get her right now. They didn't write you anything?"

"No." I feel like a guest in someone else's nightmare. I must have felt something strange was happening. That must have been why I came home. The dining room chairs are covered with cloths and marked with tags saying SOLD. The old Russian lamps above the table are gone. They were royal-blue glass, studded with bronze stars. I go faster through now, rushing into the projection room. The little rattan folding chairs for extra guests are tied into a bundle in the corner. I stand on the couch to look through the window to the projection booth, half expecting Johnny the projectionist will be there. (I remember I thought he used to live there frozen and still in his chair until the button was pushed on the intercom and then he would move about, like the postman in Joseph Cotten's mechanical bank who would come forward and take your money when the door was opened.)

Nothing is there. The machines are gone. Like two

robot elephants the 35-mm. projection machines had been part of the household for as long as I remember. They were, if you were allergic, the next best thing to having dogs.

"Susanna. Don't stand on the couch," my mother says. I jump off automatically.

"A little redecoration?" I say to her. I cannot breathe.

"Susanna. We didn't want to upset you."

"But I am . . . I am upset. What is happening here?" I am beginning to yell. "You are not selling Perdido? You can't. You just can't."

"Yes." And she turns her head and starts to cry. I hate that.

"And the studio?" I will dig into her. Her mascara will run and then she will whimper and run from me.

"Yes." Here she goes. Little steps away. Hands to her face. This time I will go first. "Susanna," she shouts, "it's my house too. I've had my whole life here. Don't be so damn selfish. Think how I feel."

"You can't do this to me—you can't keep lying—I don't care how you feel. You never tell me anything, how should I know, why should I care! I just want to beat you against the wall until you die or turn real."

I stand there clenching my fists. She gasps, she gets up and she stands right in front of me. I can feel her breath. The life of life. I hate her life because it gave me mine.

"What did I ever do to you? I gave you everything you ever wanted."

"You gave me—lies. You gave me everything to be afraid of. You didn't even tell the truth about who I am. All you ever taught me was how to lie. And how to pretend it was all fine. How was I supposed to be about this? All fine?"

"You don't like me." She looks at me like a fretful four-year-old.

"Like you? Like you? Not liking doesn't even begin to describe it, Mother. If you couldn't grow up, how could I learn? How would you imagine I could ever understand what you feel when you never say anything true?"

She gropes her way to a chair and puts her hands on it, leaning, breathless. "Does it help you to beat me? Then go ahead." I think I have really scared her. How nice to scare your mother.

"You always knew there had to be some reason." My throat tastes of steel like the way you taste and smell when you're on the train—I am becoming a sword. "You taught me your obsession with Jackson. You never showed me how to avoid it. You only showed me the destruction, how to be hurt in one easy way." I am saying things I do not know I knew. Did I learn from Carleen who learned to embellish reality with cheers, from a mother who fakes the past, who sweetens it, sugarcoats it and devours memory? Did I learn watching Val fall in love, like Lillian, with someone who hurt her and then when that was over start doing it again?

"I've never understood things like that. I'm a much simpler girl than you think."

"You're my mother—not a girl. You like not having to think about being a mother because you like to be a girl who's been rejected forever and ever and to punish him and me and Myron—and you even probably knew I'd go off to find him and get hurt and it would carry on and on and on. You didn't even check on me—you didn't even know or care where I was all these months!" And I didn't know I wanted her to until now—

"I don't understand. I just don't understand what you think I've done to you." She sits there deflating, sagging, lines and folds coming into existence, her mouth drooping open into terrible crying.

I feel myself beginning to shake with fear at what I am doing and what I am saying and understanding and I feel I am going to explode with knowing. I don't want to. I put my hands to my head.

"You are a cruel young woman." She bounces the words out between sobs.

"What are you going to do, tell Myron? Oh, how in-

349

timidating. Will I be asked to apologize to my mother? My mother." I spit the words out like an insult.

"I only did the best I could."

"It wasn't good enough."

"You might as well go ahead and kill me. Would that help, Susanna?"

"No, because you won't die. I could kill you a thousand times, Mother, and you'll always be back, reproaching me for being born, for reminding you that you couldn't keep him." And I wonder—could that have been the truth?—and I go on. "Haven't we tried to kill each other? Didn't you try to kill me?" She turns white. I can feel it happen to me as it happens to her. This terrible guess is true. It stands here as real as a stone wall. "Didn't you try to kill me? Isn't that why you never had any other children? Did you try to carve me out of you?" She was no braver than Val or Carleen—she just missed.

"Hasn't it ever occurred to you, Susanna"—suddenly she springs up, the color comes back to her face and she screams back at me—"that I didn't want any children? . . . I don't like children. And why should I? Why should anyone? Leave me alone. We have nothing."

"We sure don't. We have no home. No love for each other—and we don't either of us have Jackson. . . . He didn't," and I feel this is my killing thrust and I do not even want to say it as I do, "he didn't even ask about you."

I run up to my room. I slam the door. I rip my collection of birds' nests down from my ceiling. And I throw my birds' nests against the walls and when they will not break apart I tear them with my bare hands and when my hands are scratched I take my puppets and I take my prince puppet and I break his head against the wall and I take his arms and I take his legs and I tear them off until there is nothing left of him but shattered pieces.

And now I am at my records and sailing them through windows and when I am looking around for something else to shatter Myron is in my room. He just stands there with his arms crossed like Napoleon.

"What the hell are you doing?"

"What are you doing in here?" I scream at him. "You have wrecked everything for me."

"No, Susanna, I did not. I have tried to save what I could. And I will not tolerate you attacking your mother as you did."

I find a record I have not broken and start to fling it and he takes it out of my hand. "You," he says, "are going to listen to me. Now, sit down." And he pushes me down onto my bed. And he sits on my desk chair. I will not look at him.

"You are not my father and you cannot tell me what to do."

"No, Susanna, I am not your father. But I have tried my best. I wanted to be everything to you that your own father would not be. Your mother and I did what we thought was best. I don't expect you to thank us, no child ever does, I don't thank my own parents for certain things—but I don't, any more, blame them for mistakes they may have made. At a certain point a lot of mistakes were my own. You're getting to that age, my dear, and it's time someone told you, that you will have to be responsible for what happens to your life. You cannot blame your real father, or your mother, or me."

"I don't blame you for anything. You haven't even been that much a part of it," I say spitefully.

"I suppose I know that, and I feel somehow that that is my greatest failure. I didn't let you know me enough for that, maybe there's not enough for you to know."

I look at him. He is like a stranger sitting here, this odd, tight man, crumbled like everything in my room. We are part of the rubble. Can we put it back together without the cracks showing? I start to say something about how he is not Jackson, but . . . but I know that will only hurt him more. He is not Jackson, but he has tried. I sit down, fall almost, on the edge of my bed.

"I guess," I say, "it hasn't been easy."

"You know, Susanna," he says, "being a father, or a stepfather, is like producing a picture which everyone hates—what I try to say then in defense is we did not make a decision to make a really bad movie. We did not get together, your mother and I, and say, 'Let's make Susanna miserable.' "

"Okay. I know that." This kind of thing embarrasses me. I think he sees that and sort of half smiles to change the subject.

"In fact, I have said that, in essence, to the New York office, that I did not mean for our productions to go into the red—I know what you're feeling now, but believe me, I tried to hang on to V.L.I. . . . Susanna, I loved having this house. It may be too big now for your mother and me, but I didn't want to have to give it up like this."

"Are you broke? Is that what happened?"

"If you would like I can go into the details with you."

"Yes. I would like." If only, for once, to hear the truth before no one really remembers what it is.

"Just briefly, V.L.I. has been owned for some years by stockholders. It only takes a majority of fifteen percent to influence a major decision. There was a proxy fight and, quite simply, we lost. Their investment will be better protected by selling out to television production, and, probably, the company that will take over will sublet to independent film producers. Your mother and I are not broke. On the contrary, we feel free now, and, because you are on your own, we felt we would like to live abroad for a while. I have an offer to produce independently myself, overseas."

"Were you going to just leave? Send me a wire, maybe, sort of a Dear John letter? Don't come home because it isn't there, that sort of thing?" It's not like Val said, a jigsaw puzzle. It's like a split screen but with two movies. "You're seein' my life on one side the way you want it to be, or the way Grandmother did," I tell him, "and then there's the real one that I'm livin' but

352

I'm not supposed to know and that can make a person really crazy. I just don't want any more lies." I'm hot and red and almost bursting from trying not to cry and break down like a child.

"What would you rather have us do, Susanna? We did our best for you. Would you have been happier or more secure knowing your father was a bastard who ran out on your mother?"

"I'm the bastard around here. Remember?"

"Don't use that word like that in my house."

"You did! And it's not even your house any more. . . ."

"This isn't helping anyone," Myron says.

"And my father is not like that. He just is someone who couldn't bear being tied down. I bet he never promised he'd marry her. He's always been someone who wanted to wander. He can't help how he is. A person can't help bein' what they are. I saw him. That's where I was. I saw all of them. And you didn't even know." I hate my smug smile. Wipe it off, I tell myself.

My mother walks in.

"Susanna, stop talking like a cowboy," she says, as though nothing has happened. She is composed again. Except her eyes are laced with red and her skin is still pale. She puts her hand on Myron's shoulder and he lifts his hand to her cheek and then puts it down over hers, clasping lightly. Yes. Lightly. So he does not get stabbed by her sapphires.

"I'm not. I'm talkin' like me. You always wanted me to be perfect like Val. Well, she's not so perfect either." I stop myself in time—but now there's another big family lie, like Alan's suicide, and I'm going right along with it.

"No one's perfect, Susanna. We understand that, but there is the matter of responsibility, and, I could say, running around the country is simply irresponsible for a young girl with your background. . . ."

Did they know? Now I think they did.

"Now, which background would that be? It's exactly like part of my background. Exactly like it. Where'd you ever get the idea I'd have to turn out like you? And if you knew what I was doing why didn't you stop me? Were you looking for me?—why didn't you say something? One more lie, was that it? All of us pretending it was just fine?"

"We knew we couldn't stop you, Susanna. And we didn't know where you were—we felt, your mother and I, that you had to do it. You've always been a willful girl."

"Now, what are you going to do with me? Throw me into college?"

"Well," my mother says—her voice is very firm, I am surprised to say—"we'll expect you to make up your mind by the end of this month. You may go to college, and we will see that you are settled there, or you may come to Italy with us, and go to college there—perhaps to the Sorbonne in Paris. That's your choice." And she looks dreamy about that because it's what she would like, or the sound of it anyway. Mainly the part about going into Magnin's and Amelia Gray's and saying, "I'm going to the Sorbonne and, my God, I suppose I need everything"—when my mother comes in to shop, she always presents the need to buy a lot of stuff as work, like Val coming in from her classes with her arms full of assignments and falling on her bed with the books.

"That's no choice. It's all school and school's school no matter what they call it or where it is, you've got to be where they want you, when they want you. And I hate it and my father hates it!" She winces. Knew she would.

"That, Susanna, is life. And the sooner you get used to it, the easier it will be for you," Myron says. "And," he adds, "stop needling your mother. You know exactly what I'm talking about."

"Well, it's not life for everyone. Maybe for you. But it's no life I want any part of. Any everything's needling me!"

"You can carry on," he says. "You have no alternative."

My mother adds, "You're a young lady and young ladies, unless they're married, go to college. And that is that."

"Is that that?" I say.

Well. Married.

Married? My own little house. With my own trees no one can sell. Come and go as I please. Own charge accounts. No one checking up. Making little dinners with candlelight. Being Very Much in Love. And sex. A new life all my own with someone who will not go away. Staying up as late as you please, playing him songs. And trips for two with the top down. And sex.

Married. I will call Paul Daroff. And who could object? It is a merger, not just a marriage. How fast can you get very much in love?

I wonder if I can get Jackson to walk me down the aisle. Now that would be something. And Scotty playing folksongs on his shining silver Dobro.

Jackson walking me down, proud as punch. And Rabbi Silverberg standing, waiting for us under the little peach tree. I've got three months before we have to move. Three months to make it happen. Anyone can be in love in three months. I fell in love in twenty seconds—every time I did. All both times and look how perfect it worked out—one turned out to be—to be—well, to be Henry and the other turned out to be my father. There'll be no problem about Paul though.

Jackson walking in white next to me, and everyone in Hollywood lined up to watch like black and white glossies in a row and saying, "He must have always loved her very much—never thought we'd see Jackson Lane back in town, and for a wedding!"

And Paul will be standing up there next to the Rabbi looking shy and wise and people will be saying, "Yes, and they're going to build a new Hollywood out of the ruins." And Val and Angelo will fly out and they'll come to our first little dinner. And Val will nod at me and say, "Smart move." And she'll play piano after dinner and I'll play my guitar and we'll all sing. . . .

Jackson walking me down the aisle. Yeah, and Jesse James is showing up at Hillcrest Country Club for brunch. If you want to know, I'd a lot more likely lay my money down on that.

"Hello, Paul," I say, that evening when he returns my phone call. But can you fall in love with someone you know? Have to try to find out. "You know, I've really missed you. . . ." And I have. I have. I tell myself.

"I'm so glad you called," he says. "You had quite a trip, Val told me about it."

"Well. It was sort of here and there. But you have to go away to find out what really matters. I'm really sorry I didn't call sooner—you know?"

"I understood—those calls are always hell. By the time I get up the nerve to make them, I usually convince myself it's too late, somehow, for the subject to be brought up."

"You do understand. Listen, Paul, let's do something crazy."

"Well, what—I am keeping in mind who I'm talking to—what kind of crazy?" He's laughing around the edges of his voice.

"I will make a picnic."

"That's already crazy. Where'd you learn to cook?"

"Motlin, Illinois. And anyway you don't cook picnics. And here's what. We will take it to the fountain at Wilshire and Santa Monica Boulevard and watch the colors go round."

"Okay—that sounds like a pretty good kind of crazy. You've got a deal."

Mother I would marry and I would be a bride,
And I would have a young man forever at my side.
For if I had a young man, oh how happy I would be,
For I am tired and oh so weary of my virginity.

Whistle, daughter, whistle ...

"And I am not," I say to God, and my mother, "just whistling Dixie."

Part Four

1960

THE KNOWING LOOK THEY SAY YOU GET MAY JUST BE disillusionment. Comes standard with the station wagon which is parked under the acacia tree in front of the airy Spanish house Paul and our son, Sevin, and I live in way up on top of Wonderland Drive, not far from where Val used to live. And, yes, everyone hates Sev's name except Sev and me. (And he only likes it now because he thinks people think he is seven years old. In two years he may change his mind.) But seven is my lucky number and he was born on July 7, 1956, so what else would you call him? I said, "Well, I can always call him Jackson." No argument. If you want your own way in life most of the time make outrageous demands, then when you get right down to what you really want they say, "Oh, well. . . ." If you want the entire truth, Paul secretly adores the name because it sounds Scandinavian and that makes him think of Bergman. Ingmar, of course. Do you think I ever dreamed when you'd be at a dinner party and they were talking about Bergman it would be a man director and not the star! And, that it would be *my* dinner which is tonight and I am still here?

Of course I am the only really Scandinavian one. Or partly. Carleen did find out that was true. Our grandparents were Norwegian. We write now and then. Why don't I tell her the truth? Why did I just tell her Jackson was not in Florida when I wrote to send her my wedding invitation?—which, you might imagine, nearly killed my mother. Aunt Thelma did not let her come. I do not know why. Could be one of ten dozen reasons. Does it matter? Any of it? Carleen already has three kids (two are twins). As I said on the gift card, "That's something to cheer about."

The trust my grandmother left me gave us the down payment for this house. And Evelyn Ames released some money from Paul's trust fund for the car. But not without difficulty: "I think I'd like to wait until you've been married longer."

I called her later, after Paul was at work. "I forgot to tell you about this real estate broker I met who remembers this funny movie you made back in the silent days —which was wild. I never knew you did that sort of thing. I guess everyone's forgotten."

"It's not nice," she said, "to extort your mother-in-law." Long silence. "Well, don't get one of those little foreign cars."

"I know," I said. "Every time you turn a corner, over they go." Nothing changes.

"Is she being sarcastic, Paul?" Evelyn, who fortunately has remarried and lives in the East, rarely addresses me directly.

"No, Evelyn. That's just Susanna's way." Which is how Paul likes to see it. "If you'd only be your own sweet self," he says to me. "That kind of sarcasm is different when Val does it."

Everything is different when Val does it. She has had a successful album after doing a year of college tours. Then she married Angelo after his discovery on Broadway. Then he made *Chancel Dunes,* a sort of beatnik tribute to James Dean, and now they are out here— staying at the Chateau Marmont and hanging around with their transplanted New York "film friends." Like refugees. Except Grandfather and Grandmother wanted only to belong. They want only *not* to. They will not drive in convertibles. Or go to Beverly Hills. They spend nights at Cyrano's drinking mocha frosteds with cognac and discuss the dangers of selling out (for too little money). Paul and I spend nights wondering when you get too old to be "promising" while we watch old family movies on TV, and I say I'm going to go downstairs in a half hour and work on my arrangements of some folksongs for an album I'd like to do and Paul says he wants to do a new treatment of one of his father's four hundred properties which he has been meaning to have ready to show Angelo and Val and this new producer out from the East who are coming to dinner. And before we know it we're hooked on the next movie and feeding each other's sadness about how great it used to be. Then Paul falls asleep with one of his father's old scripts in his arms and I put it down by the bed and cover him and go downstairs and play the songs I already know, postponing again the challenge of getting material ready for a demo tape to show to Val's manager, L. C. Smith, who is out here again, looking for new talent. Tonight Val will say, "I thought you were going to call EllCee. Hasn't heard from you. . . ."

And I'll say, "Well, I'm just not ready yet."

In a half an hour I have to pick up Sevin at school, and then we're going marketing for the dinner party. Paul actually should be running a restaurant. This party is just one more prelude to the party he has been dreaming about for a year which is a Memorial Dinner for his father. "It's going to be a major event. I want every detail perfect, just as he would have wanted it—a sitdown dinner, tables of eight, tournedos—everything first-class. Every star who ever made a film for him will be in the program. We'll run a clip of the film and have each of them talk about how my father conceived the picture, and give their impressions. Of course . . . actors. I'll write the material, or get some good top writers in on it."

"I think even an actor could handle that sort of narration, Paul. Some actors can talk. Not all, I know, but some have even, one could say, the gift of gab."

"Susanna. Don't be so defensive about actors."

"I wonder if we could get Jackson to put in an appearance. But then, he never made a picture for your father. Too bad."

"Susanna, I hate to hear you do that to yourself."

"I'm not. I haven't mentioned him in months. Stop biting your nails." I used to think it was cute when he had to put down his father's long fourteen-carat gold and ebony cigarette holder in order to bite a nail. He used to think it was cute when I left my clothes right where I took them off. But he has told me (and told me, he would say) it is not always funny to wake up with my bra around his neck because I threw it on the bed the night before. "And I thought it was a fetish," I said.

"No. Why does everything with you wind up being about sex?"

"Sex?" I said. "Whoever heard of that?" Sex. It is not our best thing that we do together. Never was.

I should have noticed how neat he was on that first picnic. I, of course, had gotten plum jam on my dress. He went to the fountain, dipped a napkin in and then gently wiped off my dress, packaged all the trash and put it into the trash can, picking up some dead leaves on the way. It seems you "fall in love"—to use the phrase we grew up with—meaning: decide to marry, and you don't see anything or hear anything.

Then we drove up Coldwater Canyon to Mulholland Drive and parked. Necking with someone I had known for so long seemed silly at first.

Why were we laughing?

Were we remembering ourselves as children, because we were seeing each other as the children we were? Did we know each other too well for this? I think now it was not well enough. I saw myself as the little girl with her wet handkerchief and itchy organdy dress watching this big boy biting his nails as his father took moving pictures of him; or me, scared of the allergy shots, watching him roll up his sleeve and look away.

He pulled away and put a cigarette in his holder, lit it, rubbed the back of my neck and looked at me. "I think I love you. I've thought about it"—he considered every word—"and I really think I do." I didn't listen. As usual. If you are in love, do you think about it?

Silence. Before we ever went out that evening we both knew what would happen. But we would never tell each other. Never wreck the idea that we married for love when, of course, we married because we could create this social structure.

"And I guess we should get married."

"Terrific!" I said.

"Inevitable," he said. And I loved the sound of the word that night. When you are determined to fall in love you'll hear anything he says any way you want to.

"My God, but the furniture's all sold."

"Never mind," said Myron, "we'll tell them they'll have to wait."

Somewhere Grandmother was clasping her hands in delight.

"Susanna," my mother said to me, "do you really love Paul? Marriage isn't a school, you know, you can't just leave. Paul has always been a very nice boy."

"I've always loved Paul. Don't you think I know my own mind, honestly, Mother?"

"No. But then at eighteen no one does." We looked at each other. So she was only my age—when I was conceived. I have never learned to subtract in my head or I could figure out how old she is.

Val sent me pink roses by telegram and I called her at Hildy's. "Please don't hurt Paul. He's very sensitive."

"Everyone keeps worrying about Paul."

"That's because everyone knows you."

"Well, it's going to be perfect."

"A perfect marriage. Just like the movies?"

"That's right. You'll see."

And we were married under the olive tree. Paul looked like a dark print of Franchot Tone in his morning suit. Rabbi Silverberg studied me carefully as I walked up to the white-flowered canopy. Did he expect me to bolt for the pool? He had gone Ivy League and was wearing white bucks with red rubber soles. Dorothy winked at me as I went by, out of step with Myron.

Val had flown out for the wedding and was walking

ahead of me. I watched Paul. Was he looking at her wistfully? Was I second-best? I remember glancing at the pool where Jackson had stood that morning so long ago, looking down at me. I sent him an invitation. Returned: *Sorry. No longer at this address; no forwarding address given.* I thought he had written it on there himself to throw me off. I should have checked. Perhaps his problem is illiteracy, I thought, which would explain why I hate to read.

And so we were married.

"Is anything wrong?" Paul said, stroking my hair with his hands after we made love that first time. I could not breathe. Please, I thought, do not have an asthma attack.

"Was it nice?" I asked him.

"Yes, don't talk . . . don't talk." He was lying on me and he was wheezing too.

"I'm sorry. I'm just wondering if you're all right."

He got out and sat up. "Susanna, do you ever stop talking?"

Four and a half hours married and it was our first fight.

"No, I guess I never do stop talking," I said, "but I'll work on it. Where are you going?"

"To wash."

He came back and we did it again on our sides, then he washed and we did it with me sitting on top and he washed and we did it sort of leapfrog style and he washed and we did it on the other side and by then we had finished all the positions in the pink and blue marriage manual that came with my diaphragm.

He came back to bed with his hair combed, and neatly arranged the sheets over himself.

"Don't you want to wash?" he asked.

I got up and walked into the bathroom. There was only one thing I really wanted to do, my hand was just itching to, but if I did it to myself I wouldn't feel sexy later. God, I said, have You made me frigid for doing this for so many years? I would think You have more important things to take care of. It didn't seem too out of line to just get myself started, so then I strummed myself into low gear and bolted out of the bathroom and I ran to the bed and jumped on him. Damn!

"What the hell are you doing, darling?" ("Darling"— the afterthought of the well-brought-up groom. Say anything, but tack on "darling.")

"Do you always sleep on your stomach?" I sat unhappily astride the useless side of him. I wondered if he would think I was perverted if I rubbed a little on his back. He would only have to wash again and I had already lost the feeling.

I remember looking at him the next morning. He was sound asleep. His arm was draped over his forehead. He looked as if he had died in anguish. Sex is exhausting for them, I thought, all that thrusting. I just go through the motions, but he was feeling it. And when I really do it myself, I can just lie there, all the action is in the hand. I wondered how much of his jumping was just because he thought I liked it. I wondered if you could discuss this kind of thing with them. Maybe when we get to know each other. And to think I thought I did. Know him. Do you really ever know a man? Or anyone? And, how to define knowing?

I could not resist touching his collarbone. He has lovely shoulders, broad but also lean and his bones are so fine, cut like very delicate light wood. His cock lay nestled on his balls like a sleeping puppy.

He flinched in his sleep as though I had scared him. "It's okay, Paul," I whispered.

I got up and dressed then and asked the doorman for the keys to our car. Paul's car.

I drove down to the beach. Down Sunset. Did not look up at Perdido. And when I hit the Coast Highway I said, "Hello, Susanna."

I am still here. The wedding ring doesn't change it. I'm still looking. And driving somewhere.

And now it is to school to pick up Sevin and take him with me to shop for our dinner party. I do not like supermarkets because they are all in one place and you get very little driving done. Sevin adores the car too. His first car seat had a toy steering wheel. And whenever he was fussing, I would pick him up and we'd go out—both of us driving, him spinning his wheel and making car noises and looking over and grinning at me.

And supermarkets remind me of Illinois—of all the women like children playing at driving with their carts, in their ad-man's idea of a housewives' playschool. Staying put. Staying where they are put. I think the housewife was invented by TV to get us used to staying home so we would never think of going out to see movies.

Paul was frantic when I came back that first morning of our honeymoon.

"You sound like my parents," I said.

"You could have left a note—told me you were going out. I didn't know what had happened."

"Oh, Paul, don't, I love you . . ."

"Do you?"

We did not look each other in the eyes.

No wonder movies fade out at the wedding.

I don't like college. I don't like marriage. I am probably a beatnik. Miscast again in my own life. I am surely Jackson's perfect child. Jackson. Every time something doesn't work out I think of Jackson. And every time Jackson doesn't work out I think of something to distract me, something else to run to. This time it won't be so simple to get away.

Maybe I will grow into this. Dear Paul, sometimes even now when he is sleeping, I stroke his silky hair. To everyone else he is a Daroff; to me he is a little bit the kid who gets sand kicked in his face. And a nail biter. Sometimes he kneels on the bed and bites and thinks. Like last night. Which was one of the good nights.

"Don't," I said, kneeling on the bed in front of him, and I pulled down his hand from his mouth and held both of his hands tight between my thighs.

"No," he said, pulling his hands out and holding mine down now. And I leaned my face close to his, my hair falling down over my shoulders. "Kiss," I said.

"Kiss is it. Then I've got to get to sleep. I've got to be at the studio early. They want me to go over the budget for next week's show."

I knew we would not make love. But there's always a chance. That's one thing about marriage, you've got a fair chance to do it again. Sometime.

Then I was downstairs trying to work and he came down and said, "Ice cream time," and we got bowls of chocolate ice cream and put raspberry jam on it and I looked over my shoulder at my guitar and we went upstairs and wound up watching movies. I wanted to ask Paul if we weren't a little young to be replacing sex with food, and I thought of Aunt Thelma and Ken, but we do not discuss sex.

Any more.

We had our last major sex war six months ago. And our last sex. I remembered, as I sat there on the foot of our bed, the fight my mother had with Myron, when she complained he did not use her, when she was running out that night without her nightgown on, when he hit her. Did I marry Paul only so I can understand how she felt? I keep looking lately for the real reason.

But I do not appreciate this lesson in compassion. At least she had had her one great affair.

I wanted to figure out a way to tell Paul that there were other things to do in bed than just what we do, and that they are all right.

Perhaps I could find one of those Havelock Ellis books with the good parts written in Latin.

"Paul," I said, "did you take Latin?"

"A little, why?"

"Just wondering."

"Good," he said, picking up another script. "Hey, this is a funny notion: a musical Western with midgets. I wonder what Dad had in mind."

"They already did it," I said. "After *The Wizard of Oz*, Metro did it when they had all the Munchkins hanging around. It bombed."

"Maybe this was a sequel." He put the script aside.

"It was probably just one of those creative coincidences, an idea that terrific is bound to occur to a lot of people."

"You never miss a chance to cut me down. Why did you ask about Latin?"

"I never thought you'd mention it." I started to tell him; I wanted to. But it seemed suddenly useless.

"This is an interesting property for MacMurray and Dunne," he said, still reading. "A light young romantic comedy."

I don't want to tell him they are older. When everyone else is older, you get less promising. I don't want to be the one who reminds Paul of reality. It is the outsiders who think Tuesday Weld and Troy Donahue. I wondered if Paul and I would be found some day like the Collier brothers, buried under these old properties staring at invisible dailies and rushes, counting preview cards, imagining enterprise which was never our own.

Paul exists in a past tense which does not extend to experience beyond the Great Old Days. Would that be what they call Past Perfect?

"There's a great bit here for Lou Calhern. I wonder if I could get him to do a cameo."

"He is dead, Paul. You forgot."

He looked up at me down across the bed. "I hate when you sit there perched at the end of the bed when I'm working. Haven't you got anything to do? Sleep?"

"I already did that. Last night. I don't want it to become a habit. Could we have sex?" Perhaps it is my age. Perhaps it is the legal approval marriage brings. Perhaps it is the feeling that if we kept trying there would come a time when it is not disappointing. I wondered what it was I was so afraid of for so long. I wanted to risk running into the fear—finding out the terrible power. The thing that lurks on the other side of these gentle calisthenics. I felt it growing in me.

But sex has become something of the present tense world in which Paul does not choose to live. It was as though I said "Gardner McKay." Or asked him to go to a luau.

"I'm exhausted, Susanna."

"You always say that."

"And you always start nagging me about that when you sit on the end of the bed like that. You always bring up the same thing."

"And you always say you're too tired. Well, let me distract you." I sort of lounged up closer to him.

"It never works that way." He moved back into the pillows as though he could somehow disappear into the headboard.

"Susanna—don't you have any intellectual curiosity?" He handed me one of the scripts. "Can't you spend an evening reading?"

"I may be crazy, Paul, but I think it's just curious and not terrifically intellectual to read old scripts. I think it's also curious that you never want me. That way."

"It probably hasn't occurred to you that this is part of my responsibility to you as your husband. It's not as if we had money enough to just lie around—marriage is not a perpetual honeymoon, you know."

"Thank God." I did not need to say that. He did try on the honeymoon. Everything the manual said. Once.

"That was sweet. Maybe if you'd stop nagging and let me make the advances, maybe if you'd give me a chance . . ."

I wonder if like swimming it always comes back. Swimming, I think, is easier. There is, for one thing, no problem about taking lessons.

"I thought maybe there were some old Roman properties lying around you might have missed."

He concentrated very hard on his reading, on not reacting. It worked. I got bored and went away. I called Val in New York. They were still there, waiting for the deal on Angelo's new picture to come through. I don't think she wanted it to happen. Don't think she is happy about moving out here. I think she really hoped Angelo would stay on the stage. It will be too close, too familiar

to be living out here married to an actor. Lillian is delighted—but cautious; she sees Val's discomfort. Lillian
is tentative in her reactions to Angelo. She sees what
Val sees, but also sees something else. "He is," Lillian
said to me, "not like Alan. Angelo is not self-destructive. He has an edge of ruthlessness which will serve him
well. Alan was a softer man." Val sees the difference in
her songs. She has a new one which is becoming a hit.
"Acts Like Love."

> He acts like love
> Looks like love
> Love is a role
> He plays so well.

So when I called her that night she was up. I do not
think she sleeps. I do not think he is always there.

"Working," she said, which is her way of saying she
doesn't want to talk. There was no hello. Nothing. Just
"Working." Usually she just hangs up the phone afterward without even hearing who you are.

"Why don't you just not answer?" I said very fast.

"Because I want to show how disciplined I am."

"Well, I'll hang up. I don't want to bother you."

"You already did. What's the matter?"

"Why do you think something's the matter?"

"Safe guess. Everyone can always come up with something."

"I need to do something, with myself. I'm getting
crazy."

"I know. I'll call you right back." She hung up.

The next morning the phone rang. She said, "Okay,
you call my manager. He's going to be at the Beverly
Hills Hotel next week. He'll listen to your tapes. They're
putting together a new folk group. Now don't forget."

"I won't forget."

"No. Probably not—but you won't do it. Try to."

"Sure. All he can say is no."

"Such a positive attitude you have."

And, of course, I didn't get the tapes together. And when I did call he'd already gone back to New York. There would be another time.

I was still working on sex.

Paul was still working on synopsizing his father's properties. He had done two hundred and six of the four hundred properties. I had begun to call him Scheherazade. So long as I wanted to sleep with him there would always be one more property to do.

So I brought home a book I found in the back of Pickwick's in Hollywood. I had been looking for old songbooks with charts of Morris dances in them which I could adapt to my own songs for a show I was putting on for a SANE benefit.

"Sex: Method and Manners," Paul said, reading the title correctly. With his Eastern education I thought he would believe it more if he read it somewhere. "Where is it written that . . . ?" Easterners like to know. Here it is written. "I thought you were happy. You thought about it for weeks."

"One month and three days," I said. "And just 'cause I don't say it doesn't mean I'm not thinking.

"See, Paul," I said, handing him the book with some of the pages turned down, "I think sex feeds energy and I need it and I know I'm not wrong. Just intercourse doesn't work for me. There are these other things." I sat close beside him and talked very low, not daring to look at him. I could not say the words exactly.

"Here, read this," I said, holding out the book and closing my eyes. Will he, if it has been written, believe it works better for me with his hand?

Silence. I showed him another page.

Will he, if it is written, believe it is not traife to do it with mouths?

He threw the book across the room.

I ran into the bathroom and slammed the door. "You're a prude and a baby," I screamed through the door. "You don't know what it feels like to be frustrated. I feel I can't swallow with the longing. It's like being choked. I'd rather be dead." I stand there silently then, watching the tears come down my face in the mirror, watching my face falling like hot wax. "You're starving me," I scream. "Everyone always starved me." I think of Jackson staying away, staying invisible to me; my mother at the end of the dark hall behind the door, I have caught her starvation like a disease. Val strong-arming ambition. Everyone resisting. I felt like a baby lying in an ice cold crib being fed by a dropper.

"One drop at a time," I sobbed. "One goddam drop! Not enough to live. Too much to die."

"You are hysterical," Paul said calmly from the other side of the door.

"I know. I have a right." I listened. Was there nego-tiation in his silence?

"If you will come out," he said, "I will try."

"Okay." I came out and got into bed. He turned out the light and lay beside me. He began to stroke me with his hand.

"Is this right?"

I did not want to discourage him. "Yes. Just fine." Silence. I hear the clock ticking. "A little to the left." Silence. "Harder." Silence. "Now lighter again." He coughed. "Sorry," he said. "That's okay," I said.

"Are you asleep?" he asked.

"No, I'm just concentrating." More silence. Then his hand stopped. He was asleep.

I took his hand away and turned on my side. He did not notice, so I cried.

"Why are you crying?" he asked.

"You fell asleep."

"It didn't work?"

"No."

"I'll try again." It was the sigh at the end of the sentence which blew the fuse. I rehear it so clearly it can almost be seen in neon: TILT. STOP.

"You wouldn't be bored?" I asked, leaning toward him on my elbow.

"Well, it is a little boring," he said.

"Maybe I should try to synopsize."

"Susanna, there are more important things on my mind."

I put the pillow over my head and kicked my feet.

I got up and went downstairs to the dining room where I kept my music and my guitar and played it out; I jammed it into every line. "You are my body," I said to my guitar, "and you are my beat. I turn my hands to you—turn to you, turn to you . . ." I held it down low and moved behind it, dancing into the sound with my hips. This is all I ever really loved to do. This, and drive. This and ride. Moving: Jackson's legacy to me.

"As long as you're up," Paul said, leaning against the door, "I'd like some tea."

I slammed around the kitchen fixing it.

"Are you still mad?" he asked.

I am always mad. It is that I feel. Not sex. I am furious. And frightened. And I don't know why.

I want to run away from Paul. I have always wanted to run away, but I need something, someone to run to. I need Jackson. I need to know where he is. So I can take off toward him. I feel the running-away force gathering inside me like a movie beginning. But it has nowhere to go. I want my own present to disappear inside of it. I want it to begin. And I remember to try to concentrate on this: on Paul, trying to get me to begin, as we are back in bed.

I hear the sound of ticking. Not the clock. Something else.

"Have you become Captain Hook?"

"What?"

"I hear ticking."

"I brought up the timer."

"The timer? The egg timer, Paul? How do you want me? Hard-boiled?"

"I just wanted to see if we could do it in three minutes. I looked at that book you gave me and it said most women . . ."

"I see, and if not . . ."

"Then it isn't working."

"That's very practical." I wanted to get up and leave. But I'd never come back. I reached up as the timer went off with a terrible ringing sound and threw it at the window and while it rang angrily at us across the room, I jumped on Paul to beat him, to hurt him, astride him. I held down his shoulders and bit at his lips in a rage and screwed myself down upon him, fucking him for once, pummeling him and grating on him, all my nerves like little steel teeth attacking him everywhere and he came back at me, pushing me away and closer all at once, pulling and pushing, fighting and hating each other, years of things we have never said and never felt coming out in a hate-fuck scrimmage, like boxers going against an incessant bell calling an end to the round. And we kept at it, punching, turning, mouths biting. So this is what he loves, attack and fury. I will give it to him. I am a Kirk Douglas cow-puncher, teeth bared and raging, throwing chairs into the barroom mirror. I throw Jack Palance over the bannister, hefting him, throwing him, Jack, Jack, Jackson, God, Jackson, pitch him down to death. Jack him to a plummeting end and Paul screamed as I finished him, sitting on him, jumping jack, jacking down, my hair whirling with momentum. And I saw Jackson under me. Jackson, blond and grinning at me. Don't, I heard him say. Don't do that.

I can't, I can't, I must not. I raked these shoulders with my nails. Don't ever do that! The timer howled for attention. I jumped off, streaming sweat and come and took that timer from the corner and smashed it against the wall until it broke in little plastic pieces.

I lay on the floor in a heap and Paul came and held me tight. I sprang away from him. "I'm in trouble, Paul," I screamed. "Terrible, terrible trouble. Paul, I'm crazy, I still want him. Help me, God, help me. Take it away. Get him out, out, out of my head." And I pounded my fists against my head and beat my head against the floor until Paul held me so tight I could not move.

I look out over the canyon now from the window seat and watch the fog unrolling like gauze bandage, and I imagine I can see the ocean and hear the waves.

When I should be working or going out to get things done I think of Perdido and when I do not think of Perdido and sex, I think of Jackson and it is like hands locking in the position for "Here's the church," tight as that, right around my chest. I want to go to the phone to try to find him. But I tell myself if I don't try today, it may be easier not to try tomorrow. How many years will it take before it does get easier?

I sweat. I pull at the neck of my turtleneck so I won't feel as if I'm going to throw up.

The feeling rushes down to my groin. I'm going to want to play with myself. I try to put that off too. If I don't do that today it will be easier not to do it tomorrow. And how many years will that take until I forget?

Middle finger, center of the D chord for Do It attaches itself to the center seam of my jeans. Don't do it. I tell myself. It always makes you feel lonely afterward. I am already leaning back against the pillows. Don't. If you do it once, you'll do it three times and then you'll want to sleep and it is time to pick Sev up. I am undoing my belt. Don't. This will be the night Paul decides to try again. There is always more of a chance after a successful dinner party. I laugh and think of the line I used to say when I was very young, back when Grandfather had Seder dinners every year: *"M'ah nishtanah halaila hazzeh?* Why is this night different from all other nights?" Yeah. Why, indeed? God will do something. I have my hand on the zipper. Don't, please, don't. You'll cry. You'll miss . . . who? Someone. If you don't do it God will do something for you. Paul will get a raise. A song will fly to the page all of a piece. Or, at least, you'll come up with a second line for "Night Walk."

"I irritate the silence with my melancholy song." It still sounds like second-rate Val Benedict.

Jackson will call. He'll be out here to star in a big comeback movie and he'll want you to find him a house, with wings, so you'll all move in and you'll take care of the house for him. And you'll be invited everywhere. I do not see Paul in this plan. I do not see Jackson in it either, or anywhere. A house with wings. Flying away. That would be a house for Jackson.

Oh, to hell with it. I lift up my hips, slide down the jeans and my pants and find myself. Warm wet skin under cool pale hair. I wonder if Jackson is blond here too. Stop. Freeze. Start again. Angelo. Why do the images which come to me belong to people I cannot have? And what's the matter if no one knows? I'll go with Angelo today: Angelo hot, wiry, and moving fast. Dancing with his thighs back on the boat at C.A.'s party. Do sex fantasies always go back to when sex began? But sex began before. Pictures fly through my mind. Jackson holding that baby laughing in his big hand. Mallory bending over me in her pajamas, big breasts swinging, touching my ears. Mallory rubbing me down tenderly, tenderly. Safe to go with. When I get on enough I change her into Paul, strumming the feeling out until there is no image at all, just feeling. And as I sink back I laugh: how polite I am in abandon to throw Paul onto the screen. How useless this is. How wasteful and stupid. I told you so I tell myself. I bound up from the window seat. Wash my hands. Put cologne on them. What if one day it doesn't come off. And Paul takes my hands and smells them and says, "I want a divorce." I want Paul to take over his father's studio again one day. I want them to come and beg him and he'll find a bit character part for Evelyn when she is found, in one of those "Whatever Became Of" stories, living in a house on Hollywood Boulevard where there's a podiatrist in one room, an astrologer giving readings upstairs . . . and what if they find Jackson in one of those rooms? Jackson. Stop it. Sometimes, you know, I have to direct one foot in front of the other when I get to thinking about him and this is one of those days.

I put each foot on the floor. I will go get Sev. I actually liked it better before he went to school. I would go and watch him sleep, flat out on his back, arms and legs spread. I would put my head next to his face to feel his breathing. Breath of life, life for you must be easier. Lucky legal child, no odd lovechild, I'll never leave you. I used to pick him up—what is the sentence for the mother who wakes her child? He would put his golden head on my shoulder and his arms went around me automatically, legs around my waist. And I would take him into our room and lie with him curled into my stomach and I held him tight enough, pacing my breathing to his because he knew more about breathing than I do and I could catch his peacefulness. His hair is still like wet silk when he sleeps. My heart does not stop pounding, when I think—what if? God wouldn't. But God does. God, do not take us away from each other. Did Lillian feel this fear—did Jackson's mother? Why were there fires on both sides? How do you separate omens from fear you just have? How do you know if this connection you make today which reminds you of loss is not a sign? When is it craziness and when is it a hunch, a feeling in your bones? If I always paid attention to all my apprehensions I wouldn't let Sev out of my sight. And is that fear what I inherited from my mother? Can I sympathize now that I know what dread feels like? Just there and heavy like a chord you don't break. Lillian would say, Susanna, you've got to have faith.

Faith in You, God. Not on Your Tintype. Whatever that means. You should learn to delegate responsibility. That's what Paul wishes his boss would do, and the New York office wanted Myron to put things in the hands of a few executive producers. Maybe they were right. I think God should do that too. Is that what the Catholics believe? They've got all those Saints handling Travel, Nature, Disasters and things. And look how it goes for Catholics. Not a hell of a lot better.

Listen, God, forget Jackson. It is dangerous for me

to ask for him. Just scratch everything. Being famous too. And I'm sorry I was ever mad at Val for getting Angelo (which I never even admit as I think about it). Just let things be okay with Sev and I won't ask for anything else ever again.

I get into my wagon. Get out. Run into the house and get the list Paul and I wrote down last night. Dorothy, who is mainly doing party catering, will be coming at three. She usually comes to me only on Saturday mornings. "Who else," she says, "could ever sort you out?— he is a patient man, your husband." And she gives me this don't-you-forget-it look.

Maybe marriage is not about sex. And that is part of the knowing look.

While I'm getting the list I think of calling Val to come shopping with me. But she hates to shop. And she is probably house-hunting—which she also hates— because it implies she may really have to live here. And if she is house-hunting, Angelo will answer the phone.

And he will say things.

IT'S NOT GOING TO BE A HUGE DINNER PARTY. THAT
would actually be easier. I could make a Mexican dinner, put it on a buffet, and sit in a corner with my
serape on, playing my guitar. It's just Val and Angelo
and three New York friends of theirs who are coming
to dinner. Their friends, or the Samsons, at least, have
been living here for a year, but they act like the summertime boys who used to come out with their parents—
"The natives are amusing." They are like missionaries.
I remain a savage. Paul wants the food to be wonderful
and has had me crazy all week with changing the menu.

"Everyone," he said, "has chicken marengo. Let's do
medallions of veal with sherry and cream. And fresh
mushrooms. Slice the mushrooms very thin, Susanna.
And we'll have a light tarragon-dressed salad. Served
after the veal."

"That's ridiculous," I say.

"That's how salad is served everywhere except in
California."

"So. This is California."

"Susanna. Don't argue.

". . . And perhaps," he said, "we'll do some noodles
with a touch of garlic, but we shouldn't let it overwhelm
the veal. Get the meat at Jurgenson's, pick the wine up
at Vendome—I've already ordered it—we ought to make
a simple dessert. Peaches poached in champagne with
ground almonds in the center. And we might do some
blanched string beans . . ."

We. What's this "we" shit? Me and Dorothy. While
he's upstairs not being disturbed because he's exhausted.
Even though on the day of a party he comes home early

to rest. He thinks of himself like a prince. Can't blame him. How can you be raised as a regent and then be expected to behave like a commoner taking orders? It is hard—we console each other, mostly me consoling Paul—to be stripped of your projection room. The heart melts to think of such a thing. And Paul will be especially crazed tonight because Richard Samson is the hottest of the new producers. "Filmmakers," they call themselves—perish the thought they should be called moguls—and Paul wants Richard to buy a couple of his properties for "packaging" (another favorite filmmaker term) under Richard's new deal at the studio where Paul is currently doing a TV series it is best not to even discuss. With the Samsons, and they go very much as a set, considering themselves the new Sam and Frances Goldwyn, or, if you will, Victor and Luba Levanin—I do not give them that so fast—is coming the famous Eastern critic-playwright, Niles Henderson, who I completely do not like. With his long front teeth. He walks demolished as though his penis has been slung over his left shoulder all day. I didn't say anything. I just take notes. I have become a gopher—without even starting in the mail room. Jurgenson's. And then, at the end of the month, he'll sit there and stare bleakly at the wall and hold the checkbook balance in his hand like a dead flower.

I am in the car now—going to pick up Sev. I switch stations on the radio as always—who would have thought I'd be switching one day to catch one of Val's songs? Sometimes, when I am especially mean, I do not tell her how many times I have heard "Acts Like Love." I wonder if Angelo snaps it off when he hears it?—I do not think he exactly does a singalong.

Sev is on the corner as I turn down to his school. Cowboy hat, hanging down, waving his hands over his head like a prizefighter, grinning and jumping to see me.

"Hey," I tell him, "what are you doing way out here?"

"Waiting for you. Hi," he says. "This is a real hungry cowboy, this one."

"Oh, this is, is it? Well, it's also supposed to wait inside the school gates until the teacher takes you out to me."

"Yeah?" he says as though he has never heard of such a thing. Leaning against the seat, eyes wide, hands up on head, legs crossed at ankles. He, of course, looks like Jackson. "Everything does, to you," Val says. But he does. He flings his arms now around my neck.

I have bitten these round arms, these golden arms, so hard I have left marks and he cried once. And once he bit me back, sunk his teeth into my neck and threw his head back and laughed, tears still standing in his eyes from my bite on him. We wrestle here like this, teasing and rolling and lusting for each other. I do not want him to get bigger so that it will have to stop. I wonder if my mother lusted for me, which is why we dare not touch each other now. I wonder if she stroked my belly. And I wonder if Jackson felt this lust rush at him before he ever saw me and maybe that is why he ran. I wonder if he imagined me? A girl as big and blond and rough as he is. Maybe that is why I have to hate my mother so, or else I would want her. Or maybe I hate her because she never did lust for me. Only for Jackson who we never could have. She would not want to watch us together, hugging, running together, talking, our heads together, like me watching Angelo and Val. I wonder if Paul watches me with Sev and wonders how easy I am with him, when with Paul it is always constrained now—when we do touch I hold back because if I don't I will want sex and we will fight. Maybe we are all more physically happy with children because it will not go farther, because it is simple and open and there's nothing to expect, nothing to disappoint, nothing that can fail.

We head down to Beverly Hills now and Sev climbs in the far back seat to watch. How quickly the baby legs and arms are turning into boy legs and arms. I think the secret of childbirth is that when the baby leaves you, you are giving up the closest love you ever have. I remember the day Sev was born. . . .

I thought of the drawing Grandmother had showed me of Baba Yaga, when the witch, disguised as the house on chicken feet, went walking through the forest. It was like having that house inside of me, stretching out its legs. Paul came and sat beside me.

"Starting?"

"Think so."

"Call Dr. Harris?"

"Not yet. There's time."

I wanted to remember what I wanted a perfect mother to be so I could start to be it. One thing: it has nothing to do with anything else I have tried to be. And have I really ever tried to be anything but Jackson's daughter?

In my house with Paul and my music it was like a welcoming ceremony. I was not scared of what the baby was doing and I didn't want it to feel I was mad at it if I yelled.

"Hush baby, we're all right," I said. "Rock now, baby, gentle now. Don't worry."

Paul was on the phone. He was rushing me. He was getting dressed.

"I'm not ready yet, Paul."

"Yes, come on, Susanna." He lifted me from the chair, gentle, but insisting.

"I want to leave everyone else out." I didn't want Sev outside of me, to share. I liked the privacy. I had possession. The baby was my own, then, like my guitar, like my car. By having it, I could not keep him. No one understands that. Birth is the beginning of estrangement. Did my mother feel that? Was the beginning of my own life the end of Jackson for her? My birth must have felt like his ultimate withdrawal. No wonder she hates me.

Then, on the way to the hospital, it stopped. "It's a mistake, Paul. Take me back home."

"No—really, Susanna."

"Well, could we walk awhile?"

We stopped by Van Keppel—Green and looked at the red and orange and pink striped couch we planned to get when he produced his first picture. "And some of those marvelous little black iron and rattan square stools?" I asked. We did get them—when he produced his first TV show. And the couch has already been replaced by an old one from a Robin Hood set we picked up from an auction of old V.L.I. props a year ago. The one thing we love to do is shop and change our house around and plan for the next change. We remind me sometimes of the men who own shops on the Strip. We talk about "things" and therefore deftly avoid how we really feel. Maybe this is what marriage is. How would you know except by being inside your own?

You cannot tell by looking at other marriages. I used to watch the wives at birthday parties when I was a child, figure out who their husbands were. Directors' wives were always tanned, strong-looking, with wonderful big laughs. I think now they were steeling themselves for replacement by glamorous stars who moved in with the director's success.

A wife could hold you back, merely by having a fixed idea of who you were. You had to catch someone who saw you in full bloom to try to make the impression last. Now, writers' wives looked needed; writers had no surrogates on a set to take the place of the women who read each line and encouraged each word with a good hot lunch brought to his den on a tray. The role of wife may have been defined for all of us by writers who invented it by watching their own wives.

I thought that actors' wives tended to be mindless and cheerful, or savage wife-managers who grew to resemble male agents. The other wives did not speak to actors' wives. They did not want to hear it was not easy to be married to a hero. My mother would not want to hear such a thing, especially if it was not true—if there was such a thing as an actor who could make his wife happy.

A producer's wife was his best advertisement for his success, because no one was terribly certain what a producer did. But they were, in those days, considered quite important. Movies, then, were defined by the producer's style (as was his wife—am I Paul's greatest liability?). I think actors and writers sleep with their own wives more than producers and directors because actors and writers are more insecure and probably would not want to risk failure or gossip. They, I think, like to *look* like they play around more than they do. I sometimes think that applies to Angelo. And I sometimes fear I will find out. I also think Paul and I are not so unusual. Which depresses me, but I think there is a lot less screwing here than people think. I think the lust goes into ambition. Maybe when there is a moment of success, the night after you get the Oscar, you would fuck, furiously, gleefully, deliriously, fantasizing money and fame, with images of engraved-letter ads in the trade papers going through your head, letters from the star to a producer (which the producer's personal press people design and place), reviews in the New York papers, testimonial dinners from the trade guilds, fleeting images of competitors reading the reviews, hearing the good news, looking angry. This could make for inspired screwing; but the wanting, the working to succeed is exhausting. But when we go to parties now the men make cracks about successful sex, in between talk of deals, percentages, packages, and distribution. There are glowing stories of being a "long-distance man," of having "staying power" (which alludes, I think, more to lasting fame than what you think it means). They have always loved to talk about that. It is part of the competition. And when their studio stars had staying power, when, it is rumored, Lana Turner said that the men with the greatest staying power in Hollywood were Clark Gable, Spencer Tracy, Jimmy Stewart, and Henry Fonda, it confirmed their fame, and the executives flipped through their contract lists. What is really sexy, I suppose, is gossip—imagining what kinds of things people are doing. I am beginning to believe sex itself is not particularly sexy.

But what do I know?

Not much.

As Lillian told me that day Sev was born when I said I felt angry that my mother was not here. But I did not even tell her when I was due so she would not have had a chance to be. "Very few cases, Susanna, where motherhood changes character or imposes sainthood."

They did not tell me what it is to have a baby: I thought of the elephant inside the snake in *The Little Prince,* the hat shape—it would not get out, I would swell and burst. It was a war, not a baby coming. And they bothered me. "Leave me alone—it's my baby. Get out," I yelled. Stop putting all your fists inside of me at once. They tied my arms down so I could not hold him. Did they think I would slug them? Dr. Harris was chewing gum. Class.

"You can look in the mirror, Susanna," he said and I saw white, and red, and then I felt Sev lying on my stomach. A small weight.

"You have a little boy. He's got some shoulders on him. He's just fine."

He is here; but gone from me.

"Can I hold him?" I had to ask.

He came later down the hall, in this little swaddled blanket. He turned toward my breast and fixed on. Talk about jawlines. He was mine again.

Aunt Lillian came with a bunch of zinnias.

"You used to like these," she said.

"I used to wreck them, too."

Then Val called. She would have come but she was doing songs at some festival in New England.

"Is there summer too up there? I wonder what the skiers do?" I said.

"Some of them walk on water—How is my godson? Will you tell him for me not to listen to anything his mother says—to check everything out with me? Angelo thinks he's got a part coming up on Broadway. Keep fingers crossed, kiss that baby for me on the back of his neck."

"Sure thing." I did not suggest she do the same for Angelo.

"Have you heard from your mother?" she asked.

"No. Not a word. Not one word. But I'm not sure I told her I was pregnant. She might guess I am not a virgin."

"My mother will call her. I'm sure. You'll make up."

"I don't think I want to, Val. It is not a movie—I should be telling you—no happy endings everywhere. No way. My mother and I have nothing to give each other."

She did not ask if I have heard from Jackson. She knew better than that.

Sev's jaws clenched onto my breast. Little hands digging in like sharp little stars. Sounds of swallowing like miniature waves breaking. I wanted to show him the ocean, the merry-go-round, sing him some songs. Teach him about driving.

Do I really want to teach Sev all about driving, traveling, running away?

Low, low, breathe and blow, over the western sea . . .
Sleep my little one, sleep my pretty one . . .

How does it go?

Hold fast, little hands. Dare you count on me? Would I leave you for Jackson?

Sev, you be different. Don't be a crazy runaway. And I held him so close and so tight that he squeaked and his little hands flew off my breast.

According to the trades Jackson was in Manila then shooting a picture.

That year. That month.

So I sent the wire care of the studio producing the pilot.

"Congratulations. You're a grandfather."

"Really?" said the lady at Western Union. "Time does fly. I never knew he was that old."

"He probably doesn't either," I said.

Sev and I whisk through the stores. He picks up things to buy, quickly saying, "I did not see it on TV—" knowing that is the rule. We stop at Wil Wright's for ice cream cones and on the way home he falls asleep with his head in my lap. Dorothy helps me bring things into the house and Sev, wide awake, again goes with me up the street to the empty lot to pick nasturtiums and geraniums for the table. I notice Paul's car is here and I'm already angry that he has not come down to see us even though he never does. There are some things which you always expect even when you know they won't happen.

And some things you would never expect—I put the flowers into bowls. Sev perches on a stool in the kitchen to talk to Dorothy and I run upstairs to our room and barge into the bathroom:

Paul is standing there in the shape of an Egyptian hieroglyphic person with one of my Tampaxes up his ass and he is holding on to the string with one hand, pushing it in and out, and his other hand is flashing back and forth over his penis. "Ascot, ascot," he seems to be saying; I did not know he was so excited by races. No. He is saying, "Ass-cock, ass-cock." A little come-song— and it is too late for him to stop and he looks at me with such agony and terror and one split second after he comes he looks at me, and he says, "I got the Saks bill." Then he slams the door closed.

I wonder if I have wrecked his game for him forever. We do not say one word. It is as though that thirty seconds was a mirage. "Well, most of it was stuff for Sev," I yell through the door.

"I know, but you still think charging means you don't have to pay. And I was checking in the kitchen to put in an order to the liquor store. What are those two cans of pumpkin pie mix doing there? Why do we have two of them? How long have they been there? You never make pumpkin pie."

He comes out of the bathroom now, drying his hands

on a towel. Clinging to it, I think. His hands must be shaking.

"Well, I thought if an atom bomb raid came around Thanksgiving and we were in the cellar, I'd make a pie. I don't know, Paul. They're just cans of pie filling. Don't make a federal case out of it. I've got so much to do."

"You never make pie." This is leading up to a secondary argument about my cooking which will lead to a discussion on how much time I spend playing with my guitar (playing with myself, he should only know, and he has no more argument there) and never getting anywhere.

"Well, I will when I have the time."

I should never have said anything about time.

"You never have enough time unless it's something you want to do."

"Paul. I'll make pie this weekend. Several pumpkin pies. Paul—I'm really sorry, you know. Listen, Paul, I do that too, play with myself—need to."

"It's bigger than pie, Susanna." He speaks, deliberately ignoring what I'm trying to say.

"Bigger than both of us, perhaps?" I should not have said that.

"I'm talking about waste and extravagance."

"I wouldn't talk about that when I've spent a fortune on a dinner party you want. Can we just drop it?"

"You always want to talk, except when I have something to say to you you don't want to hear." He leans back on the bed, picking up one of his scripts. Cigarette holder in the corner of his mouth.

"I try to talk about something that matters—and you don't want to hear. Okay, we're both shocked or embarrassed or something—if it's any help I wish you'd catch me sometime—then maybe we'd understand each other better."

He's pretending to read. I could kill him. I'm trying so hard. "I'm sorry—I just think still that sex is more interesting than money or pumpkin pie mix or your scripts. Any kind of sex, Paul! Dammit, listen to me!"

"Susanna, someone has to make some money. I know that is not very interesting to you. Only spending it. And I will not discuss the other thing. Don't make it worse. . . ."

"Oh, Paul—I am sorry we both lied about loving each other. I'm sorry they lied to us. I'm sorry we both intended to marry rich. I'm sorry sex is so boring with each other we've turned it into do-it-ourselves projects. I'm sorry about everything you can think of I should be sorry about. Make a list and I'll sign it." And I slam out of our bedroom and down to the kitchen.

Sev has gone to bed in his Sputnik pajama top and car-print pajama bottoms. His hats hang from his bedposts.

Our guests arrive: Val is wearing a long Mexican skirt with a lot of this heavy jewelry Angelo gives her, pre-Columbian—all that's chic does not glitter. Although it is not as if anyone is asking, I would rather have a lot of Eisenberg ice clanking around my neck.

Angelo is in a cowboy kind of outfit with a dark-red satin tie, which he has pulled aside, so it just hangs, leaving his collar open. (I love the shadow his open shirt casts just there on his neck. Is that why he leaves his collar open?)

Niles Henderson slinks in, his cardigan sweater buttoned—only on alternate buttons—under his tweed jacket. This is so if you did not know he was a new Eastern playwright and critic you could tell by his outfit. "No wonder no one writes out here—how do you get depressed enough to write if it never rains?"

Maia Samson walks in past Niles. He reaches out and grabs the curve of her body where her short, carved Jackie Kennedy kind of dress cups it neatly. She is wearing an "interesting" pin on her chest, with her long hair twisted up and stabbed into place with artillery. Richard Samson is the nephew of a New York theatrical lawyer, which makes him think he is in the business. Angelo met him at Strasberg's school. He has his studio deal, which, as usual, he is discussing as he arrives. "I'm going over several notions now. I want to use a lot of talented people."

He emphasizes the word "talented" as though it's a new idea.

I feel on guard from the moment they arrive. Paul is always comparing me to Maia and Val. I watch how everyone turns to her and hate myself for still doing that.

I hate Niles Henderson the most. He is always implying things about sex in his vague way which is somehow dirtier. He gives these looks to Val. I don't want him, but I want him to want me anyway (then I would probably want him, probably would see him as brilliant and wonderful. I know how I am). And I want Paul to act as though he'd care if Niles looked at me like that. Angelo bristles when Niles looks at Val that way —and Angelo looks at me. Paul doesn't even notice, or doesn't let me know he notices and that, of course, is what counts. I guess everyone wants to be longed for— wants to have someone other people want. And everyone wants to be flirted with, but you also want to have someone who is going to get all ruffled up and furious about it—almost as important as the flirting.

"Niles," says Richard Samson, "is examining properties with me. I want him to do his first film—but it has to be right."

And Paul wants Niles to write the screenplay for one of his properties. He watches Niles looking at one of our pictures, a nice Warshaw charcoal of a doll riding a wombat. Niles peers at it, doesn't say anything, and turns, rubbing his thin hands over his face. "Have you got some Percodan or something? I've got a splitting headache." He's always complaining so he probably isn't a lot of fun to have in bed with you. You would move the wrong way and he would complain of concussion.

"Empirin?" Paul says. "Susanna will get you some Empirin."

"Yes. Bring me four, please, and some mineral water if you have some. And," he gives his long, thin, watery smile, "really, Richard, I can't work out here, you know I can't."

I go upstairs to get the Empirin and cover Sev, leaning over to hold him for a moment; I put his sleeping arms around my neck and by instinct he holds me tight. Did I do that with my mother—did she bend over to feel my face, to touch my cheek with her lashes?

They all get blocked the minute they cross the Hudson River. These Easterners. When Niles is not blocked or in terrible pain, he is fatally bored. I hate hearing his voice as I come down the stairs.

"What are we doing later? I'd like to get a game tonight?"

Fine," Richard says, always fast to please Niles. Like a parent with an especially difficult but brilliant child. "I think Brieley has some guys coming over." Niles is standing by the bookcase now, looking at the titles, chewing on the side of his mouth, sort of grazing.

"Paul," Richard says, "when are we eating?"

"Susanna?" Paul says, as I am passing around Lillian's practically famous chopped liver. Paul is now casing our bookshelf anxiously. Are the right books where Niles could see them? I know he will tell me later to pick up a copy of Niles's last play. Or tell me again. How could I have forgotten? How, indeed.

"Soon. I'm sorry."

"Oh, my mother's liver," Val says. "You do it well. She wouldn't give me the recipe. Susanna's a much better cook. We may not eat until midnight"—she lounges back against the couch, putting her perfect little feet in sandals up on the coffee table—"but it will be delicious."

"You are delicious," Niles says to Val, but in a removed, courtly way.

Angelo leans down from behind the couch and puts his hands on Val's breasts, right on her breasts.

"Don't," Val says, with a little look at Niles, lifting Angelo's hands away. I wish Paul was like that. Possessive about me. I look at him. He looks away. Maybe I should be more vulnerable and standoffish like Val. Maybe I dislike him because he does not pay attention to me.

"What's the matter, Cara?" This is Angelo's nickname for her. He gathers her hair in one hand, pulling it back so she looks up at him.

"Nothing is the matter." She pulls his hand off her hair and gets up. "Susanna, I'll do this, or is there something I can help with?"

Val is thinking of a song or something. Never likes touching when she is working. And I think she has been trying to work. I also think Angelo is jealous because he's not shooting yet.

"No, Dorothy's handling the last-minute part . . . it's fine. I'll go hurry things up."

"Oh . . ." Val says. "Dorothy. I must go see her."

Maia comes over to Angelo. "You can do that to me any time."

"Any time? Really?" He grins but his eyes watch Val. Dinner parties are like sexual tournaments—but movie ones, where no one really gets knocked off the horse. It's not terribly different from when we used to ride around and around the drive-ins, gunning our motors.

Except the Easterners have a sleeker style—Maia, for instance, is bold and reserved at the same time. When she flirts you have the feeling that it is because it is somehow good for business. But I still get furious when she does it with Paul. Maia arrived in L.A. tan and spends most of her time reading potential properties for Richard and going to thrift shops where she picks up things for Val and Angelo. She has a knack for picking out furniture, people, and pottery which will be very chic in six months. Her friendship is the best kind of advance publicity you can get.

Paul is staring at ashtrays, which means I should start emptying them already although he knows Dorothy will do it while we are eating. He is more like Evelyn in this way. I wonder if I am like Myron in any ways. Environment or heredity.

Val and I are in the kitchen with Dorothy who has breaded the tiny plump pieces of veal and is sautéeing them in sweet butter. I mince tarragon from my garden, which Val nibbles.

"Dorothy," she says, "I'm always glad to see you here. Guarantees dinner before we all fall asleep."

I have had enough teasing tonight I would like to say.

"Now, Susanna can do it, Val, it's just Mr. Daroff is so particular I think he's got her scared."

"You'll have to talk to her about that."

Who me? Scared of Paul? I just hate to be rushed. I hate it.

"I hear you sold another song. I'd like to come down and watch you record."

"That would be terrific. But I think I may have to do it in New York. I don't know yet. It would be so much easier to be one place or the other for a while. I mean he has to be here and me there . . ." Her voice trails off, and she wanders over and picks up a slice of mushroom from the pan and puts her arm around Dorothy.

"Then just when you get used to that it will be the other way around," Dorothy says, flipping the mushrooms into a baking dish.

"I suppose." She wanders around the kitchen, looking at things and then just drifts out.

"You'd think," Dorothy says, "she'd have known better than to marry an actor, after all Mrs. Benedict went through. She's put all that energy into that boy."

"At least they're in love. They really are." And I really believe that, even with the way he slides a look at me now and then. Or is that my protection against wanting him, to believe they are—what did I used to say?—"Very Much in Love"? I am very much in love with Sev—that's about it. My small replica of Jackson.

"Love. I thought she was the smart one," Dorothy says.

"And I'm the dumb one. That's nice, really nice."

"No. You just play dumb. I never lost a minute's sleep over you."

I'll bet Dorothy goes home and throws her broken-down shoes against the wall and shouts, "Bitch, bitch, bitch. That's all they ever do." And we spend these hours together acting close, acting like we know each other, and never tell the truth.

We are all sitting around the table. Paul smiles when Richard says the wine is "pretty good," as though that means he'll buy one of Paul's properties.

Maia says, leaning across Paul, "Val, there's a rough cut of *Marienbad* being screened tomorrow night. A very close friend has invited us and they'd love you and Angelo to join us."

"A very close friend" is Maia's way of implying someone so famous that we know who she means. It is sort of inverse name-dropping.

And I hate the way she gets so something when she talks to Val. She makes it sound like she's asking her for a date.

"What—you mean they've just rushed it over for us?" Val says. I also hate when she teases Maia. I only want her to tease me.

"Very rash," Niles says, "I hear it's seriously flawed."

"How did you hear it's flawed, Niles, it's not even finished?" Angelo says.

Paul's underlip is soft. He is hurt that we are not invited. I am furious.

"Well," Paul says, "I've heard it's going to be a commercial success."

"And what," Niles asks, "will that mean? That's exactly why Hollywood has never produced anything remotely resembling art."

He reminds me now, in his manner, of Angelo's Aunt Giordano.

"You are such a fucking snob, man."

Paul hates that word. I think he hates sex—sex that

has anything to do with me. Hates me. Will he see me barging into all his fantasies now?

"You know," Val says, "you guys have been having this same argument since you met in the Improv."

"Women," Niles says, "are always threatened by the possibility of intellectual argument, because they can't do it—it's another form of penis envy."

"Oh, Niles, you're such an ass," Val says (three cheers from me!). "Who could envy the penis? Consider the vulnerability, imagine the expectations it must live with, the comparisons it suffers; one might feel sympathy, but envy? I don't think so."

I look at Paul, expecting him not to meet my eyes. He does and there is just the smallest hint of a smile at me for the first time. Then he brushes back his hair and looks away.

"When I finish my new play . . ." Niles says, completely ignoring what Val has said, as everyone has except Maia, who winks at her (even, or especially, Angelo looks uncomfortable. He has caught Maia's wink. Does he think Val has told her something about him?), "I'm going to do a major piece on the decline and fall of Hollywood."

"How is the play?" Paul asks, politely, since no one else is really listening. Are we all thinking about our own or each other's sex lives?

Niles nods. "It's a masterwork."

I think I am going to laugh. I catch Val's eye and she looks away fast. I get up and quickly begin collecting plates.

"What I adore, Niles," says Maia, "is your honesty."

"I have to have that confidence," Niles says calmly.

"I don't know," Angelo says, "if I'm not scared, if I don't feel like I'm going to puke my guts out before I get onto a stage or in front of that camera, I know I haven't got it. I don't trust anyone who isn't scared."

"That's how I feel," Val says, "I am terrified of a song until it's done and then I don't know about it. Don't you feel that way, Susanna?"

"I don't know. Really. Does everyone want coffee?"

"I didn't know you wrote songs, too," Maia says. She does know. She just forgets because I'm not recorded anywhere.

"Susanna adapts folksongs. She has a fine repertoire. If she'd just get to work."

I feel awkward. References to my music always remind me of Gore Vidal's term "Room Emptier," for remarks like, "My sister works for the phone company." He came to Perdido one night with Alan and struck at least four of the guests into permanent social silence. How smoothly those evenings worked. How festive and quick everyone seemed then.

There were audience guests and performing guests and each seemed to know its role and those with Eastern or British accents took precedence in the storytelling or performing. An empress of Eastern theater like Cornelia Otis Skinner would continue to hold her audience even after, as was the custom, the ladies went upstairs to my mother's or grandmother's room after dinner. There they would sit, silently touching crystal perfume stoppers to their breasts and wrists and earlobes, listening attentively until it was time to join the men in the projection room where they would have their cigars and listen to John Houseman. Only during the dinner or after the movie would the others take turns talking, "dining out" on the best stories they could remember— selecting ones the others had not heard as a hostess tries not to serve the same menu twice.

I don't know where the idea got around that Hollywood was informal. People dressed for dinner. Maids wore black silk and organdy, and the ladies' gowns trailed on the floor as they sat on couches like rainbow pools of silk and satin. There were other sorts of groups, other kinds of parties, but at Perdido and at the Daroffs' and the other great houses, there was formality and a certain ritual, even, as I said, in the conversation. Especially, even—as we are doing—on another scale, you could say, when the Easterners were out. But, then too, that was quite another cut of Easterner. Niles may have the voice—but he is boring and, as Gore Vidal said, "Boring people do not get invited." Are we so desperate? Or has the rule collapsed along with everything else?

"If you have some tea, I'd prefer that to coffee," Niles is saying. He has been tapping his fingers since the subject changed from his play.

Paul is worried. He wants everyone to be very gracious. "Niles, do you think it's possible for us to have any perspective on what we do?"

Paul is trying to ask the kind of questions Niles likes, the ones which permit him to respond and quote from himself.

I walk out to the kitchen to help Dorothy with the coffee.

"How's it going?"

"I'd like to leave and go to a real party."

"Haven't been any of those going around in years, honey."

"Whatever happened to just having a good time?"

"You'll grow out of that," she says.

I come back in with a tray of cups and saucers. Niles is still on. ". . . and it was a sordid world," he is telling them, "destruction of personality, collusion . . ."

"No place like home," Val says.

"Well, you asked me," Niles replies, dipping his finger in the tea I have handed him to remove a speck of a tea leaf. "Of course, I'll have to spend a brutal summer organizing all of these concepts. . . ."

"It's going to be a devastating attack," Richard says. I think I'm getting mad.

"You see, to understand Hollywood, you have to—" I am.

"Dammit," I scream, "don't tell me Hollywood. You're all just mad that you weren't here to get the good out of it so you have to analyze and classify. I don't want to read any dissertations." (I can feel Paul's hand on my arm. At least he is touching me. So I pat it gently. But I don't stop talking.) "I want the magic shows and the razzle-dazzle and real movie stars. I want it to be not cynical. Paul, we did have a good time. People had fun with money and fame and I don't want to confuse art with Hollywood and you can do that in the East but you can't just sweep in here like carpet-baggers or something and tell me what to think about it and that's that . . . does anyone want any more dessert?"

"Susanna, really," Paul says.

"Yes. Really," I say.

Niles says, "You've just delivered a remarkable parody of what the public would expect the Hollywood Child to say."

"Well, I am a Hollywood Child," I say.

"And you're looking at it, Susanna," Val says, "like a child. I don't think my father, for one, had much fun. I'm going upstairs, if you kids can restrain yourselves for a couple of minutes."

"I think," Maia says, "we sometimes take Hollywood too seriously, perhaps that's what Susanna is trying to say." She folds her napkin neatly and rearranges three of the roses in my centerpiece. Niles, Richard, Maia, and Paul go into the living room. Angelo stays and starts piling up dessert plates.

"If it hadn't looked good, awfully good to you, Angelo, you wouldn't have worked so hard to get back here and be a movie star. I mean it."

"I know you mean it, man . . ."

"Oh, cut out that man stuff."

He shrugs. "And you cut out that movie star shit. Hey, how's your life doing, you know what I mean?" He gives me his new eighty-thousand-a-year-contract smile, which isn't much different from his old horny look.

"It's all right, how's yours?" I can't look back at him.

"Lonely, sometimes. I get a kind of fever, you know?"

"Don't, Angelo. Just don't get it . . . that's all."

"Let's have lunch some day—" he says. "Long lunch."

"You're shooting, I thought." I know he's not yet.

"You know I'm not. I want to see you.

"Maybe it was a mistake for Val to come out here for me, like she did. I guess it reminds her of everything. She really likes the city, man, and she feels she could be doing more back there—college concerts and stuff, you know." We bring the plates into the kitchen.

"Well, Dorothy, hey, man, it's been a long time." He puts the plates down and gives her a hug. "A long time."

"I was wondering when you'd get yourself out here. Movie star. How about that!" She shakes her head and stands back and looks at him. "Fresh as ever." She pauses a moment and looks at me and back at Angelo.

"Well, it's good seein' you. I'll be around." He says.

"Nothing's changed," Dorothy says. And he leaves, looking fast over his shoulder at me. "Except everything," she looks at me. "And you just watch it, hear?" Something's changed: her face looks older, ash-dark circles under her eyes, long lines deepening beside her mouth. She doesn't wear her bright lipstick so much.

What could possibly be the excuse for this? says God, Who cannot even discuss such a thing with my grandmother.

There is none I say, miserable and excited at the same time, go explain that.

Well. See, Angelo is going to do something anyway and it might as well be with me because who would think such a thing? and, two (that was one), I certainly would not tell.

And. (A weak three) Val did not call to say goodbye. C.A. called to say she had driven Val to the airport because Val decided to appear at this civil rights rally with Adlai Stevenson. I haven't even seen C.A. since her third wedding. (Her first was annulled when it turned out her husband was already married with two children. The second lasted six months. Now she is married to a veterinarian and living on a ranch in Malibu Canyon, with horses, and she has had Val and Angelo up there for some big party, but not us. Possibly because Paul is still hurt at the way her father has given him rather short shrift—about two feet of shrift, if you ask me—at the studio, which, really, should have been Paul's.)

So I am hurt and mad.

This is all horsefeathers, of course.

Bullshit says God, Who knows an appropriate vernacular when He sees it.

"I want you for lunch," Angelo said.

"You got it," I said, after spending the night before practically turning into feathers from longing and lying next to Paul and touching him until he designed himself into a position where there was practically nothing to touch. There is still no sex. He locks the bathroom door ostentatiously now. I hear the clicking as rejection. I have tried to get up the nerve to say, "I could do that for you. With you." But it does not seem possible to say. I wonder—not very often—if he sometimes, when he looks at me thoughtfully, is about to say, "There's something I'd like to try. . . ." But he is working and also planning the dinner for his father. He is probably contemplating the wine list. He has decided to make it a benefit for the Motion Pictures Relief Fund. Since so many of the old guard are on relief themselves I am not sure it will wind up very profitable—if that's what you call it. And whoever heard of a charity banquet that lost money? Always a first, I think. And I walked around in our garden before dawn this morning in my nightgown, stretching and prancing and crying until Sev was up and looking out his window.

"Hey, Mommy, what's going on? Crying?"

"No," I called up to him. "New song."

"Sounds real bad."

"Thanks," I said.

"Okay," he said. "Let's go to the Pancake House and eat a lot."

He sat very close to me in the car and I kept my arm around him and I guess he felt a lot like I felt when I watched my own mother wandering around in her night-gown, crying. He knows this from me, the thing to do is get out of the house and into the car and turn the radio on and sing as loud as you can. I dropped him off at school. When I got back Paul was gone and that's when Angelo called and I didn't think about what I was doing until I was already pulling up to the Chateau Marmont.

He is waiting for me in front in a shirt open to the waist and jeans. He gets in the car.

"Where do you want to go?"

"Let's just go. Anywhere," he says. He puts his hand on my thigh. "When you have fantasies what do you think about?"

"Being a sort of girl Woody Guthrie with fringed sequins. . . ." I know that's not what he means but I want to hear it from him.

"That's not what I mean and you know it. Don't play Susie Sunshine with me."

"Okay, don't play James Dean. What do you want to do?"

"I want to watch you drive. Go out to Mandeville, then up where you were that night."

"Of the fire? I'm not going there."

"Why not?" He's put his hand on my breast and is rubbing it lightly with his palm.

"Because. Because there's a subdivision. And it's also too far. I don't want to tease any more. Let's just do it and never talk about it, can you do that?"

"Can you?" He leans behind me at a light and lifts up my hair, brushing his lips at the back of my neck.

"Yes." I could do anything. He does not just look and talk. He knows. It's going to happen to me today with a man and that is all I am thinking about.

"Go up Franklin Drive," he says, "up above the Beverly Hills reservoir. I'm going to lay you down and look at your big, blond body until you're so hot you can't even tell me where to start on you." He is talking in his lowest, wildest voice, projecting across the front seat now from where he's looking at me over in the corner, arm out the other window, projecting so well that it sounds as if he is talking inside my own body, sounds like the dream orders I give myself. It feels like a dream. This cannot be something I would do. That is how to see it.

And we are up in the soft hills above Beverly. He leans over and turns off the motor just as I've stopped and I smell the sweet, heavy scent of his hair and he lifts his face up to mine and grabs my hair pulling my head down and his mouth is softer, wetter than I thought it would be and with our mouths still closed he darts his tongue side to side fast across my lips, and doing it firmer and firmer yet he puts his hands on my breasts and draws them up until his fingers are turning my nipples right through my bra and I feel all the feelings I've felt by myself, but more.

I grasp the tops of his thighs with my hands, rubbing along down the long muscles hard with my thumbs, moving closer and closer. This is like the sex you get from certain musical hooks where it builds and builds and breaks and builds again above the breaking point. Our eyes half closed and staring at each other, we swallow and grasp hands and let go, moving—looking at each other—out of the car, and he walks around to my side and grabs my hand again and runs with me to a flat grassy place where we stand, our arms down at our sides, hands clenched into each other's hands and press our bodies together rubbing and digging into each other in long deep circles and then he slides down to his knees and rubs his face against me, then clasps my knees with his arms and pulls me down. I cannot lie still, my body lifts and lifts to him. He slides off my jeans and we laugh at each other in the dirty husky laugh of teenagers as he sees I have no underpants on. He pulls off the jeans and I unbutton my shirt, flinging it, and it lands on a bush and I throw off my bra and lie back with my arms and legs out wide. I reach up then and toss my hair all around me in a fan and lie with my arms raised under my head, watching as he takes off his shirt and his jeans and we laugh again to see he also has no shorts on.

"Now," he says, "I'm going to do you. But if you move I'll stop. I want to get you crazy. I'm going to start you and stop you and start you and stop you and when you can't stand it I'll stop you and start again. . . . If you move around I'll stop." And he kneels between my legs and starts at me with his hands. He knows he knows. I knew he had to know. And every time I writhe he takes his hands away and pins down my hips with them and starts again, one breast, then the other, nibbling until I look to see if I have lit all up with the heat and the flashlight brightness of the feeling, and all the time he keeps coming back with his hand, stopping me, starting me.

"I've looked at you and thought, someone's got to do her, man, before that chick explodes. . . ."

"Oh, yeah. More, more." I feel like I feel when I watch a great jazz drummer, like when we danced that time and I watched the drummer's jaws move with his gum and the beat. And then when I'm limp and the sweat's coming down in ribbons around my face and pouring into my hair and my back is arching and I'm thrusting down on his hand and lifting my legs, curving them around his shoulders, he puts his jaw down to me and does what he did with my mouth with his tongue and it's like fiddles just shimmering off in my head and everything is going down deeper, harder, down to a dirty chord that will not quit and this is sex, this is it, this is what the shouting and the crying and the wailing and the rhythm and the jazz and all of that's about and he feels the feeling coming down right down there, grouping up and he presses his face down, with the mouth, such a mouth he's not, and his hands go in for the finish which goes off like the brass section's all standing up and he's done me, done me, and I wrap my legs around his shoulders and bend up from the waist clutching his head with my hands and bending down over him. "Jesus, thank you, oh my God, that's been forever coming like that."

"It just takes having a lot of interest in your work." He's straddling me, his knees at my waist now and his hands on the ground on either side of my head. I reach forward and grab his lean, tan hips and move him up into my mouth, moving up and around and gliding, circling in and out, with my hands holding tight, and then one hand holding him steady, the other going around between his thighs, feeling the soft, swinging weight of him, stopping him, starting him, teasing him and coming back for more until he's leaping, fuller, fuller, and he's grabbing my hair pulling it around like reins, pulling it tight against my cheeks as I draw him down and out and he howls like that coyote howled up on that other hill when he was thinking about having me and watching me all those years ago.

We lie side by side clutching hands. I lick my lips. We do not look at each other.

We do not talk about it. Or why or what it means or whether we should or shouldn't have or if we'll do it again. It started and happened and ended as something separate from either of our realities. Separate from each other almost. Like fantasies colliding in midair the way radio stations sometimes catch into each other and then right themselves into their assigned wavelengths. It had, undoubtedly, to do with the past, but not with the present. Or the future.

Here's selective morality; it is not really adultery if we did not go all the way.

IT IS MIDSUMMER. VAL HAS COME BACK AND IS GOING again. I have not, *not* called Angelo. I pretend it was a figment of imagination. Like Jackson.

"I think," Val says, "Angelo has walked off the set of his second film again and is under suspension. 'No cheesy Hollywood director, man, is going to tell me how to play a scene.' "

Val has taken me to watch her buy some new clothes for the trip East to redub some cuts for her new album. "I just feel like I want company," she says. "I'm so mad at Angelo. How can he be so childish!"

"He's an actor."

"That's no excuse. You're just alike, you know—no discipline."

"He has discipline." No argument, I grant, about me.

"Sometimes I wonder what I'm doing."

"Shopping," I say.

She loves this new store called Jax and is friends with the designers who own the store. I sit on the floor and watch her pose and then examine herself in the new things she is buying.

"Did I pick up this distraction from you?" she says.

"No, from my mother."

Seeing her thin elegant little shoulders, something about the line of her arms, reminds me of the little girl she was. She turns in a pale, beige, gauzy dress, her arms reaching out in my direction. She has so much, but it is not enough. Not enough to cover the fear. We both see too many patterns in lives. How much easier it would be without a past to compare to. But then why did I look so hard for mine?

My eyes fill with tears. Though, like a silly old lady watching her child, I am touched to see her buying her own clothes. It is not envy. I do know the difference.

"The only thing," she says, "is I'm sure my mother will look at everything and think it would be better if I had married someone who was buying these clothes for me. She still says, can you believe it, 'And how is *he?*' when I mention Angelo. It's like she has turned into Grandmother about actors and all that."

"She'll also say, 'I say, isn't that a little bare?' "

"Yes, I left out that part."

We see each other mostly during the day. Angelo and Paul don't get along, which is not new, but Val and Angelo also see all their New York friends. And they are being collected by some of our parents' friends, the ones who have held on as permanent fixtures, becoming now a kind of Hollywood Main Line, which really frosts me. Most of them have never called Myron and Vera on the rare years when they come to town and a lot of them talk about Alan as a kind of legend, at least to Val. "Always," Val says, "the ones who didn't talk to him then. I think having been on the blacklist is now becoming chic. They have a real knack for editing the past, cutting themselves right out there."

But she still goes to the parties. And then calls me the next day. I will wait for her to call me. Three times a day I start to call her and then I figure that's only going to bug me, because I am supposed to be working on my own new arrangements which I promised—last week —to someone who's interested in me doing a straight folk album. I said I'd go right home and get started and nothing happens. I play, I listen to myself singing, and my voice sounds thin. Then something sounds terrific and fresh and I try it again the next day and it sounds just like I've heard it a hundred times.

And then I sink into fantasies about how it's going to be. I see myself, not in chic Jax things, but something incredible like silver lamé pants and a troubadour shirt with ribbons flying from it, a real costume. I see myself somersaulting onto a stage with the audience coming up on its feet in a wave, breathing and snarling for me like a big hot wild animal and I can feel it with almost a rock 'n' roll feeling, that sexy black sound like Chuck Berry, that sound I can't do, coming in behind my folk-songs and what I want to hear, I can't get right. I want to hear this steady, drumming, rocky sound like a train, coming in real low and bass behind the guitar and I play my rock 'n' roll records to try to get it to combine and Paul says, "That's the ugliest sound I've ever heard." It is ugly and I like it like that.

Whenever I get close to calling Val over to hear some of what I'm doing, I stop. She'll laugh at me. I'd also like to write some of my own songs about her. The way she uses Alan and Angelo and the movies. It's not right there for everyone to catch, but that's what she has in her lyrics. I get ideas. And I would certainly like to write a song about a movie star who disappears and the girl who's looking for him but you can't do that. L. C. Smith says people want to hear heartwarming, tearjerking songs about love: "But your technique is good and you've got a sweet catch in your voice. Something to work with there."

"I don't know much about love," I tell him.

"Well, write about that. Mainly, what I think you'd do best are the old songs. Just package a theme, you know. . . . I can't tell you how to do it, but if you come up with a strong group of adaptations we can use I'll give you a chance. Talented family you come from, Val is going to be a big star."

"Can I be a star?" I ask—without thinking. I cannot tell what part of my longing it comes from—I just always long—for Jackson, for sex, for fame. It feels exactly alike.

He takes off his mirrored sunglasses to look at me. "You just worry about doing your work—leave all those other feelings out of it. They'll only screw you up. Good."

So now Val is back again and I haven't called. I know

they're probably going to dinner six or seven terrific places in one night and although she never tells me, I ask when I hear about things coming up if she's going and she says, "I don't know. I hate all that." Then I say how I'd love to go, or ask if I can have her tickets, or say, "Gee, we were thinking of going to that." And I'll have one of my envy fits and I won't work, I'll just lie around wondering if she did go and if she just doesn't want to make me feel left out by telling me.

So I don't call.

And then I have this dream: Val and Angelo have moved into Perdido. I think it's Perdido except all the walls are glass and the ocean is almost right outside, and just beyond it you can see Manhattan. "A hell of a view," Angelo says, as I come in. He is sitting in one of my grandfather's high-backed leather chairs, holding his silver pointer, the one he brought from Russia. Myron is vacuuming the rug. Val is bustling around in a Lanz dress like we used to wear, only it is all black. Val is holding a list of things she is doing and starts getting ready to go out. "Where are you going?" I ask.

"Well, I just have to go."

"But where?"

"I have to go, that's all. I can't tell you. I just have to go."

I see, even in the dream, parties, shopping, and lunch with everyone I want to hang around with who I imagine she hangs around with. I see their chicness in the glint in her eye.

"Well, let me come with you . . . I'll come with you."

She turns to me, so severely. Her brows straight across like they get when she really means it. "No, Susanna. You can't come with me, you really can't."

And I wake up. Furious at her. I sit up in bed angry as hell.

"What's the matter?" Paul turns and puts his arm around me. Perhaps marriage means you have a brother. Maybe I will grow out of sex.

"I just had a dream. That's all. You know I'm really hurt Val is back and hasn't called."

"Well, why don't you call her? She may have tried to call. You've been out most of the time."

"I have not. I've been working."

"Late at night. But you wander around in the daytime, Susanna. Go to sleep. Call Val in the morning."

I stop and start dialing her number for a half hour. It's always busy. I give up. Then the phone rings. And it's Val. "Who've you been talking to?" she says. "I've been trying to call."

"How was the trip?" I say.

I do not say I was trying to get her.

"It was terrific. But I'm really exhausted. I talked to my record company people. One bite and they start pressuring you right away, you know. 'When can we hear the stuff for the next album?' "

"Have you been thinking about it?"

"Well, I'm trying. But it's hard with Angelo storming around. He had a party in our bungalow at the Marmont. Some terrible crank—not in the hotel—called the cops. Thank God, Angelo had the sense to hide the marijuana." One did not think that would ever come up in the list of things to thank God about. "Susanna, he had all these jazz musicians he likes."

"What musicians?" I ask.

"No one you need to know. So don't get all frazzled you weren't invited. You lucked out of this one. Are you working on anything—I mean aside from the car?" Val always teases me about some rather unusual things I have added to the station wagon. Unfortunately the claxon horns were outlawed shortly after Sev blew them in the garage and quite a bit of plaster came down.

"Just bizarre ideas. Nothing much. What are you writing about?"

"Men and love and fathers."

"Oh—" My voice deflates. "That's what I was going to get into—folksongs, but with those themes."

"Susanna, what else are we going to write about, dummy, marching off to war? Haven't you figured out yet that no matter what we do it will be different and it will be good?"

"I guess so."

"Listen, we have to move out of the Marmont. There's no privacy. And Angelo may start shooting again. I was wrong—he's going to be okay. This week he's promised to apologize to the director, of course—I have mixed feelings. I almost wish we would have to go back. And I'm really beat—Susanna, this time I need you."

"Val—I'll be there. Anything I can do. Hey, I really missed you."

"Me, too. I love you. When it comes right down to it, it's you and me, doesn't it seem like that?"

"Yes . . ."

I feel happy, relieved, and I feel it is as if I have a sister. I feel so close to her.

And then, of course, she tells me about this beach party, a sand-castle building benefit for the antibomb group that the celebrities and artists have gotten together. And, of course, I ask if Paul and I can go.

"Well, sure, just go down and pick up some tickets. You should have gotten a call. I'm sure I put your name on the list. But that was a while ago. I'll be late. I have to go and listen to a new mix on a single I cut while I was in the East. And then I'm going over to the Biltmore. I promised the Stevenson people I'd come into headquarters. Do you know they have put them practically in the kitchen? It will be a mob scene, but I'll look for you when I get there."

"Good, and just let me know when you need me. I'm here."

"I know. Have to go now. Angelo is having lunch with this gallery owner on the Strip. I have a feeling I'm buying a painting this afternoon I won't like a lot."

When we hang up I remember I forgot to tell her about the dream. I start to call back, but she'd sound impatient, and she hates dreams. I'll tell her next week.

It is a curious feeling I have, a kind of looking forward to something I haven't felt since I used to think about a date—or when I'd think I was for sure going to see Jackson. Like that day in New Hampshire. We are finding each other again.

"You know I hate the beach."

"How can you hate the beach, Paul?"

"To begin with, it's the sand. And the water. And the fog. And, then, in this case, I loathe those people Angelo hangs around with. Sev and I will be very happy here by ourselves. And I want to work on the plans for my father's memorial dinner."

"Paul, I can't go by myself. That's ridiculous."

"Go with Angelo and Val."

"Val isn't going until later."

"So go with Angelo."

"That's not a terrific idea." (I am so evil. I am dying to tell him.)

"Why not?" Paul smooths his eyebrows as he reads, a pencil in his mouth like a bit. I could tie a jump rope to either end and ride him around, putting my own hand back into his behind until he bucks and snorts and whirls. But I just stand here placidly, tying new strings on to my guitar.

"Just because."

"No answer. Drive yourself then. I'm not going."

"Well, I think Angelo is kind of a little after me. He's a little wild right now. I guess it's Val's success."

"Probably."

"Paul. Did you hear me, aren't you jealous, aren't you furious, don't you care?"

"Susanna. You dramatize everything. If Angelo wants something on the side, he's hardly going to go after you."

"Why not?"

"You're not that kind of girl and he knows it. You're also Val's cousin. Don't be crazy."

"A lot you know!" I mutter.

"What did you say? I was thinking . . ."

"Nothing. I didn't mean to interrupt you." I want him to stand there like Jackson in a movie, holding me behind him, wild in the eyes. But even Jackson doesn't feel like that. I think that kind of jealousy was invented by screenwriters to make women adore movies.

So I ask Angelo to pick me up. To hell with it.

We drive out to the beach, up beyond the Palisades bridge which arches over the highway from the cliffs. There are torches already lit and some of the artists have made banners which flutter in the breeze, and with the costumes they wear, I think of the time when my grandparents left Russia and they gathered on the shore of the river. Grandmother was younger then than I am and she stood with her family, among the group of families from the shtetl, each one holding all their possessions and some of them had brooms and long tools around which curtains and Sabbath tablecloths were wrapped and they fluttered, she said, in that wind there like banners.

The sun has set and the beach is cool and damp, but several people have brought braziers and made campfires, which shimmer in the violet light. As the dark comes, the waves break with flashes of emerald-green phosphorus. One of the groups has injected a watermelon with vodka. Radios are playing and people are milling around from group to group shouting to friends, borrowing charcoal or ice, exchanging things they have forgotten. Most of the serious sand-castle builders were there earlier and some of the artists have brought their children, who drop off one by one into nests of old blankets and quilts. I walk with Angelo, who has been sullen and griping about his suspension, about his "stupid, fucking landlord," and even about Val. "Man, I think it's great what's happening for her, but I don't know where that leaves me. I've been alone, you know, and then she bugs me for going out. What am I supposed to do, stand around and act for the four walls?" He's stopping sulking now that he's had a few drinks and we're looking at the sand castles, like a tiny medieval town stretched along this bit of shore, although there's a pueblo, an Arch of Triumph, a large teepee with a tiny fire in its doorway, and a perfect replica of the Arroyo Seco freeway interchange. By the light of torches, some people are beginning new structures, laughing and digging and piling up the wet sand while others stretch out and just watch. It's like a big, crazy playground, but like the old birthday parties, the cliques are recognizable and, even here, there's a status to which campfire you're going to flop down by. The basic Ban-the-Bomb workers have camp chairs and a card table and are working on getting petitions filled in. The East Coast–Hollywood Axis group have the best picnic food packed in real hampers of wicker. The artists are actually making a big fish stew right here and there's a press brigade sitting around drinking martinis and complaining of the cold. Someone shoots a picture of Angelo and me walking by, and then here's Kitty Chapin who is now a regular gossip columnist trotting alongside us. "I hardly knew you, Kitty," I say. Which is what she loves to hear.

"I know. I've just gotten back from Switzerland. I had every bone in the face broken and restructured. Aren't I just gorgeous?"

"Oh, just." She has also lost thirty pounds and had her hair bleached but I'd know her anywhere. She cannot disguise insistence.

"Is this something I should know about, you two here together?"

"No. We're here separately," I say. "Val went down to Stevenson headquarters. She'll be here in a while."

"But everyone's for Kennedy," Kitty says, making a note.

"That's not true, man," Angelo says. "I'm not a card-carrying Communist."

"Oh, don't be silly with me," she laughs and trudges

off through the sand, her new nose kind of pointing this way and that like a hunting dog.

"Why did you say that? She's just crazy enough to use it, Angelo. You have to watch out for people like that."

"Listen. I don't even read that shit."

"Well, some people do, just the people who say they don't. And just the people who say they'd never look at that kind of thing, they're just the ones who believe it, even when they know because they've read lies about themselves. Half the executive wives in Hollywood hide movie magazines inside the pages of scripts when they're at beauty shops."

"Well, I'm not making films they've got anything to say about."

I decide not to say that he is not making any "films" right now. Sometimes I think I ought to be running a studio. It may be the only thing I really understand . . . you just do everything the money people tell you to do and you pay a lot of attention to gossip and politics and hire only your best friends who owe you six or seven major favors. And I'd be such a tyrant. That's the first thing. I'd make everyone so scared of me. That's how they did it. That's how Granfather did it. And that's how Myron lost it. And I'd be charming to those wives. I would be so charming and so complimentary and I would ask them—never mind their husbands—what they thought about the latest movie. That's what Paul doesn't understand. The part about being ferocious. How do you make someone mean and tough and furious for power? Paul is wistful for it, sentimental about it. That's the difference. I wonder if I care enough for him to try to do it for him—somehow. Boy, I'm going to train Sev to like it and want it and go for the throat for it, and not to run out on it like Jackson, or pout about it like Angelo, or ponder it like Paul, or fuck it up like Myron.

If I wasn't me I'd know just how to do it.

We are behind a jetty into a kind of cove. "Hey." Angelo sinks down on his back onto the sand where we have walked, him kicking at pebbles and sometimes throwing them out into the water. "Make me a sand castle."

"No, let's go back. We really ought to. Val will be coming soon."

"Okay, then, I'm going for a swim."

"It's freezing."

"No it's not . . . come on." He left his sandals back near the campfire where Maia and Richard and a couple of weird artists from New York are sitting. I know they are famous because Maia referred to them as "my oldest and closest friends." And now he pulls off his shirt and he is running toward the water and the moon is veiled by a light fog and it's an early little moon, hangnail in the sky. I see him running now like a shadow, a cutout, two-dimensional puppet of black construction paper, running to the water naked. I watch him, wanting him, trying to separate him from Val. Or me from Val. Do I want him precisely because he does belong to Val? I wonder, if, as children compete with parents—to grow beyond them in all ways: be bigger, richer, more successful—do we also try to outdo them in wickedness? What can I do to outclass my own conception but to be having an affair (and one has to call it that) with my cousin's husband? Look how I am rationalizing lust into destiny. He comes back wet, running past me and skidding down into the sand again on his back.

"Bury me," he says. It's the cast of his voice—all rowdy, breaking like an adolescent's into a kind of snicker.

"Yeah, I know what you mean. Forget that. I'll bury you all right. . . ." And I get on my knees and begin throwing sand on him, scooping it out and going at it fast and deep because I shouldn't want him like I do, because I don't see anything wrong with it and because I do, because I understand Val and how she drives him crazy. And I understand Angelo and how he drives her crazy and I drive Paul crazy and he drives me crazy and because I just love it—this, digging closer along the edges of his body, both of us screaming and laughing as he throws sand back at me and takes handfuls of it and rubs it on my breasts which he's gotten to under my top, reaching out, pulling it up, pulling up my bra. And I pull back and dig deeper, kneeling above him, getting the wet sand packed down like clay, molding it around him. "Put your arms down," I order him. "Be quiet, I'm making a statue."

"Oh, yeah, do it." He pulls his arm out from under the sand again and puts my hand around him.

"No, it will hurt you. Don't be crazy. We're just playing. We ought to go back."

His other hand toys with my breast, sand in his palm rubbing the nipple tight and hard.

"So it will hurt a little. I'm a prisoner. You're trying to get me to talk. . . ."

"Or not to talk. I think we ought to go back. Val's going to be there. I feel funny. They're probably looking for us." He puts his hand between my legs. I hear a fire engine or police siren screaming up the highway, and pull away.

"I know you like it. I'd like to get your clothes off and see you lying down on your back with the surf just coming up, all that foam just lapping at you like a lot of big cold tongues, just foaming up, making you all salty, and then I'd get down and do it to you like you've never been done. I'd tie your arms and legs down so you couldn't make me stop . . ."

And as he talks he thrusts and arches and pushes my hands down on his cock, holding me with all his strength, and I watch his eyes, we stare right at each other in the dark, as I move my hands on him, stopping, licking them, starting again. "I had a girl once who couldn't come, and when I got her to she wouldn't make any noise and one night I ate her for three solid fucking hours, man, until she screamed so loud, we were in this rooming house, man, in the city, and everyone was out there in the halls, pounding on the doors. She kept coming and coming and, oh, Jesus, sweet Jesus." And he's off in my hands, on this beach, and he's a

million miles away with some other girl in a rooming
house and I don't see her as he's talking, I see just this
crowd of startled people in their robes and chenille
wrappers, with their slippers on, holding their hands
over their mouths, affronted and dismayed, trying to
decide who will knock on the door and who will call
the police. I use my hand wet with his come to wipe
the grains of sand out of my mouth.

"And now . . . come here . . ." he says, lying back
on the sand and pulling me on my back on top of him.
He's licked his hands wet and he pushes them down
inside my pants and with one hand he opens me, the
other fingers pressing close, and he's got the rhythm
right and as I say to him, "I don't need to . . . let's just
go . . ." I know I can't stop and I begin to come, feeling
his body under me, hearing the ocean, distant sirens and
trucks and the stars wheel by as my eyes blur and my
head spins and I go into the shakes. But I don't scream.

"Okay," I say, breathless, "now let's go." I get up
fast and assemble my pants, my bra, and top. "You're
such an actor. You even have an audience in your fantasies."

"So do you." He wipes his body free of sand—will it
be free enough?—will Val wonder?—does she already
wonder and just not care? Would she be relieved?

"How do you know?" I watch him hopping around
trying to shake sand from his hair. I had no fantasy
here with him. He is one of my fantasies, which I will
never tell him.

"You told me. I remember everything you tell me.
I really like you, you know." He buttons his shirt and
puts his arm around me. "We kind of understand each
other. One thing doesn't get in the way of the other.
You understand?"

"Sure. Don't worry about it."

"I'm not worried about it, man." We walk along
quietly. He's not so playful. He's moving back into his
stage slump with the hands in the pockets.

"I'm kind of worried about Val, though. She's really uptight about moving. That was the dumbest move, having that party. It just happened, you know. I wish you'd try to explain to her I didn't mean it to happen. I'm going to do something, I think, for her. I'm going to call Slosberg tomorrow and apologize. Tell him I'll do it his way. They haven't recast yet. I talked to Dick Samson about it and he thinks if I really show I mean it, if I really come in with my hair combed and be a real pro about it, I can get it back. He thinks it's crazy for me to compromise, but, shit, who's talking? He's working in goddam TV. I feel like an ass, with her knocking herself out."

"And you don't want to be 'husband of,' either."

"Come on, Susanna. That's not it. I fucking admire the hell out of Val. She's scared I'm going to wind up like her old man. If you're going to do it, do it, I don't want to be a fucking loser, man."

Val said to me a couple of months ago, "I can tell Angelo is changing. He now says fucking more than he says man. Enriching the language."

And I remember in New York during those two months when we were hanging around and I would mimic Angelo, Val would snap at me, "Stop it. Angelo doesn't have to verbalize everything. He knows who he is. It's authentic. Not like when you try to talk like one of your old folksingers. 'Them thar hills' and all that stuff."

"I'm sorry. I'm not the intellectual around here."

"Intellectual has to do with ideas, Susanna, and the quality of the thinking. Anyone can learn to use pretentious language."

Why didn't I remind her of that when she was rhapsodizing about how brilliant Niles was? Underbelly of rock. That's what I think of him.

"You're not going to be a loser, Angelo. You already aren't."

"God, it must be late. People have split. Something's

gone on. . . ." We start running up the beach. Someone's running toward us.

"Where the hell have you been?" It's Richard. "Come on, Val's been taken to the hospital."

I freeze. Angelo grabs Richard. "Man, cut out that shit." His eyes are wild. "Where is she?—I'll break your face if you're kidding." He shakes Richard, who pushes his hands down with strength I would not have known he had.

"What's happened to her?" I am screaming.

"Get in my car, I'll tell you on the way."

God, forgive me. It is like the ride to the fire. "The ambulance took her to Santa Monica, St. John's on Twenty-second. About fifteen minutes ago. She was making a left turn—"

"Cut the crap, man," Angelo yells, his jaw and cheekbones like an iron mask in the streetlights. "Just tell me what happened."

Richard yells back, "I'm trying to, you fucking maniac. Some trucker plowed into the car and she was thrown right up onto the side of the road. Up out of the car."

Their little MG. The top down. "Susanna, don't ride in convertibles, they turn over. Sure, every time you turn around, over they go."

"How bad is she?"

"It's bad. Her head."

"Her head! Her head. I should have gone with her. Jesus."

Over and over I whisper to You, dear God, please God, let her be all right. I keep my hands over my face and try not to breathe.

"What'd they say, man?—"

"They didn't say anything. She was unconscious. It was the back of her head."

Angelo pounds the dashboard.

"Maia went to the hospital with an old friend of Val's, C.A. She was going to call Lillian."

C.A. was there. I wasn't. Stop thinking of yourself.

It doesn't matter where you were. Things happen. God doesn't know. Do you think you matter so much to Him that He'd hurt her to make you feel guilty? Contemptible ego. But that is why you do not do things. You do not do the Thou Shalt Nots because then you use them to make yourself feel so important. So powerful. You have no power. You have no power, I tell myself over and over.

We get to the hospital. Angelo has the door opened before Richard stops the car.

"Susanna," Richard says before I can get out. "She's probably gone. Stay with him until I get there."

"Don't tell me that. I don't want to hear that," I yell at him.

"Susanna, grow up. Lillian's going to need you. This isn't your big scene, okay?"

I slam the door and run into the hospital, yelling at the receptionist. "Where's Val Benedict?"

"Let me see . . . just a minute." She looks at her list.

"I haven't got a minute." Angelo has already disappeared.

"Yes. You'll have to go to the emergency waiting room, ma'am. Um, are you next of kin?"

I hate those words. Next of kin.

I run through double doors marked EMERGENCY. The word screams at me. A table with someone on it rolls by, surrounded by doctors; I stop. My hands fly up to my head.

The top of her head is covered by a cloth. Her eyes are closed. A bandage lies across the bridge of her nose. Her mouth is greased with Vaseline. I stand there frozen. The elevator doors close. I stand there watching the indicator showing the floors.

Angelo is standing punching the wall in the waiting room. Maia and C.A. come to me. C.A. puts her arms around me and her lips are puffed like someone trying not to cry. Maia is pale, reflecting green on her tanned skin from the walls. She shakes her head and cries and we hold on to each other and I'm shaking.

"Now, Susanna. Lillian is on her way. I called Paul and he went to bring her. C.A. and I thought that would be best. I couldn't tell her over the phone."

"Did he leave Sev? Who's with Sev? I should go home." I try to think. My brain is chilled. It feels shot full of Novocain.

"He got the woman from next door. Sev's asleep. He's fine. We can get you some coffee from the cafeteria if you want."

"I don't want anything."

"Susanna," Maia says, "come here. Look. This was an accident. Nothing would have been different if you had been there. I want you to understand that. Do you understand what I'm saying to you?"

She puts her hands on my arms very tightly and stares into my eyes. "There was nothing anyone could do." Women like Maia are destined for situations like this, to know what to say, what to do. She is like Lillian in that way. Rises to the occasion. I sink. In this I am like my mother. I want to run and in that I am like my father.

Two women in neat little fitted linen coats, plump women in their sixties, I suppose, walk through the waiting room to the exit. They have been visiting someone. Their arms are interlocked and they carry a cardboard pastry box wrapped with string. Women like Grandmother's friends who came with schnecken after her funeral. Women like Val and I saw going by when she was in the hospital in New York, where they marched by in round little mink coats.

"A matched set. Professional sympathizers. Can't you see us toddling along together with our schnecken in about forty years? God, don't you hope we'll have something better to do?"

Angelo is standing like a figure from a frieze, with Richard, staring at the doors. They open. A doctor walks in. "Jordan. Mr. Angelo Jordan . . ." He looks around.

Angelo goes over to him and stares at him. The doc-

tor takes Angelo's hands and puts something in them
and then covers Angelo's hands with his.

"Oh, God," Angelo screams. It is a ripping sound. I
imagine this is the sound of an animal being torn apart
alive.

"What is it?" C.A. whispers.

"Her rings, I think," Maia says. "They do that."

Richard stands behind Angelo, afraid to touch him.
We are all afraid to move.

"She is dead," C.A. says, flat.

She is dead. Val is dead? I feel. I feel. I feel with
these words that a string has been clipped. I hear the
sound of it snapping in my head. I feel it cut like I
would cut my puppet strings. And I feel myself floating
with no understanding if this is flying or falling. I feel
severed from all life. I feel I am a ghost here. And then
I feel something sink within me. I feel as collapsed and
lifeless as a puppet. I try to picture her in every year,
at every age. I try to fix her into my mind. I try to hear
her voice. I want to catch every instant of her I can
before she fades. I hold on to her like a line, reaching,
reaching across the country, on the phone, letters, running to catch up.

This is not your big scene, Susanna. I make myself
walk over to Angelo. He is sitting with his head in his
hands. One fist curled around the rings. I put my arm
around him. "I'm going to kill the truck driver."

"No, Angelo." I don't know what to say.

"She was every fucking thing in the world to me. She
was great to me, man. I mean, she was great. And I
made her miserable."

"Look, Angelo . . . Val adored you. Don't do that.
Don't think."

He shakes his head. "Listen, I don't want to be the
one to tell Lillian. You know? I don't want her to hear
it from me." I can hardly hear him. He doesn't look at
me. He puts his hand out over mine. "I first saw you
both, running around that pool. Chasing each other.
You were looking away to see if I was watching and

then she dove in and you looked around and panicked. You didn't know where she was. She had on a blue bathing suit with a little skirt."

He is doing what I'm doing. Catching every image and fixing it, putting the little black photo album corners on it. Trying to catch things we never even thought we noticed. The one I thought I noticed most I can hardly catch now. And how much time with her was wasted thinking of Jackson, seeing him in my mind when I should have been seeing her. Chasing a ghost—

Lillian comes through the door; Paul behind her. No one will have to tell her. I thought this would surely kill her, but I look at her and know it won't. She comes over to me and puts her arms around me and now I start to cry.

"I'm sorry," I say, because of everything and because I am crying now.

"Was she aware?"

"No. Oh, Aunt Lillian . . ." She has lost everyone. Absolutely everyone. I think of them around the table. A real family.

"We ought to place a call to Vera. She'll want to be here."

"I already did, Aunt Lily," Paul says and Lillian says, "Thank you, dear."

She looks at Angelo who is standing there. Almost in line with Richard and Maia, and C.A. and, as though it is, indeed, a receiving line, she embraces each of them in turn. "C.A., I haven't seen you in so many years, my God."

Paul puts his arms around me. "Were you there?"

"No." I feel so close to him, and so guilty—but so glad to see him. It is as though he is my brother. It is like being held by an old friend. I've never felt so close to him. "That was thoughtful, calling Mother." I cling to him.

"Well, Maia told me it looked pretty bad. They're flying in as soon as possible. I'll pick them up at the airport, I think that's best. Lillian's incredible. Just incredible." His eyes are red. He touches my cheek gently. "I don't think any of us believe it. I just can't."

"I saw her," I whisper to him. "Going up to surgery. I didn't think she was . . . I really didn't think so."

Lillian is standing alone with Angelo. He shows her the rings, opening his hand for the first time. She holds the rings and gives them back to him and folds his hand around them and strokes his face. And then she turns and puts her face into her hands and weeps. Maia looks at me and I go and just hold her.

"We must make arrangements," she says, finally. "There should be something nice. Oh, Susanna, dear God. Is the baby all right? Who is with him?"

"He's fine. A neighbor is there."

"Well, you must go. I will need you tomorrow. I'll need your help."

The last thing Val said to me—the last thing I remember now—was "This time I need you." I have forgotten whatever else it was we talked about. And when I think about it this minute I can't remember if it was in a dream, or some misplaced incident, but as clearly as I hear her saying, "This time I need you," I hear her saying, "No, Susanna. You can't come with me, you really can't."

I go to the airport the next day to pick up my mother and Myron. I am astonished that she has flown alone. "Myron will be here on a later flight. I wanted to leave immediately. . . . Let's get something to eat," my mother says—which is another surprise!

"Here? At the airport?"

Do you know—it is as though sitting here with her in this coffee shop has flicked on a level of memory which did not come to me on my trip. And a whole part of a trip long ago comes back which I guess I would not allow myself to think about when I was so angry at her. Not that I am not, I remind myself quickly. I remember now, though, as I watch my mother here, that on that train she would order the most incredible breakfasts. Pancakes like giant powder puffs and limp fat bacon and Danish pastries and she would have three little silver things of real jam which would sit on her tray swinging around on a tiny lazy Susan, and sausage. Somehow, on the train, I remember now, nothing was traife. I personally saw my mother eating a sausage.

She would stick a spoon in her coffee cup "to keep it from spilling" as the train swayed on along the track. She'd sit there like a traveling empress with her navy blue silk train pajamas and her special percale sheet which she would bring along—"Muslin chaps the skin." Now I remember this time as the best time of all with my mother. She allowed me to sit on her bed and she'd lean over with her fragrant arm around my shoulder, talking about the scenery to me—and sometimes just sitting there humming. I never imagined her humming at home in that big ivory four-poster bed with its three hundred yards of ivory silk hanging down. (Such dust in those drapes! Of everything, I may have been most allergic to my mother's bed.)

"What kept you from traveling more since you loved it—did you love Jackson because he was brave enough to travel? Is that how it happened? Did you start to run away together?"

"Susanna—I told you long ago—it's not something I'm going to talk about. Please." She butters the toast and asks the waitress to bring the jam back please.

Did my mother get scared and run back home? To Myron?

Rather like I did—to Paul?

My mother looks at the L.A. *Times* I have brought her. I wonder if I died it would make the front page of the L.A. *Times*. With a picture. "There you are, there's the old mean spirit we know and love," I think I imagine Val saying that, but she never said anything like that to me. She was never a mean tease. I am almost beginning to imagine she never teased at all. How long will it take me to deify her? Memory has a way of shooting through cheesecloth, diffusing character.

I wonder, watching my mother with the paper, holding it with her hands around paper napkins so she does not get ink on her skin, whether she *was* scared to go with Jackson—or more scared just to leave Grandmother, who was so very protective.

It is like all my mother's visits. I feel defensive and angry at the first minute I see her, then I relax and want her to know I am trying to be glad to see her, and then I start picking at little things again when she is getting ready to leave, which is possibly because I actually don't want her to go. I see this as a pattern, which I realize now in no way changes how I will behave or react to her on this trip.

"We got those new pictures of Severn," she says calmly. This is what she *insists* his name is. Why argue? About that—we have so much to choose from. "He looks very much the way I imagine your father looked when he was little."

I put down my English muffin and just look at her.

"You never said anything like that."

"Well, we may not have decades together. You never know. A thing like this makes us all a little different. I have never known anyone to have such a completely, thoroughly tragic life. I don't know how Lillian survives. Mother would be so devastated for her. I think your child's tragedies are even worse than your own. Anyway, I did love him, Susanna. And I wanted you. And I have decided to tell you that."

I feel myself tighten. Why would a mother have to make this major decision to tell her child she was wanted? Why do I continue to bolt at everything she says?

"Why didn't you marry him? Wouldn't they let you? Did he leave you? Didn't you want to?"

I wonder if I will adjust my memory of her when she is not here to include watching her eating now in a coffee shop.

"Nothing is ever one way. My mother knew he would hurt me—and was afraid he would leave me after we married, sooner or later. He talked about marriage and then he would disappear for a couple of weeks. And I cried for him," she pauses, bacon in hand daintily, considering kindness, "the way I know you have. And one time I knew, and my mother knew, that I couldn't bear it any more. So I wouldn't see him. I knew I had to stop it . . . or I might have lost you. I looked for a different thing then. I have not regretted it."

"Why didn't you tell me all this years ago?"

"I don't really know. I guess I thought you wouldn't want to know—shouldn't know. Then I thought it was best, when you started looking for him, for you to find out on your own. You were very persistent." She stops eating for a moment again. "It was probably a mistake, not telling you."

"Thank you."

"For what?"

"For saying it was a mistake."

"Parents make them."

"I suppose.

"Do you ever wonder what he's like now?" I ask.

She is swabbing egg with a piece of toast. But rather like an artist. Brushing. Not swabbing. "Myron said he saw some footage of him in one of those Italian Westerns. He's gotten older." It suddenly—but only for an instant—occurs to her that she may have too.

"Well, you look good, though. You really do." SUSANNA ACHIEVES FEAT OF KINDNESS TO MOTHER, says God's trade paper. A FIRST!

"Oh, thank you, dear—I haven't changed then? You never know yourself, although I do have massages twice a week and I just take very good care of myself, I suppose. Of course, my God, I've hardly got to worry about aging yet, have I?" and she laughs, with her dinner party trill sort of laugh—the one, if you were on the steps listening to the party, you could not easily distinguish from the tinkling of ice in the crystal goblets.

"Susanna, I want you to know we have something more in common than just . . ." this is hard for her to say, *"our* connection to him" (she still, I think, wants it to be *her* connection only) "—can you understand that? I spent a lot of time when I should have been working on my music. I did want to be a concert pianist. I had talent—more than talent." She arches her neck as she thinks of it, with a sad pride. "I used my drive to get over him. Do you see what I'm saying? And then, trying to be Myron's partner. Marriage, Susanna, can be a very good job."

That is a word I have never expected her to use, let alone about herself.

"But there was a lot I had to stop thinking about. Not give up. Because I hadn't done anything actually to give up. I saw myself on the stage in Carnegie Hall, seated at a concert grand in black velvet. They would talk about how I always wore black. . . ."

She sound—she sounds, my God, like me. She pays the check now and we go to the car. I carry her luggage. She still walks like a queen. Like Grandmother. Queens do not carry suitcases—or guitars.

". . . I dreamed. But I was lazy." The day is hot. The windows of the station wagon are open. She puts her arm out and adjusts the side mirror I had put on the car to make it snappier. I don't get the reflection from the road now, and she pats back strands of hair and as we drive I realize she is looking at herself. Like my father. I wonder if they made love watching themselves, not each other, in a mirror. Maybe that is why people use mirrors. I imagine trying it with Paul in a mirror— he would be making his necktie-adjusting gesture. How can sex occur to me today—or ever again?

"People like Myron didn't marry women with illegitimate children. He loved me very much. I felt I wanted to give him—not just owed him—my full attention. He also knew that I wouldn't be able to give him a child. And it wasn't—wasn't what you thought—you were so cruel that day. You know . . ."

"I just wish you had told me some of it before."

"Well, I didn't. But I have now. Try not to look back."

I will say something nice. Something I mean, even if I don't mean it exactly as she will think.

"I guess we're more alike than I thought. I mean about the music." What I fear is that I won't do more with it than she did, that I will give up. And I wonder if my marriage to Paul will be like hers. Will be! Is.

And so, I hear my grandmother say, is that such a terrible thing? Look how they are together still—and how they must have given each other the courage to move to Europe. Do Paul and I have the courage to move—closer?

"Susanna." She reaches over and twirls a strand of my hair into a long curl with her forefinger. Did she do that when I was very small? Did she forget who twirled whose hair first? "Susanna, you'll do more with it than I did. You already have. You've got your grandmother's spunk and something of your father which made him a big, big star. And you don't have anything to run away from. You have all the strength to give—to become anything you want. Do you see?" I see she is trying so hard.

Can I?

I think, of course, in my mean way, that this is probably because Lillian has lost Val and somehow that reminds her she has me. And when Lillian dies that's all she'll have. I want to do what she says, not look back. I feel this tautness with her and I want to get rid of it. I want to turn toward her, and turn away from him.

We are at Lillian's apartment. I have called Dorothy to come and help. Friends of Lillian's have come with their coffee cakes in the cardboard boxes tied with string. I wasn't certain whether to bring Sev today but Lillian insisted and he responds to a difference in the tone of things and is sitting quietly by her, working on a jigsaw puzzle she has brought out for him, and they discuss the pieces and take turns fitting them in. My mother watches. He did not know her, of course, and turned to Lillian after my mother hugged him, for a moment. But I see him glancing at her now and then, and finally he walks over and says, "Grandmother, I'd like to see that watch you've got on. If it's okay with you?" He has his hands in his pockets and he's grinning at her. She looks astonished at that smile and hands over her diamond watch. I think she would give it to him if he smiled at her like that every day and isn't it wonderful we all know why.

Angelo is wearing a dark suit, a white shirt, and a tie. I think it is Richard's. The arms are a bit long; the pants are, I think, from the way they hang, rolled up and belted tightly. His hair is sleekly combed. He looks like a young Carradine, his face skeletal and his eyes huge and hollow.

"Talk to me, Susanna. I feel like I don't belong," he says. And he says, "I don't know where I'm going to go."

"You don't have to think about that today, Angelo. Just get through it, okay?" With his color, with his rowdiness, with his language—for he is measuring every word, not saying "fucking" or "shit" once in Lillian's house today—all gone, I feel he is also my brother, but in terrible peril. Lillian feels it too. "I'm worried about that boy," she says.

Richard speaks to us privately. "I think what he needs is to work. I talked to New York today and they'll be calling him back next week to talk about an important new play. I'll tell him they called me later. He's a pro, under all the bull, he'll respond to that."

How I hate people and resent people and lust for people and envy people and then, in this time, suddenly it is all gone—all the idiosyncracies which dazzle and infuriate—and I care for everyone. We become the best of ourselves, as though Lillian is this towering conductor of emotional excellence and she pulls the bunch of us into a subdued harmony.

My mother. We look at each other now and then. Mostly she has been on the phone, spelling Lillian's friends in talking to reporters, to friends and people who are suddenly friends when there is death. I see a lot of girls going through here today, telling Lillian they were Val's closest friend in college.

"That," Maia says, catching me watching them, "was one of Val's most amazing qualities. She could convince you that you were her closest friend. It drove everyone crazy to find out she had other friends."

"I know, Maia. I know that." I am for a moment impatient. I want to say, "I was the best friend." But I wasn't. I drained her. I used her. I envied her. And she even had to tell me it was my turn to help. I didn't even figure that out for myself.

I am wondering if what shows on Lillian's face, a kind of new dimension of despair, would be on my mother's face if I died.

It has been five months since Val was killed. We walk into the Rodeo Room early to supervise the arrangements for the Leon Daroff Memorial Banquet. Paul had wanted the Crystal Room. But it was clear, after a while, that he wouldn't fill it. Although the Rodeo Room is easily filled. The menus are blue with the maroon Daroff dragon.

"It is like a retrospective of Hollywood's best art," C.A. says, looking at the people coming in, jeweled, lifted, lovely because they are so completely in the habit of being marvelous and adored; age does not change their expectant charm—the allure which goes beyond tissue and skin. Movie stars are different from real people. If you ever saw one of the big ones you know what I mean. And I am not just talking about Jackson. There are about a hundred I could name who are not like we are.

Evelyn did not come. "It's very costly, Paul, to fly out there," she said. "Bryan and I are taking the plane down to Buenos Aires later this month. I don't think we want to do both." Bryan is her latest husband. Beef importer. Evelyn eats well. Indeed, they say, she does it very well.

The old stars have taken on the manner of grand viziers. Rakish guys who roared around on cycles and polo ponies arrive in flawless tuxedos with snow-white hair. Cesar Romero, David Niven, Gilbert Roland, and Ray Milland.

Some of the blacklisted writers have come, now courted by people who kept them out of work, or—and Paul may be one of them, if I keep after him—the scions of men who are trying to make it up to them. They are back on the very best tennis courts now, tanned and swinging, and the guilds give testimonial dinners in their honor attended by the new studio heads from the East, businessmen who are not entirely certain who these men are or why they are being honored.

I think I say to Paul as I am walking back to the stage area they have set up for him, "Every winner of Special Academy Awards is here. I remember the faces from when I was a kid." (The same, but sort of crunched like paper bags.) "I want to yell every time they give those awards and don't give one to Myron."

Paul says, moving carnations in the centerpiece in some mysteriously pleasing way—I don't see a difference but he is smiling now—"They never give those awards until they get a report that someone may not live until the next Academy," and, he points out, "Isn't it interesting you think of Myron?"

"What's interesting about it?" I snap.

"I'd think you'd want them to give one to Jackson."

"I do. But he wouldn't show up."

"Just think. You could accept the award for him."

I see myself in gold sequins. "On behalf of my father, I want to thank the Academy . . ."

The party is like a college reunion for Paul (and for me. But it is his evening. I owe him that), seeing old teachers who don't recall whether he was a good or bad student but are pleased to see someone they remember.

"S. Leon Daroff would not be impressed by this party," Richard Samson says.

"Oh, don't be mean tonight. Jesus!" I snap at him.

"You don't understand, Susanna," Maia adds, ticking something invisible off the burgundy lace dress I think makes me look like a sort of San Francisco hooker. But very upper-class. And I put up my hair as a gesture to Paul. Guilt makes me a much better wife. For a while. "Paul could not give a party which would have impressed his father. If he made a triumph out of the evening he would be equal to his father. He can't do that and keep his idol."

"So," says Richard, hands in tux pockets, "this is fine —not a disaster, but surely no triumph. Very smart."

"Oh, I certainly wish I had such wonderful friends," I say.

"Don't be simplistic, Susanna. Paul would be the first one to understand what we're saying."

"Where is Jimmy Stewart—Cary Grant? Is Susan Hayward here yet?" Paul is bustling around, following his secretary like a road runner.

Although some people who promised film clips did not come through, and although some who promised to say something just stand up and take bows, and a few have not shown up or are, Paul whispers to me, "Unpardonably dull," it has the air of Miss Havisham's dining room. The way Richard and Maia talk you'd expect to see Martita Hunt materialize at one of the tables, cobwebs draping her wedding gown. The posters of Daroff films around the room look—they look impressive in their massive gilt frames. I got them out of Evelyn's storage place by bringing up her old film again. Old films do not sit well with new husbands.

"I think," Lillian says, "that it's a lovely tribute. But it's not going to do what Paul had in mind." Which, of course, was to generate interest in his father's old properties. (And that is why Richard and Maia are wrong.)

Whenever I hear the phone ring, I dream it will be a big record producer wanting to put me on the road. Paul dreams it will be a major studio head wanting to give him his own company with his father's imprimatur.

Paul gets into bed when we come home and is sitting there reading—and I hold my breath—an actual novel published this year which an agent sent him. Not that he is in a position to buy any properties, but I am just glad to see him holding something in his hands which is not covered in frayed sky blue paper with the Daroff dragon stamped on it in maroon.

"What's that novel?" I say.

"Something Richard has optioned." He puts it down, and looks at me. "I think I may do it—produce it with him. You see . . . things can change." Far be it from me to ask if that might include our sex life.

And I go downstairs to work, which means I lie on the floor with my sheets of paper spread around and think about how I am cartwheeling onto a stage, with my rainbow cape circling around me and red shiny shoes (like the sneakers I have covered with glitter which only Sevin appreciates) and I can hear the audience screaming as I catch my guitar midair and a band comes trotting in behind me playing "Night Drive," this enormous hit from my new album.

Or, maybe they are playing "Steps." Since "Night Drive" is not written yet. I've been working on "Steps" for two years. Well, maybe not two years, if you consider a line going right every month and then I have to start it all over again because I think it's better in another rhythm and another key. Crumple paper. "Steps. Cannot find the steps I climbed long ago . . ." Crumple. "From my roof I sometimes think I see another rooftop over by the dawn. I see someone there who looks at me. When I look back you have gone." Crumple. This part I have always liked:

> *Many little rooftops, all without stairs,*
> *It's time, the tone of the years.*
> *Yes, we sit at solo desks in very hard chairs*
> *Making carbon copies of our favorite fears.*

That's all. You do know, Susanna, I tell myself, how to do it. You start simple like the man said.

I want to see myself being peaceful, working somewhere serene. Serenity. Can you get any good work out of that?

I went to see Lillian last week at her office. I put it off like I put off making any connection with Val, like Jackson puts off seeing me? Like Jackson's family puts off seeing my uncle in Florida—as I will also put off seeing him again.

"I don't know how you do it," I say suddenly in the middle of talk about a new project Lillian has just encouraged the studio to buy. "Just survive it all."

"You don't survive, Susanna. You live. There is a difference. I try to stay involved with what is happening to other people. I don't have much faith in God, which is how some people do it—but I have faith in life. And time. Come, let's go to the commissary and have lunch."

She is different in her office, in one of her striking tweed suits, handing notes to her secretary, walking with such authority through the lot.

She smiles and waves at people as she walks by. Not a trace of tragic majesty. A sort of sporty competence is how she does it.

"When you're angry, Susanna, as angry as you are about someone's death, it's usually because of fear, and the fear is probably because you're afraid of some of the feelings you had—" She holds the door open for me and walks me to a table by the wall, looking out at the Wardrobe Department, which reminds me of our Wardrobe Department at V.L.I. and Val in her scarlet gown.

"Do you remember *Home of the Brave?* Remember when the white soldier died after calling the black soldier nigger, and the black soldier went mad? He couldn't face what he felt. You had a lot of mixed feelings about Val, as she did about you—she was jealous of you, living at the house, having things she couldn't, she would get furious when you never seemed to notice how she was, when she was in trouble. You ought to know that, too. No one just loves anyone. It's not very interesting if they pretend to—mainly because it is not true. The truth is always very interesting."

"I never knew how Val felt about me. Not really. We

had one big blow-up, but that was it. I never thought about it."

I wish I hadn't started this. Lillian waves to an executive walking by, one of the young new ones who think they have brought the New Frontier to Hollywood.

"You know, Susanna, when Val told me Alan was dead, for a split second, like a lightning bolt, I was relieved, which isn't a nice way to put it, but there it was, and I had to accept it. Then I talked to other people who have had the same feelings." She stirs her coffee and is looking at me, waiting.

I just said, "I know."

"A lot of people are relieved because it isn't them, and a lot of people are jealous of the celebration, in a sense, of the one who's gone. Anything you can imagine someone feeling, you can be sure someone has felt before. The only thing that makes death irreconcilable is guilt. End of lecture," she said. "Listen—you and Paul ought to be on our screening list—remind me." And this is how Lillian lives. Does it all come back to one's work? To what one does with one's day?

Angelo flew back for our benefit dinner. Which I felt was sort of an unconscious apology to Paul. We had not talked since he went to New York to begin rehearsals for the play. Richard hears he is brilliant. He is wearing a tuxedo with the shirt open and no tie. I hold his hand a beat too long and feel the electricity—and we grab each other's wrists and let go at the same moment. We do not touch each other again and we avoid each other's eyes all evening but not entirely successfully. Paul says, "Susanna, stop hanging on to me tonight, what's the matter with you?" Then he realizes something he does not think he knows and looks at Angelo and says, "You okay?—the dress, by the way, is perfect. Leon would be very proud of the way you look." Highest praise of course.

Angelo sits with the Samsons and C.A. and her husband. We have not seen any of them since that night. I'm not really sure they've seen each other that much.

As we're waiting for our cars, I see Angelo talking to Inger Stevens. I wonder if she will become a star. She is looking very sadly, very intently at Angelo as he talks. I don't want him to look at anyone or talk to anyone. I want him to be noble and grieving forever: As a tribute to Val? Or because—because of me being dog in manger? I swoop over there.

"Angelo. We're going to come to your opening on Broadway—I wanted to tell you. Paul is so pleased for you." Paul will be surprised we are going.

Our eyes skate around each other's, looking at other people—coming back. Riveting.

"I was telling Inger about how hard it was to get back to the stage. When I left the studio, Strasberg gave me a copy of *Prince of Players,* Edwin Booth's book. His brother killed Lincoln, you know."

"I didn't know."

"Yes. They were both actors," Inger says.

"Oh, really," I say. "How amazing." I want everyone to disappear. Leave us alone; to what? Our overwhelming guilt?

"Like I was so lonely," Angelo says, "I couldn't get into the part. I wasn't fighting it, there was just nothing to find. So I read this incredible thing, man, that Booth said about the night he went on, opened in a Shakespeare play, the night after his brother killed the President. He was told not to go on, that they were going to throw rocks at him. But he did it. He had the curtains open with him just sitting there. They threw the stones and he just sat there, and he held on to the scene, himself in the scene. He held on and he played it. He touched on to the role, to himself as the part, I don't remember which one it was then, and they stopped. They listened. And then they cheered. He felt himself there and they got it. So I've been trying that. Isn't that incredible, that kind of concentration? They tell me it looks good. I don't know—it's not like being able to see film. You have to feel when it's right."

The story reaches me and he knows it. It is a story

about guilt—and sitting through the stones we have both been throwing at ourselves. The thing we will never discuss.

"Yes. I'm glad you're okay, Angelo. I was worried."

"I'm here. That's all I know. And acting. Are you writing any songs?"

"Not much."

"You ought to get with that—you know. Hey, really come to the opening—I'll get you house seats."

"We'll be there."

We have fought to break that electricity in these few minutes, and when he holds me I can tell we have come to the other side of that feeling. I hope I am only relieved. I do not think so. It was something a long time coming—to go so swiftly.

I AM NOT ON STAGE IN RAINBOW CAPES OR RIBBONED
shirts or black velvet like my mother. I am right here in
my house arranging old folksongs for a new group I
might have a chance to be a part of, if I show I have
something to contribute. I take my old song sheets and
put them away. I get out a notebook of arrangements
I am supposed to be working on.

I have no feeling in my bones about it, no feeling
that around the corner something is going to happen.
After about an hour, drinking Coke, eating peanut butter and jam sandwiches, going in and holding Sevin,
taking the book which has fallen out of Paul's hands
when he fell asleep and putting it on the table and
turning out the light, and going to the john, I get down
to work, and by the time I have to get up and get Sevin
ready for nursery school, I have rearranged one song
and it's pretty good.

I take Sevin to school and wait: watching him saunter
in with his cowboy boots on and the red cowboy hat
today. Always some sort of hat.

My mother said, "Are those boots good for his feet?"
"Not at all," I said.

His teacher said, "Is it wise to let a child wear a hat
every day?"

"Probably not," I said.

I watch him begin to play with the others until he's
forgotten I'm there. "He hid from us again yesterday,
Susanna," his teacher says. "We found him in the top
of the tree. 'This cowboy,' he said, 'not coming down.'
He's still having a hard time adjusting to group activities, quite a maverick."

441

"Well, I'll try and work on that." I wonder if some day he'll run away from me. And what will he be looking for—and how long will it take me to understand? And where will I be waiting, watching for him to come back? I want to say it runs in the family, but it doesn't have to. You can fight it. But I still know how Sevin feels. I don't want to go home this morning. I don't want to work on more arrangements, or look over the one I did, and so I'm driving the long way home, which is one way to put it, past the Strip, up into the hills I'll go and then back over Mulholland. I stop at Coffee Dan's. I sit up at the counter and pretend I'm somewhere else and I'd like to feel I could run away, but I know I'd get there and still be me, and then I'd be calling home to find out how Sevin is. And I wouldn't take him with me, because he's got to learn how to do it on his own, and how to stop doing it when the time comes.

I drink my coffee and order eggs over easy, hold the hash-browns. If I get into this group I want to be snake thin. Well, not that. I would, after all, scare myself. I look at myself sipping coffee in the rosy glass mirror across from me. I watch the waitress slapping the bread into the toaster. It's a big commercial thing. She puts the soft white bread flat against this rack made of wire and the bread moves on a conveyor belt. At the top there is a toaster element under a tin hood so you can't see the heat. Then the bread falls toasted onto plates. It must have been designed by an old director. I finish my second cup of coffee and get into my car and turn right around and go home the short way and get to work.

I'm into the second arrangement and the phone rings. It will be Sevin's school. They can't find him again.

I heard myself ask him last night, "Why don't you like school?"

"Nothing good about it. That's all."

Paul said, and he put his hand on my shoulder (does that mean? . . .), "Tell him, Susanna—" And he laughed.

"Very funny," I say. "When you're trying to find him

442

all day." Or will it be the Sears man about the washing machine they do not ever really fix, or Paul to announce another dinner party?

"Yes." I answer the phone with a snap to my voice. If it is the Sears man he will be intimidated.

"Susanna?"

I am going to be very cool.

"Jackson?" You can go out looking and looking, but nothing's going to come to you until you're ready to handle it.

"I thought I'd give you a call. I'm out here doing a series." It's going to come when you're least expecting it.

"I didn't see anything in the trades." Going to happen on an ordinary Thursday afternoon when you're just doing your work like you're supposed to be.

"We haven't announced anything yet," he says, "until the deal is set. You know me, I want to keep it quiet."

I know you! I don't know you at all. I wonder if he listens to breathing. Oh, he doesn't listen to anything.

"Who's producing the series?" Oh, this is wonderful. Here I am talking like we're old cronies at Schwab's when I want to scream at him, "Where have you been all my life?" But he's come this far, I say to myself. Do not frighten him away.

"I think your husband works for the outfit, that's how I tracked you down."

"Neat tracking." Not as neat as mine was. I am shimmering with cynicism. I am betting with myself, horning in on God's game with Grandmother—what does he want, Guys? Is his deal not really so hot, not really so set at all? Does he think Paul can help?

"Hollywood hasn't changed much. These people are just the same—except they don't have any talent. But I've been wandering around out there, and I decided they've been wondering what became of Jackson Lane long enough. I was beginning to wonder what was going to become of him myself."

"I was beginning to wonder about that, too." I miss

my real cue. How neat it would have been if I had said, "Frankly, my dear, I don't give a damn." How I've been wanting to say that to someone all my life.

"I guess you were. It's a great day, why don't you drive out here and spend a couple of hours, have a couple of drinks, you're old enough for that, now, if I remember right. Or we could have a bite of dinner . . ."

"Where are you staying?" I do not really consider saying, no, I am working. I would like to think I consider such a thing, but I do not. However, I consider the distinct possibility that when I get there he will have left a note—or no note—and not be there. I don't know why I am starting it again. I'm not. It's going to be different. I don't know how. But different.

"I rented a place out here in Malibu. Not the Colony, not enough privacy there—fans sneaking in and driving you crazy, you know how it is."

"Are you still with Mrs. Rodgers?" Foolish question.

"No. She was driving me crazy. Wanting to stay put. All those middle-aged ideas about settling down."

"But she wasn't like that—" I say.

"Got that way. It happens, when people get used to you."

Would anyone get used to him?

"That's too bad—I liked her."

"She was good. We talk once in a while."

"Long while, I bet."

"Well, yes—" He laughs. "You got me figured."

"I'm very quick that way."

He, of course, is not middle-aged. My God, Jackson must be almost fifty now. I don't know if I want to see . . . to see that.

"It's not too bad to be back in the West, though. I've got a little dock out here and I've ordered a new boat. She's a real beauty. Got two sets of sails, one's red and white striped."

"Just like a barber pole." I want to let go of the fear that makes me so tight. He has reached out. "Maybe we could go for a sail. I'd love that, like we did."

"Well, not today, honey. They're doing some work on her down in the new marina over there in Santa Monica, but soon."

Does he have a boat? Is he going to be pathetic? I do not want to see Jackson poor. I'd rather not see Jackson at all. Not that way. They can rip up the poinsettia fields and tear down the backlots and sell off the studios to TV and even put that CONDEMNED sign on the cliff in front of Perdido because the Palisades are falling down, but I don't want to see Jackson different. The others can be gray and courtly and anxious, with the blur of flesh along the angles of their faces and the tired look in their eyes, but not Jackson.

I wonder if he does have a series. Paul would have told me. But maybe Paul doesn't know. They hardly tell him everything after all.

"What kind of series are you doing? Is it a good part?"

"Well, I'm the star of course. I'm not giving up my life again for some comeback cameo. It's being built around me and I've got script approval like always. The boys at William Morris always look after me."

"Jackson—actors never had script approval. I'm not a little kid any more. I want to see you and get to know you . . . but . . ."

"None of that Hollywood crap. Okay. But it amounts to that because they know I won't do any junk. . . . I'm famous for walking off the set."

"And out of town," I say.

"Out of the country, too! Don't fence with me, Susanna." And I didn't want to make him uneasy. I can hear it in his voice. He is scared to see me, too. Scared for me to see him? Afraid I will ask too many questions? I will make it easier. For him.

"Okay. No fencing . . . it will be fun to see you. No hard questions."

"There's my girl. Now here's where I'll be—" He gives me the address. "If I run out for a second, just walk in. I have to pick up a few things, okay?"

I freeze. He is already arranging his escape. But he wants something. I feel that too. He wouldn't do it . . .

"Well, you do what you have to. I'll wait for you." And I already see myself sitting in an empty house in the dark, listening to the waves pounding on the beach. I think he is including me in some game my mother played with him a long time ago. He's been getting at her through me all these years. I want him to see I'm different. If he stays to see me.

I could turn it around this time. But I won't. As I hang up I am already looking up the number of Sevin's favorite friend's mother. I ask her to pick Sev up and then I call the school to tell them to be sure he waits inside the gate. Will he be clinging to the railing, looking out for me, grinning when he sees a car that looks like ours, then disappointed when it isn't—looking for me like I looked for Jackson? It is only this once, but will I do it again—be gone longer? Am I making too much of this? Can you make too much of anything when your child is concerned? And Sevin will be concerned. I will explain. Of course, I could have told Jackson I would be there later and brought Sev with me. But I want to be the child. I haven't finished. I haven't even begun. Is that how my mother felt, sharing her father with Lillian and her mother with Val and me? And did she not even want to share Jackson with me—even the emptiness which was all there was to share? Even that had to be hers—she didn't tell me so. She wouldn't even have to share the missing and missing is itself a kind of something to own. And Paul—Paul will be furious. "He has always come first with you. He'll call one day and you'll drop everything. Think of where you'd be if you'd thought of your music first."

"Don't start," I said to him. "Don't start on father fixations, Paul, because you'll win the Oscar. I'm just a dark horse nominee compared to you."

I put on clean jeans and my white button-down shirt. Not jeans. You are going to see your father. (That is my mother speaking. My mother. Will she feel betrayed—

that we came so close, and now I run to him?) If he is there. I put on navy slacks and a red turtleneck. It will be cooler down at the beach. No, the white one. He likes white. Just go, Susanna.

Meanwhile back at the other ranch, did Jackson's family—each of them—want to own bitterness and grief in its own way? And not to be reminded—Thelma, Jackson's brother, and Jackson—that the others also suffered? How selfish I am. Wanting to think other people have the same feelings, assigning guilt so idly—or reasons for behavior to people I do not really know based upon only my feelings. Is there any other way?

It is entirely likely Sev will be delighted to go home with Tony, his friend, the way I might have been pleased to be picked up from school by Lillian, to visit with Val. Here I am again, comparing. Figuring Sev out based on myself.

My hands shake as I put the key in the ignition. And I go down our street as if I have never seen it before. I turn right onto Lookout Mountain, past the empty lot bristling with scotch broom, curving down past all the little wooden houses, the forties' stuccos hidden behind great hedges of lantana and hibiscus. I go down Laurel to Sunset, past Frascati, past Ciro's where Jackson used to go, and the Crescendo, where Bronston did not. Past Wil Wright's where Val and Lillian and I used to go after the concerts I hated at the Greek Theatre, past Sunset Plaza where Paul drove me up into the hills to neck—and wound up proposing. Does he wish when he goes by here that he had not taken that turn? Here I am guessing again. Beverly Hills where—a snap of the fingers—it folds out like an old portfolio of postcards, a change of the light and it's all green, palmy, and bright. I look at people in cars as I pass. If you knew, if you only knew who I was going to see . . . would they say, "Who?"

I know I'll spend a lot of time thinking of what he says to me and what I say to him—later. After, for instance, he is gone, maybe, when they finish the first

day's shooting and he decides it isn't working out. I'll
wonder if I shouldn't have said it this way or that and
wonder if he thinks I said some pretty stupid things.
Listen, he's not so smart. Hasn't been here in ten years
and he thinks it hasn't changed. TV people just the same
except talent—and energy and style, and, and, and. But
they are the same in a way; they stride around looking
all distraught as though they're making the decision to
drop the bomb themselves when it's only how to cut
costs and bring it in on schedule. They take themselves
so seriously. But how about the way I look when I'm
hunched down working on the floor? I am not writing
a song. I am going to detonate the whole world with an
entirely new sound. I'll wait to see that laugh he'll get
on his face, that laugh they get when they know you're
excited just seeing them. Angelo gets that laugh in his
dark way. Gets it like a smirk—"dig it"—I would like to
learn to talk like Angelo and have it sound as though I
really talk that way. That laugh . . . I switch the radio,
spinning the dial from song to song, looking for the ones I
like, skipping commercials. That laugh. It makes them
taller than they really are and then they put their hands
in their pockets and shake their stuff around and rock
back a bit on their heels and look down at you. Probably for being so silly because they know they aren't
really worth so much, but they love you loving them, do
they, man, do they. (There. That's how Angelo says it.
It's not the words, it's getting the knack of the rhythm.
You'd think I'd know that. Don't think I'd know anything so fast.)

It's the time of the ladies in their beige Continentals.
I fly by them. They dye their hair champagne and put
on their champagne minks over their champagne knit
suits and with all of the jewelry Marvin Hime has sold
their husbands at discount, they go off to lunch with
each other and compare the jewelry. In most places
people get to look like their dogs. Here they get to look
like their cars. This couple I have just passed in an

elderly navy blue Chrysler sit up square and straight to go with the lines of its body.

Being Jackson, when he gets that smile on his face, that aren't-you-glad-to-see-me smile (not, look-how-glad-I-am-to-see-you), he'll have his hands on his hips. I want Jackson to get what he wants. If it's another shot at being famous—because that will keep him here. Oh, really? Like the last time. If I had any class I would have made him come to see me, after all the chasing around I've done. Maybe I should hit him for child support. For an instant I realize I mean child support for Sevin. Do I give Jackson the role of the universal estranged father—or do I still see him, like Val said, as a lover? Will that show, and would he know the difference?

I am not actually wild about Sunset all the time now because every time I drive on it there are all these other trips—to the fire, from one or another funeral, coming home from Bronston's. And rides with Val, with us laughing—I cannot, and it's not that long ago, remember that we weren't always laughing and that the car wasn't always full of a lot of girls with Val turning in her seat to give them a look, to stare them down, to say, "Will the class please . . ." in her perfect imitation of Miss Mills. I can't remember that in the old days the sun didn't always shine. And I cannot remember that we were not absolutely beautiful and gay . . . except we weren't and there were days where we'd huddle on the beach and curse the fog, wrapping up together under beach towels, and I'd get asthma and have to go home.

I whip by U.C.L.A., see the blond boys running in their undershirts, adorable legs in their chunky white socks. Giant Sevins.

I haven't seen Jackson yet and already I'm figuring when I can see him next and whether it wouldn't be terrific to give a party for him and what we'd serve and how I'd like to have him punch Niles right in the jaw and I see Niles lying there, Jackson standing over him, picking up his glass of wine, sipping it and winking at

Paul. "Pretty good stuff," he'll say, and step over Niles, look down at him, and say, "Filmmaker!" Or perhaps Jackson will come striding into the Ashgrove next Sunday night. They always let me play on Sundays. ("They let anyone," says the voice Val has left behind inside my head, like a little clock.)

This may be it though . . . I may never see him again and then I'll get angry, pitching fits and crying and all that jazz and yet it is different this time because when I do it, I'll know what I'm doing. You're just having a Jackson attack. They should invent an antigen. Actually I thought for a while Angelo was the antigen. But it's the same item, they've just come up with a new package design this year, wears just as well, some say it lasts forever.

I wonder if he'll tell me things, answer questions and all that. It doesn't matter. I probably know more about him from deduction and hearsay than he knows about himself. And no matter what he says I'll be worrying so much about what I'm saying that I won't even hear. I'm going to do one thing straight off, though, I'm going to tell him exactly how I feel.

I slow down past a cop, who is looking at me—they know exactly who is in a hurry. Going by Veteran Avenue now. Now I'm going past Canyon View Drive where all the houses had bridges over a little stream which was almost always dry. But on one side of the road there were blackberry bushes and when we would go over and visit Ned and Tracy Wynn, Val and I would pick berries. I think you can learn about life from picking berries. The most delicious ones come easily with your hand. You do not have to yank, but they are, however, often hidden under leaves and you have to look carefully to find them. And if you did not come back quickly enough, by the next week, the ones which you did not pick would have rotted and fallen on the ground. Like songs you wait too long to write which lose their urgency. And fathers who do not like to sit around.

Why, I wonder, if I know I'll think of great things to say to Jackson just after I've left him and it's too late, why can't I figure them out before? It doesn't matter. I'm going to be sort of the strong, silent type. I'm not going to do any fancy movie running to him. I'm going to get out of my car slowly . . . pretend this is not my favorite idea. Driving past the Bay Theater in the Palisades now where we'd slide up in our limos. Once Val and I grabbed two hundred and fifty preview cards and filled them in with different handwriting, raving about a bit player named Rick Jason. "Give him more parts," we wrote. There weren't two hundred and fifty people in the audience that night was the trouble and Myron was not amused. "This is business, not a party." We were also so busy writing out the cards we'd snitched in the dark we didn't notice Rick's part had been cut out of the picture. Lousy picture anyway.

I have come to the Coast Highway. I look, because I never cannot look, up at Perdido. The entire front yard has eroded now and the house stands at the edge of the cliff, like someone with one foot out, about to commit suicide but looking around just one last time to see if the right people are noticing.

I notice you, house. I would stop and see you again as I have done twice before climbing over the fence that says you are condemned. Touching my trees. Bringing back leaves to press in my songbook. Foolish woman, stepping precariously through your bare rooms, hearing the sounds of all of our voices as I go through you looking out from Grandmother's window at the ocean where I thought I could see him sailing. I would kneel down in front of you and cry again because of everything, because of absolutely everything.

Merry-go-round—lonely-go-by . . . I'll find you soon.

Anywhere anyone lives, people and houses die and you can't rearrange the roads to avoid where you've been. If something bad happened on that road that you've gone down at least every day and sometimes two or even four times when you didn't want to do anything but drive, it shouldn't surprise you. Good things probably happened—sunny Sunday encounters, cars flirting with each other, flashing chrome bumper smiles. I remember arms around my shoulders. But I don't remember who. Why does the sadness have more impact? Why do I remember the sad songs more than the giddy, silly ones? Why do I see Jackson's brother's burned face more clearly than I remember Carleen? I would know this crazy lady on the beach in Florida, but would not perhaps place Marcia unless she had her portable loom under her arm. I remember Lillian weeping over Alan's picture more vividly than Sev's last birthday. Or is it just today I feel this way—is it apprehension darkening memory? And has expectation itself darkened into apprehension? Even on this sunny highway? I know exactly where the skid marks were. Still there. I see. They are eleven feet and three inches long. I know how many beach towels were brought to place under her head. I walked around there, made myself go there to see the place, to stand there where she started dying. I see the shoved-around debris, the sticks and rocks in the ditch by the side of the road. I tossed away some beer cans. And picked and put a bunch of mustard blossoms there. "Hey, lady, you crazy or something?" a truck driver screamed at me, as he ground on by.

No, I'm not going to run to him. I'm going to stand and shake his hand. I'm going to show I've grown up reticent and let him think that's his fault and I'm going to look wary and let him just come to me. I'll fool around in the car a few minutes and let him wonder if I'm going to change my mind. Well. That's stupid. Do I really think he notices things like that?

I turn left at the signal by the Colony and I decide that he will not be there as I go right just before the gatehouse to the Colony and up the rough Malibu Colony Road where screenwriters and young bachelor lawyers who want you to think they are writers and après success people and wily old hip political people and TV people live until the A movie that will change, if not their lives, at least their addresses, comes along. There's always been a certain kind of person living here—I think they blacklisted the entire road at one time. "A hotbed of subscribers to *The New Republic,*" one politician said. Jackson will be very happy here now, though. The young ones will collect him like an especially choice piece of driftwood. They may make him into a lamp if he is not careful.

I want to be this way: bitter and tough. But I see a white Buick convertible glinting in the sunlight up ahead and my heart jigs in its cage again. It's the light from the past and the laugh I'm going to catch. I know he has nothing to do with what I'll be doing tomorrow. I wouldn't have expected to hear me saying this, but I'm glad I didn't see him until I was ready to know all this and put the rest of it in its place and know that when I get this feeling it's just the memory of believing in magic I am feeling and that having the memory come in as quick and true as it is is magic in itself and makes me want to laugh and hug myself and say, "Susanna, look at you, beaming like one of them. Beaming like you know something," and I catch a flash of my own expression in the rear-view mirror and I'm beaming like I've never been through this feeling before and beaming like I don't know there's nothing real on the other side of it.

He's sitting up on the front deck with his legs up crossed over the railing and when he hears my car he stands up and when I see him standing there I see the blurring on the angles of his face too, and the sun does not quite catch itself in his hair any more and he's got more the build now of someone working on it. I try to fix on the distortions and the changes, but I catch them only the way you catch something when you're driving by and I only see him now as I saw him that day when I put my two hands on the edge of the pool and saw him just standing there looking down at me and laughing. I see him in a golden blue blur in spite of the too ruddy tan I trust more to leisure than to locations, I see him as light and as bright as the beginning of an idea, as a song coming on that I love and I cannot tell you the details of what he is wearing, I don't even look to see because it is so powerful just to be standing here, looking up, and I don't care what he did or what he did not do. I'm running to him and I'm running up those steps with my hair flying and I'm flinging my arms around his neck and he opens his arms and puts them all around me.